VOYAGE
TO THE WALL

VOYAGE
TO THE WALL

MANNING RUBIN

gatekeeper press™

Columbus, Ohio

This is a work of fiction. Although persons and events are inspired by the author's life and actual history, unless otherwise indicated, all the names, characters, businesses, places, events and incidents in this book are either the product of the author's imagination or his use of history. He has used real names of The Brigade and Israeli military heroes but used in a fictitious manner. It is the author's desire to honor them for what they accomplished.

Voyage to the Wall

Published by Gatekeeper Press
2167 Stringtown Rd, Suite 109
Columbus, OH 43123-2989
www.GatekeeperPress.com

Library of Congress Control Number: 2022933297

ISBN (paperback): 9781662931086
eISBN: 9781662924552

Foreword

Manning Rubin's powerful tale of Joey Goldman's experience in Europe following the end of World War II is as current as the daily headlines in newspapers, on cable TV, and in the social media.

Joey's meeting up with antisemitism, the Holocaust, the reality of a Jewish state, and the unique experience of Jews in America enables the reader to get a glimpse of the complicated history of the Jewish people—its pain and suffering and its glory and triumph over evil. It is worthwhile as context for this novel to take a quick look at that history.

The Holocaust, which Joey encounters by attending the Nuremberg Trials, did not simply *happen*. While it took the extreme evil and power of the Nazi regime to implement the murder of six million Jews, including one and a half million children, it could not have happened without the inculcation of poisonous antisemitism into the minds and cultures of Europeans for centuries. Throughout the millennia, idea after idea piled up about Jews, about their alleged evil power, that set the stage for the Holocaust.

Just as in the days of the Jim Crow South where it took something special for whites living there not to imbibe the racism that underlay society, for centuries in Europe it took something exceptional for people not to believe antisemitic tropes about Jews. First, it was the idea that Jews were responsible for the death of Jesus. Together with that was Augustine's notion that Jews have the mark of Cain on them for being Christ-killers who would wander the earth in punishment.

Then came ideas that Jews had evil powers, as reflected in medieval art of Jews with horns. Or that Jews were in a conspiracy to destroy Christian Europe, as reflected in the blood-libel charge, that they kidnapped and murdered Christian children and used their blood for their ritual purposes. Or the accusation that led to much spilled Jewish blood, of the Black Plague in fourteenth century Europe was a result of Jews poisoning the wells. These ideas remained deeply embedded and were even expanded on as Europe moved into the modern world. Already in medieval Europe, the theme that Jews would do anything for money was rife and saw artistic depiction in Shakespeare's *Merchant of Venice*.

As society became more complex, Jews became targets for those on both the right and the left. Jews were accused of being behind capitalism by Marxists, and of being behind communism by those on the right. Sometimes they were accused of both at the very same time.

Then, as religious control of authority dissipated in European societies, antisemitism veered toward something even more insidious: racial antisemitism. The tropes about Jews that had existed for centuries did not disappear, but a new layer was added, which came to imperil Jews far more than in the past. Jews were now depicted as fundamentally evil because of their blood. So no longer could they escape the charges against them. This was seen in stories of Christians in Europe, who were taken to the gas chambers of Auschwitz if they had even one-eighth Jewish ancestry.

The Holocaust could not have happened without this sordid history. It goes a long way to explain the behavior of the three elements in Europe that enabled the murder of six million: the perpetrators, the collaborators, and the bystanders. All were influenced in their behavior by the deep-seated antisemitism that had pervaded Europe for so long.

However, the history of the Jewish people is not simply about oppression and hatred of Jews. Indeed, it is a history of great accomplishments, great contributions, and great aspirations and hope despite the suffering.

Manning Rubin's story embodies that theme of hope after tragedy as the last part of the saga speaks to a Jewish revival after the nadir of the Holocaust in the land of Israel.

Just as the Holocaust was the culmination of centuries of antisemitic ideas about Jews, so the story of modern-day Israel did not *just happen*, even though the Zionist movement was formed in the late nineteenth century.

The theme of hope appeared every day in Jewish life for millennia, even in the most dire of circumstances. Central to that hope was the prayer to return to Jerusalem; through the centuries that idea kept the Jewish people alive. Famously, at wedding ceremonies, joyous moments in the life of Jews, the groom would break a glass to remind the Jewish people that Jerusalem, the Holy City, had been destroyed. Never forgetting Jerusalem was not merely an attachment to a lost past but a call for a very different future.

So, when the moment was ripe in late nineteenth century Europe, when other nation-states like Italy and Germany came into being, and when violent pogroms against Jews were proliferating, the Zionist movement began to translate that aspiration to return to the land of Israel into a reality, to win self-determination for the Jewish people in their historic homeland.

The relationship between the positives and the negatives in Jewish history speak to how antisemitism, which shares features with other forms of prejudice—stereotyping, discrimination, fear of the other—but has a unique quality. One thinks in this regard of a book that appeared in the mid-1930s by a revered Jewish historian at Oxford University, Cecil Roth: *The Jewish Contribution to Civilization*. He, like so many others, was appalled and distressed by the early behavior of the Nazis in power toward the Jews and the indifference about it throughout Europe and elsewhere.

He had a simple idea. Do a short book listing all the Jewish contributions to civilization, starting with the idea of one God, then moving to the Nobel prizes in many branches of science, the discoveries that led to the control of certain diseases, the world-class literary and economic contributions, the role that Jews played in working for peace and democracy. He hoped this book would change attitudes and prevent Nazism from growing and becoming truly lethal. Of course, Roth's book had no such impact. Indeed, for the antisemite, too often all these Jewish contributions merely confirm the deep-seated belief about the Jew, embodied in the infamous, fraudulent document, *The Protocols of the Learned Elders of Zion*, that the Jewish goal, even (or especially) when Jews play a prominent role in society, is to take over the world.

In other words, Jewish accomplishments prove the point. None of these historic antisemitic tropes have gone away. We see the surge of antisemitism, even in America, in recent years. The killers in Pittsburgh and Poway employed these tropes.

But things have also changed for the better. There exists a State of Israel, which can defend itself and which is a haven for endangered Jewish communities. Life for Jews in America remains at a high point, despite the disturbing trends of increasing antisemitic incidents including violence, the spewing of conspiracy theories against Jews on social media, and the politicization of antisemitism. This is reflected in Jewish involvement on all levels of American society and in the fact that opinion polls show that despite the manifestations of antisemitism, the

American people's attitude toward Jews remains positive. Antisemitic attitudes remain at an all-time low. Even on an international level, the adoption by large parts of the international community of the IHRA (International Holocaust Remembrance Alliance) definition of antisemitism, which includes anti-Zionism as a manifestation of the hatred of Jews.

Manning Rubin's moving story captures so many of these elements in a personal and human way. Both the challenges facing the Jewish people and the steadfast positivity of Jews in the face of horror are stories that need to be heard, whether from scholars and teachers or from a passionate memoirist like Manning Rubin, whose many experiences as his character Joey Goldman were his own for the first half of the book.

—Kenneth Jacobson, *Deputy National Director*
of the Anti-Defamation League

And don't miss the insights of these important leaders at the back of the book:

Abraham Foxman, *Director of the ADL, 1987-2015*

Mark B. Sisisky, *President of the Joint Distribution Committee*

Rabbi Abraham Cooper, *Simon Weisenthal Center*

Shoshana Bryen, *Senior Director, Jewish Policy Center*

James Patterson, *World's best-selling author*

CHAPTER 1

Ba-DUM-da-DUM-DUM, dum-dum-DUM…

The drumbeat burst from the open windows and ricocheted like gunshots off the walls of the low stone buildings across from the Panzer Kaserne in Nuremberg where the young GI was stationed. He'd heard that ominous beat in newsreels of Nazi soldiers goose-stepping and heiling Hitler. The Army had shown them during his basic training in 1945. Step after step, with German precision, in row after row, the drummers beat the sound with power in a rhythm designed to intimidate.

"These fucking Krauts are war machines. Your ass better know what you'll be fighting," his First Sergeant had shouted at the time. He had used the films to fire up the soldiers before they were sent overseas to face death.

Now, in 1946, the war over, the young soldier stood before his own set of drums, imitating that same ominous beat in his rooms upstairs in what had become the US Army Nuremberg Ordnance Depot. He had fantasized that if he saw a German stop on the street to react to this menacing sound, give a start, and look around in recognition, he would shoot the bastard. Then, a middle-aged man in a baggy grey suit walking outside the walls of this former German Army base pulled his shoulders back, first keeping step with the beat—*Ba-DUM-da-DUM-DUM, dum-dum-DUM* . . . and then moved into a modified goose-step.

Holy shit! Here's my chance! he thought.

Suddenly the man stopped, puzzled, and looked around for the source of the familiar Nazi sound.

The young soldier picked up his M1 Rifle, leaned on the sill, carefully sighted the German's head and whispered, "Goodbye, you goddamn Jew-killing son of a bitch. Ready. Aim . . . ."

But Joseph Ethan Goldman flushed and felt himself start to sweat. Could he do it? He wanted to kill. He'd been trained to kill, but he'd never had to kill. He narrowed his eyes, put his finger on the trigger, and visualized the bullet shattering the German's head, the blood spattering the crumbling wall nearby. The bastards—they all deserved death.

"Fucking murderers. Every one of you," Joey murmured.

"Joey! What the hell are you doing?" shouted Billy "Red" Blake, his roommate. He rushed in and lifted the M1's barrel.

At first Joey wrestled for the M1, then closed his eyes, bit his lip, and relaxed his grip. He bowed his head, shoulders slumped, took a deep breath, then looked up at Red.

"Jesus, Red, how did I come to this? Where I come from, we were taught better."

But this was nothing compared to the actual killing, fighting, and battles he would experience.

CHAPTER 2

How did it come to this—a naive Jewish boy from Charleston, South Carolina, now yearning to kill? He was eighteen when he enlisted. He looked fourteen, so his mates teased him: *Did you sneak into the Army?* He was short, only 5'3", with a wiry body and a face with a natural smile that often made people smile back.

"You oughta be in the Boy Scouts," his Army pal Skip Say liked to kid him. "Go get your merit badge for bird-watching and knot tying." Skip was two years older and had been assigned to the press corps covering the Nuremberg War Crimes Trials.

They'd met back in basic training at Camp Croft, South Carolina, on a freezing day in January 1945 when they were on maneuvers. Joey had put his pack down and started preparing a tent.

"Hey, you were made the squad leader, right?" said Skip, whose tent was already up. Joey had nodded, yes. What did this guy want?

Skip had quickly built a fire in front of his tent from twigs he had gathered in the woods. "No marshmallows, but you can share the warmth," he offered.

Joey almost said, "No thanks." He didn't like to depend on others. Ever since he was a kid he was practically on his own when his father was hospitalized for three years with a brain infection. His mother devoted most of her time and energy to her husband's care. This had gone on for his father's years of recovery at the expense of Joey and his older brother, Louis. "You pay attention to yourself," his mother warned him. "And be careful getting too caught up with others. You hear?"

Something about Skip's warm, frank openness made Joey hesitate as he stood shivering from the cold. Then, impulsively, he'd accepted. "Thanks. Not used this kind of weather. Freezing my ass off."

Joey put up his tent next to Skip's, drew near the fire, and they started exchanging stories. Skip's buzz cut and round, smiling face made him resemble a hairy pumpkin. He was slightly plump, even after weeks of infantry training. Because Skip was editor of his high school paper in Massachusetts, out of habit, he started to interview Joey.

"Been curious to know how come Sergeant Rooton picked you right away to be a squad leader on parade days," he asked.

"I was in a high school cadet corps, a Southern tradition," Joey said. "I knew a thing or two about drilling before I enlisted."

"I wondered how you swung that," said Skip.

"Didn't swing anything," Joey answered, frowning. "He saw how I marched when we first drilled and asked me where I learned it."

"Hey, then maybe we can share a tent on these maneuvers, and I might learn a thing or two 'bout being a soldier?" said Skip.

From then on, they hung out together when they weren't being taught to kill. They learned to fire their M1s, to crawl on their bellies under barbed wire with real bullets overhead, and to run obstacle courses with bayonets fixed and ready for the straw-man enemies that would suddenly spring out from behind trees—rigorous but necessary if they were to stay alive on a battlefield. Joey liked it, Skip joked about it, but both paid close attention.

CHAPTER 3

———

That first time on the firing range, he'd been nervous. The only other rifle he had used was his Daisy "Buck Jones" BB gun. As an eight-year-old, he fired at a robin pecking at berries on the limb of the Spanish moss–laden tree next to the yard on Sans Souci Street, then watched in horror as it tumbled to the ground. Joey saw it flapping around. He dropped his BB gun and ran crying with the bird into the house to his brother, Louis, who took the robin and gently put a matchstick splint on the broken wing and patted Joey on the head.

"Ready on the right," yelled Sergeant Rooton, startling Joey. "Ready on the left. The flag is up. The flag is waving. Ready! Aim! Fire!"

Later on, before they went out on a twenty-mile overnight hike, the sergeant delivered a warning: "You just might find your ass diving into some muddy fucking mess in the dark, and your M1 will need you to know how to keep it firing." He paused, "So, learn how to take it apart and put it back together blindfolded by next week."

"Blindfolded!" he shouted. "Got it?"

"Yessir!" they all shouted back.

That evening, as they put up their tent for the overnight, Joey looked at the clouds. "My old man would say it's gonna rain."

"Well, you told me he really knows his weather," Skip said. "So let's build a trench around the tent from the uphill side."

Rain it did, but they were dry as they studied their rifles. Rivulets flowed around their tent, but not into it. *Hmm, pretty smart!* Joey thought.

Skip yawned, "C'mon, let's use that pitter-patter to send us to a nice beddy-bye."

"Got a job to do first," Joey responded. Holding his M1, he closed his eyes. As he listened to the rain on his tent, his mind segued to a tin roof, years back, when his dad was deathly sick. It was raining and he, only three, had to stay indoors with his toys spread out in a hallway in his Aunt Minnie's house in Richmond. They were staying there while his father recuperated.

His mother walked by to sit with his father. "Clean up that mess."

His Uncle Joe chimed in, "You heard her," he said. "Put all that mess away. It's your job to make sure you don't upset your mother and make your father worse."

Joey had no idea what a "job" was or what it had to do with making his dad worse. Forever after, it made him feel the need to do the best "job" he was given. This rifle was a job, no different than others, except, it was also a dogface's protection. Do it right, or else.

One night after chow, they were listening to the news and the newscaster saying that although the Allies were succeeding, the war was still raging on both sides of the world. As infantry dogfaces, they knew soldiers were dying daily and had to be replaced. It was rarely spoken out loud in the platoon, but the question of where they would end up was always with them, especially when they listened to the radio at night in the barracks.

"Geez, this Basic shit is bad," Skip complained, "but what's gonna happen to us when Basic is over?"

Then, on May 8, 1945, the day after they finished Basic, the camp sirens sounded. Loudspeakers all over camp blared the news: "Germany has surrendered," said the voice of the commanding general himself. "General Eisenhower has informed the President that the Allied Forces have won the war in Europe. Hitler is dead. I repeat, Hitler is dead." Up-tempo band music played between more victory-in-Europe announcements.

The troops everywhere were cheering. Joey and Skip joined in the relief that spread throughout the camp.

"It's over! It's over!" they yelled. "Hitler's dead!"

Joey's friend Ruffier started singing a ditty they all knew:

Hitler has only got one ball,
Goering has two but very small,
Himmler is rather sim'lar,
But poor old Goebbels has no balls at all.

Everybody laughed, then they all joined in. The Camp Croft band formed on the parade grounds and started playing swing tunes. Nurses from the medical unit came out and danced with the guys. Skip took advantage of this and grabbed a pretty young redhead and started jitterbugging with her. He kept motioning to Joey to do the same, but Joey was too bashful. He still had acne and felt unattractive. Instead, he headed for the PX, where free beer flowed. The officers were there, mingling freely with the GIs. It was like the Fourth of July or opening day at the State Fair.

CHAPTER 4

Later, back at the barracks, hidden booze appeared, and the celebration continued until their sergeant raised his beer-filled canteen and cried, "To victory in Europe!"

"Yay! Yay! To victory!" shouted the platoon.

"And now, boys," the sergeant said, "we gotta beat those fucking Japs."

They all raised their drinks, but instead of drinking they paused, lowered their cups, and the merriment died down.

"Shit, Joey," Skip whispered, "We're fresh out of infantry Basic. That makes us prime meat to go to the Pacific. I gotta see how I can get the fuck outa the infantry."

Joey just shrugged about what fate had in store for him. He once read a Chinese proverb: "Ride the horse in the direction it's going." That was his nature. It gave him a calm that contrasted with his barrack-mates.

"Don't you give a shit?" snarled a guy named O'Connor. Joey looked at him, surprised.

"Sure," he said, "but what the heck can we do about it?"

O'Connor had been restricted several times for drunkenness and brawling. He took a few steps toward Joey. Joey was wary, but not afraid. He was short, under five feet until he was fifteen, but his Charleston neighbor Billy Muckenfuss had been a Golden Gloves boxer and often used Joey as a sparring partner in his home practice ring, so Joey knew how to box. He squinted and tightened up, ready to fight, but a group of the guys came in with a bunch of beers and O'Connor joined them.

The talk focused on the terrible things they heard about the Japs. The mood was dark. Joey kept thinking about fighting the Japs. It was bad enough for a person who got seasick even in Charleston Harbor to think about being shipped across the Pacific, but it was even worse to think about landing on a Jap-held island where they could be mowed down like the GIs on D-Day.

Two days later, they got their orders. They were to take a furlough home, then report to Fort Dix, New Jersey, to get their assignment. A proverbial wave of relief washed over the barracks.

"That's gotta mean we're gonna go to the European Theater, not the Pacific!" Ruffier shouted. There was a general consensus that this was true.

"I'm praying for France," said Skip.

"Whatever, the fickle finger of fate is in charge," Joey remarked.

"Well, I hope it's not *this* finger in charge," said Skip with a vulgar hand gesture.

CHAPTER 5

Joey went home. His parents hoped he wouldn't be sent to fight the Japanese.

"I never got into it in World War I," his father said. "Spent the whole time in the Signal Corps at the Marine base in Philadelphia."

Joey just nodded. He could count on his dad to talk about himself and about his military life, but never ask Joey about his own. Aunt Minnie, on the other hand, wanted to know everything. She had come down from Richmond to see him off.

On his last day she hugged him. "I want you to have this Magen David. It was Milton's." She put the six-pointed star on a gold chain around his neck. He had never worn one before and wondered just what it meant. Milton was his favorite cousin. He was Minnie's only child. As a P-38 pilot Ace, he was shot down over Germany last year. She was desperately holding on to the letter that said he wasn't reported dead, but only MIA. Joey's eyes misted, sharing Minnie's loss.

Milton wrote him postcards from the air base where he'd taught others how to fly P-38s until he finally lobbied his way into action in England. His loss was, in fact, why Joey dropped out of college and enlisted. In some strange way, he thought this might replace Milton for his aunt. In some ways, it had.

"You be very careful, you hear me?" Aunt Minnie admonished.

Joey hugged his aunt. "You reckon you could send me some of your famous pickles, Aunt Minnie?" he asked playfully.

"I sure will, darlin', you just write me where."

At Fort Dix, several weeks later, a young lieutenant addressed the assembled unit: "You men are lucky bastards. You're the first replacement troops for the Third Army in Germany. You'll be the Army of Occupation in Europe so the vets can start coming home."

When the young GIs heard that, a tangible sound of relief danced through the room once again. Now it was official.

Three weeks later, Joey and Skip left the base in full battle kit and were climbing the gangplank onto the Liberty ship USS Howard bound for Le Havre, France, from New Jersey.

"All aboard for the ETO," Skip called out, like a Pullman conductor. Then, to Joey, "The European *Theater* of Operations. Wonder what kind of show that *theater* is waiting to play for us?"

"One without bullets is good enough for me," someone said, and tapped Joey on the shoulder. It was Al Moskowitz, his college roommate. They had both volunteered but were sent to different camps for Basic.

"Al, holy shit. You on this crate, too?" Joey said, and hugged his friend.

"In the flesh, and happy as hell to be going to France," Al admitted.

"You and me!" Skip interrupted and sang out as they all joined in:

> *To the southern part of France*
> *Where the women wear no pants!*
> *But they all wear grass,*
> *Just to cover up their ass.*
> *When the grass falls down,*
> *It's the greatest show in town.*

Continuing to sing, they headed up the gangplank.

"We're off to who knows what!" Skip yelled.

CHAPTER 6

Joey watched the Kraut as he let Red take his M1. "Who knows what" turned out to be Nuremberg, Germany, the heart of Nazism. With World War II over, Joey had two years to go before discharge. He was part of the US Army of Occupation in the headquarters group of the 318th Ordnance Battalion at the Nuremberg Ordnance Depot.

No longer hearing the staccato drumbeat, the confused German cautiously moved away from the former Panzer Kaserne where the 318th was stationed.

"It's amazing to see how these drums cause the Krauts to get upset," Red said. "But to get you that upset . . . ."

"Okay, okay. I'll settle for that, Red." Joey spit angrily out the open window. He had come close to squeezing that trigger and was amazed at how good it felt.

Red just shook his head.

Joey had a complete drum set because he'd been picked as the drummer in the band formed to play in the officers' club on the weekends. The drumming through the open window began after Skip, using his press credentials, started taking Joey to sessions of the International War Crimes Trials held in Nuremberg's Palace of Justice. They would sit, wearing headphones set on English translation, looking down on the huge room where, on one side, the Nazi leaders sat glumly with white-helmeted GI Military Police lined up behind them, while on the other side, members of the Tribunal sat with their staff of translators and stenographers.

One day at the Trial, as he and Skip watched films supplied by the prosecution, Joey found tears streaming down his cheeks. "I can't believe this. Those bodies. Oh my God. They're just piled up like . . . like garbage."

There was complete silence as everyone saw hundreds of emaciated, lifeless bodies being stacked in a concentration camp.

"And Jesus, Skip," whispered Joey. "That huge pile of shoes by the crematorium. Who wore them? Oh my God, look at that pile. It's . . . look, Skip, kids' shoes. Little kids, for Chrissake. It's making me sick. How the hell did this happen? How come I never read about it in the news?"

Skip shook his head. "God knows."

"God?" asked Joey. "Where was God during all this?" Skip looked at him, then nodded in agreement.

Wiping his eyes, Joey bit his lip. He was really unsettled. *We never heard any details of the death camps in Charleston*, he thought. Matter of fact, nobody talked about it in Basic, either. He stared at the defendants: Goering, Hess, von Ribbentrop, Streicher—the Nazi political and military leaders. They sat there stone-faced in headphones as their crimes were enumerated. Only Goering smiled as the prosecutors challenged them with uncompromising questions about the six million Jews in Europe they had systematically murdered.

"Six million, with . . . with over a million children, just because they were Jews like me," he said to Skip. "How in hell can that be?"

"Joey, looks like you never read much of your people's history," answered Skip.

Joey frowned at *your people.* He never thought much about being Jewish.

"And," Skip added, "didn't you ever get called a kike or a sheeny growing up?"

"Never," said Joey. "I never thought much about it."

"Weren't you always made aware of being a Jew?" Skip asked.

"Well," Joey pondered, "it wasn't like that in Charleston. Least, I don't think so." He frowned, thinking for the first time that others thought of him as a Jew even though he himself never thought much about it. It wasn't that he was ashamed. It was just that in Charleston people didn't seem to care. He was glad Skip dropped it.

That night, Joey bolted upright from a nightmare about the Nazi experiments he had seen. He was screaming: "Stop it! You bastards! He's gonna suffocate. Turn the oxygen back on!"

Red woke him up. "Easy, man, easy. It's only a dream."

"No. No! You don't understand! It was real what those bastards did to their prisoners!" Joey yelled. "And they took pictures and films of it. Strapping men in airtight chambers, letting out oxygen to see how high their goddamn Luftwaffe pilots could fly before they would die."

He grabbed Red's arm. "And . . . and they would freeze prisoners to death to study what kind of uniforms to send to the Eastern Front. Medical experiments on helpless Jews—by doctors, Red, by *fucking doctors!*"

CHAPTER 7

On another day at the Trial, as if in a trance, Joey heard the prosecutors describe and show how from 40,000 camps and ghettos Jews were herded like cattle, terrified, and stuffed into actual cattle boxcars, without food or water, to go to extermination camps.

Joey wrote home:

> *My friend Skip took me to the Nuremberg War Crimes Trials again. There were photos and films of the lines at the concentration camp railway stops where going right meant slave labor and going left was to the chambers where the Zyklon B would gas those people by the millions, Dad . . . by the millions. And the films of the piles of starved bodies and piles of ashes of the victims in huge ovens. It made me cry, Dad. It was so damn horrible it even made some of the judges cry. How could people do this? How come we never heard about this at home? I am so angry at the Germans and here I am right in the middle of all of them. Did you know about all this, Dad, did you?*

When Joey first started opening his windows and playing that ominous Nazi drumbeat *Ba-DUM-da-DUM-DUM, dum-dum-DUM* he was just curious to see if it would affect German civilians passing by on the street outside, next to the Kaserne's walls. But after seeing the films at the Trials, he began to imagine killing them. First, he began to hate the Nazi leaders, both military and civilian, as he listened to the relentless challenges by the international panel of judges, prosecutors, and military experts. In solemn voices, the presenters faced the dock— Goering and Hess and von Ribbentrop and the other Nazi leaders— and asserted that they were guilty. They were *guilty of Crimes Against Peace, Crimes Against Humanity, War Crimes, and a Common Plan of Conspiracy.* Explicit examples of each were given in films and documents.

"Those crimes sound so highfalutin' when what they actually were was so low," Joey grumbled.

"Lower than low," agreed Skip.

Goering usually had a hint of a smile on his face as he sat there. "I'd like to wipe that fucking smile off his fat face," Joey spat out. "Look, look at this part, Skip, they're just ordinary Nazi soldiers doing those, those… oh, God, disgusting things—and enjoying it, too." His hatred grew, extending now to Germans in general.

On a recent visit, the Russian prosecutor, with a dramatic gesture, started to show a film of atrocities, but the projectionist had put it in upside down and there was a moment of confusion, then laughter. Even the guilty defendants actually laughed loudly and clapped their hands.

Joey growled. "All those fucking Nazi bigwigs sitting there laughing, as if they were watching *The Three Stooges.*"

However, when the film was righted, the laughter stopped abruptly. Lawyers, judges, press, and visitors were all shocked by what was depicted. Joey was so surprised it brought him to tears. Even some of the Nazis were gulping back their shame as the unimaginable scenes of torture, killing, and mountains of emaciated bodies rolled by silently on the large screen. Only the click-click-click of the projector could be heard. Joey kept shaking his head in disbelief. "How could humans do this to other humans?" he whispered to Skip.

"They demonized them," Skip said. "They treated them like vermin."

Not believing what he was seeing, Joey looked at Skip. It was making him more and more aware of being Jewish—a feeling he'd never had before.

As the films rolled on, a fragile-looking woman who was one of the invited guests in the hall began to cry out in Polish and English, "Murderers! Murderers!" She looked like the survivors in the films. Security guards raced to her and escorted her out, but she continued screaming. Running along with them was a young woman who was pleading in English with the guards to be careful.

As they passed by, Skip grabbed Joey to come with him. "There's a story here. C'mon," he whispered. They ran to catch up.

In the hall, the MPs were doing their best to calm the woman down. She was crying now, and the young woman put her arms around her shoulders. "Please, she is with me. I can take care of her." Happy to be relieved of the responsibility, the MPs backed off.

Skip approached the two women and showed his press corps ID. "Please, may we be of help?" he asked gently. "Obviously she is a survivor and those films brought it all back."

"Who can blame her?" Joey exclaimed. "Can we do anything? Maybe give you a lift to wherever you're staying?"

"Thank you so much," said the younger of the two. "I am not actually with her. I only wanted, like you, to be of help. I am Leah Chalowitz." She reached out to shake Joey's hand. An odd European gesture, he thought, as he shook the firm hand, his eyes followed up her arm and to her eyes. They, like his, were a deep, deep blue. She was his height with beautiful blonde hair streaming down to her shoulders. Blinking awkwardly, he finally managed to say, "I am Joey Goldman."

"Goldman?" she said. "A Jewish soldier—from America, yes?"

Surprised by this, Joey answered haltingly. "Um . . . um . . . yes, I am Jewish."

"Chalowitz?" Skip jumped in. "Could it be you're Jewish too?"

"Yes," she answered.

"Are you also a survivor? Of which camp?" Skip asked, already thinking of a headline for his story. Noticing his press ID, Leah became guarded, and turned quickly to Joey. "If you really can help, it would be good of you to help me get her back to where she is staying."

On the way in the Jeep, Skip continued to try to get a story out of her, but she avoided it. It was like a tennis match. Out came his question, which she lobbed back. Joey smiled at each evasive answer. Since the press corps quarters were on the way to where the older woman was staying, Joey decided to drop Skip off first. Skip protested until Joey gave him an elbow and a look. Skip nodded, grinned, and winked.

CHAPTER 8

Joey couldn't believe he was actually doing this—dropping off Skip first and then the older woman in order to be alone with Leah Chalowitz. There was something about her that made him feel suddenly courageous. It wasn't just that she was beautiful, but there was a hint of pain in her eyes paired with intensity and curiosity.

The two of them helped the woman into the small inn where she was staying with a group of fellow refugees. Now calmed down, she said, through Leah, "The others were at the Trials in the morning, and I decided to stay all day. I am so sorry to cause such trouble. Thank you for your help." She held out her hand.

He took her hand in both of his. "You are not trouble for me. Never, never," Joey said. As Leah translated, the look of surprise and gratitude on the wrinkled face was something he would remember for a long time.

Then, Joey offered to take Leah to wherever she needed to go.

"It would be nice of you to take me to where I am staying," she said.

In the Jeep, Joey asked, "What was that you spoke with her? Polish?"

"Yes, I am—or maybe I should say I *was*—Polish."

"Were you," he hesitated, "Were you in a concentration camp, too?"

"Me? No, no. I was able to survive by hiding in the forests with a group."

"Leah, I . . . ah . . . would really like to know more about you," he said. "But I don't want to pry."

"Pry? What is 'pry'?"

"It means to make you tell me how you survived if you don't want to."

She looked at him for a long moment before asking, "You are not from the press like your friend?"

Joey laughed. "No way. I'm in supply at the Nuremberg Ordnance Depot. Skip has been taking me to the Trials." He paused and looked over at her. "I've been horrified by what I've seen. I can't believe what they did to all those people."

She looked at him with a slight squint. "*Those* people are *my* people—*your* people. My whole family was killed," she said.

"Oh, my God," Joey whispered. "I'm so sorry. How did *you* manage to . . . to stay alive?"

"Over there," she pointed. "That's where I'm staying."

Joey pulled over in front of a large stone house. There were bullet holes in several places in the three-story wall. In front, sitting on a bench was a large man with a scruffy beard. He leapt up with a hand inside his coat as the Jeep stopped and peered in. *What the heck is he reaching for?* Joey thought. A pistol? What is this place? Recognizing Leah, the man relaxed, and they began to speak in Polish. When he nodded, Leah turned to Joey and asked, "Would you like to come in for a cup of coffee?"

Holy shit, thought Joey. *She wants to know me, too?* He grinned. "I'd love to, thanks, thanks."

As they entered, Joey felt eyes upon him—from three tanned young men who nodded slightly, but without expression. Leah greeted them first in Hebrew, then in English. "This is Sergeant Joseph Goldman, a Jewish-American soldier who was of great help to me today. I have invited him in for a coffee." The three shook hands without introducing themselves. One of them said, in perfect English, "Welcome, and thank you for helping Leah." With a slight bow, he gestured toward the sitting room down the hall.

"Glad I could do it." Joey followed Leah down the hall. *What was this place?* he wondered. Who were these men? Why the guard outside?

The room was furnished simply, with antique chairs; two maroon sofas; and a long, shiny, wooden table. There was no wall decoration of any sort—not even one painting or photograph. A silver samovar sat on a mahogany buffet with flowered cups, spoons, and a cream pitcher. Leah poured coffee from the samovar. "Cream?" she asked. "We have no sugar."

"Cream? Great," Joey answered. "What is this place, Leah?"

She took a slow sip. "These are, ah, people who maintain this home for Jewish visitors to the Trials. My school arranged for me to stay here this week."

"Your school?" said Joey. "You're a teacher?"

"Not exactly," she said. "I'm helping children who survived prepare for a new life." She paused and frowned.

"What do you mean, 'a new life'?"

"A life in Palestine, Israel."

"Palestine? Why? I mean—" Joey drifted off.

"Why?" she interrupted. "Because it is the only place in the world that wants us."

"Us? Meaning Jews?" Joey said.

"Us meaning Jews, yes," she replied.

"Leah, please, tell me about all this," Joey said. "I want to understand."

"About me?" she was a bit uncomfortable. "It is nothing much. I am here from Geneva, Switzerland. I'm working with a school, and they sent me here to report to the students what is happening to the Nazi leaders."

"No, Leah, I mean how does a Jewish girl manage to stay alive after her family is killed? I can't put myself in that place."

"I lived in a small Polish village, Zamosc," she began. "One day, the Germans rounded up all the Jews and made them start digging a huge trench outside the village. Men, women, and even children like me and my sister were given shovels and put to work for three days," Leah explained. "On the third day, my father woke up my sister Rael and me very early and took us to the backyard and put us into our sewer pit," she said. "He covered us with a garbage trough and told us to stay still and be absolutely quiet. Then we heard machine guns and screams— my family, knowing we were hidden and alone nearby, had refused to leave. Soldiers were laughing," she said, swallowing to keep from crying. "One of them said, 'Did you see how the old lady shit herself?'

"The Germans marched everyone, mothers, fathers, children in front of the graves they were forced to dig for themselves in the days before, and machine-gunned them all," Leah whispered, her eyes closed, lips trembling. Joey looked at her as she relived the pain, and reached over to hold her hands on the table. She looked down at them and then turned hers to hold his. They looked at each other, aware something was happening, a fledgling intimacy.

"I saw photographs of the very same thing at the Trials," he said. "Photos recorded in their efficient German way."

Leah told how she and Rael stayed hidden until dark, then fled into the forests. Joey could barely hold back tears as Leah unfolded her tale of horror and terror as she and her sister ran away—orphans now, cold and hungry with no place to go. At this point, one of the men opened the door.

"Leah, we must have this room now," he said quietly. "I am sorry." He showed no expression as, embarrassed, they quickly withdrew their hands and headed outside.

By now it was growing dark, and Joey knew he had to report back to the Kaserne. He asked, "Can we meet here again tomorrow?"

Leah sighed. "I am leaving for Geneva early in the morning," she said. "But, if I give you my address you can write to me?" As they exchanged addresses, they looked hopefully at each other.

"I will write to you, if that's okay?" his eyes moistening.

She smiled. "It's more than okay, I will be sad if you don't."

They stood staring at one another. He was holding her hands, and wanted to kiss her, but instead raised her hands to his lips, unsure of himself. Quickly she bent down and kissed his hands, then moved toward the door. She stood waving goodbye as he drove off.

"I don't believe it!" Joey mumbled as his Jeep rumbled down the road. "I . . . I think I'm in love. I'm in love with Leah Chalowitz!" he shouted. "Holy shit!"

CHAPTER 9

"You think you're in *love*?" exclaimed Skip. "After one meeting?"

Joey shrugged his shoulders in an expression of surprise, and gestured with his hands. "I mean, I think so, I mean . . . . Yeah. I- ah- mean, haven't you ever heard about love at first sight?"

Skip laughed. "Sure, sure, in books and movies, but . . ."

"No buts. This is real. I've already written her."

"Wow. Mister Shy jumps out of the nest!" Skip exclaimed. He'd seen how bashful Joey was with women when he tried one night to set the two of them up with two French press corps assistants, and Joey blew it. *Can't help it,* Joey thought.

Joey told Skip what Leah had described. The killings, the terror, the running into the night with her sister. "Those fucking Germans," Joey said. "I hate them all."

Something else was growing in Joey besides hatred, though— something he had never really experienced growing up in Charleston. It was about being Jewish. Jews had been a respected part of Charleston since the early 1700s. Like most immigrant groups, they strove to assimilate, generation after generation. His father, Louis Sr., had been a possible mayoral candidate before he got sick. Uncle Manning was associate editor of the *Evening Post*, and Big Aunt Ruth was head of the Girl Scouts. It didn't hurt that Joey was blond and blue-eyed, with lots of Gentile friends—hardly what a Jew was supposed to look like: dark curly hair; big, hooked nose; big lips; hunched-over posture.

"You don't look Jewish, Goldilocks," Skip said early on, referring to the stereotype without even thinking about it.

Joey was an empty canvas on which new experiences were like the brushstrokes of an abstract painting. He wasn't really aware of what it was that was making him edgy. His window drumming had grown from all of this.

Most of the time, he used the drum set to play in the 318th Headquarters jazz band at the officers' mess. His drumming started way back on one of the regular visits he and his brother Louis made to his Aunt Dora for supper at the Berkeley Court Apartments. He loved to use two wooden spoons to beat rhythms on pots and pans in her kitchen and sing the latest songs. She would dance a "jig," as she called it. One night, as a surprise, she gave him a set of drummer's brushes.

"You're so cute!" she loved to say. He was almost ten but very small and looked so much younger. Dora, or "Dodo" as they called her, would give him a bear hug against her huge breasts.

That night, in his room on Sans Souci Street, he couldn't wait to turn on the little Silvertone radio he'd bought at Sears with his paper route money so he could play along with the music on the *Lucky Strike Hit Parade*. He used a cardboard box as his drum and was going wild to a Harry James piece.

"I'm trying to study, damn it!" Louis yelled, slamming his door shut.

CHAPTER 10

Louis was a genius in literature and history. Joey was somewhat intimidated by him, so he turned to sports instead. With his great sense of rhythm, he excelled in every sport, a natural athlete. Louis, who wasn't very coordinated, was proud of Joey's skill, and encouraged him.

"So what, you're not big, Joey," he'd say. "You're damn good."

The drum practice came in handy when the USS Howard Victory, a just-launched troop ship, was galloping up and down, wave to wave, like a runaway horse across the North Atlantic, and the steamy, crowded lower decks lined with bunks quickly began smelling of vomit and sweat.

On the third day out, a young lieutenant came through yelling, "Anyone here play drums? I need a jazz drummer for my band."

Joey leapt from his bunk and yelled back, "I do, sir!" Volunteering wasn't usual for him, but the Army was making him more active in many ways. He was less of a loner now.

Suddenly, he was part of a little group that got to play in the officers' mess up top. Took him a little while to get used to playing on a real drum set, but he faked it fine. The other members helped cover his early trials. "Latin beat, Goldman. Latin . . . boom-chicka chicka-boom, chicka-boom," the bass player whispered. It wasn't long before Joey was thinking, *Hell, this was fun*. Maybe he could be Gene Krupa someday? They played every night for the eight-day voyage. You couldn't dance, because the crashing waves rolled the ship, so the band was entertainment for the officers and nurses who sat eating and drinking.

And the best part of the deal was the band also got to eat what the officers ate. What's more, Joey lifted stuff from the officers' mess.

"Chow time," Joey whispered to his group from Camp Croft below deck, as he unloaded a pile of goodies from his knapsack onto his bunk. "I got some chicken and steak for you."

"Jeez, lot better than the soup and Spam shit we get down here," Skip exclaimed, diving right in.

Back in Basic, he thought he might die in battle with these guys. It broke down his habit of not depending on others. *I've got your back* was something they all learned was important. Life in the Army was pushing at his belief system in so many ways, but heading for war-torn Europe was just another assignment for Joey. He didn't have a clue that it could tear up his life too.

CHAPTER 11

Now . . . here he was in the 318th HQ, where another lieutenant, Hershel Forner, was looking for a drummer too. This time, Joey ended up having a full drum set in his rooms and found himself playing weekly at the officers' club, where food and drinks also flowed freely.

He didn't find his job at Headquarters Unit hard, but it was demanding because of Lieutenant Colonel Royce Larned, the chubby-cheeked Wisconsin law professor in charge. He had interviewed Joey, who was smart and eager, and had one semester of college before enlisting. The colonel decided to put him in charge of supplies.

"How come you dropped out of college, Goldman?"

After a pause, Joey told him about his cousin Milton.

The colonel nodded in sympathy. "Sorry, son. Look, I'm sending you to supply school. I want you to run Supplies for me here. I got too goddamn many roles to cover, so make damn sure you come back knowing what the hell it requires. I know you can do it. Okay?"

"Yes, sir!" Joey snapped to attention and threw him a salute.

The colonel smiled and threw one right back at him. "See Lieutenant Forner for your orders and schedule."

Joey left and couldn't wait to tell the guys. Since it was a case of doing a job well, he had to write home.

He wrote Louis and his folks:

I'm at the Army Training Center in Heidenheim for a crash course in Supply Management. Harder than college was. Everything you need to know about Supplies in only two weeks. The center is in an old army Kaserne much fancier than where I am in Nuremberg. There are a million forms to learn, complicated procedures, and descriptions for everything from toilet paper to tank parts and weapons. You study twelve hours a day and have homework, too. All the units in Bavaria come to Nuremberg for stuff and I've got to be the one to take care of them. I guess it'll be good for me . . . . Another good part is you know how I like food. Well here there's prime ribs every night and lots of German beer. Course, there's a lot of Germans, too, which I don't like, but I do take a few strolls around the town. Here's a couple pictures of Heidenheim. Sorry they aren't better but my camera stinks.

Louis was four years older than Joey. He was drafted and assigned as editor of the Fort Benning newspaper, and never got to serve overseas. His parents said Louis was lucky, but it didn't make him very happy. He responded immediately:

Wish I could get there and go through what you are experiencing, Joey. You're a part of history and I'm just a distant observer. Keep me posted, okay? But please use words because you're right. Your pictures are lousy. Seriously, Joey, I assume you're being careful around those Nazis. I'm told a lot of them are in hiding and don't want to be caught.

Joey smiled at that. *It's nice to have him as my brother,* he thought. Louis's hand-me-down genes made him 6'1". He was always protective of Joey since Joey only came up to his chest. Louis also knew Joey suffered the most from their father's illness because he was so young and bewildered when it happened.

Joey's dad took a few weeks to write, and it was all about himself. He recalled how he was sent to be a communications expert and promoted to be a staff sergeant in the Signal Corps at a Marine base outside Philadelphia, a fact Joey already knew. He just stared at the letter, then threw it down and leaned back in his chair staring blankly at the picture of his parents on his desk.

On his return to HQ after Heidenheim, Joey was immediately faced with handling supplies not only for all the occupation troops stationed in the Kaserne, but also for the equipment for dozens of other Army units in the American Zone. It was strictly up to him to decide which requests really could be allowed, as well as being sure he kept his inventory up so he could meet the continuing needs of the huge Army of Occupation.

He visited all sixty-three buildings on the depot, taking notes about the thousands of vehicles, parts, weapons, and ammo accumulated there, and made detailed reports to the colonel daily.

"I'm busy as hell these days," he said to Skip. When Skip complained how busy he was too, Joey said, "You? Busy? Consider yourself lucky, pal. You're sitting there at a desk getting ideas for stories for *Stars and Stripes* while *I'm* getting a load of crap all day long from NCOs and officers. You should hear the bullshit stories and lists of stuff they've just got to have for their 'poor weary troops' and their 'important vehicles.'"

"Okay, okay," Skip agreed , "I got it. I got it. You win."

Joey laughed. "But I like it," he said.

CHAPTER 12

Three weeks into the job, he was flabbergasted by an urgent call from Lieutenant Forner. He walked into the lieutenant's office and stood quietly at attention, wondering what he had done wrong. Forner was busy writing something. Finally he looked up and stared sternly at Joey, who was doing his best to be nonchalant.

Joey saluted. "Sir?"

Forner saluted back. "*Private* Goldman," he said, then reached into a drawer for a large envelope, which he threw on the desk in front of Joey. "Open it."

Joey gulped, not having a clue to what this was about, and opened the envelope. Inside was a pair of staff sergeant's stripes and a document.

"Read it, *Sergeant* Goldman," Forner broke into a big grin.

"Oh, my God." He had been promoted to staff sergeant of the 318th in charge of supplies. Forner stood and reached out to shake hands.

"You're doing a very good job, Goldman. Keep it up."

Joey told no one and at day's end raced back to the barracks and found the German maid, Frau Bettina, who took care of the small building that housed the HQ soldiers. It was made of stones and bricks crusted with dirt from the many bombings that destroyed most of old Nuremberg. She took care of the eight apartments in the building, and from time to time took care of the guys with blow jobs in return for supplies otherwise unavailable to German citizens.

"Bettina! Bettina!" Joey called.

Bettina stuck her head out from a room down the hall. *"Ja, Josef. Was halten Sie da, Schatz? Was wollen Sie?"*

"Bettina," Joey said. "Look, Look. I'm a sergeant now! Can you sew these on?" pointing to where his private's stripes were.

"Ja. Ja. Gif to me," she started to put them in her apron pocket.

"No! No! Now, right now!" *"Unmittelbar, bitte."* He began taking off his shirt.

An hour later Staff Sergeant Joseph Goldman strolled into the mess hall and sat down with the group from HQ.

"Hey, guys," Joey said casually.

They were stuffing themselves, as young guys do, until Red did a double take with a mouthful.

"Holy shit, Joey!" he said. "What's that you're wearing?"

"I got promoted!" Joey flexed his arms like a weightlifter showing his biceps to make the stripes more visible, then read them the promotion notice. They all started clapping. *What a bunch of guys,* Joey thought. *I never had so many pals.*

That night he wrote home about what had happened.

> *Dad, Mom, I just got promoted to a Sergeant like Dad was! I'm a Supply Staff Sgt. with four stripes and more bucks as well. I can't believe it. I'm responsible for not only all the supplies needed here for the Depot but for all the Military units in this part of the American Zone. It's an important job, Dad. So I'm going to work at it hard. It's also a time-consuming job, but I'm glad to say I can handle it. Can you believe it, Dad? A*

Staff Sergeant like you were. That's my big news for today. Let's see. What else is going on?

The Colonel is tough, but nice, and he told me to be just like that with all those who come in begging for supplies . . . tough but nice. So I can't complain. Maybe I could complain about the food we're getting? There's a huge difference between what the Officer's Club gets compared to our mess hall. At least on the weekends when I'm playing in the band I get a few good meals. Say, could you ask Aunt Minnie to send me some of her famous pickles? I miss them. I'd write her myself but I'm really busy and I'm not much of a letter writer like you, Dad. I can't believe you got a personal answer from President Truman. Tell me what he said.

All his life, at least since he was old enough to be aware of feelings, he sought love from his father. But having suffered so long, his father had turned inward and was obsessed with his illness and the weather.

CHAPTER 13

However, Joey was always amazed how his dad would write anyone if he saw a problem. His father was proud of some of those results, like when he got his Dodge repaired for free by writing the president of the company. It was one of the things he admired about his father—action was his motto. He would write a letter, address it, put a stamp on it, and walk it to the corner mailbox. Joey tried to practice that kind of action behavior. He even wrote up a motto to go on the wall by his desk. *Think it. Plan it. Do it.*

The guys joked with him about it. Red said, "Think it—I'm feeling horny. Plan it—I'm going to the john. Do it—I'm jerkin' off!"

Carlos joined in. "I overate. I need to take a dump. Ah-h-h, I'm doin' it."

Joey laughed. "Oh yeah? Well, you're still full of shit."

It was nice having a gang to hang around with, he thought. But coming back from an afternoon at the Trials he was silent at dinner. Noticing this, Carlos said, "Those Nazi bastards got you down again?"

"They're gonna get theirs, so why worry?" Smitty said. Red agreed.

Joey just nodded. He was flipping back and forth between anger and depression thinking about what was done to the Jews, but he didn't feel comfortable saying what he felt. *I wish that one of them was Jewish. The lieutenant is Jewish but he's an officer so I don't think that would fly.*

Guess I could talk about this with Skip, but, shit, he's not Jewish, either. Strange to feel part of a group, yet not completely comfortable. A new burden to carry. One he'd never felt before. He wrote about it to his dad.

> *I'm still going to the Trials with Skip. I'm intrigued by what went on in this war and startled by how terrible the Germans were, especially to the Jews. I mean terrible. Murdered just because they were Jews. Village after village machine gunned standing in front of pits they were made to dig for own graves. It's been giving me nightmares, but I'm so excited by the new job. Maybe this will help me sleep better.*

Weird how it helps to be able to express yourself, he thought as he read it over. *I haven't been able to do that very well. Ah, what the hell,* he thought. *I'm still a teenager.*

A week later, Lieutenant Forner asked Joey to come to his office.

"Any idea why he wants to see me?" he asked Red on his way there. Red shrugged. Saluting as he entered, Joey was introduced to Captain Dick Bartlett from SHAEF Headquarters.

"Sergeant, is Louis D. Goldman, Senior, your father?" the captain asked. Joey began to sweat.

"Yessir." *What in hell is this about?* he thought.

"Seems your father reacted to your saying in a letter that the food sucked on the base," said the captain.

Oh, shit, Joey thought. *I'm in for it now.*

"He sent a letter to General Eisenhower that said, and I quote, *As a Marine Sergeant in World War I, I know how important it is for morale to keep soldiers as happy as possible in difficult situations. My son mentioned that everyone on his base complains about the lousy food they are eating in the mess hall even though the war has ended."*

Unbelievably, Eisenhower sent the captain to check it out and improve the situation. Joey's heartbeat slowed back down. Bottom line, the mess was vastly improved, and the word got out it was because of Joey's dad. From then on, when anything irritated someone in his group, the request was, "Hey Joey, write your old man!"

One of the German secretaries in HQ had seen Joey kneel down in the Kaserne and scratch a stray dog's ears one day, and she asked if he would like to buy a puppy from her dog's litter. He bartered for it with a box of Hershey bars. "Schatzie" was now his constant companion and helped soften the homesickness he sometimes felt. When he went to the mess hall he always had his canteen cup hooked into his boot so he could bring her a treat. Back in his office, Joey picked up his pup and thought about what had just happened.

On the one hand it made him feel good. He was embarrassed, and at the same time flattered and admiring of his dad, but as he thought about it, he was sad realizing his father had only reacted to what he wrote about food quality without responding to what he had written about the Nazis' "Final Solution" that Lieutenant Forner referred to as "The Holocaust." It disappointed him. Since he knew his father had become critically ill and was hospitalized for three years with a brain abscess when Joey was only a toddler, Joey had always been sympathetic. His mother was a sweet young thing from Richmond who never had to do much, but suddenly, faced with running the family she turned to taking care of his father without giving enough attention to her children. Then his father became self-absorbed with his illness. He took to analyzing every little physical thing happening to him. The impact on Joey was profound. He was forced to become self-sufficient, self-protective, and task-oriented from then on. It also saddled him with a self-imposed perfectionism at age five so that he wouldn't do anything that would "upset his father."

Schatzie brought him back to the moment by jumping down and whining at her empty water bowl. Growing up, Joey always had a dog. When he would come home from school, his father would usually be napping and his mother would shush him, but his hound dog, Petey, would rush out to greet him like he had been away for ages. He took his canteen out to the water cooler. Then his phone started ringing.

CHAPTER 14

"Hey, Goldman, the phone's ringing in your dog pound!" yelled Red from his office next door. Joey finished filling his canteen cup with water for Schatzie, walked into his office and poured some into the doggie bowl next to his desk, and answered. "Hello, Staff Sergeant Goldman, 318th Supply."

"Hello, Staff Sergeant. This is Corporal Moskowitz calling! How the hell are you?"

"Al, you S-O-B. How the hell are *you*?" Joey exclaimed. "To what do I owe this honor? I've been wondering where you were since we were on the SS Howard V-I-C-T-O-R-E-E-E." They both shouted and laughed.

Al Moskowitz was stationed in Wiesbaden. He and Joey had met through S.A.R, a high school fraternity, before they ended up as college roommates.

"A staff sergeant—in supplies, yet? How'd you manage that so fast?" asked Al. They exchanged stories. Al, it seemed, maneuvered himself into getting a military occupation specialty as an "Entertainment Specialist."

"That mean you're an actor or what?" asked Joey.

"To be or not to be, that's me," answered Al in flowery, accented English.

"So, Shakespeare, maybe you could use something I might have here? Got lots of stuff."

"I can, but it's got nothing to do with supplies. My mom asked me to try to locate a relative of my dad's barber in Wilkes-Barre. She was told he was a survivor of Dachau."

"Dachau?"

"Yeah," said Al. "The concentration camp down near Munich. They told her he's likely in the displaced persons camp in Fürth. That's right next to you, right?

"Fürth? Yeah. It's close. But I don't know anything about it," Joey said, thinking of the awful sights he had seen of wasted refugees. "Why don't you just give 'em a call?"

"I tried," said Al. "Too hard to get through to those camps. Bureaucracy at its height. Then I realized it's so near you, maybe you could try to find him."

"Well . . . um . . . I don't know . . . I . . . ah . . . I got a lot to do here," Joey said. "Isn't there some kind of organization for this kind of thing?" *Bad enough to see them in a film,* he thought, *but what if he met an actual survivor who had been starved and tortured?* His mouth went dry. What if they looked like the corpse-like people he had seen in the films? He clutched the phone.

"But Joey, you won't believe this. His name is Joseph, too. That's what made me think of this. But it's J-O-S-E-F with an F, Josef Weizenbaum," Al said. "If you could find him you could help get him in touch with his family and get to the US."

"Um, I don't know . . . I mean what . . . um . . . exactly . . . um . . . what would that take?" *Getting involved with someone from a death camp?* he thought. *Do I have the balls to do that?* It was his childhood warning *Don't get involved!* versus his new experiences here.

"C'mon," Al continued. "You'd just have to arrange certain papers to go to the International Refugee Organization as well as the . . . lemme see here what it says . . . the American Joint Distribution Committee. No big deal."

Joey began to sweat. *I wouldn't even know how to communicate with someone like that,* he thought. *Seeing films was hard enough, but in person . . . .*

"She sent me info about them which I can send down to you," Al said. "How about it, Joey? This is important. Please, Joey, you know what the fucking Germans did to our people, and you can help give this guy a chance to get to America."

"Yeah . . . but I'm not sure of this at all," Joey stammered. *Our people* again.

"What's not to be sure of?" asked Al.

"Al, have you ever seen those people?" Joey said. "They're . . . they're human wrecks . . . scary."

"Oh, c'mon, Joey. You find him. You put him in touch with his brother. You're done. Period."

"You make it sound easy, but I don't know." Al was silent. Joey could almost feel his disappointment.

"Joey," Al said softly, "being a good Jew means being a giver, to . . . to . . . umm . . . help others in need." It was what the rabbi had taught him as a kid.

"Well, okay, I'll give it a try," said Joey. He stared at the phone after they hung up. *So I'm to be a good Jew. What does that all mean?* Schatzie started whining. Joey realized he was anxiously rubbing the pup's ears too hard. He lifted her up and nuzzled her into his face. Schatzie licked his face. What had he just agreed to?

After feeding and watering the pup, he walked next door and told Red about the call. "Whattaya think, Red? It would be like to help one of these concentration camp survivors? I mean, they have to be really screwed up people, you know. Sorta gives me the creeps."

"Yeah, probably is a little freaky," said Red. "But with what you've been telling me about the Trials, seems to me you . . . you gotta do it, Joey, don't you think?"

"I guess," said Joey. Truth was, he was aware he'd grown up being told not to get too involved with others. That instinct was something he was learning to fight, but how was he going to communicate with this guy . . . if he was even there? He didn't speak much German, and no Yiddish at all. He stared at Red.

*Ba-*DUM*-da-*DUM*,* DUM*, dum-dum-*DUM*.* The sound came to him again, and he saw the SS marching. He knew he had to do it.

CHAPTER 15

———

It was an unusually cold Friday. Joey backed his Jeep out of the motor
pool and headed for the displaced persons camp in Fürth.

"Damn glad I got this heater today," he muttered. He had
arranged for the German POWs who worked in the Kaserne repair
shops under his supervision to weld an old Ford top and sides onto his
Jeep and install a heater, a radio, and a plush leather driver's seat so he
would be comfortable in any weather. Today he really needed that.

The road to Fürth was in pretty good condition. There were no
bombed-out roads and bridges to bypass. The clouds were gray and
threatening. *Stratocumulus opacus,* he could hear his father say. Besides
his obsession with his illness, his father was obsessed with the weather
and had become expert at forecasting by looking at cloud formations.
Somehow, conversations would always end up about one or the other—
more on the weather these days. Joey took a deep breath and felt a chill
in his lungs. His thoughts were cold too. What would he find in Fürth?

Lieutenant Forner, the HQ adjutant, was, as least as far as Joey
knew, the only other Jew in the depot HQ, so he had asked him about
Fürth. Neither of them was religious, but they acknowledged they had a
connection. In some strange way it was comforting. "M-O-T," his SAR
frat brothers would describe it: Member of the Tribe.

It started, Joey remembered with a cringe, when at Christmas
he brought a small tree to his office. The lieutenant, walking by, did a

double take and entered. "A Christmas tree, Goldman? Just what kind of a Jew are you?"

"What do you mean, sir?" Joey asked, surprised. "We always had a little tree at home."

"You celebrated Christmas, not Chanukah?"

"Well, yeah, sort of. I mean . . . we gave gifts at Chanukah, but we lit up a little tree like . . . well, like most folks did in town. You know, just for the season."

Forner, who was from New York, shook his head and sighed. "I heard of Reform, but not that Reformed! Never heard of our people celebrating a major Christian holiday." Embarrassed, Joey tossed the tree out right away, but not that memory.

Afterwards, he had asked the lieutenant about Fürth. He'd summoned Joey about a letter he waved. "I called the area's rabbi chaplain for you about Fürth and that DP camp and what he knew about it. He wrote back and included a little travelogue," he chuckled. "Probably does long sermons, too."

> *Yes, there is a DP camp for Jewish survivors in Fürth. It's interesting that when the Emperor deported the Jews of Vienna in 1670, a large group of upper-class Jewish families moved to Fürth, and the Jewish population rose to almost 20% in the early 1800's. But their synagogue was destroyed in Kristallnacht by the Nazis and the remaining Jews were deported.*

Just like a rabbi to throw in some Jewish history. It was actually interesting, though. "Kristallnacht, huh?" Joey said.

"Yeah, when the Nazis trashed everything Jewish they could find," said the lieutenant.

"Oh, yeah, the Night of the Broken Glass."

"They broke more than glass," the lieutenant nodded and handed Joey the chaplain's report.

"I also called the camp for permission for you to visit and they told me there were 850 inhabitants there," said the lieutenant.

"I hope to hell this Josef Weizenbaum is one of them," said Joey softly.

CHAPTER 16

———

He drove down narrow streets between dark, medieval buildings. There was little evidence of the war. Fürth had escaped most of the Allied bombing. No two houses looked the same. It was like time traveling through history, with literally hundreds of buildings dating back as far as the 1500s. He turned into a plaza where he was amazed by a beautiful ancient fountain. Stopping to admire it, he read a bronze marker, *Der Gauklerbrunnen*. It was set amid surrounding architecture of perfectly preserved buildings from the 1600s and 1700s. How could people with such a sense of beauty become such senseless murderers? Fürth wasn't like Nuremberg, which was eighty-five percent demolished, so broken and battered that the Army advised GIs that it could be dangerous to walk through the old city since a Nazi sniper was rumored to be hiding in there.

Identifying himself to the MP at the gate of the group of buildings, he parked and went into the office. To his surprise, the UNRRA official found Josef Weizenbaum quickly. "Funny way to spell Joseph," said Joey.

The official gave him a look. "I think you'll have to go to his room," he said. "I'm not sure how easy it would be for him to come down here."

"Whattaya mean?"

"You'll see, Sergeant. You'll see . . . . There's a lot of that here."

He sent Joey to Building 4, Room 333. Joey walked through the courtyard of the complex of weathered sandstone buildings. They were once the magnificent homes of the wealthy, with wrought iron balconies and large casement windows. Joey became aware he was being watched. When he glanced up at the windows, the refugees housed there moved back quickly, as if afraid. Following a massive granite walkway, he stopped short as he came upon a number of emaciated men and women in drab, oversized clothes, looking much like what he had seen in the Trial films and photos. Their brows were furrowed almost like they were of stone, sculpted and frozen in time with harsh memories and the loss of loved ones. Their eyes stared at and away from him as if they were still trapped in the camps. They stood in close groups, like cornered animals, unable yet to grasp what was happening to them.

The conversations stopped as he passed each group. He tried smiling but they remained solemn. They watched him suspiciously but deferentially, with very little movement of their fragile bodies. This stranger was a soldier. Soldiers were to be feared, for soldiers could mean torture, humiliation, degradation, and random death. *Oh, my God—* they looked like ghosts to him. He wondered how they would ever be able to recover from what those Nazis had done to them. Gritting his teeth, he felt his anger at the Germans again.

Coming to a large, once-opulent entranceway, now with a hand-painted sign, "Building 4," he stopped, inhaled, and shuddered. What will I find here? What condition is Josef Weizenbaum going to be in? What did the UNRRA guy mean? *You'll see.*

Joey straightened, shoulders back, and slowly climbed the damp, darkened marble stairs. The hallway was wide, with marble floors, and wallpaper that was beginning to shred, and dimly lit ceiling lamps. You could see the dead insects inside them. Uninviting. Knocking gently on a door, also marked with a hand-painted 333, Joey waited, holding his breath. Sweating, he knocked again, with a bit more force. From inside came a voice.

"*Hereinkommen . . .*" it said, haltingly.

As he slowly opened the door, Joey looked around and saw two figures seated near the huge casement windows. They were both in silhouette, motionless and staring at him.

"Josef Weizenbaum?" Joey asked softly.

The partially bowed head of the man on the right raised slightly and in a somewhat hoarse voice answered suspiciously, "*Ich bin Josef. Wer sind Sie?*"

Joey searched his meager German. "*Ich bin Joseph, auch. Joseph Goldman. Ich bin ein amerikanischer Soldat,*" he said. "Do you speak English? *Sprechen Sie Englisch?*"

"*Nein, Ich spreche nicht Englisch,*" the figure replied.

The other figure stirred, and Joey approached the two. He could only swallow at what he saw. Both were thin, gaunt, with expressionless faces wiped clean of emotion from endless torture and deprivation at the hands of their *Judenfrei* believers. They were motionless. Only their eyes moved.

Again the drums: *Ba-DUM-da-DUM-DUM, dum, dum, DUM*. He bit his lower lip and thought of slowly inching back out, but the other man looked up at him. His left arm hung lifeless. His right twitched as if to make up for its deadened mate.

"I can speak English," he said, with a German accent. "I am Karl Joelawitz."

Joey stammered, explaining his mission about Josef's relatives, and how he might help Josef get to America. Karl translated, his voice getting excited as he realized the implications for his roommate.

Josef himself began to transform from a lifeless statue, looking back and forth from Karl to Joey, and finally reached out to touch Joey's arm.

"*Du . . . Amerikanischer Soldat,*" he said. "*Warum würdest du so einem Juden helfen?*"

Hesitantly Karl translated: "Why would you help a Jew like this?"

Joey, his brow furrowing, looked into Josef's ruined eyes and put his left hand on the bony, fragile shoulder. With his right hand he slowly opened his coat collar, then his shirt, and pulled out first his dog tags and then, slowly, the gold chain around his neck that held his Magen David. The two stared at the six-pointed star, then looked up in wonder at Joey, whose hand trembled as he held it.

"*Jüdisch? Sie? Sie sind ein Jude?*" Josef cried at the sight and rose to his feet to embrace Joey.

"*Ja, bin ich gerade wie Sie jüdisch!*" Joey answered with a hesitant smile. He bit his lip to keep tears from flowing. Why was he crying? He hadn't thought of the Magen David as making him Jewish. It had just been a memento from Aunt Minnie, but here it meant something that moved these slight, frail men to excitement.

Karl joined the embrace and the three of them turned in a slow circle. It was a strange, dancelike mixture of joy and sorrow. For Joey, that mix also included questions.

His Jewishness . . . the universality of it.

CHAPTER 17

For an hour they sat and exchanged experiences. Karl was once a university professor. "But all Jews were fired and forced into ghettos. My wife, Rachel, and I were sent to Mauthausen in cattle cars, standing together like wheat bound tightly together. When we arrived, they stripped us naked and marched us into the camp, beating us on the way with clubs, rifles, and whips. Suddenly, our women were separated from us." He paused and swallowed several times. "Rachel showed me where she quickly buried her wristwatch before the march started and we were separated. Later I found it." A look so desolate shivered across his face. "It kept me alive when I bartered it for food. But Rachel . . . Rachel . . . I . . . " he shook his wizened head before saying. "I never saw her again . . . nor any of her family or mine."

"How did you manage to stay alive?" Joey whispered.

Karl looked at Joey, then closed his eyes, "That I could tell stories of German history interested an SS officer, but only for a while, so I was then assigned to . . ." He stopped and looked away, recaptured by a memory of horror.

Josef patted Karl's shaking hand. "*I war auch in einem Lager und verlor meine Familie.*"

This prompted Karl to rise from where his memories had lowered him. "Josef also lost his whole family. He was in Dachau. Josef owned a bakery. It was burned on Kristallnacht." Karl lowered his head. "Many were killed, and many were sent to the camps."

"I've heard of Kristallnacht and Dachau," Joey said.

"We just couldn't believe what was happening to us," Karl said. "Josef's brother did believe it and managed to buy his family a way out in 1937 and ended up with those cousins in Pennsylvania. But Josef was like me. He just couldn't believe this would continue." He shook his head and continued, "His brother knew better. He was a very successful tailor. Tailoring wasn't in demand in the coal mining area where he went," he chuckled. "Hair, however, grows everywhere . . . so, he used his skills with scissors to become a barber."

He stared for a long moment at Joey. "I can't believe you have found Josef. His brother will be so happy." He took a long breath. "It is rare to find someone alive."

Joey told them about the call from Al and about the American Joint Distribution Committee. The two men eagerly asked Joey what it was like being Jewish in the Army and life in America. They were fascinated about a Jewish-American soldier and wanted to know what it was like growing up in Charleston.

"It was all right being a Jew there?" Karl asked.

"Oh, sure. That was never a problem for me or my family," Joey replied. "We were Reform."

"Reform? Zo, not very religious."

"Not very religious," Joey replied, a little embarrassed. "No Yiddish at all. Charleston didn't even have a deli."

"A what?"

"A store that sold Jewish kind of foods. You know, Pickles and corned beef and . . . " Seeing Karl's puzzled expression he stopped. "Never mind."

"You were *bar mitzvahed*?"

"Me? No. Our temple—"

"Temple?" Karl said.

"We called our synagogue 'temple,'" said Joey, embarrassed again.

"That's Reform all right," said Karl.

"I was what we called 'confirmed' at fifteen. Never had to learn Hebrew."

"But you are Jewish, yes?"

"Well, yeah, I am," he added, getting a little more embarrassed. "Look, I have to get back to base in Nuremberg. I promise I'll be back soon with things for you. And hopefully some information and papers about getting Josef to his family in America."

He held both men at arm's length, looking at each, then impulsively kissed them and left.

On the way to his Jeep, he slowly laid his hand on his chest where his Magen David hung. It was unsettling to him how they reacted to it.

When he looked up, he was startled to find he had crossed the courtyard and was standing next to his Jeep. Getting inside, he noticed a young man nearby staring at him. He was leaning against the huge wrought iron gate. He didn't look like a refugee, more like a soldier of some sort. Joey squinted his eyes at him, and the young man nodded. *Who the hell is that, and why is he staring at me?* thought Joey. But he dismissed it in the strangeness of the moment. All the way back to the base he replayed the meeting. He was glad he had come. He thought about how vastly different it was being a Jew in Charleston compared to being a Jew in Europe. His history teacher had once said, "We take our freedom for granted here." And it was true. *These people were forced out of jobs and then murdered by the millions just for being—being what*

I am. How could that be? If I lived here I could have been murdered, too. I could be on that horrible pile of bodies. Dr. Raisin called us "The Chosen People" when I was confirmed. What a joke.

CHAPTER 18

Joey was walking away after parking the Jeep back at the depot when he heard someone speak.

"Sergeant, Sergeant. Can I show you something?" It was the German POW who was in charge of Joey's Jeep in the motor pool.

Joey turned back. *"Was ist los, Braun?"*

The German looked carefully around, then took out a camera from a briefcase. He handed it over. It was a beauty, especially compared to the crummy Kodak Joey owned. Then Joey realized someone was standing silently at the entrance, watching them. He looked suspiciously at Braun.

Braun whispered, "Ach, don't vorry. He is my . . . how do you say . . . vatchdog assistant." Joey eyed the assistant, then relaxed.

Braun's English was good. "I learned in ze German press corps," he said. He had been captured in Nuremberg in the final months of the war and had been designated as a trustee and put to work here with two hundred other POWs. They were also guarded by a Polish Army unit.

"It's a Leica Three, *Herr* Sergeant," he said in a low, confidential, deferential voice. "In mint condition. Auto rangefinder. Beautiful lens, one thousandth of a second speed. It vas Oskar Barnack's last design before he died."

The beauty and precision of the camera's design was obvious. It was this same German precision that had allowed them to overrun

Europe and kill millions so efficiently. Joey shook the thoughts out of his head, then addressed Braun harshly.

"So, whattaya want, Braun? To sell it? What?" He felt like punching the German. But he knew instinctively that this was a great find, even though he didn't have the faintest notion of who Oskar . . . ah . . . who-the-fuck-Bar-r-nacky was.

"Yessir," whispered Braun. "But I need things, not money."

"What kind of things?"

"You know . . . on ze Black Market. Seegarettes, zoap, chocolate," Braun whispered. "Especially seegarettes, sir!"

Cigarettes had become money. Several times Joey had used his rationed smokes to acquire stuff. Some of his buddies were even importing cigarettes from home. Red Blake had recently gotten a Luger that he kept hidden. The cigarettes were rarely smoked. Instead, they were traded dozens of times by the Germans for things—mainly for food from farmers, who were the ones who ended up lighting up.

"How much, Braun?"

"Excuse me, sir, but here's a list that vould do."

A list. German efficiency, Joey thought. "Okay, lemme have it." And looking it over, Joey growled, "I'll see you tomorrow with the stuff."

"*Danke*, sir," said Braun obsequiously. "And it iss already loaded vith a roll of new film. Sir."

Walking out of the motor pool with his new toy, Joey laughed. Now he could send some really good pictures home. He'd show his brother a thing or two about his photographic ability.

As he passed by the ballfield that the USO had provided, Joey was surprised to see two horseback riders trotting toward him on the field. It was Lieutenant Forner and the beautiful young Frenchwoman all the guys knew he was shacking up with. She was connected with the press corps as a translator. Somehow it reminded him of the Bill Mauldin cartoon in *Stars and Stripes* of two French girls reacting to an approaching war-weary GI: "Don't look now, but here comes old *Voulez-vous coucher avec moi* again."

The riders stopped and looked down at him, at which point he aimed the camera and said, "My new camera, sir. How about posing for my first award-winning portrait about life in the ETO?"

They nodded, and *click, click*! They were recorded for posterity. He used the new camera right away to take a picture of himself and later sent the photo to Leah in a letter.

> *Dear Leah,*
>
> *I have been thinking about you from the moment you left. How I wish you were staying close by. If you don't mind, I have enclosed a picture of myself so you will, I hope, remember me.*
>
> *Am I too overconfident to ask if you would send a picture of yourself to me? I don't want to be pushy but there is so much I want to know about you. Are you planning to live in Geneva? Is there a way for you to be a teacher here? Please write to me.*
>
> *Fondly, Joey*

He reread the letter and changed "Fondly" to "With much care." *Wish I had the balls to write what I really feel,* he thought: "*Love, Joey.*"

CHAPTER 19

"Can I take this into the Trials next time?" Joey asked Skip, proudly showing him the new Leica. Skip took it and examined it closely.

"Are you kidding? No way!" said Skip. Joey could tell he was a bit jealous.

Skip had arranged dinner for them with two Russian girls who were translators. He was good with women and looked pointedly at Joey. "We're gonna have *two* great meals tonight. Okay?" he said. "Don't get bashful on me like you did last time with the French babes."

Joey was uncomfortable with girls. When he was growing up, most of them were at least a foot taller than he was, and not interested in "cute little Joey." God, how many times had he heard those exact fucking words. His high school pals had called him "Shrimpy."

"Okay, okay," Joey said, a little embarrassed, and started to put the camera away.

Skip looked again at the Leica. "Hey, I got an idea," he said. "Let's do a photo weekend. You got the Leica, and I got my Agfa, which ain't so bad. Got it with this set of Flak Binocs. Look, came with the works— even has this wooden case and tripod."

"What'd it cost you?"

"A carton."

"Of what?"

"Lucky Strike Whites," Skip said in a *Radio Hit Parade* announcer's voice. "Lucky Strike Green has gone to war!" They both laughed.

Dinners at the press corps were great, especially compared to the more basic mess hall chow Joey was used to. Afterwards, upstairs in Skip's room, the couples took to the bed and the sofa. The translators were both very sexy and spoke English well. In the midst of the boys' grunting, groaning, and thrusting, the girls began speaking Russian to one another.

Jeez, Joey wondered, it's like they were doing this as a job.

"Are you sure they're really translators?" he asked Skip afterwards.

Skip laughed. "Who knows? They're either spies fucking or fucking spies. But who cares? We get laid and give up nothing but ourselves and a few lonely sperm! Not a bad deal, huh?

That weekend it snowed yet again. Joey and Skip set out, ostensibly to take lots of pictures to send home, but since they had also talked recently about sending gifts home, Skip suggested they make the trip end up in Oeslau, the largest of the community units making up Rödental, and the home of the W. Goebel Porzellanfabrik, makers of Hummel figurines.

"Their stuff is world famous," said Skip. "The folks back home would get a kick out of them. The spoils of war, so to speak."

"Be nice to send something special to my Aunt Minnie," Joey said.

"Your cousin's mom?" Skip said and paused. "Tough way to go."

"Yeah. Thing is, they've called him MIA. So she still thinks he might turn up in some hospital," said Joey. "I'm thinking the Red Cross in Geneva keeps records on all that. I wanna go there and see what I can turn up. But a Jew landing safely in Germany wouldn't have a chance—officer or no officer."

CHAPTER 20

A s they headed north from Nuremberg, comfortable in the heated Jeep, Joey drove, and Skip navigated from a map he had picked up. Along the way they stopped and took pictures in the small villages and farms they passed through—quaint, with no evidence for miles of the destruction from the war their Fatherland had caused. The snow had stopped, but it covered a lot of the landscape, so later when they came to a Y in the road they had to stop and figure which arm of the Y to take.

"I think it's left," Skip finally said. "We should be near the factory."

Joey pulled into the narrow left lane. For twenty minutes they drove slowly through wide-open fields, strangely empty of any animals.

"Wow," Joey said. "Looks like the North Pole. See anything of the factory?"

Skip picked up his new binoculars and peered ahead. "I think I do see something up there off in the distance. Keep going."

"Is it the factory, I hope?" Joey said. "My butt is getting sore."

"Nah, doesn't look like a factory. It's more like a . . . *holy shit!*" Skip suddenly shouted. "Turn around. Turn around, Joey. Quick! That ain't a factory. It's a fucking Russian outpost! And they're running to an armored car! Move it, man. Move it. They're after us!"

Joey swerved, gunned the accelerator and skidding wildly did a 180-degree and headed back to where they'd come from. Now he realized that what they were driving on was not a lane. "This ain't a road, Skip. It's a fucking frozen creek bed!"

Skip twisted in his seat to look back with the glasses. "We must be in the goddamn Russian Zone . . . and they're gaining on us. Floor it, Joey! If they catch us, they'll lock us up for sure!"

But the Jeep was no match for the Russian half-track, and before they could make it back to the intersection, the Russians passed them and spun around directly in their path. Stopping as best he could, Joey halted as the Russians piled out with automatic weapons drawn. A young soldier motioned for them to get out of the car.

"Name, rank, and serial number only," whispered Skip.

CHAPTER 21

"**ID**z pliz," the young soldier demanded. They handed over their IDs, and he handed them to an officer who was approaching. After examining them, the swarthy, handsome young officer asked, in perfect English, "What are you doing here?"

"We're looking for the Hummel Factory, sir," Joey said.

Skip whispered, "Keep quiet."

The officer noted this and continued to direct his conversation to Joey, who was sweating. "And entering Russian territory," he said, gesturing to a sign in English and Russian at the intersection.

"I, we didn't see that, sir," Joey said, swallowing hard. "We're sorry for that. We are just looking for Hummel gifts to send home to our families."

Skip interrupted, "We are American soldiers and cannot be held. I insist that we be allowed to be on our way."

The officer gave him a fierce look. He pulled his revolver and placed it against Skip's cheek. "Wrong," he said. "You have violated our zone and *can* be held." He cocked his pistol and reached for his handcuffs

Joey gasped, reached for his Magen David and said, "Sir, I am a Jew! Wouldn't you rather hold me?"

Shocked by the outburst, the officer looked at him, glanced at Joey's ID then motioned to where he knew GIs wore their dog tags. "Show me," he said.

Joey, puzzled, reached for his tags.

The officer took them in his hand, saw the H on them, and looked up at Joey. *Oh God, now I'm in for it,* Joey thought. But to his surprise the man gave a faint smile, lowered his pistol, and relaxed his demeanor. "You should be more careful, soldiers, and learn to see signs." He pointed to the sign. "Be on your way." He turned and directed his men to return to the half-track. As Joey and Skip got back into the jeep, the Russian looked at Joey. "We have suffered too much," he said, saluted, and left.

We? thought Joey. "We?" he said aloud. "Does that mean what I think it means?"

"That he's Jewish?" Skip said. Breathing heavily. "Jesus. How lucky can you be?" They drove back to the intersection and looked at the sign.

"ATTENTION! YOU ARE ENTERING THE RUSSIAN ZONE!" Skip read. The Russian equivalent was posted below it. "How the hell did we miss that?"

"Looking at the damn scenery I guess," Joey said. As he drove the Jeep onto the real road, he started to slow down.

"Keep going. Keep going!" Skip said. He kept his binocs focused on the Russians, who had headed back into the distance.

"I should have known," Joey said. "This one is paved, not ice." Coming around a curve they came to a village.

"Pull over," Skip said, still breathing hard. "You realize what could have happened there?" he said as he slumped back in the seat. "Maybe you don't know those fuckin' Russkies are holding some of our military who wandered into their zone. Jerks were looking to buy a goddamn dog and did just what we did. Only they didn't know it and got caught and are being held as spies. We coulda been in prison and fucked by the Russians . . . and I don't mean *getting* fucked by Russians, like last week."

"We were lucky," said Joey shaking his head. "Being Jewish in Germany was lucky for a change. It's so damn strange. You can be Jewish in one country and it's bad, and in another, it's okay . . . even good."

It was puzzling to Joey. The Russians were Allies. Both of them had seen the Russians as angry prosecutors at the Trial, deploring the fate of the Jews as well as of their own citizens and soldiers. *Yet here they were pursuing us,* Joey thought, *and only letting us go because I am a Jew.* He shook his head. The whole experience was crazy.

CHAPTER 22

"Maybe we should just turn around, Skip," Joey said. "Who needs a figurine anyway? They'll probably just be more Nazi stuff."

"No way, Staff Sergeant," Skip replied. "My office said this'll make great stuff to send home . . . to your Aunt Minnie and all. We've come all this way. Lemme just ask someone here how close we are to Oeslau." And he jumped out and headed into a small *Bierhalle* next to where they had stopped.

Joey looked at the timber-frame buildings across the road, some with painted facades and ornately carved gables, untouched by five years of death and destruction elsewhere. Two minutes later, Skip came out with a big smile, two sandwiches, and two large paper cups.

"*Bier* for the *Vonderful Amerikanischers*," he said, and held up a small brochure. "This factory, believe it or not, is only about a mile up the road. So eat, drink, and be merry, sonny boy!"

Pilsner foam on his lips, mixed with thick mayonnaise, Joey let out a loud burp and they both laughed. Ten minutes later they pulled up in front of the Hummel factory. It was built of ancient, faded red brick with small windowpanes of wavy antique glass, and a huge oak double door with brass fittings. It was nestled in the snow much like the corny Hummel versions of barns and villages in the brochure Skip had just been given at the beer hall. Reading from it, he translated, "The

Hummel figures are based on the artwork of Franciscan Sister Maria Innocentia. Okay, Innocent Sis, show us your stuff."

Reaching for their supply of cigarettes, they jumped out and went to what turned out to be a locked door with a sign *"geschlossen bis morgen"*—closed until tomorrow. "Closed my ass," Skip said. "The folks in the beer joint said knock hard on the window on the right." He did, and lo and behold the heavy wooden entrance door creaked open, revealing an old man bent over like a cartoon character in a fairy tale.

Looking up suspiciously, the old man asked in a grouchy voice, *"Was wünschen Sie?"*

"Öffnen Sie die Tür, JETZT!" Skip commanded. And, looking very official, said in gruff German, "We are here to inspect the factory!" And out of the side of his mouth to Joey, "Look official, because we're here to inspect the place." Slapping the side of his pants with his gloves as he had seen German officers do in films, Skip barked, *"Sprechen Sie Englisch?"*

"Ja, ein Wenig—a little," the old man replied.

"Gut. Show us everything," Skip ordered. Joey rolled his eyes.

Inside, after repeating this stern request, they were given a tour of the works where the sprightly little Disney-like characters were made. There were hundreds of tiny, colorful figurines . . . little cherubic blonde, blue-eyed girls and boys in classic German folk clothes, braided pigtails and lederhosen, plus angels and animals and folk scenes and quaint houses.

"Vunderbar, ja?" said the old man with pride. "Ze work of Sister Maria Innocentia." *Innocent, my ass,* Joey thought. *What happened to all that innocence? How come it turned so easily into the killing and torturing of innocents . . . by the millions?* Skip meanwhile was taking pictures and urged Joey to use his new Leica.

Joey refused. "I don't want any of this shit."

"C'mon, you said you wanted something special for your Aunt Minnie, so trust me. This Hummel stuff is special."

So they bargained for ten figurines—five each—and coughed up the necessary cigarettes, Camels this time. They had figured which relatives they needed to send something to and, mission accomplished, they returned to the Jeep and headed back in time for dinner call.

On the way back, with Skip driving, Joey kept looking at the catalog and muttering to himself about how unreal and un-German the Hummel stuff looked. "Fucking bastards," he muttered. Skip, who was behind the wheel, looked at him, said nothing, and drove on. Joey just stared out the window, thinking angrily about how Sister Innocentia's country had turned out. Now, whenever he saw people in the snow, he thought of footage of Jews standing naked in the snow, waiting to be machined-gunned to death and fall into the ditches they had been forced to dig.

CHAPTER 23

———

The next morning at mail call, Tech Sgt. Steve Bowen was handing out mail and gave a letter to Joey. "Something from your broker?" he said, smiling.

"What the hell do you mean by that?" Joey snapped.

Bowen did a double take. "I was joking about your investment portfolio."

Joey blushed. He meant *stockbroker*, not pawnbroker. Bowen wasn't joking about him being Jewish.

Embarrassed, he said, "Sorry, I was thinking about something else." Bowen gave him a puzzled look and continued the mail call.

Joey was jumpy. The week before, at the mess hall, a drunken combat vet corporal confronted him at the table as he sat down with his food tray. He'd leaned in, eyes red and widening. "You headquarters people seen the redeployment list?"

"Well, yeah," Joey said, startled. "I've seen it."

The vet tapped his name strip. "Carlyle," he snarled. "Was I on it?"

"Carlyle? I . . . I don't think so."

The vet grabbed Joey by the neck and pushed him back so his chair tilted. "You Jew bastard," he shouted. "You're putting all your friends on it first."

"I got nothing to do with that list!" Joey said, trying to get his footing. "The officers make it. Let go of me, goddammit."

"Let go of him, goddammit!" growled Smitty, grabbing the GI by his hair. Carlos twisted the vet's hands free of Joey's neck. They dragged Carlyle outside and threw him down. "Listen, you drunk asshole," Smitty snarled, "you even *look* at him again and your antisemitic ass will be in jail instead of getting home. You hear me?"

Carlyle looked up at the two hulking soldiers standing over him and nodded a sullen yes.

"Now beat it," hissed Carlos. The two turned and went back inside. Joey was still in shock. They stood on each side and patted his shoulders to reassure him. All was okay now.

"Son of a bitch forgot what he fought for," Smitty said.

"But he won't forget what we just told him," Carlos said and winked.

Being Jewish was becoming so different from what Joey had realized growing up. It marked him as something different, even though he didn't feel he was. Or was he? It had been a good thing being Jewish when he met Leah and the Russians. Just now it was a bad thing. How could it be both? It wasn't fair.

CHAPTER 24

———

The envelope was light blue. He smelled it and smiled. It was fragrant. In his office, he carefully slit it open and took out a photo of Leah. He examined it slowly, moving it closer and then back. Standing in front of a building that looked like a home, she was smiling. On the back it read, *This is the school where I teach*. Holding the photo in one hand and the letter in the other he began to read:

> *Dear Joey,*
>
> *I had to ask the rabbi exactly what "pushy" meant. And when he explained, I had to laugh. If you hadn't been pushy asking for my picture, I would have been so upset. How could you ever think I would forget you? I am feeling the same as you, "With much care." Much, much care. It is surprising to me and pleasing. I am only in Geneva for a while. I wish I could be a teacher near you, but I am destined to go to Palestine like the children I teach. It is, as I said, the only place that really wants us. And needs us as well. The British are making it difficult for us, however. I have been told to be ready at a moment's notice, but I don't think it will come soon. Is there any way that you might come to Geneva? Do you get, what do you call it, a furlow? Your picture is on my nightstand.*

Joey read the rest of the letter and started all over again. He was about to kiss the photo when Red walked in. "Some chow, pal?" Red said.

Blushing, Joey quickly put the letter and picture in his desk and jumped up. Red cocked his head and gave him a look, then they left.

CHAPTER 25

During the week, Joey arranged with Lieutenant Forner to help him get the necessary papers for Josef from UNRRA and the American Joint Distribution Committee. The JDC came through quickly with an agreement to help. The UNRRA bureaucratic system dragged on. Joey planned to visit the camp on the next Friday with a load of goodies from the PX . . . not just what his rations allowed, but extras—Colonel Larned was also the PX officer for the Post Exchange. On hearing Joey's story, he gave him a note for buying extras at the PX. "Here, Sergeant," he said. "Let me know what I can do for those poor souls. I was part of the 42nd that liberated Dachau and I'll never forget what I saw there."

"Dachau? You were there?" said Joey. "Down near Munich, sir?"

"Correct," the colonel said, and paused. "You're Jewish, right?"

"I am, sir," Joey answered, wondering where this was going.

"Might be something you'd want to see, Sergeant. You'd be shocked," the colonel said. "But if I were you, son, I'd get there before it's all cleaned up, so you'll understand just how bad it was."

"Bad?" Joey asked.

"Right," the colonel said. "The news hasn't been very forthcoming about it. Apparently the film footage is too raw to show in theaters."

I ought to ask Lieutenant Forner for a pass to go there, Joey thought. *Maybe he might even come with me.* Then again, it'd be weird going somewhere with an officer. He looked at the colonel's note and headed for the PX.

○○○○○○○○○○○○○○○○○○○○○○○○

CHAPTER 26

————

As he maneuvered the jeep through the narrow, winding streets of Fürth the next Friday, Joey wondered just what in hell the colonel had meant about Dachau. Could it be worse than the films he had seen at the Trials? He hit a pothole and the large bag of goodies from the PX bounced in the seat up against the passenger window. He had collected a variety of things he thought would be needed—cigarettes, soap, chocolate, snack packs, T-shirts, socks, two fatigue caps, razors, mints, coffee—little things displaced people probably hadn't seen in years.

The thought of men and women and children dispossessed of all they owned haunted him now—not just of little things like these, but of everything they owned, most of all their freedom—standing naked in lines in freezing weather like this and being prodded with guns and sticks by overcoat-clad soldiers as he had seen at the trial.

"Sons-of-bitches," he said as he stopped beside the MP at the DP camp entrance.

"Sergeant?" said the MP peering in the jeep's window.

"Oh, sorry," Joey said, embarrassed. "I was thinking about the ones who put these people here."

The MP eyed him carefully. "What's in the bag, Sergeant?"

Joey opened it carefully. "Just some stuff for the folks," he said.

The young MP walked around to look inside. He looked up at Joey and back to the bag and gave him a close-lipped nod of approval and ushered him in. Joey headed for 333, carrying the bag over his shoulder like Santa Claus. Joey again noticed the tall, muscular, olive-skinned young man in the courtyard watching him. *What the hell is he? He doesn't look American . . . definitely doesn't look like a recovering refugee. Why was he always here?* Joey nodded sternly and was puzzled when the nod was returned with a smile. He turned into the ornate entrance and climbed up to see Josef and Karl.

He entered the room and saw Karl quickly grab his hat and put it on. The two men rose and embraced him, and both began speaking at once.

"*Willkommen, schöner Sergeant,*" cried Josef.

Karl translated. "Welcome, beautiful sergeant," he said. "Joseph, you have breathed some hope back into our lives. You don't know what it means to us. We wished you'd come in time for services."

"Services? Services? Oh . . . right. It's Friday," Joey said, slightly embarrassed. "Nah, that's okay." *What could they possibly do at services?* he wondered. *Pray to a God who deserted them?* After a moment he said, "Please call me Joey," and placed the bag he carried onto one of the beds. In a deep voice, he called out, "Ho-Ho-Ho. It's Saint Nicholas," then grimaced. "No, wait a minute . . . it's . . . um . . . it's . . . it's Judah Maccabee, bringing Chanukah gifts!"

Karl laughed aloud and translated for Josef, who joined in laughing and clapping his painfully thin hands together. In amazement they examined the treasures, holding each of the items up and showing them to each other. Tears made their angled way down both the bearded, deeply wrinkled faces, bringing them back to life, it seemed to Joey.

Karl said softly, "You know, Joey, that Chanukah symbolizes many things. It is the victory of light over darkness." He repeated this to Josef.

"*Bitte Gott aundzer fintsternish hat geendikt,*" whispered Josef in Yiddish. "Please God our darkness has ended."

To bring back the lighter mood, Joey picked up one of the fatigue caps and, turning, he grabbed Karl's hat and raised the fatigue cap to replace it. But what he saw stopped him cold. Karl's bald head was almost conelike. There were deep indented rings all the way around it leading up to the top. Karl stiffened, and with his good arm slowly put his fedora back on. Josef put his arm around Karl. "*Die Nazi Doktoren experimentierten mit Karl,*" he said.

"Oh God," Joey said, reaching out and removing Karl's hat gently. He felt the pain in Karl's eyes. "What experiments did those doctors do?" His heart beat faster, then it started to sound like the drums, *Ba-DUM-da-DUM, DUM-dum-dum-DUM.* "Please, tell me, Karl."

Karl waited a long moment before replying. "When the SS officer got tired of my history stories, I was put into medical experiments, like many others. I became part of Herr Rosenberg's Aryan desire to achieve what he called, 'To Advance The Third Reich's Racial Ideology.' So, they bound my head with rawhide and hemp and . . . and kept them wet so they would shrink and," he swallowed hard and continued, "and improve my head, they said. But it was simply a way for them to experiment and torture."

Joey blinked rapidly, rattled. Then he leaned over and gave Karl a kiss on his head and carefully placed the hat back on. None of them moved or spoke for over a minute. Joey thought of his own father lying in bed, his head bandaged from brain operations, and his Uncle Joe saying, "Sh-h-h! You want to make your father sick again?" What was he getting into? Should he have come here? He saw himself pulling the trigger on that German from his apartment window, and with a struggle of will he closed his eyes and shook his head.

"To hell with them all!" he shouted. "Let's drink to the future!" And from his shoulder bag he took out a bottle of Schnapps and three paper cups. Turning toward the window, cup held high, he offered a toast: "To the victory of light over darkness and to the future!"

"To the future!" they shouted in unison toward the sunlight. Glancing down outside as he drank, Joey saw that young man again. He was playing and speaking with two children. He looked up, saw Joey and smiled. What they could be speaking about? Their lost family? Their lost parents? A horrible thought.

CHAPTER 27

Collecting his belongings, Joey hugged the two. "I'll be back next week," he promised, "and I hope with news of Josef's papers." He glanced back down at the young man in the courtyard again. *Jeez . . . could he be some kind of government intelligence guy and report what I'm doing here? Shit, am I gonna get in trouble for this?*

Coming out of Building 4, Joey crossed the courtyard to the young man, and in a serious voice said, "Hi. What's going on here? Just who are you? Who are you working for?" The man was young, sharp-featured, and handsome. Maybe early twenties, Joey guessed, but noticed that his eyes were older and reflected something intense.

"Please," the man said. "I mean no harm. I am a Jew here from Palestine. I was a soldier also . . . with the British Jewish Brigade."

Joey frowned. "The Jewish Brigade?"

"Yes," he said. "From Palestine. Part of the British Eighth Army. My name is Micah Zuckerman, from Kibbutz Navon in Palestine."

"A British soldier? So what are you doing here in a DP camp and out of uniform?"

"It's a long story, but I am helping and encouraging those who want to get to the Promised Land," he answered.

"Well, why are you always watching me?" Joey said, staring at him intently. Looking back just as intently, the young Palestinian said, "I am interested in why an American soldier is helping us Jews."

"I am Jewish as well," Joey said, feeling a bit defensive. "And we American soldiers have helped liberate the Jews and everyone else those Nazi bastards have tortured and maimed."

"You have . . . we know that. I'm sorry if I offended you," the man said and smiled and reached out to shake hands. "Shalom."

Looking down at the hand, Joey took it. "Shalom," he said. He had never used that word before. "I'm Joey Goldman from Charleston, South Carolina, the United States of America. Glad to meet you," he said.

"Charleston? Really? Charleston, South Carolina?" asked Micah. He seemed excited about it for some reason. "So what are you doing here?"

"Helping arrange passage to America for the cousin of a friend of mine."

"Why not help him get to Palestine?" said Micah, his expression changing from a smile to an intense, concerned look. "He would be among his people."

"He has people in America who want him safe with them," said Joey.

"Of course . . . he will be safe there, but . . . ."

"But what?"

"I . . . I have to be careful."

"Careful? Why? Of what?"

"I do not know you."

"I don't know you either," said Joey.

"Can we have a cup of coffee then, and talk more?" the young Jewish Palestinian replied. "I believe you could be of help to me." He pointed to the buildings. "And to them." Joey looked up at the faces staring at them from the windows above and felt himself frowning.

"Look, I'd like to know you, too. But I'm late," he said. "I have to get back to base. I'll be back in a couple weeks . . . on the Friday."

"Shalom. Till next time, then," Micah said.

"Shalom," said Joey, and they parted. Shalom, shalom, shalom, he said slowly to himself.

As he headed back to Nuremberg, a thousand thoughts competed in his head. Now he remembered: Skip had said something about members of the Palestine Jewish Brigade as a part of the British Army. A Jew from Palestine helping a camp full of survivors? How?

CHAPTER 28

"He said he was one of them," he told Skip the next time they were together.

"They were a fierce force," Skip said. "The Brits kept them in various deserts far away from the fight. Finally, on Churchill's orders, they allowed them in, and they beat the shit out of a lot of German army groups in Italy."

"He was such a young guy, but very serious," said Joey.

"According to news reports, after VE Day they secretly killed a lot of high-up Nazis, especially SS and Gestapo," said Skip. "Probably still at it, but mostly now they're getting refugees out to Palestine, and the Brits don't like it."

"How do they swing that?"

"Our folks are turning their heads the other way," said Skip. "The Russians too."

"The Russians?" said Joey. "The ones who chased us are helping the Jews? Seems weird that our natural allies the Brits are *not* helping the Jews get to Palestine and the Russians are."

"At least for now," said Skip.

It's so damned complicated, Joey thought. He was curious about Palestine. All he knew was that Jerusalem was there and Jews had been there for centuries. "Next year in Jerusalem," he said aloud. It was something he heard every year at the family Seder. Creepy, being a Jew here where they murdered you just for being one. Maybe Lieutenant Forner knows more about it. So he asked, "Lieutenant, you know anything about the Jewish Brigade?"

"A little," Forner answered. "I know they were the Palestine Brigade and then became part of the Brits' Eighth Army. I'm told the Brits hesitated to train them because they were afraid they'd be trouble later in Palestine."

"Trouble? What kind of trouble?"

"Joey," Forner said kindly. "The Brits are in charge of Palestine. They want the Arabs, not the Jews, to have it when they leave."

"But aren't the Jews from Palestine in the first place?" Joey asked.

"Yeah, but the Arabs don't want them back."

"Because?"

"Because the Arabs have the oil and the Brits think the Arabs can help them stay important in that part of the world, especially with the Suez Canal."

"So how come they let them get into the war?"

"There was a lot of world outrage when the death camps were discovered, so Churchill forced the Army to allow the Jews to join the fight against the Germans in 'forty-four," Forner said. "And they proved themselves on . . . um . . . the Senio River in Italy." He pointed to a spot on the huge map of Europe on the wall behind his desk.

Joey walked over and looked. "You know anything about what they're doing now?"

The lieutenant now looked closely at Joey. "What's this about, Sergeant?"

Joey turned quickly back. "Nothing, sir. I . . . I met one of them at the DP camp in Fürth."

"Well, we've been warned a number of times by the Brits that they're illegally helping refugees," Lieutenant Forner said. "So that's not a surprise. But you should be careful around him."

"Careful?" Joey said. "Why? He's a Jew helping Jews. Isn't that good?"

The lieutenant smiled slightly. "Yeah, sure that's good. It's just that we don't want any trouble with the Brits."

Joey saluted and walked slowly back toward his office thinking he'd better question this young guy Micah about Palestine on his next visit.

CHAPTER 29

S tanding at his office door with two javelins was his friend Smitty. "Hey Joey. You ready for the lesson? It's a perfect blue sky day for it."

"Jeez, Smitty, I forgot. Gimme ten minutes," Joey said. "Got to check on something."

"Smitty"—Terry Smith—was a hulk of a guy. Blond, with a cherubic face and grin, he had been an Olympic hopeful for the javelin back home in Indiana. It was a specialty that had come in handy several times as his unit fought its way through Belgium and into Germany, as when his platoon was ambushed by a German machine gunner as they approached Kirchgarten, a small, peaceful-looking village. They had all scrambled for cover, Smitty had told him. Smitty had crawled behind a stone wall that had been there for probably two hundred years. And, as he and his squad leader had done several times before, he whistled. The squad leader pumped a barrage at the gunner's location as a diversion to give Smitty cover to stand take aim, and toss a grenade with unerring accuracy into the window of the building where the gunfire came from. That was that. Now the village was peaceful.

Joey always managed to become friends in the army with someone huge, strong, but likeable as well. Most big guys, he found, if they were intelligent, were also likeable. Their size assured them that most people wouldn't pick on them. It started back at Basic at Camp Croft. One evening in the barracks, when Joey was polishing his boots,

Kevin O'Connor had staggered in drunk. He was a stereotypical Irish guy from Boston's South Side, heavy drinking, always arguing. Joey'd had trouble with O'Connor before. He was jealous of Joey for being named squad leader, and he didn't like Jews.

"Whattaya doing, you shiesty little gump?" he slurred. "Polishing up your boots like you polished up Sergeant Rooton?" With an angry laugh he grabbed his bayonet from beside his cot and stumbled down toward the wide-eyed Joey, who was the only other GI there. "Think you're so fucking great, you little Christ killer. How 'bout I give you another circumcision? One you'll never forget."

It was the first anti-Semitism he had experienced in the army. *Did O'Connor really say that?* Joey thought. As he moved back, he wrapped a towel around one arm and was getting ready to throw a boot at the advancing drunk when his friend Emile Ruffier, a 6'3" weightlifter, also from Boston, came up the stairs behind O'Connor.

"Put that fucking bayonet down, you drunken Mick bastard," he shouted.

O'Connor turned angrily. "Go fuck yourself, Frenchie, or I'll put it down *your* throat."

Ruffier lunged forward and kicked O'Connor in the stomach. The drunk, waving his bayonet, flew backwards into and through the screen door at the barracks' end, into the air, and crashed down onto the ground a story below. He broke a wrist and was court-martialed and sent to the clink for his fifth drunken fight in two months.

"I can't believe what he called me. I don't get it," Joey said to Ruffier.

"You don't live in Boston or you would, Joey," Ruffier said. "His kind grow up hating Jews. They pass it on like a fuckin' virus in their families . . . and in their church, too."

Joey was startled. "I . . . I feel so dumb about . . . well about being Jewish," he said.

Ruffier laughed. "Jews dumb? Are you kidding?" He patted Joey affectionately on his head. From then on, maybe subconsciously, Joey ended up friends with big guys like Ruffier and Smitty—big guys who were also smart.

Ten minutes later, he and Smitty took off for Soldier's Field, the notorious stadium the Nazis had used for mass events. He had seen it in the basic training films and in the Nazi books Skip had shown him. So he had suggested that was where to go across town so Smitty could get in some practice throwing the javelin and also teach Joey how to throw one accurately.

"Look at the size of this place, Smitty," said Joey. "The Germans called it *Zeppelinfeld*. This is right where Hitler spoke to, I don't know, thousands of Nazi troops and civilians."

They spent the better part of an hour as Smitty taught Joey how to throw the javelin accurately. He finally got it, and three times in a row landed it in the circle Smitty had drawn. Then turning to look up, Joey said. "C'mon, let's go up top there where Der Führer himself would be." They climbed the steps. "There was a giant swastika up there at the very top that the Army blew up when they took Nuremberg last year," he said, pointing.

Standing where Hitler had stood, they took photos of each other with Joey's new Leica. Smitty laughed and saluted like the Nazis, right arm and hand outstretched, and with the other he used two fingers to imitate Hitler's mustache. But Joey just stood silently, looking out on the field, reflecting on the enormity of the results of Hitler's murderous rants here. It had wiped out so many Jews. "Our people," Lieutenant Forner had said.

As he stood there visualizing the thousands *sieg Heil*ing, he heard that ominous drum beating in his brain. *Ba-DUM-da-DUM-DUM, dum, dum, DUM.* He gulped, and felt his anger rising in his chest. His hands curled into fists, and he suddenly spit over the balcony. Smitty looked at him, puzzled.

CHAPTER 30

A week later, Joey was back in Fürth. Both of the survivors had grown stronger and livelier in the weeks that Joey had cared for them. They were eating better and doing some light exercise walks and, of course, feeling hope for the future—powerful medicine in itself. "I have some papers to fill out for you, Josef," Joey announced. "And I've got a bunch of clothes for you. I hope they fit."

Today it was almost a lighthearted lunch in the courtyard. Spring was about to begin, and the trees showed that slightly reddish cast that said so. Karl and Josef were enjoying the goodies Joey had brought. He was telling them about being at the stadium, as they sat around a small table in the courtyard.

"I was at Soldier's Field last week."

"Soldier's Field?" asked Karl.

"*Zeppelinfeld*," Joey explained.

"Ach," said Karl. "Where the Nazis really took over." He shook his head slowly.

"I know," Joey said. "I know. But it's also where *we* took over."

Changing the subject, Joey said, "They told me the date for Josef's departure could be within four months!"

Karl translated this to Josef, who rose and put his hands on Joey's shoulder, "*Danke, Joseph, danke.*"

"*Sie sind willkommen, lieber Freund,*" Joey said softly.

Looking across the courtyard, Joey spotted Micah with a group of DPs around a table. Joey had left a second bag of supplies from the PX there for others to take and Micah was helping them. He waved to Joey and Joey waved back. Seeing this, Karl cleared his throat, leaned over and said. "I have news about a departure also."

"A departure?" Joey asked. "What kind of departure?"

"To Palestine," whispered Karl. "Me, to Palestine."

"You?" Joey almost shouted.

"Yes," said Karl. "That young man, Micah, says he is arranging it!"

"Palestine? That's hundreds of miles away," Joey said. "How in hell is he going to get you there? And you'd run into all kinds of obstacles and red tape."

"Red tape? Red? You mean the communists in Hungary and Russia?" said Karl.

"No, no," said Joey. "That's just an expression that means bureaucratic gobbledygook." Karl frowned, not understanding.

"It means official details that are long and boring," said Joey.

At this point Joey stood and motioned to Micah to join them, which he did enthusiastically, seeing the assortment of goodies on the table.

"Dive in. There's plenty here," said Joey.

Micah gladly accepted. "And you brought that other big bag for others in the camp. You're a good man, Joey. God will reward you."

Joey stared at Micah. It was justice he had thought of in helping here, not God. He frowned. "Thank you, Micah. You, too. But I need to hear about what you've promised Karl here. It sounds like a very difficult thing to pull off."

"I don't say it won't be difficult, far from it," Micah said. "But we're doing it every day all over Europe. There are many of us here from Palestine. We keep a low profile."

"Because you're doing something illegal?" Joey said.

"Illegal to some, yes," Micah acknowledged. "But not to these poor souls who want to come to *Yisroel*. So we're here to help them."

"How can you be sure you're helping and not hurting them again?"

"We have ways. There are friends who help us along the way."

"Friends? What kind of friends?"

"Especially in Italy they help us get to seaports and on ships to Palestine."

"You're telling me the US Army doesn't mind this?" asked Joey in disbelief.

"That's not always the case," Micah shrugged. "But usually they look the other direction, thank God. Our biggest difficulty is with the British."

"The British?" Joey exclaimed. "Weren't you fighting as part of the Brits?"

"We were, yes. But now they try to stop us at every step."

"The British Army? How come?"

"Because they control Palestine!" Micah exclaimed. "It's their mandate . . . and they are more interested in barrels of Arab oil than in letting the Jews, our people, find a safe home there."

Our people again, thought Joey.

"It's control and economics, not ethics, to them," Micah smirked, then said, quietly, "Joey, there are fifty million Arabs who don't want what's left of the Jews to come back to our land . . . our land for almost four thousand years. They're being encouraged by the Grand Mufti of Jerusalem, who sided with Hitler."

"He sided with Hitler?"

"Yes, with the Germans," Micah said. "And he is now pressuring the British to keep Jews out . . . and the Brits are caving."

"Why?" Joey said.

"For lots of reasons. Including a very antisemitic foreign secretary. They are not our friends, Joseph."

"I don't get it. They're our allies."

"Your allies, Joey. Yours, not ours. They don't want to help the Jews!"

"We joined in to help England and now they won't help these poor Jews?" Joey said.

"England, hah," Karl said. "Don't you know England once expelled all the Jews? For over three hundred years. It's the same vicious circle we have suffered forever."

"Vicious circle? Whattaya mean?" Joey's knowledge of Jewish history was limited basically to the Passover story of Moses and the Exodus from Egypt, something about Purim and Queen Esther saving the Jews. And the Chanukah story. That was about it.

Micah was getting exasperated. "For God's sake, Joey. Where have you been? Don't you realize that throughout Europe, Jews were not allowed to be professionals or teachers or farmers or anything but moneylenders?"

"Which they did only because the church declared moneylending off-limits for Christians," Karl said. "So . . . . "

"The church?" said Joey. At Camp Croft, his friend Ruffier had talked about the church in Boston. "The church fixed it so the Jews would become moneylenders?"

"Yah," Karl said, "und when the debts got too high, instead of the borrowers paying back what they owed, they just blamed the Jews and did horrible things to them. Und in England, instead of paying back what he borrowed, King Edward the First ordered all the Jews to leave the country."

"How do you know all this?"

"I told you that first day, Joseph," Karl said. "I was professor of history at Freiburg University. Until the Nazis declared it illegal for a Jew to be a teacher under the 'Law for the Reintroduction of Professional Civil Service.'"

"Reintroduction? What did that mean?" Joey asked.

Karl sighed. "It meant they reintroduced us to living in ghettos and in poverty."

Joey was silent for a while. He had an "H" on his dog tags, for Hebrew, but he went to Temple only on Rosh Hashanah and Yom Kippur, the two holy days that most Jews celebrated in his community, plus the family Seder at Passover. It wasn't something that had been on his mind. The feeling inside him wasn't exactly religious, it was more emotional, a kind of growing recognition of his identity. He looked from Karl to Micah and back several times.

"I see."

"So for me it could be a new life in Palestine," sighed Karl. "I could even teach again. They want me there."

Micah smiled. "They do want him there," he said. "What does your Statue of Liberty say, Joey? I know it by heart." He raised his hand: "'Give me your tired, your poor, your huddled masses yearning to breathe free.' Well, we can say it a little different, but the same. 'Give me your wretched refuse from your murderous shores. Send these, the hopeless, homeless, torture-tossed to me. I lift my lamp beside God's ancient promise of a homeland.'"

There was a long silence, each man absorbing what had been said.

"You can help us, Joey. You can help us in many ways." Joey stared back, tight-lipped. *How could I help? Getting refugees through all those zones? How the hell did they do it, anyway? It would be a violation of the Army's policy. Is it worth a court martial? But then, is it worth even more to get the thousands of Karls to safety after what they have suffered?*

"This . . . this is a lot to swallow . . . a lot. I'll have to think about it." He rose to go. "I'll be back on Friday in . . . umm . . . three weeks and . . . and we'll talk more." Karl and Josef both rose and gave him a long, sweet hug.

CHAPTER 31

I'll have to put this on my scale, he thought. *Be a good boy and don't upset your father.* That's how he started his "scale," worrying about how his father had become extra sensitive to noise, and whenever any noise or voice was loud he would squinch his eyes and cup his hand to his right ear and wince with a hiss, "S-s-s-t." That sound so unnerved Joey when he was young that he would put the pros and cons of whatever he was doing around his father on either side of a scale and see which might cause that hiss. Thereafter it had become a habit to put anything that was confronting him on his scale and measure its pros and cons. It was part of his routine.

The drums floated in his mind. Karl and Josef on one side and Army regulations on the other. He reached up and touched the six-pointed star around his neck. He had just thought of it basically as a good luck piece from Aunt Minnie. But now it was beginning to feel like much more than that. The Germans had made all Jews wear a yellow Magen David on their clothes or armband to point them out before they began deporting them to death camps. He would have had to wear one himself. It was so unlike growing up Jewish in Charleston.

Suddenly he realized he'd missed the turn and was about to drive into the off-limits Old City. He slammed on the brakes, startling an old woman picking pieces of unbroken blue tile from one of the thousands of piles of rubble which was once the old walled city. He turned around quickly, remembering there was a sniper hiding in there.

A sniper was indeed caught in the ruins of the Old City. He wounded an off-duty MP who was making out with a Fräulein in part of a damaged tavern. Pants down and skirt up, they were coupling in such a way that the bullet had gone through his buttocks and continued into hers. But the former SS officer's gun jammed, giving the MP enough time, even with his pants at his knees, to wing him and bring him in.

Red Blake did routines about the incident for days: "The Purple Hard-on was recently awarded for scoring twice in ass-to-ass action in the face of enemy fire!" But Red also started carrying his Luger tucked into his belt.

"Just in case. You never know," Red said.

The tension around the Kaserne was rising, not only because of the sniper but because the word was that verdicts would be given soon at the War Crimes Trial, and maybe there would be a German uprising. Joey had already ordered gas masks and ammunition to be distributed to all on the depot. Maybe it would actually give him a chance to shoot a few Germans, he thought. So, good . . . let them try something. What they did to the Jews should be repaid in kind. An eye for an eye. Yeah. He would like that. He reached into his desk drawer for one of the three .45 pistols he had requisitioned—one for Lieutenant Forner and one for the Colonel: *Automatic Pistol, Caliber .45, M1911A1.* The third was for himself.

They never examined his orders, since he was doing such a good job and giving them detailed reports of his activities weekly—not so detailed in this case, he thought, smiling to himself. Checking to see the safety was on, he slowly raised the pistol, and as those drums started in his head he aimed at an imaginary German. "Pow. Pow. Pow. You Nazi bastard," he said. Schatzie looked up at him and whined. He looked down and put the pistol away. "Don't worry. Puppy dogs don't count," he said as he lifted Schatzie up onto his lap.

Next time he went to Fürth, Micah was away. "We don't know where or why," said Karl. "He just disappears sometimes."

Maybe on one of those missions, Joey thought. "Killing SS, I hope," he muttered.

Karl looked surprised. Joey saw that Karl did not know about such missions. And why would he?

"You are angry about something, Joseph?" Karl said.

Realizing his error, Joey turned toward Josef and his frown softened. "I don't know why they're taking so long with Josef's papers, but don't worry. I'm on the case."

Karl translated, and Josef stroked Joey's face, saying, "I know you are, *Liebchen*." Though they were the dependents, Karl and Josef had come to think of Joey as their son. It was important to their mental stability, since their own children, their whole families, had been murdered.

CHAPTER 32

Joey and Skip were at the Trials again and were listening intently as the prosecution made its careful, concise case. You could see the Nazis' worried looks now. Especially Von Ribbentrop, who had earlier doubled over with laughter when the Russians had loaded their atrocity film upside down. He had nothing to laugh about at this point. The verdicts would come at the end of the summer. There was a hanging now hanging over him.

Skip and Joey felt the tension building. When they left the Palace of Justice, Skip suddenly grabbed Joey. "Let's get the hell out of this burg for a few days. It's July Fourth coming up. We're due a furlough. My friend Stan Lanning at *Stars and Stripes* told me the Rest and Recreation Center in Garmisch-Partenkirchen was a blast. Whattaya say?"

"Garmisch? Where's that?" said Joey.

"Down below Munich. It's in the mountains where the bastards held the thirty-sixth Winter Olympics," said Skip. "The Third Army took it over last year for R & R. C'mon . . . a little wine, women, and song?"

"Munich?" said Joey. "Isn't that where the Nazi party started?"

Skip sighed, "Yep. But we won't stop there, Joey. So relax."

Skip was no dummy. He saw there was a hatred growing in Joey and that he had to be careful in some ways with his pal.

Bundling into Joey's Jeep, papers in hand, they headed south, singing "Ninety-Nine Bottles of Beer on the Wall" at the top of their lungs. As the weather turned from warm to hot, they rolled down the windows and continued into Bavaria toward Munich, passing through many small villages. Usually the townsfolk just stared at them.

"Joey, look at that. Is that a Hummel village or what?" said Skip.

"A village of innocents, right?" Joey said.

Periodically they would pass an Army checkpoint and have to stop to show their papers and bullshit with the MPs. The Jeep with the Ford top was always the main topic of interest.

"Good thing we ain't on the run," said Skip. "Wouldn't take long to spot us. Hey, look at that sign! *Dachau.* Wasn't that what your Colonel told you to see?"

Joey slammed on the brakes, pulled over and looked back. "Dachau, yeah, that's the concentration camp. It's supposed to be an awful sight."

As Joey started backing up, Skip looked thoughtfully at him. "That could ruin our stay at the Eibsee, man," he said, gently. "You'll be depressed as hell. Maybe we should do it on the way back, not now, Joey."

"I guess . . . I guess you're right. Okay," Joey agreed. "We'll wait. But on the way back."

"Deal. On the way back," agreed Skip.

They drove on without talking for a long time. Finally Joey nodded up and down several times and switched on the Philips radio the POWs had found and installed in the jeep for him. It was set to AFN Munich. Frank Sinatra was crooning "Nancy with the Laughing Face."

"Hey, all the comforts of home," Joey laughed. Skip smiled with relief.

CHAPTER 33

———————

Bypassing Munich, they pulled into the parking lot of the Hotel Eibsee on Lake Eibsee in Garmisch, just as the sun was setting. The hotel was nestled at water's edge, looking across at the Zugspitze, Germany's highest mountain. It stood snowcapped, even in July. Four stories high, the hotel stretched for two hundred feet along the lake, with layers of gray, rocky, mountains looking down at it. Each room facing the lake had its own wood-railed balcony. Joey stood still, staring. He had never seen such an amazing place. Skip had to pull him inside.

As soon as he and Skip checked in, they headed for the long front porch that faced the mountains. There were huge sofas, with overstuffed pillows. They flopped down and ordered beers. The lake was a beautiful thing to behold—snowy peaks looked down on water turning pink from the sunset. It calmed them down so much that they were nodding when a GI strolled by and laughed at how relaxed they looked.

"Doesn't look like you're up for the Carioca, guys," he ventured.

"Carioca?" asked Skip, sitting up. "What's that?"

"The Casa Carioca. Hottest spot in town. We, the US Army I mean, built it. Dancing. Ice skating. And lots of be-e-e-e-you-ti-ful Fräuleins looking for action," the GI said. "Hi, I'm Frank Sturdevant. Down from Wiesbaden for a few days." They introduced themselves because this sounded interesting.

"I got a buddy stationed up there," Joey said. "Al Moskowitz, he's stationed . . . "

"Holy shit," Sturdevant broke in. "Al Moskowitz? He's in my unit. I can't believe this. How do you know Al?"

"From high school days. You a Special Services actor like him?"

"Which Special Services?" asked Skip.

"MOS 03B. Entertainment," said Frank. "We put on shows. You know—plays, theater, music—to entertain our fellow American Occupation Forces. That's us." He laughed.

"Sounds great!" said Skip, laughing back. "But hey, let's get back to the Fräulein entertainment forces here. Where's this Club Carioca?"

"Casa Carioca," corrected Frank. "C'mon let's grab some chow inside. It's really good here. Then I'll lead you to a night of . . . heh, heh, heh—'who knows what evil lurks in the hearts of men?'"

"Heh, heh, heh, 'the Shadow knows,'" said Skip picking up on the radio reference. "I'm ready for a little Fräulein evil! Heh, heh, heh, heh."

Having eaten and washed up, Joey and Skip met Frank and headed for the Casa Carioca. It was next to the Olympic Ice Stadium, and from it, big band swing blared, played by a GI orchestra. "Pennsylvania six-five-o-o-o!" the band shouted.

The dance floor was crowded with couples of all sorts. Some pairs were in military uniforms, but most were a sexy Fräulein hanging on to a GI. All the tension they'd felt back in Nuremberg was floating away. Joey, always the drummer, was keeping time on the table with the silverware when two young German girls approached. One boldly asked, "You vont to dance mit us?" She reached her hand out to Joey. He stood and slowly took in her classic, blue-eyed, blonde-haired Teutonic beauty. Skip leapt up and grabbed the other girl and whirled out onto the floor. And dance they did—waltzing and drinking and jitterbugging and drinking and eating and drinking and more drinking until finally Skip's partner said, "Zo? Let's go home, und, you know . . . have zum more fun."

Upstairs, in their room, it was only minutes before lights went out, clothes were thrown on the floor, and naked bodies were rolling around on the beds. The boys forgot for the moment their roles as occupiers, and the girls forgot their national defeat, and its accompanying hardships. Being with Americans could mean a lot for the girls, but underneath all that was just plain sexual desire making itself rise to the top. The moonlight shone through the windows, revealing the boys on their backs and the girls mounted on them as if riding bucking broncos. Seeing this just as he climaxed, Skip combined it with another popular radio saying.

"Hiyo, Silver! Away-y-y!" Skip shouted, and he and Joey burst into delighted laughter at the reference.

The night went on and on like this. In the morning, the four were awakened by the hotel's maid service. Shyly they all dressed. The girls, delighted to connect with Americans, anxiously suggested plans for the nights ahead. "I am Katja," the one said shyly to Joey. "Und you?"

Joey smiled. "Call me Joey."

"Joy like in happiness?" Katja asked.

Skip laughed. "That's perfect. Mr. Happiness himself."

Frieda, Skip's companion, laughed also and sang, "Joy to zee world. Zee Lord has come."

Jeez, thought Joey. *This is fucking nuts. If I hadn't been wearing rubbers she'd have seen I was circumcised. Then what?* And only now did he think about Leah. But this wasn't love, it was just sex. They were under a lot of stress. Just young guys having fun, he rationalized.

As the girls were leaving, Joey handed them a whole carton of cigarettes.

"Danke!" they shrilled. *"Danke vielmals! Wunderbare Soldaten. Danke Ihnen für Alles!* Zenk you for all this!"

Skip smiled back enthusiastically. "Well, thank you for *Alles . . .* and I do mean *Alles."*

When they left, Joey flopped back onto the bed, exhausted, satiated, and, at least for this moment, free of all care. "Think they got room service in this here establishment?" he said.

"Didn't you get enough service last night?" said Skip, laughing. Joey joined in.

CHAPTER 34

———————

They spent the next four days lying in the sun, swimming, boating on the Eibsee, eating, drinking, and being very merry with the Fräuleins. Joey had never experienced anything like this. The girls, like many of their peers, knew that most of the Americans were open, generous, and fun-loving. It was something they needed . . . to be carefree and hopeful again. Joey wondered about Katja and what she had been through.

Maybe there were some decent Germans after all. On the last day, Joey and Katja were out in a rowboat checking out the sunset. He was pulling at the oars, and she sat facing him and pulled up her dress to show she was wearing no underclothes. It quickly led to them screwing on the bottom of the boat. Shy Joey couldn't believe what was happening to him. The ripples from the rocking spread concentric circles from the rowboat across the pinkish waters toward the shore. Later, Skip told him he'd been sitting on the porch with his binocs and figured out what was happening out there. He'd laughed out loud; "Proud of that boy," he'd said.

At the Casa Carioca that night, the foursome was drinking and dancing as usual when Sturdevant joined them with his date. "Lieselotte," he said introducing her. Eyeing her huge breasts that wanted out of her tight black dress, Skip said, "A lot, yeah, a lot." Joey having just taken a sip of beer spit some out laughing. Seeing this, Lieselotte raised her stein and said, "Our *Bier* too much for you, ja?"

"It's different than our beer but I like it," Joey said. "Yah. *Ja.*"

"But the way you zip it . . . too slow. You don't trink it like us." With that, she downed a huge gulp.

"Too slow, huh? Well, I'll bet you I can down a mug faster than you. Wanna bet?"

"Bet? Bet? Vot do you tink? I vould bet like a Jew? A Jew?" She laughed.

Before he knew what he was doing, Joey threw his beer into her face. "Goddam German. I *am* a Jew and, yes, I'll make you a bet . . . I'll bet you'll rot in hell . . . all of you!"

Skip reached out and grabbed Joey and pulled him back as the girl fled.

Sturdevant said, "Easy, man, easy. She's just a dumb Kraut bitch."

The girls didn't know what to think. Katja put her hand on Joey's neck and said softly, "You, you are Jewish? You are so nice." She began to cry. "We did terrible things to the Jews. God will punish us."

Joey turned to look at her. It calmed him down. He patted her head gently and said, "*You* didn't do it, Katja. Don't cry."

CHAPTER 35

That night Joey said, "I'm outta here." Skip agreed. They checked out in the morning and headed north back into reality—and Dachau.

"I'm ready for it now," said Joey, his mood still altered from the night before.

As they drove up to the gates of the concentration camp, they noticed how close it was to the town. Above the entrance was the sign, *Arbeit Macht Frei.* "Work sets you free," Skip read aloud. "Do you fucking believe that?" It was the first time Joey heard him angry about this. Usually, Skip would only agree with Joey's angry comments.

"Remember at the Trials," said Joey. "That lawyer said the people of Dachau claimed they knew nothing about what was going on at the camp?"

"Nothing my ass," said Skip. "I can already smell it, and my CO said the cleanup was almost finished."

Using the letter Colonel Larned had given him, Joey got the MPs to allow them to drive in and see the situation. There were still piles of clothing from the thousands of prisoners who had died there.

Joey walked up to a PFC sitting at a table outside one of the grim, gray, cement buildings. He had a stack of photographs and documents he was organizing into a report.

"Excuse me," said Joey to the soldier. "But we're visiting here and wondered if you or somebody could tell us exactly what went on here.

I'm Joseph Goldman from the 318th Ordnance in Nuremberg, and this is Skip Say."

The soldier looked up in surprise. "You're visiting? What do you mean, *visiting*?"

"Sorry," Joey said. "That's a stupid way to put it. See, I'm Jewish and my CO suggested I come here so I can tell others just how rotten the Nazis bastards were, and . . . "

"Oh, okay, I see. Well, you ain't gonna believe what you'll see. It's pretty hard to describe. My name's Harold Porter. I'm with the 116th Evacuation Hospital. We came in here and . . . you wouldn't, you couldn't, believe this scene. I've been sent back here to organize information for the Doctors' Trial." He looked at them and squinted. "I'll give you a looksee you'll never forget," he said. "If you're up for it."

Joey wasn't sure now that he *was* "up for it." Skip glanced over at him, so he gritted his teeth and nodded okay. The PFC turned a stack of pictures around and began flipping through for them to see.

"There was a marshaling yard back there where the trains full of prisoners came and went. There were some fifty cattle cars full of corpses—fifty goddamn cars piled up with men, women, and children," Porter said. "All dead from hunger, thirst, suffocation, beatings, shootings. Thousands of them." Joey and Skip screwed up their faces in shock at what they were seeing.

"You can imagine what actually seeing this does to you," continued Porter. "The GIs went crazy. They shot every fucking Nazi here they could find."

"Good for them," Joey muttered.

"C'mon," Porter said, and motioned them to follow him toward a small, dismal-looking gray building. It was the crematorium. The remnants of a small flower garden stood in front. Joey shook his head and pointed to it. Skip nodded in disgust.

"There was a huge stack of corpses in two rooms piled up, all nude so that their clothes wouldn't be 'wasted' by the burning," Porter said. "Here, look at this." He handed Joey a photo.

"Jesus, they're stacked like kindling," Joey said, and felt the gorge rise in his throat.

"Like for a fire," said Skip. "Like in hell."

"They were *in* hell," Porter said. They walked inside. Ashes still lay in the furnaces. "These furnaces were for burning six bodies at once, and over there and there those rooms were crammed to the ceiling with more bodies—one big, stinking, rotten mess, their faces purple, their eyes popping, and with a weird grin on each one."

He shuddered. "They were nothing but bones and skin. If you can believe it, those hooks up on the wall were where they hung bodies, like beef, before they tossed them in the ovens. I vomited three times when I came in there."

"How many bodies were there?" Skip asked.

Porter shook his head. "Thousands and thousands. I wrote my folks about it, but I don't know if they can really get it."

"And how many live prisoners were left?" Joey asked softly.

"If you want to call them alive . . . maybe thirty thousand," Porter said. "Mostly Jews. While we were inspecting this place, some of them drove up with wagonloads of corpses from the compound. Watching the unloading," he shook his head. . . "it was horrible. The bodies squooshed and gurgled as they hit the pile and you could almost see the odor. It took months to bury the dead and then process and doctor the survivors and move them out."

Two hours later, after seeing much too much, Joey and Skip said goodbye to Porter and headed back to the Jeep. "Now you really know why we fought this war," Skip grunted.

Joey nodded. "It was so much harder seeing this shit in person than on those films at the Trials." He felt battered by the pattern of experiences he was living . . . the Trials, Karl, Josef, Micah, the Jew-hating Fräulein, and now . . . Dachau. Again, the drums beat in his ears.

CHAPTER 36

That night, another nightmare. This time he was a prisoner in a camp in a situation that a Treblinka survivor had told Josef about, and that Karl had translated for him. "The commandant, Kurt Franz," Karl had said, "was particularly brutal and would kill at least one prisoner a day. He would practice boxing by using the head of any Jew passing by—male, female, child—he didn't care. He would grab his victim's shirt and strike with the other hand. The victim would be ordered to hold his head straight so that Franz could get a good blow in. And he did this expertly. The sight of the Jew's head after a 'boxing session' of this sort is not difficult to imagine." Karl had been visibly upset. Joey screamed in his sleep, as if *he* were being beaten, until Red once again shook him awake.

What was happening to him? Back in Charleston he was just like his friends, wasn't he? Then he remembered the time little Donnie Murphy asked him to come out and play, and how when he said he couldn't, because it was Friday dinnertime, Donny had yelled, "You Jew!" His Dad had scolded Donnie and told Joey not to worry about it. Donnie knew very well that on Fridays the Goldmans lit candles and Joey's father read aloud from a brief booklet of prayers from the Temple. Obviously, Donnie learned things at home from his parents. Joey had the hots for Donnie's older sister, Barbara, so he let it pass. But there it was—hidden for years in a brain storage compartment that was only now being pried open.

CHAPTER 37

On his next visit to Fürth, Joey sought out Micah and sat with him in the courtyard. "I need to know more about the Jewish Brigade," Joey demanded. "And about what's happening in Palestine. I want to make sure Karl and those people," he looked toward others in the courtyard, "aren't going to be hurt again."

"Those people are not '*those people*,'" Micah said. "They're *my* people, the living and the dead are *my people*, . . . and *your* people, Joseph!"

Joey turned to look at Micah, then back at the refugees down at the other table enjoying the treats and other things he had brought them. He nodded slowly.

"Joseph, I cannot reveal things to you just because you ask," Micah said quietly.

"Whatta I have to do to know?" Joey said, almost shouting. Karl and Josef looked his way, concerned. "I need to know," he said more quietly.

"There are things," said Micah. "But I will have to discuss this with others." He paused for a moment, thinking. "I *can* tell you some things about Palestine—that it is part of the British Mandate from after World War I."

"I do know that," Joey said. "I wrote my brother for some facts, and he told me about British rule and the White Paper."

"The White Paper, yes, 1939," Micah said, almost snarling. "Instead of all the promises the Brits made about establishing a Jewish homeland, what they promised instead was a future Arab state. And they stopped allowing Jewish refugees fleeing Hitler to immigrate into Palestine. They also stopped allowing us to buy land."

"So what did you do?"

"What could we do? We fought with the bastards so refugee ships could unload their passengers." Micah shrugged and frowned. "We gave the Brits a really hard time until the war started. And then we wanted to have a Palestine Brigade, so we could kill Germans."

"And they let you, right?"

"They refused us for a long time. But then they finally allowed us to join the Buffs."

Joey had never heard of the Buffs.

"It was their infantry regiment already stationed in Palestine," Micah said, shaking his head. "At least it gave us the training we needed."

"So when did you get here?"

"When they were pushing the Nazis back and uncovering the death camps," said Micah. "The public pressure was so great to let us get a chance to fight the Germans that they finally let us form the Jewish Brigade. And then Churchill ordered them to let us go into Italy as part of the UK army."

"My lieutenant told me that," Joey said. "He said you kicked German ass there."

Micah laughed. "We did. We did just that."

"He also said you—ah—took care of a lot of SS and Gestapo officers."

"We . . . we handed in lots of names to them," Micah said, hesitating slightly.

"And that now you're smuggling refugees to Palestine."

"Smuggling? That's a good word for it," Micah said, his nostrils flaring. "The British consider homeless Jews *contraband*. So, yes, we have to smuggle them out."

"We? You're not in uniform," Joey said. "Who is 'we'? I . . . I'd like to help you but . . . ."

"But what?" Micah said, and frowned slightly. "You are afraid?"

"Afraid? No . . . no, not afraid. *Concerned*. It's against regulations," Joey said. "I could be court-martialed."

"Against US Army regulations, perhaps, Joey," Micah said, gently. "It is *not* against humanitarian regulations. And it is surely not against the need for Jewish survival."

Joey realized that Karl had been translating their conversation for Josef. Of course—because it affected the future of all four of them. Looking at their anxious faces, Joey wanted to help. He could tell that although Micah hesitated to reveal the secret activities of the Brigade, he wanted Joey to join in. The two looked into each other's eyes, searching for the right words, waiting to see who would blink first.

Finally Micah closed his eyes, took a long breath, and decided to chance it. "I *am* a member of the Brigade. We fought our way through Italy. Yes, we—how did you say it?—'took care' of important SS and Gestapo officers in hiding, and we still have more to find. But our most important task is to help get Jews to Palestine. They are needed there. They are wanted there."

"Why aren't you in uniform, then?" Joey said.

"I guess your lieutenant didn't tell you. The Brits demobilized us in June and forced us to return to Palestine," said Micah. He looked into Joey's eyes. "Joseph, Joey . . . I am really trusting you now. Please don't disappoint me."

"I promise, Micah," Joey said. He reached out his hand to shake on it and Micah smiled as he took it. While clutching Joey's hand, he turned his smile onto Josef and Karl. You could see the relief on their careworn faces. They closed their eyes and bowed their heads for a moment. *They are thanking God we are friendly,* Joey thought. Even now? Even after what he allowed them to suffer?

"But you are still here . . . not in Palestine, Micah?"

"I am, but I am not," Micah said, smiling. "You know how in the movies the stars have doubles for the stunts? Well, the Brits' way of stopping our rescue efforts was to send us home. But we picked doubles from the refugees, and trained them how to wear our uniforms, how to stand, how to march, how to salute, and how to use a weapon.

It's a whole *megillah*."

"You mean guerilla?" Joey laughed.

"No, *megillah* is Hebrew for 'a long story,'" Micah said.

"Oh. You sent them back as you! That was brilliant!" Joey said. "But . . . who *are* you? I mean, what if you get stopped and asked for ID?"

Micah glanced carefully around, then showed his ID card. Joey read aloud from it: "Micah Zuckerman, Refugee Department, The Jewish Agency, 12 Hasharon St., Tel Aviv, Palestine." He raised his eyes slowly in amused admiration. "How many of you are here now?"

"Enough," Micah smiled. "But we need all the help we can get, Joseph."

"What kind of help? he said, though he began to suspect what the answer was, and felt himself start to sweat. "I don't know what I could do."

"You're *the* supply sergeant for the Nuremberg *Ordnance* Depot," said Micah. "Ordnance. My god, Joey, that's vehicles and weapons.

We need vehicles to transport survivors from here to the ports, and weapons and trucks to go to Eretz Israel when the British leave and the Arabs attack."

"You think the British will really leave?" asked Joey.

"We will make them leave," said Micah. "And *that* will guarantee the Arabs will attack us."

"Vehicles and weapons?" Joey said, frowning, knowing that would create real difficulties. "I don't know how I could pull that off."

"We can help you," Micah said. "The TTG has experience with that. It can be easy."

"TTG? What's that?"

"An 'army' group called in Hebrew *Tilhas Tizig Gesheften*," Micah replied.

"Loosely translated it means 'Kiss-My-Ass Business,'" Karl broke in with a chuckle.

Joey laughed, but then suddenly stopped. "This requires a shitload of thought," he said, slowly shaking his head. "I can't say yes or no to this, Micah. But I promise I won't reveal anything to anybody. You have my word. But you've gotta understand, this is *not* what I came here to do. I have to think. I *have* to."

"I understand, Joey," said Micah. "But it *is* what I came here to do. I hope you can understand that." He got up from his bench and paused a moment. "Joey, I want you to meet some Brigade leaders and hear what they have to say. Will you do that?" He held out his hand. Joey looked at him, then at Karl and Josef, and slowly nodded yes, and shook on it.

"I will set it up on Sunday, September first," Micah said. "The day before your Labor Day, if you can meet me here?"

"I'll be here," Joey said. He gave the two older men a hug and a kiss. "Okay," he said.

As he walked slowly back to his jeep, Joey wondered how Micah knew such details about all that was going on, including about Labor Day. *I like him, though,* he thought. *Guess he has to be very smart to be getting away with all of this.*

CHAPTER 38

Everything he was finding out kept Joey tossing around that night. He had to tell someone and that could only be Louis.

Dear Louis,

I went to the DP camp again since Karl and Josef, my two wounded birds, wanted me to talk with Micah, the Palestinian Brigade guy. Louis, you have always been the only one I've ever told my secrets to so please don't tell ANYONE about him. Our mail isn't censored anymore so I will tell you what's going on. You remember when I shot that robin with my BB rifle on San Souci Street, and I brought him home and you helped me fix his wing? How I hated using a gun, and now here I am thinking about killing Germans. I have found out so many bad things about them and good and bad things about being Jewish that I am getting stressed out. Micah wants me to meet some of their leaders and I just have to admire them. You won't believe how they risk their lives to help Jewish survivors get to Palestine . . . and he's pressuring me to help them with stuff from the Depot. You know, trucks and weapons and ammo because I am THE Supply Sergeant for the Depot and Colonel Larned leaves supplies completely up to me. Louis, what do you think I should do? And for God's sake don't let Dad know about this. He would have a shit fit

and try to order me to stay out of it. I wonder if he even knows
about the Zionists and Palestine. I doubt it.

Joey felt upset saying this about his father. On the one hand, he realized how terrible it must have been for him to be struck down at a time in his life when he was a rising star in the new world of electricity. Joey knew all about how the store in Charleston had been a citywide attraction. "The talk of the town," Dodo would say when she showed the boys the album she kept of the store window displays with the latest appliances . . . radios, irons, heaters, washer-dryers. Plus, she had clippings from the *Evening Post* about General Electric calling his father "The Dixie Dynamo." Then, Louis explained, almost overnight their father was down, and then out, for close to three years. He lost everything, but he didn't give up. That took guts that Joey admired, but it also changed his dad from the up-tempo, fun-loving father his brother told him about to the anxious, self-involved person Joey knew. Joey longed to be loved by his father, but he hated the rigidity and distance that, growing up, he felt from his father. *Louis is the only one in the family I can explore my feelings with,* he mused. Louis wrote him back immediately.

> *Dear Joey,*
>
> *I've given this a lot of thought. You know I can't tell you what to do . . . only what I think. My first inclination was to say you're risking not only your Army career, but a court-martial that would haunt your life forever. Then last week we were shown some Signal Corps footage at HQ—the kind you've apparently been seeing at the Trials—of the camps and survivors and mounds of dead Jews and I felt like throwing up. I was so shocked and angry I yelled out during the screening. And now I see why you're so taken with the Brigade. At least*

they are trying to do the humane thing. Palestine seems to be the only place that wants Jewish refugees. Joey, you just have to think about whether you can safely do things without getting noticed. Remember how we used to plan our baseball games inning by inning? Step by step, what one move might do to the next. Who would you walk and who would you pitch to? That's what you have to do before you make up your mind.

Love, Louis

CHAPTER 39

That evening, he sat in his office long after everyone left. So, how would he plan this? It was far more complicated than the games Louis and he had planned. Louis had known that, small as he was, he could get a hit every time he was at bat. In a close game, Louis would put him in to bat in the late innings when several runners were on. The pitchers would feel sorry for the cute little guy when he came to bat and ease up on their pitches, and Joey would smack a base hit into the outfield, knocking in the winning runs. Louis was always protective of him, so he reciprocated in the way he could, by making sure Joey always got a hit. It was their bond. How to get a hit now, so to speak, was next.

As a first step, he looked at the records of what was actually on hand at the depot. He listed the various kinds of vehicles—tanks, trucks, Jeeps, artillery, and self-propelled equipment—then hand weapons of all sorts, ammunition, and food. That was his "starting lineup." Jeez, he thought, *if only I could just hit a bases-loaded home run and airlift everything to Palestine. Wouldn't that be a gift!* That made him sit up straight and start to sweat: *What am I thinking? I could get in terrible trouble!* That kind of dreaming by the Jews that this would pass was exactly the kind of thinking that allowed the Nazis to enact their plan, which was why the Jews of Palestine were saying "never again."

Because the depot was the combat vehicle collecting point for the Third Army, it held thousands of vehicles. He learned to drive all of them, from the M-90 Pershing tanks down to the "deuce-and-a-half," the two-and-a-half-ton trucks. He leaned back in his chair. *I guess I could manage something*, he thought, *but what if I get caught? It will be the end of me.* He heard Micah responding, "But if you don't get caught it could mean you will help prevent the end of Eretz Israel." *Israel*, he thought. Israel, a place for Jews to be safe.

A homeland for these poor souls . . . my God, what they'd been through nobody would believe. He closed his eyes, and the trip to Dachau filled his mind. He thought, *They're still almost prisoners in these fucking camps.* He remembered the saying Karl had told him:

"Dear God, make me dumb,

That I may not to Dachau come."

"I'm Jewish!" he said aloud. "I gotta help them. Somehow, I gotta help them."

CHAPTER 40

Rolling into the DP camp in Fürth later that week, Joey spotted Micah waiting for him. Micah was dressed as a businessman this time—a neat, dark-blue suit, lavender-and-gray striped tie, and a white handkerchief peeking out of his jacket pocket.

"Sorry I'm late, Micah," said Joey, "but I had to fill an order for a unit in Bad Groningen. Just who are you today? You look important." Joey smiled.

"Don't worry. It's never too late to help us," said Micah. "I have an appointment after our meeting to purchase some—ah—expensive equipment."

They drove out of Fürth to a small farm. Several old cars and a horse-drawn wagon stood in front of the seemingly peaceful farmhouse. Sitting on the wagon, smoking a cigarette as if idly taking a break from farm chores, was a thickset man dressed in somewhat shabby clothes. Then he reached for an automatic weapon on the wagon seat. Joey thought it looked like a Johnson M1944, but maybe not, and guessed the man was a Brigade member. He nodded to Micah to proceed. The house was typical, half-timbered with dark brown boards forming patterns on the white walls. It sat in the middle of an apple orchard, with apples on the ground and a weather-beaten horse munching on them. Leaves were beginning to fall as the trees prepared for their cold winter sleep. Micah knocked, and the door opened. Inside, around a scarred oak table sat three men, all apparently members of the Brigade, who eyed him closely. One rose and smiled. "Welcome, Joseph, welcome. I am Alon. Come sit and meet Mordechai and Pinchas and have a cup of coffee."

They shook hands and stared intently at Joey. Joey stared back, noticing the long, thin white scar on his face that Mordechai unconsciously stroked tenderly and often. Smoke from cigarettes was illuminated by a distinct shaft of light cutting through the small four-paned windows.

It made the situation look like a movie mystery. He expected George Raft to walk in packing a pistol.

"You look a bit hesitant, Joseph," Alon noted. "Relax. Sit. We're so happy you came, really. Micah has told you a little about who we are, and why we're so hopeful to get your help. But I want now to take you into our confidence if that's all right with you." The others nodded their agreement.

"It is not something we do lightly, Joseph," said Mordechai in a German accent. "I hope you understand this."

Joey nodded. "I do. And I am willing to help. I just hope you're not expecting too much of me."

"You have been to Dachau and the Trials, Micah told me," said Mordechai. "So, you have seen firsthand what these animals have done to our people."

"Well, not exactly firsthand," said Joey, "but, yes, I have."

"And you have seen in Fürth the pitiful remnants of our people," added Pinchas. "We are here to help them go to Palestine, where they are wanted, not hated."

"Where they can come back to life," Mordechai added. "The British," and here he spat into a brass spittoon, "the British are preventing this in every way they can."

"But we have so far outsmarted them," Alon broke in. "We have several routes established and IDs and official papers prepared so that our transports can smuggle survivors to and through Italy to ports where ships are taking them to Palestine."

"*Next year in Jerusalem* is more than just a prayer now," said Pinchas. "It is a promise we have made."

Joey smiled. "You and the Kiss-My-Ass Group?"

"Good! Good!" Pinchas shouted, and laughed.

Alon cocked his head and lifted his bushy eyebrows in approval.

"So, what do you think I can do to help?" Joey asked

"What is the function of the Nuremberg Ordnance Depot, Joseph?" asked Alon.

Joey stared at him. "The function?"

"What do you *do* there, yes?" Alon responded. "I don't want you to reveal any secrets, Joseph, just to tell us what's accepted as the mission of the Nuremburg Ordnance Depot."

Joey looked slowly at each of them. Just how much information did he want to disclose? These were Jews who were risking their lives every day for their people. *My people*, Micah had said. *They're . . . they're my people, too*, Joey thought, and swallowed several gulps from his coffee. *Jeezus, I've got something they desperately want, or they would never have revealed themselves like this.*

Micah spoke softly. "Joey, I know what you're thinking. Would you be a traitor to America if you helped us? Or would you be a traitor to . . . to the children of Israel if you let them rot and die in detention camps after they have suffered such unbelievable horrors? This is not about hurting America, Joey. It's about helping Palestine become once and for all a home for homeless Jews, so this can never happen to us again."

"Joseph," Pinchas broke in, "we have been chased for centuries. Our mission now is what we call the *bricha*—that means 'escape' or 'flight.' Jews are not allowed by the Soviets and the Allies to leave the countries of Central and Eastern Europe controlled by them. We have to help them escape."

"I understand that," Joey said. My friend Josef told me about what has happened to survivors who tried to return home."

Mordechai stroked his scar. "Did you hear of Kielce, Poland?" he asked. "On your Independence Day last year, Joseph, a pogrom there by the Poles—forty more Jews killed, and many wounded. I think the Russians helped provoke it. The Polish Catholic Church said the Jews brought it upon themselves." His lips curled with disgust. "Even the pope wouldn't condemn it. So, Joseph, the Polish Jews who are left need the *bricha*. They need to escape, and soon."

Joey nodded his head in sympathy. He thought of the stories Karl and Josef had told him. "But how can I help?"

Alon moved close to Joey. "Your depot's mission, Joseph. Tell us of it."

CHAPTER 41

———

Like a schoolboy in third grade, standing by his desk, Joey closed his eyes and stood a little straighter, and recited from memory. "Our mission is to process combat vehicles for overseas shipment and for long-term storage, and to issue serviceable vehicles as needed by the US Occupational Forces." He opened his eyes. "Also, to remove and dispose of weapons, live ammunition, and explosives left in the vehicles we receive."

"Since you're the supply sergeant for the depot," Micah said, "you no doubt know how many of those things you have?"

Joey nodded. "Last count in August was . . ." in his head he saw the report he had submitted, "13,005 vehicles, 2,471 .30- and .50-caliber weapons, 422 boxes of ammunition and explosives, and many boxes filled with handguns."

Alon's eyes widened. "Joseph, how do you think we get the refugees to Italy and the boats? In vehicles—two-and-a-half ton trucks, usually. How many of those do you have in storage?"

Joey's eyes squinted in realization. "I would guess about five hundred."

Micah bit his lips. "And as *the* supply sergeant, couldn't you manage to arrange to issue thirty or forty or fifty of these five hundred 'serviceable' vehicles to the TTG without anyone knowing a thing?"

"Well," Joey said, a little surprised, "if I had the right paperwork I guess . . . I guess I could. But . . . "

"Joseph," Pinchas interrupted excitedly, "trust me. We could provide you with foolproof orders, signed by General Eisenhower himself if we needed to, for vehicles and some for weapons, too."

"Pinchas can give you a document as soon as you decide to help us," Micah said. And, looking straight into Joey's eyes, he placed both hands on Joey's shoulders. "Think of Karl, Joey. Think of Karl in one of *your* trucks going to La Spezia on the Ligurian Sea, and sailing to a new life, a safe life in Eretz Israel."

Oh my God, Joey thought. *I could do this. Ba-*DUM*-da-*DUM*-*DUM*, dum, dum,* DUM—the drums were there again, urging him on. He looked at each one of them and, taking a deep breath, he said, "I will do it if I can. But I must think a lot about this."

Mordechai beamed. "Pinchas will send you a test order, whenever you ask."

CHAPTER 42

On September 30, 1946, the Nuremberg War Crimes Trials would deliver verdicts. The Army was concerned there would be some sort of German uprising when this happened, so orders were given zone-wide to be on alert. At the 318th, gas masks, ammo, and machine guns were distributed to all the troops. Joey was responsible for this, and after dispensing everything he stopped off at the latrine on the way to the mess hall. There, sitting toilet bowl by toilet bowl—there were no privacy partitions here—were six of his pals from the headquarters group, all wearing their gas masks and mock-grunting and groaning.

"Yay, Joey!" they yelled, pulling their masks down and laughing hysterically. "It's about time you issued these."

Joey laughed. Just then, one of the guys let out a monstrous fart. Everyone looked around and slapped their masks back on. It was Carlos Aimone, called "Frenchie" because of his heritage and his obsession with food. Sounds of muffled laughter behind masks mingled with Joey's howling. Frenchie looked back and forth and spread his hands and shrugged. Laughter was such a good feeling in these days of foxhole mentality.

Firing practice was also required. Joey had several photos of Hitler, Goering, and SS officers printed up, and when he and Red went to the firing range, Joey stuck them over his targets. Pulling the trigger ever so slowly on his M1, Joey cursed them as he accurately shot them to bits. "Die. Die. Die," he whispered. Red looked at him carefully, sensing that something had changed. No longer was his roommate the same nice young boy from Charleston. He was someone who took pleasure in imagining he was killing Germans.

CHAPTER 43

October 1, 1946—the day of the verdicts. A siren sounded. Colonel Larned's voice came over the depot's loudspeaker system. "The Nuremberg War Crimes Trials have handed down the verdicts and eleven of the Nazi defendants are to be hanged. All personnel should man practiced posts ASAP. We do not know what might happen, so be alert."

Joey, Red, and Frenchie, in full battle garb, set up a machine gun position behind a thick stone wall facing the depot's main entrance. Joey wanted something to happen. He was itching to kill some Germans and kept clicking the safety on and off on his .45 automatic. Red was nervous. He envisioned a full-scale attack and was afraid. "Whattaya think the bastards will try?" he whispered.

Frenchie, on the other hand, was calm. "They ain't gonna do crap," he said. "Listen, they ain't all bad. Look at the girls in the office. They don't seem like killers to me."

"Yeah, well, ask them what their fathers were doing for the last four years," Joey said. And he told them a story Josef had told him. "A bunch of ordinary German soldiers . . . ordinary soldiers, not anything special, were using a Jewish infant like a soccer ball . . . kicking her, *kicking* her back and forth, until she was dead. They weren't SS either . . . just fuckin' soldiers like us, and . . . . " He stopped suddenly. A figure moved in the dark near the entrance. Joey clicked on the machine gun, held his breath, and drew a bead on the figure.

"Who goes there?" Red shouted, as directed. "Password!"

"New York Giants!" the voice shouted back. It was Lieutenant Forner himself. He jumped in with the guys. "I've made the rounds and so far so good. You guys got rations?"

"We got rations sure, sir," Frenchie muttered. "But rations ain't really food."

"That all you can think about, Frenchie?" said Red.

He turned to the lieutenant. "He says nothing's gonna happen. You think anything will, sir?"

Forner looked at him quizzically. "You be ready, Blake. But I agree with Aimone. I don't think a goddamn thing is going to happen. These Krauts obey orders and their orders on May 8 last year were to surrender. The war is over."

As night settled in, and they crouched behind the wall, nothing more was seen or heard. The colonel came to their post the following midday. "No trouble anywhere, lads," he reported. "I'm ordering an all clear."

When it sounded, the boys hurrahed happily, but Joey just nodded. He might have had a chance to shoot a few Germans. He thought how close he had come to firing last night, and headed back to his office.

They were all put on alert again, however, on October 15, Rosh Hashanah, when the alarm siren sounded and on the loudspeaker the colonel called out more news. "Attention. Herr Goering has committed suicide somehow, using a cyanide pill smuggled into his cell. We do not know whether this is a sign for some action, so man your posts immediately."

The alert continued the next day, when ten Nazis were hanged. It was bizarre to Joey that all this was happening right at the time of Judaism's holiest days. Red had asked what Rosh Hashanah and Yom Kippur were about, and he explained it. "It's the Jewish . . . *our* . . . New Year, number 5707."

"Whatta you mean, 5707?" Red asked.

"I mean," said Joey, "that we Jews have been around for 5,707 years."

"Jeez," said Red. "I never knew that."

Neither did I, Joey thought. Karl had told him that. It was a first for Joey, talking openly and proudly about being Jewish. "It's sort of poetic justice that these murderers of Jews should get it at this time, don't ya think?"

"Damn right," Frenchie grunted. "Damn right."

On the next day, Sgt. John C. Woods, the Army's executioner, used the standard drop method to carry out the executions of the ten remaining Nazi war criminals on three wooden hangman's platforms.

CHAPTER 44

Ten days earlier, Joey spent a Yom Kippur ceremony with Karl, Josef, and Micah at the DP camp in Fürth. A tent had been put up in the courtyard earlier for Rosh Hashanah, and the refugees gathered in it for services. "To atone for our sins," Karl said to Joey. "That's a cruel joke. We have lost everything. Our sin is to still be alive."

Joey gave him a hug. In a profusion of languages, the outpouring of grief over their lost families was mixed with joy about the news of the upcoming hangings of the Nazi leaders

"Justice," Karl said.

Justice, yes, but at what a price, Joey thought. Watching the refugees swaying back and forth as they prayed, Joey said to Karl, "How can they still pray when all their prayers didn't stop the massacre?"

Karl took a long time to reply. "I cannot answer that. It has destroyed my faith in a God," he sighed, "but not my being Jewish. That confuses me."

"I'm not even sure what being Jewish is," Joey said. "I never really thought much about God . . . or being Jewish. But now it's sinking in that I *am* Jewish. Still, I have no feeling about praying. None."

Karl nodded. "For me, being Jewish means being kind, charitable, willing to stand up for justice, and being courageous."

"Courageous?"

"Jews have faced more persecution than any other people . . . and we're still here," Micah said. "Even this *Shoah*, this catastrophe, won't defeat us. We never give up, and now we're going to have our own land again."

"That's what they're praying for," Karl added.

It won't take prayers, Joey thought angrily. *It needs action.* It needs the Brigade, and they needed his help. It was customary at home to make a New Year's resolution. He had never made one, but maybe "to help" should have been his Rosh Hashanah resolution. He knew the colonel wouldn't find out if he turned over some trucks and weapons to the Brigade. Even if he did, he was the kind of man who might just look the other way. He knew in gruesome firsthand detail what was done to the Jews. *After all, he told me to see for myself and tell people what happened at Dachau. I'm gonna do it. I'll help.* Once again, Joey's fast-beating heart turned into the ominous beat of those drums. He would help. But when would he tell them?

CHAPTER 45

November 1946. On a cold Monday morning, a package arrived for Joey from Richmond. It was from Aunt Minnie. With a broad smile, he grabbed a boxcutter and, just as he had anticipated, took out a big jar of Aunt Minnie's pickles carefully and safely wrapped in pages from the *Richmond Times Dispatch*. *Oh man,* he thought. He saved the paper for its news, carefully twisted off the jar top, and reached in for one of those small kosher dills. Ah-h, they were just like he remembered them. He closed his eyes and bit in. The crunch said they were fresh, and unaffected by their overseas journey, unlike his own. Memories flowed in, stimulated by the smell and taste of the pickles—of happy times spent at Minnie and Joe's beach house, and games played with his big cousin Milton. He still had a postcard from Milton from the US Air Force Training Center out west dated 1942. "Dear Little Buddy," it had started. "Fucking Germans," he said aloud.

As he munched another pickle, he noticed a letter in the box and opened it.

Dear Joey,

I hope these reach you in one piece. I know how you love my pickles and, Joey, darling, how much we love you. I hope all is safe and sound. Uncle Joe and I have a favor to ask you. This month on November 29 it will be the third anniversary of Milton's being shot down. They tell me even

now he is still listed as MIA and that maybe the International
Red Cross in Geneva might have a record of him as a POW.
Is it possible for you to see what you can find out from them?
I have finally resigned myself to this loss, but your uncle still
can't let go. Perhaps you can help him by seeing for once and
for all that Milton is truly gone from us. His wife, Elaine, as
you may know, has also given up. I don't know how you can
find out anything but please try.

> *Love, Your Aunt Minnie*

Joey put the letter down and reached for another pickle, which he rolled slowly in his fingers. He started to cry as he thought of Milton spiraling to earth as some Nazi bastard gloated in his Messerschmitt and zoomed away. Thrusting the pickle into his mouth, he bit down angrily, gathered the box, the letter, and the pickles and marched down to Lieutenant Forner's office.

"Sir, would . . . would you please read this?" he said

Puzzled, the lieutenant reached for the letter and began to read it, then looked up at Joey with appropriate sympathy. "You want to go to Geneva, I surmise?" he said.

"Yessir, I would do it as fast as possible . . . and I'm sure Red . . . um . . . Billy Blake would cover for me if something came up."

"You have my permission, Joey," said Forner. "Is that last big requisition for the Frankfurt unit completed?"

"Just about, sir," Joey answered. "It will be by the weekend. I would go after that, if that's okay with you." There was another important thing on his schedule he had to do before he left . . . a meeting he'd asked Micah to set up with Alon, so he could agree to accept a test and get involved.

"Pick up your authorization paper for the trip tomorrow," Forner said, interrupting Joey's thoughts. "And can I taste one of Aunt Minnie's pickles, Sergeant?"

Joey laughed and watched as the Lieutenant's face lit up on the first crunchy bite, a not uncommon reaction.

That night he wrote to Leah. At last, he said, he had a way to get to Geneva. Getting that letter from Aunt Minnie—fate, he thought. To verify the end of one life and the beginning of another.

CHAPTER 46

Driving up to the Fürth DP camp entrance the following Friday, Joey noticed a TTG vehicle parked under a classic linden tree, whose sturdy trunk stood like a solemn sentry protecting the truck. Snow clung to the maze of branches and a small snow owl sat motionless on one of them. Micah stepped out of the truck. He was in a UK officer's uniform and motioned to Joey. He looked around carefully.

"After you see them, we'll go in my truck to our meeting. Okay?"

Joey nodded and headed into the courtyard. *Jesus, I've got my hands full here,* he thought. The Brigade, Karl and Josef, and Geneva for Milton and Leah. Then there was always the supply shit that never stopped. And . . . oh . . . Skip had been insisting they take a furlough before discharge to see Paris. "How ya gonna keep 'em down on the farm after they've seen Paree?" Skip had sung, then crooned, "and we got to spend a foggy day in London Town." The responsibility was overwhelming sometimes. Only thing to do was to keep going and not look back.

When he did look back at what he always thought was a Tom Sawyer life, growing up in Charleston, he realized now it was only sort of Sawyerish—just in living next to a river. He was never mischievous like Tom. His street was called Sans Souci. French for "without care." And it was just that in so many respects—especially compared to today.

He thought now about what life was like there. Because of his dad's sickness he'd been on his own a lot from a very young age and was often lonely. Now, with these two refugees, Micah, the guys, and Leah, he was less lonely than he had ever been. *What's happening to me?* he thought. He stood quietly in front of 333 for a minute, then knocked and went in with his usual bag of goods. He hugged both his friends. They always greeted him like he was Superman. It made him feel both good and bad. Good in that he could help them. Bad, because who really knew what was going to happen to the two of them? It was not in his control.

"Joseph, kind, kind, Joseph," Karl cried out, taking the bag. "It's so nice of you. I could almost believe again now that you have appeared."

Joey gave them both another big hug. "I can't stay today," he said. "I just wanted to see you for a minute and tell you I'm going away to Geneva for a few days."

"Ah, yes," said Karl remembering. "To the Red Cross?"

Joey nodded. "Yeah, to see if I can find out anything about Cousin Milton. Aunt Minnie says he's still listed as MIA, so maybe he's in a hospital or somewhere and is unidentified so far."

"That would be nice," said Karl, sadly.

We know your families are not missing in action, Joey thought. *They are missing forever.*

"I know it's probably useless, Karl," said Joey, "but I will try to find out about my cousin once and for all."

Karl patted him on his shoulder. "We wish you luck. But you know, Joseph, even if he landed safely in Germany and had his identification on him, they wouldn't care that he was an American officer. To them he was first a Jew, and for that they would kill him. Even without any identification, his circumcision would give him away."

"I know. I know that," Joey said. "But I must try to give my aunt some peace . . . small as it may be."

When Karl translated, Josef nodded his head slowly, sighed, and reached for Joey's hand. "So many. So many. So many," he muttered.

Explaining that he and Micah had a meeting, Joey said goodbye and left the two standing as still and solemn as the Linden in the parking area below.

"When are you going?" Micah said when he arrived downstairs. "And for how long?" He looked a little upset.

"Just for a few days next week. Why?" said Joey.

"Nothing. Nothing," said Micah. "It's just something we've learned that may need some help."

"I only have a few months till my enlistment is up, so I have to do this. I promised my aunt." And he had promised Leah he would be there, but he did not reveal that to Micah.

"Sure, sure. I understand," said Micah. "I'll tell you about it later."

CHAPTER 47

A lon, Pinchas, and Mordechai had been told by Micah that Joey had something good to tell them. Knowing how significant this new resource could be, they had gathered from various places in Europe for the meeting. The men closed in around him. "You have news for us, Joseph?" said Alon. They could hardly contain themselves, but they struggled to keep straight faces. Joey looked around at the three.

"I will help you," he blurted out. "I will help the Brigade!"

They closed in to hug him, lifting him into the air as they would a Jewish groom at his wedding. Two of them were in UK uniforms and one, Mordechai, was in an American lieutenant's outfit, which startled Joey. He was amazed at how realistic they all looked. *They don't fool around*, he thought. *This is real, what I'm getting into.*

Sensing this, Alon smiled. "We can also be Russian or Italian as the need arises."

They were in an isolated area outside of Fürth across the Pegnitz River near Poppenreuth. They never met in the same place. This was a small cottage like the ones he had seen on the trip to the Hummel factory. Charming, folksy, but who knew what kinds of killers had lived there. Had the man of the house smashed a Jewish baby's head against a wall? Had he raped young Jewish girls and then killed them? Had he stolen all his Jewish neighbors' belongings? The thoughts raced through his head.

For the next hour they told him how the Brits would not permit refugees to proceed to Palestine, even though the US president supported the Jewish Agency's request to Britain for 100,000 immigration permits. Also, how British Foreign Minister Bevin refused, and only allowed 1,500 a month. To see just how and where Joey might fit in, they outlined the activities of the Brigaders. Codes were determined for communication and identification. The stew in his head was simmering with anger toward the Germans and the Brits, pity for the Karls and Josefs, and admiration for the idealism of the Brigade members.

Finally, they discussed sending a test requisition for several trucks and some weapons. "We will send it to you in a day or so," Mordechai said.

Joey nodded, then stopped suddenly. "No. Wait until I return from Geneva and get in touch with Micah," Joey said. "And I want you to send it to our adjutant, First Lieutenant Hershel Forner, not to me. He receives all official communication. If it passes him, I'll try it. But I gotta say, if it doesn't, I will have to wonder right along with him and be asking what the hell this is."

"Fair enough," Pinchas said. "He will okay it, you'll see. But it won't be from Eisenhower. It will come from a Third Army Officer in charge of the region. We know who, don't worry."

"Since you will be in Geneva," said Alon, "here is the address of one of our projects." He wrote something on a pad and handed it to Joey. "It is a small school run by the Jewish Children's Relief Organization, where we have established a training program for a group of refugee children from Buchenwald to ready them for their life in Palestine. It is called The Foyer, or the Hôtel de la Forêt."

Joey's heart pounded and he stood straighter. *The Forêt. Leah is still teaching there, as far as I know,* he thought.

"Joseph?" said Alon. "Is something the matter?"

"No, no," stammered Joey. "It's just that I know someone who works for The Foyer."

"Well," said Alon. "That's good. He can help show you everything."

Joey blushed. "She . . . it's a she."

"Oh," said Micah with a smile, remembering Joey's story about the Polish refugee Leah at the Trials and their meeting at the Brigade safe house. "Wouldn't that be nice, eh?" He winked at Joey.

The men grouped around Joey and each shook hands, wishing him a good trip. They were grateful he had agreed to help, and they let him know it.

He was thinking anxiously about what he was now involved with when he finally said goodbye and was taken back to his jeep in Fürth. Driving back to Nuremburg, Joey became happy about his decision. It was a chapter in his life he could never have imagined. He shook his head. *Instead of shooting Germans, I'm now going to help get to safety in a Jewish homeland people whom the Nazis had tried to destroy*, he thought. *How could I be so unaware of what went on?* It wasn't in the *Charleston Evening Post*, where Uncle Manning worked. "Leah, Leah, Leah," he said aloud. The Foyer School. He was going to see Leah. *Please still be there!*

Excited at this thought, he banged on the horn with his fist, which made an old man leap in fear to the side of the road and shake his fist at the jeep. "Sorry! Sorry," yelled Joey out the window. "Um, *Entschuldingung!*" *What the fuck*, he thought. *The Krauts are the ones who should be sorry. Screw him.*

Back at Headquarters the next day, Joey examined the inventory in detail. In Building 21, fifty two-and-a-half ton trucks were stored. Their batteries were on trickle charge in Building 27. Of the seventy-three buildings the German cavalry had operated in the Kaserne, all but six were badly damaged by bombings, but the Army had now rebuilt sixty-three for the depot's use. It was a goldmine for the Brigade—if he could just sneak the stuff out without being caught and, court-martialed. *Shit*, he thought, and gripped his pencil so hard it snapped in two.

Schatzie jumped up onto his lap for attention. *I hope to God those papers are okay*, he thought, scratching the pup. "You're about the only goddamn good thing about Germans, Schatzie. The rest . . . ." Then he remembered Katja. "At least most of them are for shit." He made a list and hid it in his desk to await his return.

CHAPTER 48

————

Four days later, as Joey's train pulled into Geneva, he was remembering other train trips he had taken. Like Louis, he had always loved train rides. It was ten years ago when, at age nine, he was sent by himself on a train from Charleston to visit Aunt Minnie and Uncle Joe in Richmond. They had tipped the conductor to watch out for Joey, and he did. That was how self-sufficient Joey was early on. "Small in size but big in stature," was how his English teacher at James Simmons School described him to the assembly when Joey had won a statewide art contest. A lot had happened in those ten years, like now.

It was very late when he checked into the small hotel. *Damn it,* he thought, *too late to try to see Leah.* Then he realized he didn't even know her address—only her post office box.

Joey sat alone outside at a sidewalk café called the Splendid and took his bearings. He had a map of Geneva and the address of the International Red Cross Prisoners of War Agency, which he would visit tomorrow. Newsboys were shouting about a US Air Force plane crash in the Swiss Alps. Miraculously, no one was hurt. On the street, almost everyone used bicycles—not because there was a gasoline shortage; it was a European thing. *People looked the same over here,* he thought, *but they're different as hell.*

Joey also had the address for Leah's school, given to him by Micah. He couldn't wait to see her. He had written her about his visit, but she hadn't responded. He hoped she hadn't suddenly been summoned to a boat heading for Palestine. The children there were training to go to Palestine, and Micah suggested Joey meet Rabbi Schacter, the US Army chaplain who brought the children there. It was another example for Joey of what the Brigade was doing. Pinchas had told Joey about Theodore Herzl and the formation of the World Zionist Organization, whose first meeting in 1897 was in Switzerland. So this trip was a meaningful one for Joey in so many ways. The whole thing sort of energized him.

"*L'Agence Centrale des Prisonniers de Guerre*," Joey said the next morning, as he climbed the steps to its office. "Prisoners of war. Oh God, I hope, I hope."

He waited to be helped for an hour. Finally, a stout, sour-faced woman of about fifty took his information. "Come back in two days," she said. Joey explained that he had to report back on duty in Nuremberg. Couldn't it happen in one day? She gave him a look that said "forget it." So, he forgot it and set out to find the Foyer and Leah.

Her building was in the middle of a block of interesting residences, each a bit different but all of a kind. Each building had trees surrounding it. *The street was clean enough to eat off of,* he thought. The school was in a three-, maybe four-story structure with an attached tower pointing up into the gray Swiss sky. Rabbi Schacter greeted him warmly and invited him to come for a talk with some of the children, but Joey's first question was about Leah. She was still here, the rabbi assured him, and would come in the late afternoon. Relieved, Joey asked about what went on in the Forêt. Rabbi Schacter beamed. "They are learning Hebrew and facts about Palestine as well as crafts they will need there," he said.

One of the boys, Wolf Nehrich, was being interviewed by someone doing research. Joey was introduced to the interviewer. "This is Sergeant Joseph Goldman, Doctor Boder," the rabbi said. "He is here to see what we're doing to get these young survivors to Palestine."

"David Boder," said the bearded, sad-eyed, stoop-shouldered man, and shook hands with Joey. "We know very little in America about the things that happened to people who were in concentration camps. I want to educate them about it and get some of these Jews to America, not Palestine."

The boy was thin and fragile looking, as one would expect of a survivor. He was telling the doctor about SS doctors taking pus from sick prisoners with a syringe and injecting it into others to make them die.

"Did you see that yourself?" Boder asked.

The boy grimaced. "Experienced it myself, saw it, yes."

Joey sat in silence as the boy slowly unfolded his horrific journey from his home in Poland, through years of torture by the Germans who had rounded up his family and killed all but him and a brother, until the Americans saved him and a thousand other boys when they liberated Buchenwald.

As with Karl and Josef, hearing in person what had happened was worse than seeing films at the Trial. *Ba-*DUM*-da-*DUM*-*DUM*, dum-dum-*DUM . . . The boy's monotone recitation of unimaginable horror summoned the deadly drumbeat, and Joey could take no more. He forced himself to walk away from this and see the other things being done with the boys.

In his heart, Joey knew he wanted to, he would, he must help the Brigade, no matter what happened. "Damn the torpedoes, full speed ahead," he said to himself, remembering the story his high school history teacher, Mrs. Fleet, had told the class about Admiral Farragut at the Battle of Mobile Bay in 1864. A lot of Americans died in the Civil

War—600,000. But ten times that number of Jews had been killed by the Nazis, and damned if he was going to fail to help those who were left.

Suddenly, he felt a tap on his right shoulder, and turned. Leah! Both inhaled deeply and grabbed each other's shoulders and started to kiss, then realized that all the boys in the classroom were staring and laughing. Leah laughed along with them, then took his hand and led him into the dark mahogany-walled hallway and kissed him happily, longingly, lovingly.

This was like in the movies, he thought as they were kissing—the beginning of a romantic, a *very* romantic few days.

CHAPTER 49

Joey insisted they go to a nearby café. Yes, she nodded. Sitting across from one another as they drank coffee, they exchanged stories. He told her about his unsatisfying visit to the Red Cross.

"It is odd. You are searching for a life that was ended," she said sympathetically. "I am waiting to start a new one." *Strange,* he thought. *Just what I was thinking.*

"A new life in Palestine?" Joey said. "Maybe it should be here?"

Leah laughed. "Oh, no! You know how I want to go to Palestine."

"Leah," he said seriously, "you have never told me how this is going to happen."

"I am sworn to secrecy," she answered, wringing her hands.

"The Jewish Brigade and the Jewish Agency are organizing it for you,"

She sat up startled. "You know about the Jewish Brigade?"

"Yes, I know a lot about the Brigade," he said.

"How . . . how do you know about the Brigade?" she asked, frowning.

"I also have been sworn to secrecy," he stated with a smile.

"They started me in Italy and now to Geneva," she said. "Next, I will be going to the Adriatic and on a ship to Haifa."

"From La Spezia."

"You *know* these secrets?" Leah said. "But we must not have secrets from each other."

"Never again, but I can't reveal exactly how I am helping the Brigade."

"I understand those kinds of secrets," she agreed quietly. "I have been where they were required."

"I need to know about that . . . about you and the rest of how you survived," he said. "Come, let's go to my hotel for dinner."

Back at the Splendid she started to reveal a little more of her escape from her hometown, but she stopped suddenly.

"I don't want to spoil our time together with my past," she hesitated but Joey insisted. He knew how Josef and Karl had spent their years in the camps, but he wanted to know how a young Jewish girl managed to survive not being in a camp, about her exploits fleeing through the forests.

Joey moved his chair around to her side of the table and put his arm around her. "Please," he said. So, she continued her story about how the two girls had managed to make their way south.

"We were blonde and blue-eyed, so we weren't immediately suspected of being Jewish," Leah said. "Sometimes, when we were starving, we went into villages to get food. But there was always someone who we could just feel was onto us, so we never remained anywhere for long. Our torn clothes would give us away."

"You're a long way from Poland now," Joey said. "How did you do it?"

"We were sleeping in a barn in Relavka when the farmer who had given us shelter came running in and said the local police were searching for Jews. He cried out, 'You must run now, or it will be bad for all of us!'" She told how they had rushed out into the woods and kept running for over an hour. "Suddenly, a huge man stepped from behind a tree and pointed a rifle at us. 'Halt!' he said in Polish. 'Where do you think you're going?' Rael began to whimper. We were shaking with fear. I told him we were running from the police. He stared at us, then asked why we were running."

She was quivering with the memory. "I didn't know what was right to answer, then my sister blurted out, 'Because we are Jewish.' 'I thought so,' he said, 'but you don't look it. So, come with me. We are Jewish and you can hide with us.'" Leah described how they followed him for miles, into and through a swamp, until they arrived at a camp of Jews who had escaped the roundups by German troops of several villages.

"They were armed and wanted nothing more than to kill Germans," Leah said. "We stayed with them for weeks and we were taught how to fire rifles and pistols. Several times we went on raids to blow up railroad tracks. We were cared for by a huge, loving woman who would brush Rael's hair and sing lullabies to her at night."

Joey was stroking Leah's hair as she said this, and she grew suddenly silent.

"Did," Joey stopped stroking her hair and said softly, "did something happen to Rael?"

"I was assigned to go hunting for food with one of the men and . . . and when we returned hours later there were bodies everywhere," she sobbed. "A German patrol had found the camp and killed all of them."

Joey hugged her and whispered, "I'm so sorry . . . so very sorry, Leah." His hatred of Germans was boiling within him. He visualized himself with the sisters behind him as he fired a machine gun, mowing down German after German. "What happened after that?"

"We—Meir Ghovertza, the man I was with, and I—headed west. We traveled only by night and stole food from bars that we passed until, miracle of miracles, we met a Red Cross unit and I convinced them I was Italian," Leah said. "They gave me papers that got me from Poland to Czechoslovakia. Then I took a train to Austria, but I ended up in a British camp. They detained me like a prisoner."

"Goddamn British," said Joey. They were tops on his shitlist now that he knew from the Brigade how the Brits were preventing the Jews from getting to Palestine. "How did you escape from there?" he continued.

"One night, some soldiers came and took several of us away. We had to hide under tarpaulins in a truck," she said.

"The Brigade?" asked Joey.

"Yes. They were the Brigade, and they took us to the border where we were met by others who brought us here."

"My luck," he said.

"Yes, but I am now all alone," she said, and leaned against him as he held her in his arms.

"You are not alone. You are not alone. You will never be alone again." He kept repeating and pledging he would find a way to be together. "In America," he said.

"Or Yisroel," Leah said.

He nodded in agreement, "Or Israel."

The waiter came over and told them the hotel restaurant was closing. Joey led Leah upstairs to his room. In the room they stared at one another shyly, then slowly moved into each other's arms. It was as if this was how it was meant to be . . . that they were brought together by fate and knew it. They made love all night long—not in a wild, sexual passion like Joey had experienced in Garmisch with the Fräulein, but with tenderness—almost with gravity.

CHAPTER 50

The next day, they went to the Red Cross where, as expected, he found no record of Milton. Questioning the woman to make sure she had done her job, he showed her the picture Aunt Minnie had sent him. She looked at it, then up to Joey. "Joel?" she said. "Is that Jewish?"

Yes, Joey nodded.

"Even if he landed safely, they would have killed him, American or not," she said, matter-of-factly.

Just as Karl had said.

"A Jew is an insect to them," Skip had said.

Leah rubbed his back sympathetically. He thanked the woman and they walked arm-in-arm outside.

"Goddam Germans," he swore. He took a picture of the building to send to Aunt Minnie and then asked a passerby to take one of him and Leah, which he promised to give her later.

They wandered the city for hours, telling one another more about their lives up until now. In a small jewelry shop, Joey bought Dreyfuss and Zentra wristwatches for himself and Skip, and a necklace with a small silver heart for Leah. As he put it around her neck he whispered, "I give my heart to you."

She laughed and kissed him. He laughed back. "Man, that sounded so corny."

"Corny? What is corny?" Leah asked.

"Um-mm . . . not very *hep*," said Joey. "I mean . . . let's see . . . not *fashionable*. Old-fashioned. Yeah, that's it."

"I think I understand," she smiled as she caressed the heart.

As they walked along, Joey spotted a sign in a store window and pointed excitedly. "Look! Speaking of 'hep,' the Don Redmond Jazz Band from America is playing here tonight. Let's go dancing!"

* * *

Entering Victoria Hall that evening, they pushed their way down to seats next to the dance floor. Joey's American uniform helped make it easy. The band was composed of Black musicians who blared out tunes familiar to Joey. It caused a few moments of homesickness as he remembered listening to the *Lucky Strike Hit Parade* from his bedroom on Sans Souci Street. But when he looked at Leah, that all seemed like a story from far, far away. It was *now* that mattered to him, and being with her from now on was what he wanted more than anything. When the band started playing *All the Things You Are*, he took her hand and moved out onto the dance floor. As the familiar lyrics flowed through his head, and he began to sing them softly into her ear.

> *You are the promised kiss of springtime*
> *That makes the lonely winter seem long*
> *You are the breathless hush of evening*
> *That trembles on the brink of a lovely song*
> *You are the angel glow that lights the star*
> *The dearest things that I know are what you are*
> *Someday my happy arms will hold you*
> *And someday I'll know that moment divine*
> *When all the things you are, are mine.*

The evening went on and on like this. *Jeez*, he thought to himself, *this can't be happening to me. How the hell am I gonna go back to base without her?* He started to think maybe he should just stay here and go with her, but he knew he couldn't . . . for so many reasons. "But we *will* be together," he said aloud.

"What?" said Leah. "Together? Yes . . . together. Is that corny?"

"Corny but true," he laughed.

Leah looked at the band of all Black musicians. "They are all Negroes," she said. "Is that how it is in America? They do not mix?"

Joey sighed. "The colored people . . ."

"Colored?" she interrupted. "You call Negroes 'colored'?"

"I . . . I guess that's what we do," he said, embarrassed. "They have suffered much in America." He thought of his nanny, Florence, who helped raise him. She was loved as part of the family, but she lived in the segregated, run-down part of Charleston that still existed.

"At least in America we didn't murder them all," Joey said sadly. "Many of the Jews in Charleston have sympathy for the color . . . I mean *Negroes*. But there is little they can do besides being kind and generous. They came as slaves, and I hate to say it, but they've been treated in many ways like the Germans consider the Jews . . . not really human."

Leah stopped dancing and just stared at the band. Joey looked at the musicians. They were all smiling and nodding approval at one another as they played riffs. Their color seemed to mean nothing to the Europeans—only their musical talent counted.

Joey spoke softly, almost to himself. "They're still oppressed at home, yet here they are smiling . . . it's like survivors still believing, even though their prayers were never answered."

Leah wrapped her arms around him and pulled him close.

They spent the night in each other's arms, but never went beyond kissing this time. He wasn't sure why, but it just felt right. It was overwhelming, this feeling. Not at all like his crush for Betty Jean

McCleary in Charleston, when he was fourteen. She was a foot taller than he, and just thought he was the cute little guy next door that she liked to talk with. He used to jerk off thinking about her until one night at a party he saw her necking with his pal, Jimmy Todd. He stopped talking to her after that. "Puppy love," they called it. This was different. It filled him entirely—his body and his brain.

The next morning, they went sightseeing. He noticed the streets of Geneva were unbelievably clean, as if no one would dare to drop even a gum wrapper. Strange, these Swiss. Always neutral but, according to Lieutenant Forner, not really . . . whatever that meant.

They went to see the League of Nations complex. The buildings and grounds were magnificent, but Joey wondered what had gone wrong with the League. The "War to End All Wars" was what they had called World War I, but once again, the damn Germans had brought death and destruction to the world. Magnificent buildings didn't mean squat.

CHAPTER 51

O n the third day, they went to the train station, clutching each other as if afraid the wind would blow them apart. Finally, Joey boarded the train for his return to Nuremberg. As it pulled away, he kept leaning out to see the platform, waving and blowing kisses. On this trip he had made two discoveries. As expected, a conclusion of death for his cousin Milton, but unexpectedly, as Leah had said, a beginning of a new life with her. As he settled down into his seat, he smiled, thinking, wouldn't it be great to go to Palestine with her! Or maybe she would come to America? One way or another, I'll be with her, he thought as he fell asleep.

There was no nightmare in this sleep. A dream, yes. He was in a bed, a wounded soldier in a military hospital. Around him were soldiers in various states of suffering. He felt a pain in his chest and put his hand on it and winced. Another hand was placed on his, a soft, female hand. His eyes followed up the arm to a beautiful face with deep blue eyes. It was Leah, now a nurse. Bells were ringing. "It's your heart," she said. "It was empty, but I gave it a transfusion from my own." She leaned down and kissed him, and the pain was gone. "Corny, yes?" she said and smiled. "But so true." The bells grew louder. A conductor ringing a handbell woke Joey up, announcing Nuremburg as the next stop.

Handing the Swiss watch to Skip in the press corps dining room, Joey showed him the pictures he had taken of Leah and told him about what happened. "The pain of leaving her to come back was crazy, Skip," Joey said. "I've never felt anything like that."

"Jesus, Joey. All this happened in three days?" Skip asked. "Pain?"

"Right, pain," said Joey. "I even had a dream of heart pain on the train coming back."

"Damn, and what about your cousin, Milton?"

"That was a different kind of pain," said Joey. "But on the other hand, it gave some closure to it." He told Skip some of Leah's stories of her escape and about the Brigade helping her to get to Palestine.

"The Brigade?" said Skip. "Again the Brigade?"

"Yeah, the Brigade," confirmed Joey.

CHAPTER 52

The following week, Joey wanted to head once again to Fürth. He was ready now to learn details about the test with the Brigade, and his time at the Foyer with Leah had helped him feel more strongly about his involvement. On his desk that morning was a phone message from Sergeant Zucker, Micah's code name, that he would pick him up at Fürth Saturday morning.

At yet another isolated farm east of Fürth, Micah pulled in and was directed to drive into a garage. The doors were quickly closed behind them and Joey and Micah entered a side door to greet the Brigaders. A new face was apparently in charge.

As he shook hands, the main said, "Johanan Peltz. I am sorry to be abrupt, but we have just learned of something that must be attended to tonight. If I may, I will show you what we have in mind for your test so that you may start to think about just how you will arrange for them at your depot." He laid out on the table two pages of items they would like to have. It was a very businesslike meeting.

Joey could sense that Peltz had something else he was intensely concerned about and wished to get the meeting over as quickly as possible. His manner was curt, but not arrogant.

"Please commit this to memory, Sergeant," Peltz said. "I don't want such papers out of our hands." Nodding to this, Joey spent a few minutes studying the list. He made memory hints so he could make his own list in code later. Meanwhile, Peltz talked in a low voice with Micah.

"Okay. I have it," Joey said. "I'll have to let Micah know when I think we can do this. Probably not until spring."

Peltz reached out to shake hands again. "Thank you," he said. "You are doing a courageous thing, I know, Joseph. I must ask you for another favor. We need Micah to stay with us. Will you drive his vehicle back to yours?"

"What?" Joey frowned. "Why? I mean it's a UK vehicle."

Peltz smiled. "Not anymore. It has US Army plates on. Here are directions back to the DP camp. Leave the keys under the seat. It will be all right. Trust me."

Joey realized what was happening. Obviously, they had located an SS bigwig.

On his way back, he pondered the incredible ability of the Brigade to operate in so many ways—license plates, IDs, uniforms, information, hideouts, transports—you name it and it seemed they could do it. Tonight, there was no doubt in his mind they were getting revenge on another Gestapo or SS higher-up, whose hiding place they had found. I'd like to see one of those, he thought, and watch the bastard cry for mercy. As he drove, he kept repeating aloud the equipment Peltz had asked for. He was realizing just how important he was to them.

CHAPTER 53

At the end of a long day at the office, with four different groups coming in for supplies, Joey went into the lieutenant's office to report that all were handled. They were both tired. Forner offered him a cup of coffee. It was black and had been cooking for a long time, so it was bitter, but it helped perk him up.

"Lieutenant," Joey asked, "what's holding up Josef's papers for so long?"

"UNRRA and the military," said the lieutenant. "They both tried to send these refugees back to their own countries until they found out that instead of being given back their homes, they were being beaten and killed by their fellow citizens. Now the task is to try to convince other countries to take in the Jews."

"Why is it so damn hard to be a Jew, Lieutenant?" wondered Joey. "I never realized it."

"I don't know, Sergeant. Maybe it's because we seem to have something that makes others jealous. They don't like that we're the 'Chosen People.' Ever been one of those *not* chosen by your schoolmates to be on a team, Sergeant? Know what I mean? Not a happy feeling is it? Maybe that's it. Hell, I really don't know."

"Yeah, but I wouldn't kill someone for not being chosen," Joey said.

"Well, obviously there are those who will, and not just the Nazis," he muttered after a long pause.

They were both silent for a while, then Joey saluted and left. *Chosen for what?* he thought and gritted his teeth.

Just as he was walking back into his office, the telephone rang. *Who in hell can that be at this hour,* he wondered? "Hello, 318th Supply," he answered.

"Joey, wow. Glad I caught ya," said Al Moskowitz. "Hey, Frank Sturdevant said he met you down in Garmisch. Said you had a 'Three-F time.'"

"Three-F?" said Joey.

"Fun, Food, and *Fuckin'!*" Al shouted.

Joey laughed. "He's right. Definitely a 'Three-F time.' Except at the end." He told Al about Sturdevant's Fräulein, and the last night at the Casa Carioca.

"Listen," Al said. "My father and me, too, are really grateful for your finding Josef and helping him to get to Wilkes-Barre."

"I'm glad you asked me to do it," said Joey. "I've really enjoyed meeting him and his roommate, Karl. They're a remarkable pair."

"His relative is my father's barber," Al continued, "and he has promised my father *and you* free haircuts for the rest of your lives. 'Course it would be expensive to go to Wilkes-Barre from Charleston for that." He laughed. "But you never know when you might visit me there."

"Hey, you never know," said Joey. "So, how's things in the world of stage and screen?"

"You can see for yourself, I hope," said Al. "I wanted to invite you to a Seder to be held here. There was one in Munich, but it's the first really big one in this area since the war. The military just announced it's holding it for all Jewish soldiers in the area, for all the survivors who are in the DP camps around here, and also for members of the Jewish organizations helping refugees in the area. You meet any of them at Fürth?"

Joey paused for a moment. "Yeah, I've met some of them. A Seder, huh? Jeez, that could be interesting. Tell me when and where."

"I figured you'd need some advance warning so you could get a pass," Al said.

"My adjutant's Jewish. I think I could get a pass," said Joey. "I'd say Wiesbaden would be about a two-hour drive from here."

"Great! It's the sixth of this April, on a Monday. You can stay with me a couple of nights," Al said. "Afterwards we can have, well, at least a 'Two-F time.' If we're lucky, there might be some other Fs around. I'll put a map in the mail for you, and, Joey, thanks again for the Fürth thing."

Joey sat back down again at his desk, and marked the date on his calendar, April 6, 1947. He thought about the family Seder at Uncle Joe and Aunt Minnie's in Richmond when he was little. He remembered looking at his father, with the bandages around his head. Only recently out of the hospital, his father just stared into space. He remembered feeding Trixie, Uncle Joe's terrier, under the table, and how his brother and sister were giggling at the Hebrew being recited. Hebrew was a strange sound to them. Wasn't much used in Charleston by their friends and family. This would be such a different Seder experience—something the Krauts had prevented for years, more triumphal—but maybe, if they're like his Fürth family, they would instead be torn up by all those they lost.

He sighed and came back to now as his little dachshund stood on her hind legs begging to get on his lap. "Holy shit, Schatzie," he said to the puppy. He had taken to speaking to her as a friend and confidant. "April . . . that's only three months before my enlistment is up. I'd like to see about a furlough, so I can see Paris and London with Skip before I go home. He insists that's an absolute must, Schatzie. Whattaya think?" Putting Schatzie down, he wrote himself a reminder to apply for that, first thing in the morning. Then he picked up one of Headquarters' new issues of *Stars and Stripes,* which came first to Supply for distribution, cut the light, and headed for bed.

CHAPTER 54

Red was sound asleep, but Joey was too wired, so he got into his bunk with the paper and read. He laughed aloud at a Bill Mauldin *Willie and Joe* cartoon of a GI in a foxhole as bullets whizzed overhead, saying, "I wish I had more than one life to give for my country. I'd like to have another to go home on." Then he jerked his head back as he saw a list of spouses of military officers that were scheduled to arrive from the states. There was "Mrs. Hershel W. Forner." Wow . . . what's *Mademoiselle* gonna think about that! He laughed.

In Lieutenant Forner's office the next morning, he asked for two weeks leave. "So I can see Paris and London before I go home in June, sir."

The lieutenant looked at the calendar and then up at Joey. "Sergeant, I'll think about it, but I'm afraid the regulations state very clearly that no leaves are to be granted if the discharge is scheduled within six to eight months. And that, I'm sorry to point out, seems to include you. Be happy you're finally almost home, instead of Paris and London."

Joey was surprised at this according-to-the-books behavior and argued a bit more, then saluted and returned to his office. He opened his desk drawer to get Skip's number to deliver the bad news when he spotted something. "A ticket to Gay Paree?" he said aloud. There, smiling up at him on top of his stack of pictures, was Lieutenant Forner and his French mistress on horseback, taken way back when. *Son of a bitch. I wonder? What the hell, why not. He knows what I've been going through.* He smiled. Picking up the photo and the *Stars and Stripes*, he marched back into Forner's office, saluted, and dropped the photo— with its negative showing very obviously—onto the Lieutenant's desk, "Just remembered I wanted to give this to you, sir."

"Ah, your new camera that day," Forner said. "I look pretty snappy, eh? Thanks."

With that, Joey about-faced, then turned back. "Oh, and here's your latest *Stars and Stripes*, sir. I see your wife is on the next arrival list. That's great."

Forner looked at the list, then at the photo, noticing with relief that the negative was also attached, which meant Joey was telling him his lips were sealed. Looking again at the list, then slowly up at Joey, who was hoping desperately he hadn't overstepped his relationship, Forner frowned, which made Joey's stomach flip-flop. Then the lieutenant's expression slowly broke into a grin, and Joey grinned as well. Both now laughed.

"I see, Sergeant. I see," Forner said. "Thanks for the negative. Let me think about it." Joey saluted with a sheepish grin and about-faced.

CHAPTER 55

Three weeks later, Skip and Joey were tasting a fine Bordeaux in the bar at the hotel Le Meurice on the Rue de Rivoli. Joey, who had never known anything much about wine, was watching Skip.

"Swirl the wine around in the glass, sniff the aroma, and swish a bit around in the mouth. *Comme ça!*" Skip said, raising his eyebrows with a look of aristocratic haughtiness.

They were staying in a recently renovated hotel famous for its international clientele. The Louis XVI style of the restoration dazzled Joey. He had never seen such opulent decor. The flowered, upholstered, gold-painted chairs in the lounge seemed too beautiful to actually sit on. Standing in front of the huge, carved marble fireplace, the two GIs timidly asked for two glasses. "Bordeaux, *s'il vous plaît,*" Skip said. Heating in the hotel was intermittent, so they figured a lot of wine was essential to keep the chill out of their dress uniforms. Sufficiently stoked against the cold, the two went out and began roaming the streets of Paris, which were once again becoming lively and beautiful.

"Beautiful, because the Frogs caved in for the Krauts so Paris wouldn't be destroyed," said Skip. "A good thing in hindsight, because Baron Haussmann did an amazing job redoing Paris." Skip, in a faux French accent, told Joey how Napoleon III "commissioned zee Baron to redesign Paree and turn it into a *cite* of wide boulevards and *magnifique,* architecturally-controlled buildings."

Walking down toward the Place de la Concorde, they heard an amazing variety of languages. Displaced refugees from all over Europe flocked to Paris in the hope of finding a visa to some safe country where they could start a new life.

Crossing the Place de la Concorde they came upon the Hôtel de Crillon just as a bunch of photographers and onlookers crowded around several beautiful young models. Pushing his way closer, Skip asked a photographer in French, "What's going on? Who are they?"

"It's Fashion Week! The first in years," he said in English. "See that guy with them? He's who we're after." Joey saw a balding middle-aged man being kissed by one of the models.

"The bald guy?" Joey said.

"That's Christian Dior. He's making fashion news," said the photographer. Skip pulled Joey past the group and into the hotel lobby.

"C'mon, this place has heat!" he said. Joey felt it, too. "Maybe we can change hotels," Skip said.

A smartly dressed young American woman overhearing this, laughed, "It's Fashion Week here, boys. Also, they're signing a bunch of peace treaties here, too. So, you're lucky you got in anywhere. You on furlough?"

Skip turned on his best smile, "Yes ma'am, and we're looking to paint the town chartreuse. I'm Skip, and this is Joey."

"Well, nice. I'm Rosamund, and I'll buy you heroes a drink if I may?"

She told them all about Fashion Week and Christian Dior's "New Look." She was here from New York for *Vogue*, and Skip turned on every ounce of his charm. "Since you seem to be in the know, how about a recommendation for a great restaurant for tomorrow and join us on our last night here?" Skip tried, but it was of no use.

She gave them some suggestions, then said, "Sorry, love. I'm working day and night." She paid the tab and rose to leave. "Got to go to work, boys. Enjoy the Sébillon tomorrow. That's where I'd go." Off she went, and off they went to dinner as well.

"What the hell," said Skip. "I tried."

That night, as they dined at Au Pied de Cochon, Joey said, "In the five days we've been here, I find it weird that we've heard almost nothing about the war." Then, as if by some Jungian synchronous cue, he heard someone laugh. *"Pas plus de Juifs à s'inquiéter sur,"* they said. He recognized *"Juifs."*

"What did he say about Jews?" Joey demanded.

"Forget about it, Joey," Skip advised. He didn't want to get Joey started. But Joey insisted, saying he wouldn't start anything.

"I won't start anything—I just want to know."

"He said 'no more Jews to worry about,'" Skip said, softly. Joey stared at the speakers' table for a long time. The men felt it and looked back. Seeing they were American soldiers; they lifted their glasses to them. Skip reciprocated, but Joey just stared.

Yesterday, when they had walked across from the hotel into the Tuileries Gardens, the concierge told them, pointing with a flourish of his arms and a proud tone, "Go to the left for the famous Louvre Museum and to the right for the Place de la Concorde with its famous obelisk."

"To the left and to the right," said Joey. "That's a lot different from what they meant at the death camp railroad stops."

Skip nodded. He thought about the Vel' d'Hiv roundup of Jews in Paris—thirteen thousand of them rounded up, not by the Germans but by the French police, women and children separated, and all sent to death camps. But he wasn't about to tell Joey until they got back to

Nuremberg or it would be the end of the new "three Fs"—fun, frolic, and food.

And food it was on their last night—at Le Sébillon, a famous restaurant in the Neuilly suburb. They took a taxi, and the driver wouldn't let them pay. "*Merci*," he said. "*Pour notre liberté.*"

"The milk-fed Allaiton de l'Aveyron leg of lamb is legendary," said Skip, reading the menu.

Joey laughed. "I can't believe what they eat here. Brains, cheeks, balls, hooves, tails, lungs. . . ." He whispered, "What about penises? Do they eat that?"

"But of course," Skip said, in a French accent. "But only if it's zee live one!"

Joey almost spit out his wine with laughter. "And I can supply one!" he said.

The friendship between the two had been a saving grace for both: an education for Joey and a balancing for Skip, whose tendency was to take life as fun and games. It was affecting his advancement, but Joey had lectured him about taking his job more seriously, and Skip had listened.

Their infectious laughter was noticed and approved by the women at the next table, who sent over a bottle of red wine. "*Domain de la Passion—Haut-Brion—1946*," Skip read from the label. "This must be some great wine. C'mon, you be the taster, Joey." Going through the steps Skip had taught him, Joey twirled, sniffed, tasted, and smiled, and lifted his glass to the women who smiled back. The French were visibly appreciative of the Americans as liberators and, as many GIs experienced, physically appreciative, too. It wasn't their luck that last night, however.

CHAPTER 56

Crossing the Channel in freezing weather the next day, Joey thought about the storms of D-Day and the stories he had heard about the terrible battle casualties on the beaches of Normandy from one of the vets at the depot who was in it. Then he looked up and thought of Milton. His hatred of Germans was now a fixed part of his mind.

In February 1947, London was having a snowstorm such as it hadn't had for years. On the one hand it was beautiful and covered up the terrible destruction from the German Blitz, but on the other it made things tough for the Brits to endure with all their shortages. On a sightseeing tour, Joey and Skip saw shattered buildings everywhere.

"Not as bad as Nuremberg, but it must have been pretty bad here," Joey said. "You have to admire them for going through it." He thought about how conflicted he felt about the Brits and their treatment of the refugees compared to his sympathy at how they suffered through the Nazi Blitz.

"It's been snowing 'ere every day," announced the guide on the sightseeing bus, a pudgy-faced, round-bodied troll of a fellow, "and we ain't seen the last of it yit." Looking around to make sure there were no women aboard, he added, "Freezin' me bloody arse off."

Joey and Skip laughed along with him. As they passed Trafalgar Square, the guide pointed out the National Gallery, and in his speech over the loudspeaker said, "Over there, you Yank chaps, is a statue of Colonel George Washington of the British Army in Virginia."

The boys again burst into laughter. Each day they went on a tour of London's famous sites. "It's nice to be able to know what everyone's saying for a change," said Joey.

"Right-o, old chap. It jolly well is," Skip agreed. "But the food is jolly-well awful. These Roz Biffs don't have the Frogs' talent with food."

That night, Joey was happily reading the *Times* of London and the *Manchester Guardian*. "It's great. They're in English!" As he put another shilling into the small gas heater in their room, he reported the news to Skip.

"It's the coldest, snowiest February on record. Just our luck. The army had to help dig out the rail tracks." Then, as he flipped pages, he discovered an article about Richard Crossman, a Labour Party member. "'Crossman denounced as 'wrong and inhumane' Foreign Minister Bevin's positions against allowing the immigration of Jewish refugees into Palestine and his calling the UN's partition plan' . . . let's see . . . 'manifestly unjust.'" Joey read. "It's just like Micah told me."

"Who's Micah?" asked Skip.

"Um, well, um . . . he's someone I met at the DP camp in Fürth."

"Another refugee? What exactly did he say?"

"Well, not exactly a refugee," Joey added "but he said the Brits are 'enemies of the Jews.'"

"Joey . . . what's going on with you? Is a nice, not-so-Jewish boy from Charleston turning into a . . . a Zionist?"

"I'm not. No. I mean, I've learned some things that, well, make me think about Palestine as a justified place for Jewish refugees," stated Joey. "And the Brits are making it impossible for that to happen."

"The Brits, as you put it, are going to get out of Palestine soon, according to what their prime minister just said. He called the Mandate unworkable. Then what?"

"Then the Arabs will attack," Joey countered, "and who knows what will happen. It's not fair."

The cold wave continued as they were finishing their stay in London, and Joey took pictures of all the places to send home: Westminster Abbey, the Houses of Parliament, Big Ben, the Charles Dickens house, and the River Thames. He would send them all to his brother. *Louis will be so jealous,* he thought with a smile. On their last day, Joey went to see the Changing of the Guard at Buckingham Palace by himself. But as he watched the soldiers marching and freezing in the record snow drifts, he couldn't help thinking of Nazi victims freezing in tattered clothing as they stood in life-or-death lines.

The pictures he had seen at the Trials were embedded in his brain. Naked Jews being ushered in for what they thought would be a shower. Children screaming for their parents as they were hauled away. The Guards' drumbeat transformed into his Nazi drumbeat but intermingled with it in his mind here in London were the sounds of the bomb bursts as described by the tour guide. Walking through snow-clad streets and seeing the enormity of the destruction from the Blitz, Joey felt a genuine sympathy for the wartime Brits. Turning onto Duke Street, he came upon a small synagogue building next to what was called the Great Synagogue. Joey went in.

"It was destroyed by German bombs in 1942," said the cantor who was rehearsing inside. "This is our temporary synagogue."

Joey was somewhat unsettled by this. "Are you comfortable here in England?" he asked.

"Comfortable? What do you mean?" The cantor didn't understand.

"I, ah, I mean the British are refusing to let Jewish refugees from Europe go to Palestine. They are stopping ships and imprisoning the refugees in Cyprus."

"I . . . I've heard something about that," said the cantor nervously. "But we're perfectly free here. Perfectly. Ah, w-would you like a look around?"

Joey sensed his discomfort and decided not to pursue the point. They walked through and ended up in the library. Looking around, as if he thought he might be watched, the cantor picked up a book and thrust it at Joey. "Here, you might want to read this," he said softly, and gave Joey a small paper bag as well. Joey looked at the title—*Israel, The Forgotten Ally,* by Pierre Van Paassen.

"The Americans published it several years ago," whispered the cantor. "It tells you a lot about how badly my country is treating the Jews in Palestine."

"Why? Why are you so nervous?" asked Joey.

"Our rabbi is definitely not a Zionist," said the cantor. Puzzled, Joey thanked him and left. That night he stayed up for hours reading the book, which was by a Dutch journalist who had spent years covering Palestine. He was astonished.

The next evening, Joey and Skip were at the hotel bar downing a few. "You won't believe what the Brits did to the Jews in Palestine for years," Joey said. "This book is shocking. There's a part about how the Arabs massacred a rabbi and his whole religious school while a British policeman just watched."

Skip just nodded. He was thinking more about the date he was lining up with the young Scottish nurse sitting next to them at the bar.

"It's so goddamn complicated, Skip," Joey grumbled. "I feel sorry for all the destruction here, but I don't understand how they could change so much about the Jews."

Skip just nodded again, winked twice, and got up and left with the lass. Joey watched them leave, but he stayed at the bar drinking Guinness. He thought about his "sexy time" at the Eibsee. He wished he were more aggressive with women, like Skip, but it didn't come naturally. At least he wasn't a virgin anymore, but it was ironic it had had to be with a Russian spy, then a German, then finally Leah, a Polish girl. Joey shook his head and laughed. *Wonder if American girls would be different? Well, poontang is poontang, I guess.*

But then again, it was such a different experience with Leah. He wondered just where she was at this moment and when and how he could be with her again? *Crazy . . . this trip is only making me more confused about the Brits.* They had suffered, but then again, not anything like the Jews. You'd think they'd be more sympathetic. But they weren't. Oh well. Tomorrow, back to Germany. The vacation was over. *France and England were the experience of a lifetime.* But it also was a couple more nails in the coffin of his Germanophobia. He was more convinced than ever about being involved in the urgent plight of the Jews and Palestine.

CHAPTER 57

As they rode the train back to Germany, Joey looked out on the devastation of towns and cities and dwelled on the horrors the Nazis had brought to England, Europe, and Russia. Of the millions killed, the murder of so many Jews, and what they still faced now. On the other hand, here he was getting a little joyride before he went back to the safety of America.

"How could they do that?" he said aloud.

"How could who do what?" Skip said. Joey just shook his head.

Back in Nuremberg, he was concerned he hadn't heard from Leah. They had exchanged several letters but it was her turn to write, and he was getting anxious. What could it mean? Was she now in transit, on the way to Haifa on some rattletrap ship that the Brits might capture—or sink, as they had done before?

"Leah. Leah. Leah," he sighed aloud. Love presented a variety of feelings to Joey. The pain of not holding her. The fear something bad had happened. He remembered their first kiss. "Corny," he said aloud, and laughed at that memory. This was a first for him. This was real. The next morning, as if he had ordered it, he found a letter from Leah waiting for him.

Dear Joey,

It is happening! I am to be on a ship in two days that will take me to Haifa. I don't know its name or which port

I am going to, only that I am to be picked up here. They tell
me to only bring one suitcase. As if I had more. I hope we
leave from that Italian port. They are much friendlier than
the French and seem better able to fool the British. How I wish
you were with me! I keep thinking back to our Geneva days.
It is as if someone placed us together knowing that we should
always be together. Sometimes at night I close my eyes and
pretend my pillow is you. Never has a pillow been so kissed.
When I am settled in Palestine, I will immediately write to
you so that I can get your letters and hear of your plans. Think
of me always as I think of you.

    Love and kisses on this very page,
    Your Leah.

Joey kissed the page and her name several times. *How could he be with her?* He would be discharged in a couple of months and had hoped she would still be in Geneva. It would have been so much easier to convince her to come home with him then. But now, what would this mean? She loved the idea of a Palestinian homeland for the Jews. *How could he handle this? Go home and hope? Go to Palestine?* He lifted the letter and read it again.

Friday came, and Joey drove to Fürth to check on his survivors and found that Micah was not around. "Micah is off on another one of his missions," Karl told him.

Joey was irritated. It meant he couldn't get an answer for the test date, one way or another. But it helped him decide that he would have the test after his trip to the Seder in Wiesbaden, not before. He didn't want to be preoccupied before then. He wrote that in a note. "Please give Micah this," Joey said to Karl and Josef. "You know you're my secret communication men with Micah."

Karl took the note with an excited look and showed it proudly to Josef before slipping it carefully inside his jacket. Joey held back a smile. He pretended to look suspiciously into the courtyard, then gave them a hug and left.

How I love those two! The next morning, looking at the Brigade list with his secret code, Joey closed his eyes, trying to visualize the actual transfer of stuff. His phone jangled him back to the now.

"Hello, Joey?" Al Moscowitz said. "It's me, Al. I didn't hear from you. You coming to the Seder on April sixth?"

It was mid-March, and Passover was approaching. "Darn tootin'," Joey said. "I already talked about it with Lieutenant Forner. I even asked him to come."

"Great, will he?"

"He said he envied my being able to attend, but Mrs. Forner had arrived, and they were busy being reunited."

"Reunited? Is that what it's called?" They both laughed. "How long can you stay?" Al asked.

"I'll leave that morning and stay two nights," Joey said. "I got your directions so it should be a piece of cake."

"Splendissimus! See you on the sixth."

CHAPTER 58

Joey had permission to take a two-and-a-half-ton truck from the depot, but he preferred to take his Jeep, and it was okayed by the lieutenant. The motor pool sergeant gave Joey a map and suggested it could take at least three hours, not two, to get to Wiesbaden, so Joey set out before noon on April sixth to make sure he was there by sundown. This was something he didn't want to miss.

The road was paved, but not always two lanes. As he headed north, he realized the traffic was basically nonexistent. He didn't want to be late, so he stepped on the gas whenever the stretches were straight. He was two hours into the trip and listening to Vaughan Monroe singing "Ballerina" on AFN Radio Frankfurt, when he rounded a bend at the small village of Wertheim am Main and was startled by two US MPs standing in the road with machine guns aimed at him and signaling him to stop. He jammed on the brakes and pulled over. They approached on both sides of the Jeep.

"Your ID, Sergeant," they demanded.

Joey handed over his papers. "What's going on? What's this all about?"

"You were speeding, Sergeant," a beefy-faced MP replied, with a look of disdain and importance that the gun he held gave him.

"Speeding? Me? Maybe forty-five, no more."

"Wertheim am Main is a thirty-miles-per-hour zone. Get out of the Jeep please."

Joey got out and they pointed to where he should go, a small official-looking stone building. Standing in the doorway was a captain looking at Joey and his Jeep. He nodded to his men, turned, and disappeared into the interior. Joey followed and saw the captain sitting behind a long oak table with a number of trays filled with documents. His name plate was prominently displayed on the desk—Capt. Gerard Finn. The captain's shirt was pressed in precise military style, two creases in front, three in back. *Not a good sign, means he's over-conscious of his role, probably. My officers don't dress like that.*

One of the MPs handed a paper to the captain which he read, then reread aloud.

"Exceeding the speed limit by fifteen miles per hour." He looked at Joey's ID, at Joey, then back to the ID card. "Sergeant *Gold*-man." He almost spit the name out, over-emphasizing the first syllable. "Why in such a hurry, *Gold*-man?"

Joey was stunned by the whole thing. "I didn't think on a such a small road, with no traffic at all, that I was speeding, sir."

"My men are using the new radar, Sergeant. I assume you've heard of that? So, if they say you were speeding, you were speeding. And just where might you be speeding to, Sergeant?"

"I am on the way to Wiesbaden, sir. I need to be there before sundown."

"Before sundown? What? No lights on that elite, souped-up Jeep of yours, *Sergeant*?" Every time he said "Sergeant," it was snakelike, as if he wanted to spew poison.

"It's not that, sir," said Joey. "I'm invited to a Seder that starts at sundown. It's the first Passover ceremony there since the war began."

"Passover, huh? That's a Jew thing . . . a Jew ritual, huh?" It was said almost with a smirk.

"It's not a ritual, sir. It's a holy religious service," replied Joey.

"Where you from *Gold*-man?"

"The 318th Ordnance Battalion in Nuremberg, sir."

"No, I mean where you from . . . New York, right?" asked the captain.

"New York?" Joey answered. "No, sir. South Carolina."

"Well, Sergeant *Gold*-man from South Carolina, you will be fined eighty dollars, to be taken from your pay, for breaking the speed limit. Give this paper from us, the Third Military Constabulary Squadron, to your payroll officer, who we will also send a copy. You got any questions?"

Joey looked at him squarely. "Yes sir. Where are *you* from, Captain?"

The captain squinted, puzzled. "From Boston."

"South Boston?" Joey asked.

"South Boston, yes."

Joey nodded his head. "I thought so," he said softly.

"What's that supposed to mean?" snapped the officer.

Joey saluted. "Nothing, sir. Am I dismissed, sir?"

The officer returned the salute with a slight sneer, thought for a moment, then nodded yes. Joey did a snappy about-face and returned to his Jeep.

"Son of a bitch," he said. "Second damn time." Again he headed north.

CHAPTER 59

Pulling into Wiesbaden, Joey was again amazed by the destruction still evident on almost every street, as in many German cities. *Serves 'em right for what they did to the Brits and Russians.* Mounds of debris were everywhere, sometimes next to buildings miraculously unscathed by Allied bombings. The horrors of war were impactful on so many levels. Many of which were not so easy to notice.

At a corner, he stopped to determine which way to go. Looking up at an unscathed three-story building, with little balconies bordered by iron railings around bay windows, he saw a woman using a wooden paddle to beat pillows and quilts draped across the railings—something he'd never seen before. She stared down at him. He noticed the apartment next to hers had one window with curtains, and another boarded up where blasts had shattered the glass. It was impossible from a human point of view not to feel sorry for people amid such destruction, but in the next breath he shuddered, remembering the films he had seen of the emaciated bodies stacked like kindling at the various German death camp crematoria.

He looked up at the woman and wondered where her husband was. Was he an SS or Gestapo officer who cut the beards off of old Orthodox men then beat them to death, or who machined-gunned men, women, and children so they would fall into graves they had just been forced to dig for themselves? He spit out his window thinking about that. If he could have spit on her at that moment he would have. He visualized running over a bunch of Nazis, when suddenly she smiled and waved at him. He was so surprised he nodded and smiled back.

Joey drove away, frowning at what just happened. After asking several passersby, who again to his surprise, were quite friendly, he found the Hotel Grüner Wald where Al was stationed and parked. As usual, his souped-up Jeep was the object of curiosity of both GIs and civilians. Checking in, he found Al snappily dressed and anxious to get to the Seder services.

"I was getting worried, buddy," Al gave Joey a bear hug. "So let's get your stuff into my room and head out." Al was a handsome guy who, as usual, was smiling. "Soon's I get discharged, I'm heading for the Big Apple and trying my luck," he said, then broke into song:

> *Give my regards to Broadway.*
> *I'm coming there to be a star!*

Joey laughed. "Moskowitz wins for Best Actor." Then he stopped and thought about his anti-Semitic exchange on the way here. He told Al about it. "Maybe you have to change your name, you know?"

"Yeah . . . ," said Al. "I heard about actors having to do that . . . like John Garfield is really John Garfinkle. I'm thinking of Al *Markim*. Whattaya think?"

"Markim?" said Joey. "Sounds okay. You could be a *goy* with that."

"I know, but it's hard to be Jewish in Hollywood," said Al.

"Hard to be Jewish in most places, I'm realizing," answered Joey.

"Yeah," said Al. "Where we're going now, we'll see the awful results of that. C'mon, let's go."

Joey put on his dress uniform, his cap, and stared in the mirror for a moment with a sad expression. Then, arm around each other's shoulders, they walked out to catch a ride to the Seder. They would remain arm-in-arm friends for life.

CHAPTER 60

In what was once a gymnasium for Nazi officers, the US military prepared a Seder for some four hundred people, including Jewish soldiers from the US and the UK stationed nearby, survivors from the DP camps in the area, and members of the nearby Jewish Agency from Palestine. Entering the building, Al and Joey felt the emotional excitement all around them. The sound of different languages hummed like bees around a spring flower bed. They crossed to the rabbi, a chaplain from the 3rd Infantry Division, who was going over a hand-held list.

Al saluted and addressed him. "Sir, Al Moskowitz from the 14th ENT here. Can we help in any way?"

"Thanks, but ETO HQ has ordered everything amazingly well. Look at this place," the rabbi said. "Four hundred beautiful place settings, candles, flowers, Kosher wine . . . looks like the Ritz, right?"

"Never been to the Ritz, sir," said Al with a smile. "But it sure looks swell."

"Who all's here, sir?" asked Joey. The rabbi pointed out the US and British soldiers' section, the survivors' section, and a section for Jewish Agency members and others who were actually representatives of the various international Jewish organizations helping refugees throughout Europe.

"But I'm thinking to change that," said the rabbi. "I want everyone to mix it up." He turned to Joey. "What do you think, Sergeant?"

Joey gulped at the question. "It'll certainly be more emotional, sir. It's like . . . like you'll turn it all into one big family."

"That's exactly what I had in mind, Sergeant." With that sentiment, the rabbi went up to the head table, tapped on the microphone, and asked everyone to "mix it up" and forget the section signs.

There was a melody of excitement and anxiety as they did what he asked.

The service began—in English, Hebrew, and Yiddish. Looking around, Joey saw soldiers looking embarrassed at being alive and healthy in front of the gaunt, sad survivors, some of whom cried frequently during the service. Others seemed joyful and drank more than the four cups of wine called for in the *Haggadah*. Unknown to Joey, disguised Brigade members were proud, angry, and crying as well.

Sitting next to Joey was a solemn-looking young man. "I am Solly Ganor from Lithuania, and I was in Dachau," he explained. "My father also is here," he said pointing to a sad little man at the next table.

"I went there not long ago," said Joey. "I've had bad dreams from what I saw, so I can barely imagine your nightmares."

"Not just nightmares," Solly sighed. "I have day-mares most of the time."

"'Why is this night different from all other nights?'" asked the rabbi.

"Look," Solly pointed. "The rabbi is asking the four questions." He began to sob. "Who usually answers them? The children, that's who. The children. Do you see many children here?" He shook his fist. "*Do you? No!* They killed them. Killed them by the thousands." Joey hugged Solly, as pity, anger, and sympathy all swelled within him.

After the meal, which was served following the unusual, beautiful *Haggadah* prepared by the Army, the rabbi pronounced the final traditional prayer. "*Shehecheyanu*: Blessed are you, O Lord . . . who kept us alive to reach this season."

As all said "amen," a member of the disguised Brigade suddenly stood, and in Hebrew started to sing the *Hatikvah*. Rising together all around the hall, other members stood and joined in. The young man next to Joey leapt up. "The Czech Jews sang this in Auschwitz as they went to the gas chambers," he said.

"Can you tell me the words?" Joey asked.

Solly sang in English,

> *Our hope will not be lost,*
> *The hope of two thousand years,*
> *To be a free nation in our land,*
> *The land of Zion and Jerusalem.*

He quoted the lines in English after each line was sung in Hebrew. Soon, everyone was standing, singing, and crying. When it ended, the silence seemed louder than the singing. Joey realized he too was crying and was holding hands with the youth and the British soldier next to him. He stared at the group across from him and suddenly he recognized Micah. He walked over to him, and they both stood, looking without expression at one another, until Micah slowly smiled and reached out his hand, which Joey took.

CHAPTER 61

"*Shalom Aleichem*," said Micah. "I didn't know you would be here."

Joey's expression was part smile, part curiosity. "*Gut Yontif*," he responded, which was all he could recall from his childhood days at Sabbath School in Charleston. "And I didn't know you would be here, or where you were."

"I had . . . things to do," said Micah. "Come sit with us."

"I'm here with my friend Al," said Joey. "He's the one who asked me to find Josef. Can he come also?"

Micah frowned. "No . . . no. Does he know about us, or what I asked you to think about?"

"No, I promised you I would say nothing to anyone." Then suddenly Joey realized he had in fact told someone—his brother. But this was such a possibly life-altering thing to discuss, and Louis was his sounding board for so many things, so he knew it was really safe to have told him.

"Thank you for that," Micah said. "Just say hello, then we can meet at another time. Okay?"

They walked to a table nearby. There was a lot of paper being exchanged by survivors with American and British soldiers.

"What's all that about?" asked Joey.

"They are trying to connect with relatives or friends in the US or the UK," said Micah.

"But we want them to come to us. We need them." Micah took Joey's arm and led him to a group of Brigaders in civilian clothes. "Come say hello to Alon, Joey," said Micah. Joey reached out to shake his hand.

"Supply Sergeant Joseph Goldman of the 318th Ordnance Battalion," Alon gripped his hand. "Surprised to see you here." This time, Joey thought, "Goldman" was said with admiration—not like this morning.

"Micah has said recently how helpful you've been to the refugees in Fürth," he smiled. "And that means a lot to us." For the first time, Joey looked closely at Alon. Like Micah, he thought, not a "typical" Jew, like his small, pudgy Polish-born Uncle Joe who had shushed him, or his mother's "Jewish"-looking brothers, Abe and Sam. This was a different breed. He glanced from one to the other at the strong, young men grouped around Alon. Amazing—these Palestinians were fighting for a Jewish homeland and risking their lives to save these survivors from further terror and hardships.

"Joey?" Micah asked. "Are you okay?"

Joey nodded and came back to the moment. "Sorry, I . . . I'm sort of overwhelmed by all this. It's so much to take in."

Alon stared at him, with tenderness, sympathy, and approval on his tanned face. "I know. I know," he said softly, and he placed his hand on Joey's shoulder. "Can we meet for breakfast tomorrow? I'd like to discuss the test. Micah could pick you up at eight?"

Joey nodded "yes," shook hands, and went back to where Al was waiting.

"Who are those guys?" he asked. "How do you know them?"

"They're just some Palestinians," Joey said. "We met at the Fürth DP camp. I just wanted to say hi. So, what's next, Shakespeare?"

Al gave him a slow, quizzical look, then turned and pointed to the rabbi. "He asked if we could help in the cleanup here. I said sure. That okay with you?"

CHAPTER 62

An hour later, they sat at a table with the rabbi and several survivors who had also volunteered to help. They were a little worn down after piling up the various components of the occasion and helping lug them out to the Army trucks that the drivers called the "Matzah Ball Express."

Joey looked carefully at those around the table. A US Army rabbi, a couple of Jewish GIs, three refugees—including the young Dachau survivor—Al, and himself. *What the hell is this all about?* he wondered—this pride in being Jewish, and the outpouring of such emotion in a Seder, the Holocaust slaughter of the camps, and the Brigade guys sending refugees to help build a homeland. A totally new world for him.

Raising a glass of wine, the rabbi said, "*Shelo ahad bilvad amad aleinu lehaloteineu! . . . Vehakadosh Baruch Hu, matzileinu m'yadam.* Many have risen in every generation to destroy us, but God, may his name be blessed, saves us from their hands."

Everyone drank to this toast. There was a long silence until one of the survivors, young Solly, put his wine glass down with a bang. "Yes, but where were you, *Ribono Shel Haulam,* when millions of our children, mothers, fathers, sisters, and brothers, went to the gas chambers? Where were you, God?"

The rabbi lowered his eyes.

Solly continued, crying now. "I'm sorry for thinking these terrible thoughts, Rabbi, at a time when I should be rejoicing in our freedom, and the fact that my father also survived." He paused and looked around the table. "My father wants me to go with him to Canada. But what this Seder did for me was strengthen my desire to go to Eretz Israel and fight for the Jewish state, a state where we can defend ourselves with weapons against anyone who wants to destroy us."

Everyone seemed moved. Then, slowly, the rabbi turned to Solly and raised his wine glass in a toast. "To Israel," he said.

One by one the rest did the same thing. "To Israel."

"To Israel."

"To Israel."

Finally, Solly raised his glass. "'Next year in Jerusalem.'"

Joey turned to Al, frowning and shaking his head. "It breaks my heart to see all these poor homeless souls hoping to get to Palestine. I want to help them. And, and . . . I mean . . . I never felt anything like this before. I'm not religious but it's making me crazy . . . you know, about being Jewish."

Al shrugged. "Jeez, I dunno, Joey. Maybe you should talk to the rabbi?"

As they walked out of the building and watched the convoy leaving and the soldiers and refugees going their separate ways, Joey saw the rabbi chaplain shaking hands with the Army officers who had made the Seder possible. He waited, then walked over to him.

"Excuse me, Rabbi, but do you have a minute to, well, explain something to me?"

"Explain something?" the rabbi asked, cocking his head to the side. "What something?"

"Um . . . about being, you know, being Jewish." Joey looked down.

"Aren't you Jewish?" the rabbi asked, looking puzzled.

"Um, sure, but I mean, I never thought much about it . . . and . . . and when I see all this happening here, so many different kinds of people . . . soldiers from the US, the UK, France, Russia, survivors, and Palestinians all being so . . . so excited about going to a Seder, I'm not sure what's going on. But . . . but I'm *feeling* a part of it."

"Come on. I'll give you a ride back to the hotel and we'll talk," said the rabbi. They got into his Jeep and with Al they rode back through the shattered streets of Wiesbaden.

CHAPTER 63

In the hotel bar, the rabbi sat at a booth-like table and bought them both a beer. Joey was comparing him to Rabbi Raisin back in Charleston, a gentle old man who was always smiling. This rabbi was younger, more like a regular guy than a religious figure. He said he was from a Conservative temple, *Har Zion*, in Philadelphia. Joey felt comfortable with him.

"You identified with the emotion that filled the room during the service?" asked the rabbi.

"I did, I did!" Joey exclaimed. "That's what made me ask you to help me understand. Since I've been here in Germany I've learned about the camps and the killing. I can't believe the Jews of Europe could suffer such terrible things just because they were Jewish."

"Yes, It is terrible," the Rabbi said. It's a holocaust. Some are calling it 'The Holocaust.'"

"Holocaust? *The* Holocaust? Jeez," Joey continued. "I hate the Germans for this. Hate them! They should all be punished."

He was silent for a moment, considering. "I've been tempted to seek revenge," he confided. "But Rabbi, even in our own Army I've experienced anti-Semitism twice. So, being a Jew, you can get it from everywhere. And yet everyone here seems so . . . so committed to being Jewish. I'm not religious, Rabbi, I hope that doesn't offend you, but . . . ."

"Relax, Sergeant," said the rabbi. "You don't have to be religious to be Jewish. Think of it this way. We're a family, and like most families we don't always agree or believe like one another. But there is a bond between us all, and we have a mission as a family to look out for one another, and also, as the Bible commands, 'to be a light unto the nations.'"

"I guess I'm feeling that bond for the first time in my life and it's, well, unsettling, but . . . but it's a good feeling, Rabbi. I mean, I want to help these poor bast . . . ah, poor refugees."

"I hope you will," said the rabbi. "But, Sergeant," his expression changed, "beware of revenge."

Joey frowned. Revenge was uppermost in his wishes. *An eye for an eye, a tooth for a tooth. That's even in the Bible. How could you not think of revenge? That Christian "turn the other cheek" stuff isn't for me.* But how could he tell that to a rabbi?

"Thank you, Rabbi, sir," he said instead. He saluted and rose to leave just as Al entered the bar with two girls in uniform and waved for him to come join them. He was in no mood for socializing, but he closed his eyes for a moment, paused, and opened them up with a smile.

CHAPTER 64

"**Y**ou're a cat?" Joey said to the amazingly beautiful girl Al introduced to him.

They were finishing dinner at the Club, enjoying lots of German beer, and having a generally good time. She was in her early twenties and wore a military-type outfit that showed off a very sexy body. She was so beautiful that every GI passing by just stared. Her ID tag said, Sondra Fisher, C.A.T. Joey looked at it and raised his eyes to her. "Sondra, C-A-T, eh?"

Brushing red hair back behind her ears with a shake of her head, Sondra smiled. "Right! C-A-T—Civilian Actress Technician," she said. "We're here to entertain the troops. Actually, we're in the Special Service shows so you guys won't have to dress up as girls anymore in the plays, like in Shakespeare's day. They do call us CATS."

Across the table, Al mouthed, "Meow . . . wow." Joey tried to stifle a laugh by gulping his beer.

"What's so funny?" Sondra teased.

"I was just thinking I might actually be allergic to cats," Joey said quickly, grinning.

She laughed and leaned over. "I hope not," she purred in his ear. They ordered another round.

He woke up the next morning in his room at the hotel. Blinking his eyes to focus after a night of heavy drinking at the Eagle Bar, Joey was startled to find he was in bed with Sondra. *God, I must have been plastered! She's an American, too . . . from New Orleans.*

"Time to get up, soldier boy," she whispered in his ear, and up it went.

No sooner had they finished there was a knock on the door. It was Al. "Joey, there's a guy named Micah downstairs looking for you."

"Oh my God!" Joey exclaimed, and leapt out of bed, and started dressing.

Giving Sondra a quick kiss on her head, he rushed out, still combing his hair with his fingers. As he stepped into the elevator, a rush of guilt hit him. Not about being late, but about Leah. *How could he do this to her? Do what? I was drunk and Sondra was . . . oh, God . . . what if Leah were doing that to me! But we're not actually engaged . . . yet.* His value scale was flipping up and down like a seesaw.

Micah took one look at him and burst out laughing. "A little, how do you say it? R and R last night?"

Joey grinned sheepishly. "Not much rest, actually, but a lot of recreation. Sorry I'm late."

"Don't worry. It's never too late to help us," Micah said.

They drove out of the city, to a horse farm this time. Galloping along the fence that ran besides the truck were two beautiful horses; one was dark rust and the other looked just like Tonto's pinto. What the hell was a pinto doing here in Germany? He soon found out. The farm belonged to an American Jew, Ernie Compain, who had stayed here after his discharge. The pinto was his, left by an American Wild West show before the war. Joey was introduced to him inside the neat little farmhouse. Ernie had met the Brigade and joined in to help.

"Seems they like my talent for, what shall we call it? Smuggling," he said. "I decided to take my discharge here. I figured I'd take advantage of the unrest, confusion, and black market to make the bucks I'd never be able to accumulate in the States. You can do the same, and team up with me!" Ernie put his hand on Joey's shoulder. "You could go home a rich man off the Germans, Joey." He handed Joey an expensive-looking cigar, which Joey refused.

"That's not exactly what I have in mind to do with the Germans," Joey responded politely. *Not me, what I want is more like what Micah told me about, a* bricha *member who had poisoned a supply of bread served to German POWs.*

Alon came in a few minutes later, this time with a stocky fellow in a tailored suit that clearly made him uncomfortable. "My name's Carmi and I hate wearing this suit—so you'll know," he said, and shook Joey's hand. "I've heard a lot about you, Sergeant. You don't know—or maybe you do know—what you're sitting on can be a godsend to us."

They laid out the details of the plan to test the help Joey could provide. It would take place, as he wanted, in late April. Micah would be part of the group that would come to the depot to pick up the trucks and weapons. The requisition would, as Joey had asked, be sent to Lieutenant Forner, and Joey would get a "go" or "no go."

"So you'll know either way," Carmi explained. "If you don't hear from us after you receive the requisition, please call the number on this card, and please don't leave this card around. Just say you can, or cannot, fill the order, as if it were one of the units you supply. We will react accordingly."

Afterwards, Ernie set out a spread of the most mouthwatering delicacies. "You could be eating like this every day, Joseph," he said once again, this time offering some Russian caviar.

Micah laughed. "If you took a discharge here, I would hope you would join us, not Mr. Entrepreneur there."

Jesus. What a weekend. Every part of Joey, from head to heart to toe and in between, had seen action. It sure hadn't been like life on Sans Souci Street in Charleston.

○○○○○○○○○○○○○○○○○○○○○

CHAPTER 65

———

A week later, Lieutenant Forner called him into his office and handed him a bunch of papers and requisitions without paying much attention to them.

"Three reqs, and a letter from your brother," he said.

Joey flipped quickly through the requisitions. Nothing. Forner was looking at another document. "And here's another req. From the TTG. For a pair of two-and-a-half-ton trucks and twenty-five .50-caliber guns to be sent to a unit in Leipheim. Hmm. What's TTG? Never heard of them." Joey swallowed and anxiously blinked twice. This was it. "Go" or "no go."

"Well, it's signed by Colonel L. J. Phillips, SHAEF Headquarters, and the First Military District. Luke's a good guy so . . . ." He stamped the document *Received by Lieutenant Herschel Forner, 318th Ordnance Battalion,* signed it, and handed it to Joey.

"So, how was the Seder?" he asked.

"Holy shit," muttered Joey.

The lieutenant looked up, surprised, "'Holy shit?' That's how you describe such a memorable Seder?"

"No sir. I mean, I . . . I was thinking, how the heck I'm gonna get these reqs out in time. I haven't completed the last batch yet."

"Oh," said Forner, chuckling. "I thought you meant the holy ceremony sucked."

"No sir!" Joey exclaimed. "It was the most emotional thing I ever experienced." He told the lieutenant everything, leaving out, of course, getting laid and meeting with the Brigaders. His questions he kept to himself.

Walking back to his office, he thought about the logistics. Sitting down, he read the requisition again, then stared out the window. *This was fucking scary. Would it work?*

That afternoon, Micah called, using the name of a sergeant from the TTG.

"Sergeant Goldman? This is Sergeant Frank Nicolo of the TTG. Have you received our requisition 4501 for materials?"

Joey held the papers in front of him, knowing Red was in the next office. "Yes, Sergeant," he said in a low voice. "I have them here. I can fill this order. When do you need these things? And how will you get them?"

"We will have drivers for the two vehicles there Wednesday, the middle of next week. You'll provide assistance loading the boxes of materials as discussed?"

"Sure." Joey was nervous, even though all he had to do was deliver the things, and the TTG would take over. "I will have four POWs on hand to help. Have your drivers report to me in the 318th Headquarters Building, just on the right after you enter the depot on the Schweinauer Straße . . . um, I mean, Schweinau Street."

"Thank you, Sergeant," responded Micah. "Our men will be there Wednesday at 9 a.m. sharp with the necessary papers and identification. Good-bye."

Joey held the phone in his hand, amazed. It was so easy. Just take the two trucks out and load the boxes, and that was that. Or was it? *What about Lieutenant Forner? Maybe I should tell him. He's Jewish.*

He'd understand. But no, he would never allow it. He was military, all the way—said he was gonna stay in, as a career.

As he sat at his desk, filling out the papers for the transfer of the trucks, he thought of Karl, smiling and waving goodbye from the back of one of the trucks. That felt good. It was a better way than just killing a goddamn Kraut. Maybe the rabbi was right about revenge. Or at least about other ways to get it.

That night, however, the whole thing brought on one of his nightmares, based on a story Josef had told him. In the dream he was Josef, in Dachau. He was going to work as usual when the SS officer in charge shouted at three other men. "Halt! Benario, Artur Kahn, Erwin Kahn, over there. Against that wall." The three moved, shivering with fright. They knew what was happening. "Fire!" commanded the Nazi *Sturmführer*, and the three fell, with bullets in their foreheads. The officer turned to the rest. "It is a good thing these Jewish insects are dead. They have been hostile elements and had no right to live in Germany—they have received their due punishment." In his dream, Joey pulled a gun and screamed, "Nazi bastard! You must die!"

The SS officer turned his pistol on him just as Red shook him awake.

"Wake up, man. Wake up!"

"I wanna kill 'em! I wanna kill 'em all!" Joey yelled.

Red shook him again. "Calm down, Joey. It's a dream. Only a dream."

CHAPTER 66

"Sergeant Goldman, there's a couple guys here from the . . . the, lemme see, the TTG, with orders to see you from Colonel L. J. Phillips, the First Military District," said the MP on phone duty at the Kaserne's entrance.

"Oh, okay," said Joey. "Show 'em how to get here."

Ushered into his office by Lieutenant Forner's German civilian secretary stepped three men, in US Army uniforms. Startled, but hiding it, Joey saluted back to a first lieutenant and looked next to him into the face of Micah, now Sergeant Frank Nicolo, US Army.

"Here are our papers, Sergeant," said the lieutenant. "Can we get right onto it? We have a long drive ahead of us."

As they walked to Building 21 Micah spoke softly to Joey. "Our papers are in order, right? No problem, right?"

"When I see your taillights, I'll agree," whispered Joey, glancing around. As they examined the two trucks, a group from the Polish Guard unit drove up with a truckload of boxes of weapons, and four prisoners of war to unload them into the two-tonners.

Suddenly Joey jumped. The colonel and Lieutenant Forner walked around the corner of the Headquarters Building and looked over at Joey. They walked over and Joey saluted. Micah also saluted. The colonel looked at his watch. "Still at it, eh Sergeant?"

"Last one today, sir," Joey said, saluting and trying to sound casual. Forner, however, took the papers from Joey and asked Micah, "Where is this TTG from, Sergeant?"

Joey felt disaster coming. *I knew it. I knew it . . . .* Micah saluted, "We are not the TTG, sir. They are a British Eighth Army unit."

Forner nodded and walked over to look into the trucks. Micah stepped in front, as if he would pull open the tarps. "We're handling this for them since SHAEF doesn't want them in our zone and requested instead that we bring materials to the Brits at the Zone border."

"Oh, I get it," said Forner, apparently satisfied. "I wouldn't want them roaming around the American Zone either."

At that point the colonel called out, "Let's go, Lieutenant."

Forner threw Micah a salute. "Carry on," he said, then headed off.

Micah smiled an *I told you it would be ok*ay as Joey slumped with relief. Then they both got into one of the trucks and headed for the main gate.

As they showed papers to the MPs there, Joey jumped out with Micah and watched the two trucks roar off. "Jesus," Joey said as they walked to Micah's US Army-licensed Jeep. "I thought we'd had it. But you guys are amazing." They shook hands, and Joey told him he would be at Fürth on Friday.

"See you then," Micah said, driving away. *I'm committed now*, thought Joey.

He glanced up at his apartment window across the way, and heard the drums,

*Ba-*DUM*-da-*DUM*-*DUM*, dum-dum-*DUM*. They had come to mean many things to him: anger, hatred, uncertainty, and now . . . hope.

CHAPTER 67

"**I** had a dream the other night about an SS officer in Dachau," Joey told Karl, who translated for Josef. Joey continued, "For no reason, he suddenly executed three Jews in front of everyone. It was the story you told me, Josef."

"SS Hauptsturmführer Stengl," Josef said bitterly, and talked on.

Karl translated: "You couldn't afford to even look him in the face. He would shoot you for that." Josef closed his eyes and frowned at the memory. Again, Joey wondered how any human could act that way, and how anyone could ever get over things like that. They were in the courtyard and Micah, now a civilian again, came to join them.

"*Shalom*," he said. "The journey was successful."

"Journey? What journey?" Karl said.

"A ship that just got to Haifa," Micah made up quickly. "Like the one I want to get you on as soon as I can."

As Micah and Karl talked about the possible trip to the Holy Land, Joey thought about his fantasy of killing the next German to stop at his drumming. When he got back to his room, he very lightly played the riff but thought again of what the rabbi had said about revenge. *Getting refugees to Haifa is the best revenge.*

Haifa was still on his mind as he sat with Skip in the press corps dining hall. It was the first day of May, and Skip raised his wine glass in a toast:

Hooray. Hooray.

The first of May.

Outdoor fucking's back today!

Joey looked around, a little embarrassed, but no one seemed to notice. "I can't believe it's May already," he said. "Our tour of duty ends next month."

"Damn right," said Skip. "Back to old Charleston for you and who knows where for me," and burst into song: "'How you gonna keep 'em down on the farm after they've seen Paree?'"

Joey laughed. "It sure would be different to be back on Sans Souci Street."

"You'll be sans wine, women, and song," said Skip. Then, reconsidering, he asked, "Heard anything yet from Leah? She get there okay?"

"Got this today, believe it or not," Joey took a letter out of his jacket. "From a Tel Aviv PO box. Sort of wanted to talk to you about it. Lemme read it to you, okay?"

"Hell, yes," Skip said. "I'm glad you got it."

"Dearest Joey," he read softly, and looked up at Skip with a smile.

> *I am finally here, my love. They have sent me to a wonderful kibbutz in Givat HaShlosha. Here's my address to write to. Please. Please. Please write to me. How I wish you were here. I am learning to be a nurse. And you know I already know how to be a fighter, so they also have me teaching others how to use rifles, pistols, and machine guns. I'm busy day and night. But never too busy to think of you. Joey. What will you do when your discharge comes due? Will you come here? What will you do and what will I do without you? I dread thinking about it. Please write me soon, my love.*
>
> *Yours always, Leah.*

"What do you think I ought to do, Skip? I miss her something terrible, but I just don't know what to do. Not go home? What will my family say?"

"Look, Joey, how the hell can I advise you?" Skip said. "I don't know how you feel. Shit, you haven't known her a long time. Do you really love her? Can you really know that in such a short time? I've seen you change about being a Jew, growing to hate the Germans, and wanting to help the refugees. Joey, you don't have to tell me, but I know you're getting friendly with those Brigade guys. I know it, and trust me, Joey, they'll want *you* to go to Palestine and help them get ready."

"I've thought about that, Skip, even before I met Leah," Joey admitted.

"But *thinking* and *doing* are different," Skip said. "Talk about a life change from Charleston! That would literally be a world of difference. I guess if it were me, I'd ask her to join me in the States, but that's me. You got to put all this on that scale you're always talking about."

Joey nodded and held the letter to his nose and took a deep breath. Skip noticed this.

"Damn," he said, half to himself. "You're gonna go there. Jesus."

CHAPTER 68

———

Joey sat at his desk, lining up the day's requisitions, and heard a knock on his door. There stood a staff sergeant.

"Sergeant Goldman?" he asked.

"The very same," said Joey. "Can I help you?"

"I'm Sergeant Heaney from the Third Constabulary Squadron," he said.

Joey squinted. This struck a bell. "Third Constabulary Squadron. Where's that, exactly?"

"Wertheim am Main," he replied

"Captain Gerard Finn?" said Joey.

"Right!" Heaney said. "You know him?"

"I met him last April. April sixth, to be exact," smiled Joey. "What is it Captain Finn needs?" He took the requisition and looked at it, then looked slowly at his inventory lists and walked over to a group of filing cabinets, where he pretended to search. He couldn't believe his good luck. Finally he turned to the sergeant. "I'm afraid we're all out of these, Sergeant."

"You're kidding," said Heaney. "These ain't special or unusual kinds of things."

"I know but it's, well, I see it as a special request," said Joey.

"What does that mean?" asked Heaney.

"Means tell Captain Finn you'll have to try the depot in Berlin."

"Berlin? Jeez, Sergeant . . . that's a lot of days and lots of red tape away!"

"Yeah, I know," said Joey, "but tell Captain Finn that Sergeant *Gold*-man is sorry, but that's life. Accent on the *Gold* is how you say my name to the captain, *Gold*-man." Joey stood up. "The captain ought to fit well into Berlin."

The Sergeant looked puzzled. "I don't understand."

"It was Nazi headquarters," said Joey. Confused, the sergeant walked out, his shoulders slumped at the rejection.

"How about that, Schatzie?" Joey said, picking up the dog after the sergeant left. "Turnabout is fair play, wouldn't you say?" Schatzie licked Joey's face and squealed happily, as if she knew this was poetic justice.

PART TWO

CHAPTER 69

_____

Tel Aviv—

"Leah Chalovitz, eh?" said Stef Eisner, reading Leah's information on his clipboard. "Polish, survived your family's murders and escaped into the Cratchna forests." His eyes jumped from his clipboard to her. He paused, then looked back down and, nodding ever so slightly, continued. "Fought with a Jewish partisan group. They were wiped out and you ended up making it to Italy?"

Leah shifted uneasily in her chair at this interrogation by the tall, young Palmach leader. Standing over her, he stared down, his face expressionless.

"Yes," Leah stared right back. "I . . . was out foraging for food when a German unit ambushed my group and killed them all." She looked down.

"Including your younger sister," Stef added quietly, looking at the report.

"Including Rael," Leah nodded her head slowly. The memory came at random moments like this.

Seeing this, Stef waited a moment. "I'm sorry, Leah," he said. I have lost family there, too. It is why we are preparing ourselves for what will happen if the Arabs do as they threaten and attack us in force. But . . . ." He paused. "They will find Jews can kill better than they can."

He looked again at her folder. "You say you can fire rifles, pistols, and machine guns?"

"I know the German Kar 98k and its sniper sight, and the Russian Mosin 91/30," she said, straightening in her seat.

"Oh, the Mosin-Nagant."

She could tell he was impressed, so she waited a moment. "I have killed Germans with both," she said.

His eyes snapped up from the clipboard. "And you want to be part of our Palmach?" His expression changed now from stern to one of slight approval.

"I do," she said. "I was told you are the fighting part of the Haganah, and I want to fight anyone who tries to attack Jews. Anyone."

Stef looked closely at her. He could see a muscle in her cheek moving angrily. Reaching over, he raised her chin so that she looked directly up at him. "For thousands of years they have been killing us, Leah. They use any excuse to blame us for whatever they've done. We are their scapegoats. No more. No more. No more . . . . Never."

She was accepted into the Palmach, and he told her of the secrecy required, of how she would be sent to a kibbutz to work. "Each month you will have eight training days of weapons and combat."

"I know weapons and combat!" she said, interrupting.

"This will be a little different, you'll see," he said, smiling. Then, as an example, he told her how he had helped in the blowing up of eight bridges, and how the British reacted. "Operation Agatha, they called it. Raiding kibbutzim and arresting thousands of Jews, confiscating our hard-earned weapons. Ruthless. You will use fourteen days to work for the kibbutz and then seven days off. It will not be easy."

"I am not looking for easy," she said, rising from her chair. "I am looking for a home."

She wrote Joey about what she could.

> *Dearest Joey,*
>
> *I am now at a kibbutz as part of a training program in many things. It is all so thrilling. But it is also hard, really hard. The land is beautiful and so are the people. They are from all over Europe and Russia. I have not been this happy since I was a little girl. I would be the happiest in my life, however, if you were here. I am pledged to be careful what I write so please understand.*

* * *

Joey read and reread her letter telling him about moving to the kibbutz and undergoing training. "As part of the "*Hach'shara Meguyeset*," Joey told Micah on his next visit to Fürth. "What does that mean?" he asked.

"It's a training program," Micah said. "She will learn, how do you say . . . the Three Fs—farming, fighting, and fraternity—as part of the Zionist Program."

Joey burst out laughing. "That's not the Three Fs I've experienced." Micah looked a bit confused. Joey continued, "You remember . . . in Wiesbaden when I was late to meet you?"

Micah laughed. "Oh, yes. You told me your three Fs. Ah, let's see . . . food, fun, and . . . fucking." They both broke up. "Well, she can learn *those* Three Fs after we have a secure homeland."

"*Those* Three Fs she's going to learn with *me*," Joey said, suddenly very serious.

"What are you saying, Joey? What do you mean?"

"I have kept your secrets, Micah. Now you must keep mine," Joey insisted.

Micah searched Joey's face and said softly, "I promise, Joey. I promise."

"I am planning to take my discharge here in June. I want to join your work," he said. "I haven't told my family yet. It will be hard."

Actually saying these thoughts out loud of changing his life, perhaps forever, made Joey so uneasy he shivered and broke into a sweat. How could he desert his parents and Louis? What could he tell them to help them understand that what he had been through here had convinced him that Jews . . . what's left of them . . . desperately needed a homeland? In his mind's eye, he saw his family at the dinner table on Friday nights saying a few prayers and sipping grape juice—his father wouldn't use wine—but it was unemotional. Routine. Not heartfelt. Now, here he was, not really religious but really a Zionist, an in-love-with-a-survivor Zionist. His private scale told him he had to get to Leah, be with Leah, take care of Leah, and God knows, how many other Leahs there were who needed help—help he could give them to get to Palestine. To Yisroel, Alon had called it.

Micah put his hands on Joey's shoulders. "You are making a very loaded choice, I know, Joey . . . Joseph. But, you have an opportunity to make a difference in this world of hatred and genocide of our people. It is against so many odds that it will not be easy, but it will be done."

Joey lifted his hands, placed them on Micah's outstretched arms, and stood looking him in the eye for a long moment. "Yes, it will be done," he said.

CHAPTER 70

The next day, mail call gave Joey a lengthy letter from Louis. It was a reply to Joey's telling Louis of his decision and asking for his blessing. He knew that letters were no longer being censored, so he had struggled to describe again his feelings for Leah, the Wiesbaden Seder, the care he gave Karl and Josef, his visits to Dachau, the War Crimes Trials, and his admiration for the Brigaders. He was no longer the naïve little brother, and Louis realized it. He had always been Joey's confidential sounding board.

> *Dear Joey,*
>
> *This is so hard for me to write. I understand that you're deciding to go to Palestine and help the displaced Jewish survivors you have met and cared for to find a homeland. I understand and even encourage your wanting to do that because they have no other place to go. You have seen the unimaginable and cruel destruction the Nazis have done to the Jews. I hate to feel I'm preaching to you but . . . even when this genocide became known to the world, the gates of most nations, including our own, were not opened to our landsmen. But Joey, it has been this way forever. We Jews have been blamed for every conceivable ill and murdered in every conceivable way. Now we have been cut in half. Think of it . . . we are now only six million. They are almost a billion*

each, the Christians and the Moslems. They have found every imaginable excuse to confine us, enslave us, and blame us since time immemorial. They are cowards, bullies, afraid to let us live in peace.

Lots of our Jewish Americans have fought and died alongside the British and helped save their ass, and now, as you know at first hand, they are doing every possible thing to prevent these poor Jews from reaching Palestine.

So, my brother, my dear little brother, I am tortured with indecision. I am afraid for you. I am scared you will find only misery and hardship by going to Palestine. You have been lucky so far to be alive. I am torn between identifying with your plans and wanting you to come home and help Jews from here. We're still restricted from many things in America but at least we aren't being killed, and things will change. Mother and Daddy are getting old. They have prayed for your safety every day. Milton's death gave them nightmares about losing you. Think of them, Joey, and think of how you would survive there as a civilian.

How would you live and support yourself? Where would you live? Would this be dangerous? You learned to be self-sufficient at an early age but being alone in a war-torn country is a lot different. Would these Brigaders really take care of you? There is so much to think about, Joey. Please consider all this carefully.

Love, Louis

CHAPTER 71

"Goldman, here's another requisition from that TTG unit. Look it over and handle it if it's okay, please," said Lieutenant Forner, signing and handing papers to Joey. "I'm up to my butt trying to satisfy my wife's demand for better living quarters." He sighed. "Many of the officers now have spouses arriving, so the competition for apartments is increasing."

Good. It makes made things easier for me. He glanced down to see a request for four more two-and-a-half-ton trucks, and seven machine guns, with ammo as well. Micah was pressing Joey to get as much as possible before his discharge in five weeks.

Back at his desk, Joey was thinking that he hadn't even discussed getting his discharge here with Lieutenant Forner and the colonel. *I'm pretty sure they would help make it happen, since they knew of his care for the two DPs, but suppose they make it difficult for me? I gotta ask Ernie Compain in Wiesbaden how he managed it. Micah would know how to reach him. Maybe I'll go visit Al again.* The Three Fs flashed in his mind. Was Leah doing the same in Palestine? He shook his head rapidly, *No.*

"Why are you saying 'no' when I haven even asked you yet?" asked Red, looking at him from the doorway.

"W-what?" Joey stammered. "I mean . . . I was thinking about something else. Whattaya asking about?"

"There's a dance at the Opera House tonight with the Redman Band from the States. Thought we might go and have some fun."

"The Redman Band?" The memory of that night in Geneva with Leah had made Joey feel even guiltier about shacking up with the C.A.T. in Wiesbaden. "Um, ah, yeah, okay," Joey said. "Let's do it."

* * *

"What the hell is with you, Goldman?" Red asked as they drank beer in the Opera House and watched the dance floor "There's Kraut pussy all over waiting to be meowed at, and you're just sittin' there."

Nodding, Joey took a long look at the dancers and got up to go onto the dance floor with Red. *Might as well have a little fun.* Then the band struck up "All the Things You Are," and Joey froze in his tracks. Two Fräuleins approached, but he was staring and kept shaking his head "no," and they backed away from him, somewhat fearfully.

Later, at their quarters, Red said, "Something's up with you, Joey. You been quiet for days now. What the fuck's going on?"

They'd been roommates for two years now, and Joey wished he could tell him, but he just couldn't. Once he knew the details of the job Micah and Alon were arranging for him with the Jewish Agency from Palestine, maybe he could say something, but not yet.

"I'm thinking about something different, but I just can't talk about it yet, Red," Joey said. "As soon as I've thought it all through you'll be the first to know. I promise."

He had a meeting in a few days with Forner and would find out just what the response would be when he made his decision. It would keep him up nights, he knew, and he imagined all sorts of different reactions, from an excited "okay" to a threatened court-martial, or God knew what else.

In the meantime, Joey busied himself with work, arranging the transfer of items to the Brigade and visiting Karl and Josef. It was like he was leading a double life—maybe a triple life: the supply sergeant, the secret Brigade aider, and the DP protector. His correspondence with Leah was a bright spot in all this.

> *I am working in the orange fields in the kibbutz. They have figured out how to irrigate the fields that were just sand and grass for centuries. It's almost fun. Especially compared to the long night hikes with full backpack. They drill you with attack strategy lessons as well. My teammates are all men, but don't worry. Here is a kiss for the only man I am interested in.*

Her lipstick signature at the end of each letter was a thrill.

> *I only wear it for these kiss signatures. Never otherwise. This is no place or time for cosmetics.*

Each time, he kissed it several times.

CHAPTER 72

One midweek afternoon, a storm blew in just as Micah had come to the depot. This time he was a US second lieutenant. The rain was so hard it forced everyone who could to stay indoors. In rain parkas, he and Joey supervised the transfer of material to two of the four two-and-a-half tonners being passed over.

A sudden thunderbolt made them both jump. Micah grabbed Joey's arm. There was alarm in his eyes and sweat on his face. Joey had never seen anything but calm strength there, so he pulled Micah over quickly into one of the trucks. "You okay?" he asked.

Micah was breathing heavily. "I am afraid of lightning," he said. Another bolt struck nearby. Micah put his hands over his ears. Joey put his arm around Micah's shoulders and said, "It's okay. We're safe in here. Lightning doesn't hit cars."

"I was in a storm, one worse than this," Micah said. "And we were running around the track at the athletic field and the coach told us to get inside the gym. One of our units, a big, heavyset guy we called Tiny, said he wanted to do one more lap and kept running." Micah shook his head. "A bolt came down just as Tiny passed a metal drain and went right through him into the drain. He was literally fried right there as we watched."

Joey stared, wide-eyed, as Micah gritted his teeth, remembering. "And the lightning kept smashing down near us for half an hour. So we couldn't go out and get him."

"Jeez, that was awful. Where was this?" Joey asked. "An athletic field? At a school?"

Micah turned to face Joey, "Yes, at a school. I . . . I never told you this before. And . . . and . . . you know the school."

Joey squinted, pulled his shoulders back, and cocked his head, puzzled. How the hell would he know a school Micah went to?

"Remember when I said I would set up our September meeting after Labor Day," he said, "and you looked surprised I would know about an American holiday."

"Yeah, I do remember that," Joey replied. "So . . . so does that mean the school was in America?"

"The Citadel," Micah said.

Joey stared, open mouthed. "In . . . in Charleston? *The* Citadel? You were at the Citadel?"

Micah gave a rueful smile. "*The* Citadel. I was sent there in 1938 by the Jewish Agency to attend courses in battle strategy and deployment and . . . "

"I can't believe it," Joey said. "I was eleven then, and I'd go see the cadets parading once a week. Were you part of that?"

"Oh, no, no. I was there by special arrangement as a civilian. The Agency tried to get me into West Point, but your government wouldn't allow it."

"So you got into the 'West Point of the South,' as we called it," Joey said, amazed. That Micah's leaders had the foresight to send him to the Citadel gave Joey fresh hope that Israel might once again become the Promised Land.

"And you know something about Charleston, I guess?"

Micah jumped as another bolt exploded, now more distant. "I met your rabbi."

"Rabbi Raisin?"

"Yes," said Micah. "I may have even been at services at your temple, as you call it, when you were there."

"If you believe in fate, this would be something to prove it," said Joey.

Micah laughed. "Fate is what you make happen, not what happens to you. Maybe because I spent quite a bit of time in the South I felt a bond with you right away?"

Joey was moved. He, too, had felt it draw them closer. In some way, it made Joey feel more secure in what he was doing. They talked about Charleston while the storm passed. When it was over, they got out and Micah, embarrassed, thanked Joey. As the trucks departed, Micah promised Joey that arrangements were being expedited to set him up as a representative of the Jewish Agency and that he would be given an apartment in the DP complex in Fürth.

"So," Micah told him, "you now can feel safe telling your superiors of your plan without being specific—just that you will be officially helping refugees. And, Joey, you should start making the necessary military arrangements for your discharge in Europe."

"I will," Joey reassured Micah.

"We'd also like to make another requisition, soon."

Joey thought for a moment. "Micah, the TTG won't work again. It will raise suspicions."

Micah nodded. "What if it came from a US Army unit?"

"You can do that so it's, um, really authentic?" Joey asked.

"Sho'nuff. Y'all'll be completely happy. As happy as if you had a big bowl of she-crab soup," Micah said in a surprisingly good Southern accent.

"Sho'nuff?" Joey drawled in reply. "Ah loves she-crab soup." Micah shook hands and led the four-truck convoy out toward what was hoped would be its ultimate destination in Palestine, or at least would be carrying refugees to get to Palestine. Joey stood for a long time watching. He was doing something good, something that made him realize for the first time how proud he was to be a Jew.

That night he sat in his office, composing a letter to his parents. Already balled up and thrown away were six tries. As Joey tossed them, Schatzie would jump at each of the paper balls, growling and attacking them as if they were stray mice. Joey rested his head on his hands. "God, I wish I could do this in person," he said aloud. "It would be so much easier." But he knew it wouldn't be. He could hear his father: "You're not a Palestinian Jew. You're an American, goddammit." His mother would just wring her hands and cry. So he bit his lip and rolled another sheet into his typewriter. Schatzie sat and watched, waiting for the next ball. Joey closed his eyes and rubbed his forehead, trying to pull out the right words.

CHAPTER 73

A fter many failed attempts, he finally completed the letter.

Dear Mom and Dad,

I've told you some about what I've experienced here over the past couple years. It has affected me deeply. Dachau, the Trials, the survivors in the Fürth DP camp, the Jews from Palestine who are here to help survivors get to Palestine . . . it has all made me aware of so many things . . . especially that I am a Jew and . . . how hard it is to be a Jew. How very hard.

I'd never thought about this before, Daddy. Growing up in Charleston, I knew I was Jewish, but it didn't mean to me then what it does now. I still can't believe that millions of Jews were just slaughtered like animals just because they were Jews. And not just gassed and incinerated. They were used as subjects in horrendous medical experiments, as targets for German rifle practice, as slave labor, as playthings for various tortures; unimaginable, inhuman, indescribable treatment by the Nazis. They make our terrible treatment of colored, I mean negroes, almost seem tame in comparison . . . almost. Thankfully, we never killed them like the Germans killed us. It has made many sleepless nights for me.

A tear dropped onto the edge of the paper and slowly settled into a circle of wetness. Joey wiped his eyes and continued.

> *I believe firmly that once and for all the Jews deserve their own homeland. The British promised it once and now have changed their mind. They are preventing the remnants of European Jews from coming to Palestine to start a new life in a nation of their own. They have even sunk ships filled with refugees trying to reach Palestine—refugees who managed to last through the torture and starvation by the Germans only to have their lives taken by the British.*

> *All of this is leads up to a decision I have made that I know will upset you.*

Joey paused and visualized his living room on Sans Souci Street. His father in his overstuffed wing chair. His mother sitting on the long, padded bench where as a little kid he had brushed her hair as she lay down and read him a story. Now, pacing back and forth. "Shit," he said aloud and started writing again.

> *I have become very involved with the members of a Jewish group. They are from Palestine and fought for the British during the war but are now helping to get thousands of refugees to Palestine. Daddy, this is extremely confidential. Extremely. Promise me you will not write a letter about this. It could be very hurtful to me and many others, so promise me. In my position I have been able to help them get much-wanted supplies, which they'll need at home when the British leave and the Arabs attack. And, trust me, the Arabs will definitely attack. They don't like or want Jews there, but the Jews are finally back there in numbers after two thousand years. Back to the land that was theirs for thousands of years.*

*They want what remains of these Jews to come join them.
God knows nobody else wants them. I'm gonna do whatever
I can to help . . . .*

Joey paused here and swallowed to summon up his courage. All
his life, he had been careful to protect his father from excitement. What
he was about to write, he knew would make his parents frantic, but he
had to do it. Swallowing again, he continued . . . .

*So instead of taking my discharge in July and coming
home, I will take my discharge here. I have been promised a
job to help refugees get to the Promised Land. Promised by the
Brits and by the Bible. I never realized what we always paid
lip service to in the Seder . . . 'Next year in Jerusalem.' Now I
know, and I aim to make it come true for these poor beaten-
down souls who have no home anymore. Mom, Dad, this
isn't impulsive. I've thought and thought about it for months.
Ever since I went to that Seder in Wiesbaden. Please try to
understand. Please. I will be all right.*

Much love, Joey

He read it over three times before putting it an envelope,
addressing and stamping it. Even then, he sat looking at it as he reflected
on what he had decided. "Schatzie," he said, picking up the pup, "this is
gonna be a hard thing. I hope I know what I'm getting into."

The pup licked him and wagged her little tail, as if saying
Whatever makes you happy, go for it. Joey rose, turned out his light, and
headed for his room. As he passed Lieutenant Forner's office, he knew
that tomorrow he was scheduled to tell him his plans and would be in
for a tension-filled discussion.

"'Next year in Jerusalem,' Lieutenant," he whispered, and saluted
the office door.

CHAPTER 74

In the morning, Joey got up early, carefully pressed his shirt and pants, and made sure his uniform was clean and his boots shined. He looked in the mirror and squinted his eyes. *Is that the uniform of a very professional soldier I'm looking at?* It would help his proposal to them. His father had always proudly shown him a picture of himself in his full-dress Marine uniform at the Pennsylvania Navy Yard, where he had been stationed during the first world war. Knocking on Lieutenant Forner's office door, he licked his lips several times and entered. He closed the door behind him and saluted. Noticing the closed door, the lieutenant frowned, "What's up, Sergeant? Something wrong?"

"My discharge is coming up very soon, sir," Joey said. "And I want to discuss my plans, sir." The lieutenant pulled himself up in his chair.

"What's all this 'Sir' business?" he asked. "Sit down and spit it out."

Joey sat, placed both hands on the desk, and leaned forward. "I want to get my discharge here and go to work in Europe helping refugees," he wet his lips again.

The lieutenant pressed his lips together in a faint smile, nodded his head ever so slightly, and looked at Joey as a parent might look at a child with a wild idea. "Better slow down and give me the whole story, Sergeant. What you're asking is possible . . . just not, I think, very practical."

Joey was ready for this. He had rehearsed his pitch, which was very much like the letters he had written to Louis and his folks. While he talked, the lieutenant listened patiently and pulled up Joey's records from the file in his desk. When Joey finished, Forner opened the file on his desk, studied it, then looked up at Joey. "Son, you have a sterling record," he said. "Not just here, but in everything you've done so far in school and the Army." He frowned slightly. "You will be putting yourself in a very peculiar position by doing this."

"What do you mean, a peculiar position?" Joey was alarmed.

"An American civilian, jobless, alone, with no clout, trying to deal with the aftermath of a world war?" said Forner. "How in the world do you expect to do that?"

Joey started to explain the Brigade but realized he couldn't. "I have a connection, Lieutenant. It will help me find a job and a place to live and work. I'm sure of it."

"The Jewish Brigade, huh?" Forner said. Joey was shocked. He stammered, "I can't say, Sir. I just can't."

"Sergeant, Joey," the lieutenant's tone was gentle. "I know a lot more than you think. I'd like to help, too, but my career will be in the Army and yours could be as well. The colonel said only last week he wanted to talk to you about becoming an officer candidate. Coming from him, that's quite a compliment."

Joey closed his eyes and leaned back slowly. *I wonder if he actually has known all along about what I've been doing with Micah. I can't believe he could, but then again, what about telling me to handle that last TTG order with the excuse that he was looking for a better apartment? If I'm that obvious, how can I expect to be in a secret organization? Maybe my plan is stupid. Maybe I'm stupid.*

Forner interrupted his thoughts. "I've seen the stuff you've been taking to Fürth, and I approve of that," he said. "And I surmise you met a Brigade member there and my guess is that he's been working on you, right?"

Joey breathed a sigh. He didn't know. "I met several people from the Jewish Agency of Palestine. They've been the ones 'working on me,' as you put it. I can get a job with them."

Forner closed the file. "Tell you what, let's discuss this with Colonel Larned. Okay?"

Joey nodded. Forner must feel that the colonel could convince him to stay put. But the lieutenant was actually sympathetic, maybe without knowing it. Joey was sure now he could resist the colonel. *I am on a mission, like . . . you know, Theodor Herzl.*

CHAPTER 75

The colonel began his talk with Joey about the glory, adventure, and security of being an officer in the United States Army—like a recruiter. He went on for fifteen minutes about the history of America, and how the Army had been instrumental in making it all possible, before he suddenly switched gears and explained how he thought the Jews didn't stand a chance of having their own homeland.

"The Middle East is oil country, and the entire world relies on fossil fuel," he said. "That's the main reason why the Brits have sided with the Arabs. A few thousand Jews simply won't be able to stand up to that. So for you to hang your future on that would be a sad mistake, son. A very sad mistake."

Joey looked at him and felt his stomach churn. The colonel had a warm, assuring look. Maybe the colonel was right? Then Joey inhaled deeply and, looking away at the huge map of Germany on the wall, he lowered his head and thought of the horrors the Nazis had committed in that very country. Joey shook that feeling off. After all, the Colonel hadn't seen the strength and ingenuity of the Brigaders. He had no idea of the weapons stockpiles and defense planning the Jews were preparing. Joey remembered the young survivor at the Seder who would give his life to establish a homeland. *Maybe I would do the same if I had to?* For the next half hour, he listened as the colonel tried to get him to become an officer. In the end, he promised he would sleep on it.

But he didn't sleep on it. Instead, he rolled around all night not sleeping but thinking of all the ramifications of his decision. He filled his "scale" with the pros and cons. A life of actively helping fellow Jews finally be free of torture and go to safety, versus a life of just contributing, to help them from afar. A life of adventure but with possible danger, versus a life of safety at home. A life with Leah, versus a life with his parents and Louis. The scale was teetering up and down in his brain just like the Howard Victory had pitched and yawed as it crossed the Atlantic. He saw Josef and Karl facing off against his aging father and mother. It was a seesawing night, to say the least.

When he got up to go to the office, he realized it was Saturday, and he wouldn't be seeing the colonel until Monday. He had nothing to do until playing in the band that evening at the Officer's Club, so he grabbed Schatzie and headed for the motor pool to get his Jeep. He drove to the PX and picked up things for Josef and Karl and headed out to Fürth. He stopped at the famous fountain and got out. As he leaned against the hood to think about what he was going to do, two small boys approached and laughed as they petted Schatzie.

"Hallo, Captain," one said. "You hef candy für us, pleess?" Joey smiled at the boys and reached into the Jeep and gave each a Hershey bar. "*Danke*, Captain! *Danke!*" they cried and ran off.

Joey sighed. *They are innocent. but what happens when they learn their legacy is genocide? How will they handle that? Will they be up to it? They couldn't possibly feel about it as I do.*

CHAPTER 76

The JDC had finally given Josef the necessary papers, and Josef and Karl were thrilled to show them to Joey.

"He will be going to a boat in Marseille in two months according to these instructions and sailing to New York City, America," said Karl.

Josef grabbed Joey and planted a big kiss on both cheeks. "*Vielen Dank, ausgezeichneter Junge. Danke!*" he said.

Joey blushed. "You are so welcome. So welcome." Tears clouded his vision. Schatzie was running around the room yip-yapping in delight. *What I want to do with my life is right. I know it's right.*

Karl picked Schatzie up and drew her to his face. He closed his eyes, and the pup licked his face. Joey looked at him—he must have had a pet for his kids. *Had.* A word so many of them knew. *Have . . .* that's what he wanted for them.

That night became a night to remember. His band had been playing at the Officer's Club for about an hour: "Peg O' My Heart," "The One O'Clock Jump," "Ballerina," "Open the Door, Richard," "Near You." Joey looked at the dancers. All happy, well fed, dancing as if they hadn't a care in the world. As they took a break, he closed his eyes and in his mind compared them to the Seder crowd. Without thinking, he began playing the drumbeat that had pursued him so relentlessly—*Ba-*DUM-*da-*DUM-DUM, *dum-dum-*DUM . . . .

The room stopped and turned to the bandstand, startled and wondering what was going on.

Lieutenant Forner and his wife came quickly up to the stand. Joey stopped and came to meet them. "What the hell's happening here, Sergeant?" Forner demanded.

"I . . . I . . . I'm sorry, sir. I'm sorry," Joey stammered, near to tears. "I've been so troubled by what I talked with you about and I know now that I want, I must, stay and take my discharge here. I'm sorry, sir. It just overtook me."

The lieutenant stared at Joey in anger. The whole room was starting to crowd up to the bandstand.

Then as he said, "This is no place for you to do this, Sergeant," his wife put her arm in his and gave a gentle tug, and he slowly softened. He put on a big smile and waved the crowd away, then put his hand on Joey's shoulder and said, "It's okay, son. It's okay. Get yourself a drink and we'll talk tomorrow."

Joey swallowed. "Thank you, Sir, I'm really sorry, really sorry."

CHAPTER 77

A response to his letter to parents arrived.

> *Dear Joey,*
>
> *Your Mother and I are extremely upset with your idea of staying in Europe. Helping refugees is a noble thing but there are Jewish organizations and the UN who will do that. You have your whole life ahead of you to create. Helping Jews who survived can't be that. We, our family, already gave up Milton to this war. To give you up would be a terrible thing to do to us and that is a possibility you can't ignore in war-ravaged Europe. GIs have been killed by Nazis who went underground. Please, Joey, come home and discuss all this with us. Don't just let some impulse change your life forever. You've done your duty as a good soldier. I promise I won't write any letters.*
>
> *Love, Dad*

Sitting in his apartment Joey reread the letter several times. It made him squirm. He didn't want to hurt his family, especially his mother. But how could his father measure Milton's loss against six million who were murdered? Six million who didn't have a chance to fight, who were imprisoned and tortured and killed, and more who were still being kept in camps and prevented from finding a homeland?

Picking up the picture of his parents from his desk, he stared at it. "This is not an impulse, Dad," he said aloud. "You don't understand. I've realized I'm a Jew. Jews need a place of their own and, dammit, I'm gonna help them get there."

He turned to his drum set and very lightly with his fingers beat out the sound:

Ba-DUM-da-DUM-DUM, dum-dum-DUM. . . . Ba-DUM-da-DUM_DUM, dum-dum-DUM . . .

Strange, he thought, *how I've gone from wanting to shoot at a German out of the window, ending his life, to wanting to help people, my people, get a new life.* "My people, Dad," he said aloud. "*My* people."

When he told Skip about his decision, Skip just shook his head. "You're out of your fucking mind, Goldilocks," he said. "It's like they just let you off the reservation and you're drunk with freedom for the first time."

"You're wrong," Joey said, shaking his head. "I'm not drunk, Skippo. I'm sick. Sick with the thought that half of my people . . . " he liked using that term now . . . "half of my people have been turned into ashes, and the world still doesn't give a fuck." He told Skip about his plans of getting a job with the Jewish Agency and living in Fürth. "I'll still be around to hear your dumb jokes for a while, at least." The thought that their friendship could be over made them both silent for a bit.

"Well," said Skip. "I'll still be good for a real meal to help you through your ration starvation. Or maybe you can find a Fräulein to move in with. . . . Oh," he stopped. "I forgot about your Leah. She wouldn't like you getting local pussy."

"Don't you ever think about anything besides food and fucking?" Joey laughed.

"You forgot the third F," Skip answered with a big fake smile. He saw that he couldn't change Joey's mind.

CHAPTER 78

Kibbutz Givat HaShlosha—

Leah sat in her cot at the kibbutz reading the letter from Joey that said he had made up his mind. He had decided to change his plans, his identity, his life.

I'm so glad . . . but her arms holding the letter slumped. Instead of coming to Palestine, he would be remaining in Europe.

She wrote that, although she was glad he would be helping others like her come to the homeland, she wished he could come to help the homeland directly. But this was her first day back from an eight-day secret training with the Palmach, and she could barely keep her eyes open.

They had finished a thirty-two mile night-and-day hike with full field pack and rifle. At one point, they were passing an Arab village at night. Suddenly a barrage of stones was thrown at them. Stef fired a warning shot.

"Shoulda aimed better, Stef," Yossi Rubin had said.

Stef glared at him. "There'll be plenty of killing before too long, Yossi," he replied. "And it will *not* be pretty. So save your anger."

Leah woke to a ringing bell and realized she hadn't even undressed. The paper and pen were still on her cot. The kibbutz's two-week working period had started, and she went out to get breakfast at the community mess before she reported to the medical building where she cleaned, helped, and took classes to learn to be a nurse. When she wrote Joey that night, she told him about the schedule:

> *. . . two weeks working for the kibbutz, eight days of training, and seven days off . . . but not really off. I still have to attend nursing classes. When I go to training they have given me a cover story to tell the kibbutz that I'm going to school in Tel Aviv to learn accounting and Hebrew. They think the kibbutz doesn't know the truth but I'm not sure of that. I'm leading a double life, being taught to kill and at the same time to save lives. But I'm not complaining. I love it here doing what I'm doing. I feel at home.*

CHAPTER 79

Now that the war was over, the various Jewish organizations were doing everything possible to get the British to leave Palestine. But with the British essentially siding with the Arabs, and doing everything they could to prevent Jews from coming to Palestine, the Irgun and Haganah's Palmach and the radical Stern Gang united in blowing up British facilities. It was an undeclared war, with casualties mounting in Jewish, Arab, and British populations.

Micah told Joey how important it was to get more and more refugees there to help when the British finally gave up. "And they will give up," he promised. "We will make them give up. It is our land."

Earlier, when Joey raised the question that the Arabs say it is *their* land, Micah banged his fist on the table between them in the Fürth courtyard. "Their land? Well, how come you're living in America. In the Diaspora? Because they *took* our land, that's why."

"The Diaspora?"

"Yes," Micah growled. "The Jews who fled Palestine centuries ago to other lands before they got slaughtered," he explained. "To Spain and the Inquisition. To England where they were exiled. To the pogroms in Russia, Poland, and Lithuania." He paused to calm down. "It is our land that we will return to . . . that we will fight to own again."

Joey felt chills as Micah spoke. He looked around at the courtyard, the buildings, the refugees. Yes, he, too, would fight for a Jewish homeland.

CHAPTER 80

Lieutenant Forner began reading aloud. "Army Regulations 615-360 states, 'Individuals serving in overseas command who are authorized to be discharged will ordinarily be returned to the United States where their discharge will be accomplished.'" He went on reading the details. Joey frowned and bit his lip hearing Forner read, "'Overseas commanders may separate eligible military personnel in overseas commands under applicable procedures provided that the consent of the government of the foreign country involved has been obtained and the laws of the country complied with.'"

He looked up at Joey, who looked uncertain.

"So I have to get the Krauts, um, the Germans, to okay it, too?" Joey said, almost hopefully.

"That's what it says, Sergeant," Forner replied. "But it also says first *we* here have to approve it, and *you* have to waive your transportation home. And *we* are also the 'government of the foreign country' at this time."

"And you're gonna okay it, aren't you sir?" Joey said, almost pleading.

"Goddammit, Goldman! Your old man has written another of his goddamn letters to General Clay at SHAEF, and we have an officer coming tomorrow to investigate all this."

"My father? Oh, shit!" *I can't believe it! I asked him not to write any more letters. He wants to control everything!*

The lieutenant sighed. "I need this like a . . . ." He shook his head. "Never mind. Nine o'clock sharp tomorrow." He closed the file with a slap that implied *dismissed.* Joey returned to his office and started to write an angry letter to his father, but then he looked at the photo of his parents on his desk and crumpled the letter. *Maybe, maybe I should go home first to get my discharge and then come back. But . . . what if I can't get back. I'd be just another American sitting on the sidelines. No way. No way. No way.*

That night was another tosser and turner. Red had long ago started using earplugs so he could sleep soundly and get through the nights of Joey's bountiful dream life. In the morning, Joey told Red everything he was planning, except about the Brigade. Red had heard about the drumming at the officers' club, so he knew something serious was up.

"It's not just helping the refugees," Joey said. "There's a need for military supplies for the Jews in Palestine." *A little groundwork,* he thought.

Red looked puzzled. "Military supplies? What the hell for?"

"It's . . . well, it's because the Brits are gonna leave Palestine and when they do the Arabs are gonna attack the Jews. And the Arabs have got lots of armies and weapons and planes." Joey balled up his fist and banged it on his knee. "The Jews need weapons or there'll be another goddamn Holocaust."

Red gulped. "Holy shit, Joey. That would be awful . . . terrible. But . . . where are you gonna get weapons from?"

Joey had already told Lieutenant Forner that Red would make a good replacement for him. He hoped he would be able to convince Red to help in this, but he knew not to suggest it now. When you live with somebody for several years, you share a lot. Over the past two years, he often talked with Red about the survivors and the Trials. He knew Red was sympathetic.

Red saw the change in Joey. "I've seen you sort of, well . . . grow. Never thought about you being Jewish at first, but you've changed."

"Never thought about it either," Joey said. "I realize it now. Not being religious, but being part of a culture, a history, a people. Know what I mean?" They talked for a long time before Joey jumped up. "Holy shit," he said. "I gotta be in Forner's office in half an hour!"

CHAPTER 81

He saluted the captain from SHAEF, who looked Joey up and down with a steely glare, and carefully answered question after question about why he was asking for his discharge in Germany. He spoke of his discovering the Holocaust, being at the Trials and Dachau and Wiesbaden, the survivors at Fürth, being Jewish and realizing the desperate situation of the survivors and their need to get to Palestine, and of meeting people from the Jewish Agency. The officer's expression turned sympathetic, and he nodded ever so slightly, then suddenly broke in.

"Are you mixed up with the Jewish Brigade, Sergeant?"

Micah had warned him this might come up. Joey had rehearsed what he would say . . . the same thing he had already told Lieutenant Forner.

"The Jewish Agency, you mean, sir? I've been meeting with them at Fürth. They have offered me a job here, sir."

The captain looked over at the lieutenant with his eyebrows raised, as if for verification. Joey realized that his father hadn't mentioned the Brigade, only that he wanted Joey to come home.

"When the word 'Brigade' comes up, he who hesitates is lost, as the saying goes," Micah had warned. "Without a beat, tell them it's the Jewish Agency you've been talking with, and Joey, be patient. Let *them* do the talking."

Joey remembered their Charleston conversation about she-crab soup, and how, when he was a kid in Charleston, his mother had taught him to catch crabs down at the little weather-beaten wharf on the edge of the marsh under the ancient, moss-clad oak trees next to their house on Sans Souci Street. Sitting on small folding chairs, she had shown him how to lower the string with the bait slowly and wait patiently as a crab cautiously moved up and grabbed the bait. "Now pull him up really, really slow," she whispered. "Wait till he's near the surface then swoop him up with your net." It was calm patience she had taught. He must apply that now, he thought.

Forner slowly nodded to the captain, as if to say "okay."

After a long pause, the Captain said, "Okay, son, your record in the Army has been spotless and positive. I'm going to approve a European discharge if your commander submits it. I hope you know what you're doing. You understand that the US Military authorities under General Clay have to say okay as well."

"Yessir, I understand. What about the Germans?"

"The Germans?" said the Captain. "Oh, you've read the regulations. Well, the Germans don't have a goddamn thing to do with it at this time. We tell 'em what's what."

"Thank you, sir. Thank you," Joey said softly. *Here goes . . . .*

CHAPTER 82

Several days later, Joey was expecting another arrival of Micah and three GIs. This time they were prepared with IDs from a Constabulary Unit near Munich.

Joey was always amazed at how their papers and IDs were so professional. Forner never suspected a thing. It was this way with the Brigade all over Europe. No obstacle seemed too big for them. "This is our destiny," Micah had said. "Anything to assure a homeland."

On this trip, the supervisor of the POWs who were ordered to load the four trucks was Braun, the POW who had gotten the Leica camera for Joey.

Impatient to get the loading done Micah spoke out with a stern German command demanding Braun hurry it along, "*Beeilen Sie sich!*"

"*Zu Befehl,*" Braun quickly answered, and started moving faster. *Zu Befehl,* "at your command"—not the usual *jawohl,* "yes, sir"—He had used an SS reply.

Micah casually took out his camera and photographed Joey. "Smile!" he said. Then, among others, he took a shot of Braun and said nothing. A week later, Micah met Joey on his Friday visit to Fürth with a picture of Braun as an SS officer.

"Untersturmführer Otto Golboch, wanted by every intelligence service for his misdeeds at the Treblinka camp," Micah said.

"Braun, an SS officer?" Joey said, amazed.

"A murderous SS officer during Operation Reinhard," Micah replied.

"Operation Reinhard?" asked Joey. "An operation with a person's name?"

"Reinhard Heydrich, the coordinator of the *Endlösung der Judenfrage* . . . the 'Final Solution of the Jewish Question,'" Micah said. "Somewhere between 700,000 and 900,000 Jews died in Treblinka's gas chambers." He held Braun's photo up." This son of a bitch was in charge." He spit on the picture. Joey was speechless. He had his Jeep cared for by a mass murderer.

"We want him, Joey," Micah said. "I want to come get the bastard."

Joey was startled. "But, but . . . he's our prisoner. I can't just give him away."

Micah raised his head slowly and looked into Joey's eyes. "He is a murderer of our people, Joseph. He's very clever . . . a trusty at your depot. Just report that he escaped."

Joey let this sink in. What Micah said was true on all counts. It was a risk, but . . . should he take it?

"What if you're wrong?" he said.

"The proof will be the SS tattoo in his armpit," Micah said. "Since he is a prisoner of war, if it's not there, you can send him to another unit, but I know it will be there."

"You have to tell me exactly how you would do this."

Micah laid it out quickly. "I will come with a US Army truck to pick up some . . . some weapons for which I will have a valid requisition. You have Braun be the one to bring them, and I will have him put them up into the inside front of the truck. There we will hold him and tape his mouth and remove his upper garments." Micah went on.

"What . . . what will you do with him?"

Micah waited before responding. "You have pledged to help us, Joey. This can be your chance to see another part of what we do. But it is strictly your choice."

"You mean . . . ?"

"Yes." Micah answered, staring at him. "You can follow our truck with another vehicle. Not your Jeep."

CHAPTER 83

Three days later, the Brigade truck with its US Army ID arrived. Joey had received the approved requisition from Forner. He picked up Braun, aka Golboch, himself to drive to where the ammo was stored. Braun was joking about the pretty girls who worked in Headquarters. Joey was so anxious about what was happening he couldn't even smile.

Braun looked at him, puzzled, which made Joey feel even more uncomfortable. Quickly he brought Braun and the single box of ammunition requested to where the Brigade truck waited. A young "US Lieutenant" was in charge. He ordered Braun to get up into the truck to receive the box. Braun saluted, and pulling aside the flaps covering the back of the truck he climbed up and turned to receive the box lifted by the lieutenant. Then the German turned to place the box down inside the truck and as the flaps fell back into place behind him, two Brigaders hidden inside grabbed his arms and Micah slapped tape across Golboch's mouth.

The German struggled only for a moment, his eyes wide with fear. Micah grabbed his shirt and undershirt and pulled them up as Golboch's arms were raised above his head. Micah shined a flashlight. There it was—the double lightning bolts of the SS—under the left armpit.

"*Untersturmführer Otto Golboch, ja? Wir haben Sie gesucht,*"— We were looking for you." Micah whispered. The German shook his head to plead, no . . . it's a mistake, but was quickly tied up and thrown onto the floor. Micah whistled.

Outside, the young lieutenant turned to Joey, and saluted. "We'll be leaving now, Sergeant. We have what we needed."

Joey returned the salute. As the Brigader stepped up into the two-and-a-half tonner, Joey looked around to see if anyone had observed the operation. Convinced it was all clear, he got into the truck he had just used and followed.

One hour later, the first truck pulled off the quiet country road in the Zerzabelshofer Forest and followed an overgrown dirt road through giant pine trees to a bluff high above a small but fiercely flowing river. Micah and his men pulled Golboch from the truck and walked him down to near the edge and tied him to a tree. Joey followed them. The German had wet his pants and was frantic.

Micah showed him the official Nazi photo. Golboch saw Joey and made animal-like sounds to get Joey to stop this. Joey gritted his teeth and stayed silent. They were both sweating, one out of fear, the other from anxiety.

Micah quietly pulled his pistol out and placed a silencer on it, pulled the tape off Braun's mouth and in German said, "Make a sound and I shoot." Braun looked at Joey and pleaded, "Don't let them do this. It's a mistake. I have been a very good prisoner."

Micah interrupted, "You were a very good murderer, too."

"I was only following orders," Braun whined.

Micah snarled, "Following, hell. You *gave* the orders. How many times? Seven hundred thousand? Eight? Nine?" Braun was whimpering, in tears, and looked at Joey, who turned away.

"In the name of the Jewish people, I sentence you to death for murder," Micah said. With that, he turned to Joey and handed him the pistol.

Joey stood, staring at the pistol, then slowly faced the quivering Braun. He looked at Micah, who slowly nodded. *Thou shall not kill. An eye for an eye. Never again,* Micah had said. Next, Leah's tears as she told of her murdered sister came to mind.

Joey closed his eyes to calm down. It was the first time he would kill someone. He would cross a barrier of sorts. A place in which killing was allowed, for justified revenge. But could one life make up for hundreds of thousands? Even when he had played Cowboys and Indians in the woods around Sans Souci Street, he felt bad for the Indians . . . and the memory of shooting that robin with his BB gun had made him cry.

But this was different. These Germans had tried to eliminate a whole people. *His* people. And Micah had told him, as had others, that it wasn't just the members of the Nazis. No, there were plenty of willing German executioners. Men and women. Plenty.

Taking aim, Joey had to steady his pistol hand with his other hand. His shot rang out. Although muffled, it echoed through the tall pines and inside his head.

Braun' s body slumped, his head blown open. Seeing it, Joey drew in an audible breath and blinked. Tears flowed down his cheeks. He watched as Micah went through Braun's pockets to remove any identification. Then the Brigaders untied him and threw the body down into the river.

Micah came up to Joey. Without speaking, he put both hands on Joey's upper arms and looked at him, sternly but sympathetically. He knew how life-changing this was and nodded slowly. Joey held a long look back, then nodded "okay." As if in approval of what he had done, the clouds broke and a shaft of sun lit up the area.

CHAPTER 84

"Joey, what in hell are you talking about?" Al Moskowitz asked. "Staying in Germany now that we can get home? For what?"

Joey had told Al about his plan since Al was due to go home at the same time. "I'll be living at the Fürth DP camp, so don't worry about Josef," he said. "I've been bugging the JDF to get his papers final and his plan and they've come through. Tell your dad I'll stay on it. How's my friend Sondra? If you see her one day, say 'Hi.'"

"I . . . ah . . . do see her. Every day. Nights, too. We've become a thing, you know. She and I are in love." Al giggled like a schoolboy.

"Al, that's great!" Joey yelled. "I hope you're very happy. Like I am with Leah."

"Leah? Who's Leah?"

"It's a long story, Al. She's a refugee who is now in Palestine." They talked awhile and Joey told Al all about Leah.

Joey's plan had shocked his friends. Skip was the only one who understood, at least to some degree. "Jeezus, Goldilocks," Skip said. "To do something as drastic as this? I've seen how you've changed, but jeez, I dunno. What about your family?"

"Yeah, well, I know." Joey's thoughts were ping-ponging in his head. His father had written another long letter to him.

"You're an American, Joey, not a Palestinian," his father had written. "You've done your part for your country. Don't get involved in another country. It never turns out well."

How the hell would his father know anything about getting involved with another country? It was absurd. In some ways he wished his family could see the footage he had seen at the Trials, the ashes and smells at Dachau, and the Seder in Wiesbaden. Maybe then they would understand that Jews must have their own homeland. He sighed. *The world doesn't fucking understand. They gotta have a scapegoat, and they outnumber the hell out of us.*

"They'll just have to understand . . . like Louis has," Joey said.

"And Leah, what about Leah?" Skip said.

"She's doing her part and, and I'm thinking that sooner or later I will get her to come to America with me," Joey said. It was the first time he had said that even to himself.

Skip looked at him for a long time saying nothing.

CHAPTER 85

———

"Herr Sergeant," a voice said. Joey looked around. It was Braun's "watchdog." Joey was making another survey of weapons and ammunition in the warehouses. Somehow, to his surprise, the assistant had come up behind him.

"Guermann, is it?" Joey said, looking at the POW's name tag.

"Heinrich Guermann, sir," he said. Joey recognized the disdain when he said *sir*. "I wish to know what happened to Herr Braun."

"He was transferred to Frankfurt. They had a need for someone with press experience."

"Transferred? And he did not even say goodbye to me? I am his assistant."

"They told us to send him immediately," Joey said. *What the hell is going on here?* he thought.

"And without his personal things? They are still here," Guermann said.

Joey stared at Guermann. "Frankfurt had a vehicle just leaving here and told us that Braun could get everything he needed there."

"I do not believe this, Herr Sergeant," Guermann said angrily.

"What are you getting at, Guermann?" Joey said, angry also.

"I want you to tell me what you did with him, *sir*," Guermann said.

"It's none of your goddamn business, Guermann. Now get your ass back to work before I report you."

"No, Sergeant," Guermann said. He had drawn a Luger and pointed it at Joey. "You get into that room."

"Are you crazy, Guermann? Don't you realize you'll probably be killed for this? Give me that gun."

"And you might get killed if you do not tell me the truth and provide for my escape," Guermann said, pushing Joey into the room, which no longer had a door and was filled with spiderwebs and dust. Taking Joey's belt, he tied Joey's hands behind him on a chair, making sure Joey was visible to the outside. Then, walking to the door, Guermann fired two shots into the warehouse ceiling. He returned and positioned himself behind Joey with the Luger aimed near Joey's right ear.

"They will come now, and if you want to live you will tell me what happened to private Braun."

"Colonel Golbach, you mean," Joey growled.

"Ah, so that is what happened. He is imprisoned now."

At this point, two Polish guards and two MPs cautiously entered the warehouse, arms drawn.

"Over here," Guermann shouted.

The four separated and approached the door from both sides. The MP sergeant held out a rod with a mirror on it and looked inside.

"Do not be afraid. I will not hurt him if you do as I say," Guermann shouted.

"Tell them to provide a Jeep for us right away. We will leave and I will drop you off after we have gone," Guermann said to Joey.

"No way, Guermann."

"You are stupid enough to die for this?" asked Guermann, pushing the pistol barrel into Joey's ear.

Joey thought about it, then called out, "I'm not hurt, guys. He wants a Jeep and will take us outside and release me somewhere out there."

"You believe that son of a bitch Kraut?" the sergeant asked.

"Don't think I have much choice, Martin. That is you, right?"

"Yeah, Goldman," said Sergeant Ralph Martin. "I'll get a Jeep."

Five minutes later, a Jeep driven by Lieutenant Forner with Red Blake skidded to a halt at the warehouse door. They hurried into the warehouse and observed the situation.

"You sure you're okay and we have to do this, Goldman?" Forner shouted.

"Guess so," Joey called back. "Now, he wants you all to leave the warehouse after you back the Jeep straight inside and leave it running. Lieutenant, as we drive out if he sees anyone hiding on the door sides, he says he will kill me, okay?"

They did what was asked. Guermann untied Joey, then retied his hands, and prodding him in the back together they walked to the Jeep. He tied Joey's hands around the back of the passenger seat and headed around to the driver's side.

Suddenly, out jumped a POW who savagely smashed Guermann's head with a shovel, knocking him unconscious to the ground. Picking up the pistol, he rushed around and untied Joey's hands and gave him the Luger. Joey ran around to the fallen POW and called out, "Lieutenant, Martin, you can come in. I've got the gun!"

Running, with arms drawn, the group immediately handcuffed the dazed Guermann and started to handcuff the other POW.

"Wait, don't," Joey said. "He's the one who conked Guermann and released me." With that he shook the POW's hand and thanked him.

"He was a Nazi SS bastard," the POW said in German. "He and Braun both. They wanted nothing to do with the rest of us."

Hearing this, Joey tore Guermann's sleeves off and raised his arms. There it was, the double lightning bolt symbol. He then wondered whether to try to give him to Micah or let the others turn him in. Better let them hand Guermann over, and that's what he did.

The next day he promoted his rescuer, putting him in charge of his Jeep.

CHAPTER 86

The party in Fürth started the night Joey was handed his discharge papers in Lieutenant Forner's office. So much had gone down. The Brigade had organized everything for him. They had the Jewish Agency give him "official" papers appointing him to a job with them as a refugee coordinator. He received his savings from his Charleston bank in the form of a packet of money orders in US dollars, which the Agency promised to cash for him. His salary would also come in US dollars from the Agency. His room and board were arranged in the Fürth DP complex.

Looking over the apartment with Micah, Karl, and Josef, Joey felt a sharp sense of homesickness. He sat on the small, iron single bed. It was so spare compared to his double bed at home. He looked around at the grayish walls with their faded wallpaper. It seemed prisonlike. Once this had been a luxury building with fine apartments and wealthy inhabitants. Today, it was a ghostly complex with ghostlike survivors.

Karl and Josef had tried their best to cheer up the small apartment with lace curtains on the windows, which opened onto the small, wrought-iron balcony. They had found a drab, olive, easy chair with worn arms. Joey had brought some lamps and kitchen items and a fine Oriental rug he had bought on the black market. *More likely than not the rug had been confiscated from a Jewish family—a family that no longer existed.*

"Zo? What do you think?" Karl asked eagerly. "Now you are our neighbor."

Josef clapped his hands in appreciation.

Micah was quiet. He knew the apprehension Joey was feeling. He'd said to Joey that he had undergone a similar transition when he was younger and left his parents and moved to a kibbutz the Palmach had picked for him. He had brought a painting of Jerusalem for Joey.

"Next year," he said as he presented it. That brought Joey back to reality. This was to be his home for who knows how long, so make the most of it. From his duffel bag he brought out a bottle of French champagne, and they all made a toast.

"*L'chaim,*" Karl said. *To life,* thought Joey. So many millions could no longer say that. He was obsessed with the number. Six million. Almost a hundred times the number of everyone, black and white, in Charleston.

Josef and Micah raised their glasses and said in unison, "*L'chaim!*"

"Thanks for my welcome party," Joey said. "To a new chapter in my life."

After the toast, Karl presented Joey a little box with a blanket. "For Schatzie!" Karl said. He put it down and Schatzie immediately jumped in and barked. She had already become the pet of everyone on Joey's floor and was putting on weight from all the treats.

CHAPTER 87

Joey's official goodbye party was in the 318th Headquarters Meeting Room. The Nazi officers previously stationed there had redesigned it extravagantly, with carved mahogany paneling, crystal chandeliers, parquet floors, and a huge gilded mirror to make the room seem even larger. Colonel Larned had resigned himself to Joey's decision and wanted sincerely to thank him for his job as supply sergeant, which Joey had handled faultlessly.

The colonel raised his glass. "To Sergeant Joseph Goldman, RA 13181510, with our wishes for success on his mission." He took a sip. "Having personally seen the hell these poor souls have gone through, I wish the barriers the Brits have put up will soon be taken down." Everyone raised their glasses, shouted various good luck phrases, and downed the bubbly wine. Champagne was something new to many of them, young as they were, and they didn't know they were supposed to sip it.

Joey was well liked by everyone in the headquarters unit. He always approached others with love, and received it in return. But now inside him there was anger that he had to hide. He had been assaulted by what he had undergone in his two years in the land of the Third Reich, and the scar was etched into him, probably forever. Red had already been assigned to replace Joey and had offered to help him in any way. *He doesn't know what he's offering.*

"Living among the Krauts ain't gonna be easy," cautioned Frenchy. "You gotta be on guard all the time."

Joey smiled. "I'll be safe. Don't worry." At Fürth he had already met the Jewish policemen who took over as the DP camp guards after the Americans had left. As survivors themselves, they did everything possible to make sure no more ill came to those in their care in the camp. They were the opposite of the capos in the concentration camps. These were men who were only appointed to keep things organized and helpful, especially for the children. Honor courts were established to find and prosecute Jews who had used their positions as capos under the Nazis to cause trouble and often death to their fellow Jewish prisoners.

At the end of the party, Lieutenant Forner and Colonel Larned asked for quiet, and then the colonel held up a set of keys and jangled them. "No doubt some of you envied that special Jeep with the Ford top, heater, and radio that one of us had gussied up," he said and laughed along with many. "Well, you won't have to look at it any longer. I have authorized its transfer as a going away present for our departing honoree."

Everyone applauded, and Joey couldn't believe it. He took the keys and with tears saluted the two officers. The colonel gave him a big bear hug and then saluted back. The lieutenant handed Joey papers to make it official, then returned the salute.

CHAPTER 88

It was a night Joey would often think about. He wrote Louis about it. His letter ended with this:

> It is so hard to leave this bunch. We have become a family and the thought of leaving them gives me a pain. A pain I'm sorry to say that is more severe than what I feel about not coming home now. I love Mother and Daddy but in, well, a less personal way. That's hard to admit but I'm sure you know why. With you it's different. I know you're always there with and for me ... like these guys are. I've enclosed some pics of my new apartment and of Karl and Josef. Micah wouldn't OK sending one of him. Tomorrow I leave and it has led me to the voyage I'm about to take. It has been a life-changing experience.
>
> Take my address and write to me, please, Louis. I am involved now as I've never been involved with anything in my life. It's a good feeling but scary.

He put the pictures in and dropped the letter into the HQ mailbox.

CHAPTER 89

"*Ma shlomkha.* How do you do?"

"*Ma shlomkha.* How do you do?" Joey repeated after the Hebrew teacher.

One of his daily duties was to learn Hebrew. "You'll need it to deal with us," the Jewish Agency representative had insisted and Micah agreed. "It'll be necessary to know Hebrew to work closely with the Brigade."

Joey had never been required to learn Hebrew. The language was in disuse for several thousand years, but had been kept alive by the very religious. Now, here it was—the language of Palestine and the future state of Israel.

"*Ma ze?* What's this?" he repeated. "*Ma ze sham?* What is that?" Joey shook his head slowly. He had never been good at languages, but he was determined to learn this one.

On his first "trip" with Micah, he had visited a school for refugee children in Pontebba and seen what they were being taught. The instructor, a small, wiry kibbutznik named Meyer, had described it proudly: "They have to learn Hebrew, and, I would add, are eager to. We also teach them the geography of Israel, and farming and fighting. The children want to get to their 'promised land.'"

Micah patted him on the shoulder. "The underground Brigaders are helping to get them ready, so they can soon make the risky journey through the British blockade."

Joey heard a slender, young teen survivor pleading with his instructor to teach him to shoot: "I vant to fight, not farm!" the young man pleaded.

"You will do both. You *must* do both," the instructor replied. "We will turn our deserts into pastures and pray. As Isaiah said, 'We can turn our guns, rather than beat our swords, into plowshares.'"

Micah sighed. "The Arabs will not let us put our guns down. It'll take a lot more than prayers."

Joey thought of Leah learning to farm and fight. Her last letter had told him how hard it was.

> *Dearest Joey,*
>
> *I have just returned from a sixty-kilometer hike with full field pack to a new kibbutz in the Negev. You would not recognize me. I look like one of the musicians we saw in Geneva. This is a very hot country and the winds that blow through make it worse. They call it the* hamsin. *Sometimes you cannot see your way. If windblown sand were edible I would be fat by now. It's great you are learning Hebrew. It will make it so much easier for you when you get here. ARE you getting here? I miss you so every day.*

The letter went on, very carefully and with no detail, implying that she was doing real things, not just training.

Joey was both afraid for her and proud of her. It was unnerving to him that she was there and he was here. But both were doing something really important, he felt, and it helped to keep him calmer. Looking into the mirror in his room he said aloud, "Little Joey Goldman is in love with a girl who is risking her life helping others, and he could be risking his own, too. Jeez."

* * *

He would have been really unnerved had he known about Leah's latest exploit on a night patrol to blow up a bridge the British often used to supply a unit of the Arab Legion.

Leah wrote about it in her diary, but was careful not to write it to Joey:

> *Tonight we went out dressed as British soldiers in case we were discovered. We were silent and almost walking on tiptoes for over an hour. At one point tonight we passed by an Arab village. A dog came up and started to growl. I was sweating with anticipation and, well, with fear. Mendel Cohen threw him a piece of hamburger and we were able to continue unseen. Our sappers planted the explosives and we pulled back a distance. The bridge went flying into the night sky, and we went flying back to our kibbutz. It is terrible how the British confiscate our arms, while letting the Arabs keep theirs.*

CHAPTER 90

———

"The papers! The papers!" shouted Karl. "Josef vill at last get to America!"

He was in the courtyard waving a large envelope to show Joey, who was having coffee on his small balcony up above.

Joey jumped up. "Fantastic!" he yelled back. "Bring them up! Bring them up!"

Karl, followed by Josef, entered the dark hallway leading to Joey's apartment. It might have seemed like running to them, but running it wasn't. Those abilities had been left in the camps.

Joey and Schatzie met them on the landing, and he grabbed the envelope. Sure enough, it was all the required official documents from the Joint Distribution Committee, including the schedule of Josef's departure from Marseille on the SS America.

Micah came by that same afternoon with information about a mission. They were to bring six truckloads of refugees from a British DP camp near Leipheim to Marseille to meet a Palestine-bound ship, the SS Providence. This could coincide with Joey's commitment to get Josef to Marseille to meet the SS America. For the mission, Joey tried on a US Army lieutenant's uniform supplied by Micah that was complete with a fake ID and passport (he was now Lieutenant Forner, he noted with alarm). Looking in the mirror, Joey frowned with surprise and concern: here he was, honorably discharged but not so honorably disguising himself as a US officer—something he had never thought of till now. To calm himself, he remembered something Micah had said: "You are not being a traitor to America, Joey. You are helping your people in need."

When the day came the following week, he became Lieutenant Forner and went next door to get Josef. Karl and Josef were holding both hands together like children. When Joey entered the room they looked at him and began to cry.

Joey looked at the floor and pressed his lips together tightly. They will never see each other again, he thought. How hard that must be after what they have gone though. Josef, at least, has some family, but Karl has no one. At least I have the comfort of knowing I have family safe in America. Looking tenderly at them, he thought, *I will make sure Karl gets to Israel, no matter what I must do.*

Josef kissed Karl and leaned to pick up his battered valise. Joey rushed over and took it. Schatzie sensing something began to whine. Joey placed a hand on Karl's shoulder. "I'll be back in a few days," he said. Karl just nodded and patted Joey's hand. He could not speak. Joey helped Josef down the stairs and into the courtyard. Josef looked up and saw Karl at the window and waved. Karl, holding Schatzie, blew Josef a kiss. Schatzie was barking now. Joey sighed. *Gonna have to leave her to the survivors on his floor.*

They turned and Joey bundled Josef into his truck and headed for a rendezvous the next night with Micah. The convoy of six trucks, now with British Royal 78th Division identification, drove through the night. On reaching the British Zone, Micah asked Joey to convince the guards at the gate to allow them through.

"I am authorized to pick up POWs from your detention center in . . . ," Joey said, scrambling for a name, ". . . in Linz, and to transport them to a prison in our American Zone."

The guard, looking at the 78th emblems, had no idea where Linz was, or even if there were a Linz. As he examined the papers he looked at Joey with suspicion. "No one told me to expect this," he said. This was Joey's first mission in disguise, and he fought to control his fear. He remembered what Rafi, one of Micah's fellow Brigaders, had said when Joey asked him how they withstood all the stress. "But for the grace of God, they are you. You have to make up lies, steal things, back up others, and never ever fail your mission."

He motioned to Micah. Micah was dressed as a UK sergeant major. He offered two bottles of French champagne to the guard in a perfect British accent: "Wot say yew 'ave a bit of Frog champagne on us, guv'nor, for your troubles?"

The guard promptly grabbed the booze and stamped Joey's papers. With a smile and a thank-you, he ushered the convoy through the gates.

"Blimey, mate," Joey said in an almost British accent. "Yew are amizing."

They laughed and raced on. Josef, however, hiding in back under a blanket, was sweating with anxiety. His experience in captivity made him afraid of soldiers on duty. In the German concentration camps one had never known if it might be your last moment. He'd told Joey about when he was walking with a friend, who had suddenly slumped over and fallen with a bullet through his head, fired by an SS officer from his balcony. Target practice. Had the officer picked the prisoner on his left, Josef would have died.

At the British camp, using a different set of papers now from SHAEF, it was relatively easy to convince the officer in charge to turn over the Jewish refugees to the Americans. The Brits wanted no part of the Jews—not in their detention camps, nor in Palestine. Foreign

Secretary Bevin, speaking about refugees, had recently announced, "Jews should not push to the head of the queue."

"Chaim Weitzmann once said, 'The world is divided into two parts,'" Micah told Joey. "One where Jews cannot live. And the other where they cannot go." But the Brigaders were determined to change that, even at the risk of their lives, and so was Joey.

The refugees were crowded into the trucks. The convoy stopped an hour later on a quiet dirt road and the refugees were fed a brief meal.

It was sunset and calm up above. Below, the anxiety circulated through the group.

Micah asked for their attention: "You must be very quiet when we reach the Zone's border crossing." He showed them how the tarpaulins at the truck's ends would be pulled down and tied shut.

"But what if we have to . . . to urinate?" a girl asked. Some boys laughed.

"Unless you want wet knickers, hold it in," said Micah. The boys laughed again. The girl stuck her tongue out at them, and the laughs were even louder. Somehow the young ones managed to leave their horrors behind better than the adults. Only time would tell.

As they rolled back to the crossing they had previously gone through, a different British guard demanded papers. It wasn't so easy this time. In the lead truck, Micah had been supplied with a stack of officially stamped transfer sheets listing the names and titles and unit info of hundreds of prisoners. This was normally sufficient to allow passage, but this guard was cranky and decided he wanted to open the tarpaulins to examine the trucks. Micah insisted this was unnecessary. The guard, however, wasn't cooperating. As he reached for the first rope, shouting was heard and a pistol shot rang out. The guard spun around, drew his pistol, and cautiously staying close to the trucks worked his way down the line of vehicles. He came upon Joey, in his US officer's uniform, holding his .45 and peering into the darkness.

"Wot's going on 'ere, sir?" the guard challenged.

Joey pointed to a loose truck flap and said, "One of our prisoners cut his way out," he said, sternly. "He's headed into those trees."

The soldier blew his whistle and the sergeant who had received the champagne three nights before came running. The sentry told his sergeant about the escaped German: "It was just about when I was going to check the cargo these chaps are carrying."

Just then Micah appeared, and the sergeant recognized him. "Forget these chaps, Camberry. These 'ere are the blokes who treated us to the bloody champagne. Let's report the bloody Nazi quickly." The two rushed off.

"Thank God for champagne," Joey breathed. "I could do with some myself."

"Leftenant," Micah said, "Oi'm 'appy to see that yer such a bloody quick thinker."

CHAPTER 91

Every few hours they would stop at prearranged locations, where the refugees were given a meal and a chance to move about. They would then be hurried back into the trucks for the next leg of their journey. Occasionally, one of the trucks would erupt into songs in Yiddish or Hebrew, and the drivers would flash their lights to stop the convoy and Joey or one of the Brigaders would good-heartedly berate the passengers for making noise. They passed through the American Zone into France, easily for a change.

"Eat, drink, and be merry," Micah said to the two sentries on duty, and handed them a case of whisky and three cartons of Lucky Strikes. It was a common practice, and the Brigade took full advantage of it. Such was the currency of the day and the yearning for relief from the tension of the recent war. Two days later the convoy rolled into the camp set up by Munya Mardor, a Haganah officer in an American captain's uniform.

"Welcome, Lieutenant," he said. "It seems I outrank you."

Joey laughed and saluted. "Yes, sir. At least on this trip."

They both laughed. Uniforms and ranks changed depending on the mission. *Even so, as a Haganah officer he does outrank me. He's an officer in Eretz Israel.*

There was a row of tents for the six truckloads of refugees, along with warm clothing, shoes, toilet articles, blankets, cots, and hot meals. The refugees were overjoyed to be on the brink of an end to their horrors and the beginning of hope in Eretz Israel. As he knelt to help a teenager put on his new boots, Joey thought of the film of the piles of shoes outside the gas chambers he had seen at the Trials with Skip.

"You are American?" the boy asked in hesitant English.

"I am," said Joey. "Where are you from?"

"From Poland," the boy answered. "But I cannot go there anymore."

"No? What happened?" He knew well what kind of horror had happened.

"The Germans make all the Jews come to the square," the boy said softly, remembering the long bursts of machine gun sounds. "But I hide under a metal roof from one of the buildings they blew up." Tears filled his eyes. "I stay there till dark, then I run away into the mountains."

How many stories had Joey now heard like this? Each one made him angrier. Sometimes he felt like going back to Germany and machine gunning a German village. Micah would often calm him down. "Focus on saving Jews for Eretz Israel," he would say. "Revenge now comes second."

Since leaving the Army, Joey had been part of four acts of revenge. When the boy said "mountains," Joey remembered the last one. It had taken place on a mountain road, very similar to the one they had just traversed. They were in an Austrian forest, at another cliff, high above a river. The Gestapo officer acted with bravado, as if he could force his captors to submit to a superior will. Bound hand and foot, his mouth gagged, he tried to spit. Micah walked up close and spit twice, once in each eye. "I sentence you to death, in the name of the Jewish People," he said. Micah aimed his gun at the German's forehead, then paused and lowered his pistol, to the German's relief. Micah then nodded to Joey and motioned to him to give the German a push. Joey realized what he was to do. The muscles in his jaw trembled as he gritted his teeth. He drew his knife and cut the ropes tying the German to the tree. Looking him in the face, he hesitated. The German smirked, thinking he was being set free, but Micah held up a picture of the man in his Gestapo uniform, and Joey nodded and pushed the shocked officer over the cliff. He watched as the German splashed, hands bound, into the waters below and sank out of sight.

An eye for an eye . . . sometimes. Micah had nodded yes, several times, as if he read Joey's mind. Then he motioned him to get rid of the rope.

Shaking his head to draw himself back into the present, Joey addressed the youngster: "Where was your home in Poland?"

"Krasnystaw," he answered.

"I have a friend . . . my girlfriend. Leah is her name," he said. "She is from Zamosc."

"Zamosc!" the boy cried, excited. "That is so nearby to my town! Is she here?"

"I wish! No, she made aliyah to Palestine months ago. Like you will soon."

"Do you promise?"

"We will do our best, I promise," said Joey, and gave the boy a hug.

CHAPTER 92

Early the next day, Joey and Josef left the camp in a Jeep labeled "US Army," headed for Marseille. Staying overnight in the camp had made them late, because just as they were ready to leave, Micah had asked him to wait while he found something. Turned out it was a bottle of Russian vodka.

"A rare find," Micah said. "Just as a thank you for your help on this trip."

"Ah, I'll enjoy this," Joey thanked him. "But I gotta run to make that departure!"

He raced to reach the harbor before the ship was scheduled to leave, passing Port-de-Bouc, where the refugees from the ship Exodus had been returned to France from Haifa by the Brits. After the thousands crowded on board like animals refused to debark, even with a shortage of food and horrible sanitary conditions, the British sent them back to Germany. World public opinion was outraged by this act of cruelty.

The Brits had then changed their policy of returning refugees to Germany, but not their attitude. The Royal Navy continued to pursue and capture refugee ships, and after subduing the outraged refugees, sometimes killing them, they sent them to detention camps on Cyprus. The conditions were spare but reasonable, but they were painful reminders of the Nazi death camps where the refugees had spent hellish lives.

That the Jewish Brigade had fought so bravely for the Brits but now had to fight against them was hard for Joey to understand. Even more baffling was the fact that anti-semitism would continue after what the Nazis had done.

"You're always looking for justice in an unjust world," Louis had told him in a recent letter. The rabbi in Wiesbaden had told him that was one of the things that Jews believed in—justice.

Rushing into the port where the SS America was to depart, Joey had to flash papers at a French soldier who looked them over with suspicion. "*S'il vous plaît*," Joey said. "We are in a hurry. The ship is ready to leave." The soldier eyed Josef. Recognizing him as old and weak, he softened and handed the papers back to Joey and pointed them where to go.

Josef was bewildered by all this. "*Ich habe Durst, Joseph. Bitte, einen Kaffee, Joseph.*"

"I understand you're thirsty, but we don't have time for coffee, Josef," Joey snapped, and slammed the accelerator before screeching to a stop next to the huge ship. Its gangplank was roped off, and a young French soldier was there. "*Non*, Lieutenant," he said. "The ship is already loaded. No one else is permitted to board."

"But we have come all the way from Nuremberg," said Joey. "This poor man survived Dachau. He is going to Pennsylvania in America to be safe with his brother at last."

"Sorry, sir, but I am only following my orders," said the soldier.

Joey settled back slightly and looking into the Frenchman's eyes he put a hand on his shoulder. "I followed *my* orders to land in your Normandy on June 6, 1944. Is this what I get in return?"

The gendarme's mouth opened in surprise. "I thank you for that, sir," he said, sympathetically. Then, looking around, "The ship is now rescheduled to sail at noon tomorrow. Bring him here at eight in the morning and I will help you. My name is Marcel."

Joey shook hands with the soldier. "*Merci*, Marcel," he said. "I am Joseph, and this is . . . " He turned. Josef was nowhere in sight.

"Josef!" he shouted and ran from the gangplank area.

Down the dock, Josef was shuffling along toward a café.

"Sir!" a nearby gendarme called. "What are you looking for?"

"*Kein verstehen*,"— I don't understand. Joseph said, bewildered.

The gendarme tried in German. "*Wer bist du? Wo gehst du hin? Ihre Papiere, bitte.*" But Josef, of course, had no papers. They were with Joey.

After several attempts to get an answer, the policeman ushered Josef along to a small police station near the café. He shoved Josef gently into a small room that was salt soaked to a gray hue like driftwood. There was an empty cell in the back usually occupied when freighters had docked to unload. At a small, metal desk sat a young policeman reading a soft-porn magazine, which he hastily put into a drawer.

"What is this?" he asked as the gendarme helped Josef into a chair.

"I found him wandering the dock. He has no papers."

"Looks like one of those refugees," the young policeman said.

"My guess, too," said the other. "Let him spend the night here, and Capitaine André will speak with him tomorrow. He speaks only German."

"Okay, but André won't be here until one o'clock tomorrow."

"Well, feed the poor old guy until then," the older policeman said as he saluted Josef and left. Josef sat terrified, once again held captive by someone in uniform.

Joey ran along the dock shouting Josef's name with no response. Coming to the café, he ran up to two old men drinking red wine and chewing on strange-looking sausages.

"*Parlez-vous, anglais?*" he asked.

The men stopped chewing. "*Non, Monsieur. Que le français.*"

Summoning his high school French in desperation, Joey managed to ask if they had seen Josef. To his surprise they nodded and pointed to the nearby police station.

"*Merci! Merci beaucoup,*" Joey exclaimed and turned and ran to the station. Inside he felt almost faint with relief to see Josef sitting with a cup of coffee the young policeman had given him. They hugged each other. "Where were you going? I was so worried."

"I wanted coffee," Josef answered innocently. "See?"

Joey just shook his head, then turned to show the young man Josef's papers. "*Un réfugié Juif,*" he said. As he helped Josef up to leave, the policeman stood and told Joey that Josef had to stay until the captain released him tomorrow afternoon. An argument ensued until the policeman began to get angry and threatened Joey that he, too, would have to stay. Seeing the futility of this, Joey backed off and said he would return in the morning with help.

Where the hell am I going to get help? He stepped outside. *There's no Haganah members near here. Wait, maybe on board there are?* And he hurried back to the gangplank.

The young soldier was still there and greeted Joey warmly. Hearing the story he sympathized, but "*Quel dommage,*"—What a pity. He still couldn't let Joey go aboard.

Joey leaned his elbow against the gangplank's end post, closed his eyes, and bent his head into his hand. *What in hell could he do? How would Josef ever make it to America in his state of mind?* Watching this, the soldier tapped Joey on the shoulder.

"Sir, I am to be relieved in ten minutes. Maybe I can speak to the policeman?" Joey was amazed by this act of friendship. Maybe the French, unlike the British, really did understand the magnitude of what the Nazis had done to the Jews. After the soldier was relieved of his post, they started up toward the police station. Joey reached into his backpack and pulled out the special bottle of vodka he had been given by Micah as a thank-you.

"Maybe this will help get him released?" he said.

"Oh-h-h . . . Russian! That's scarce! This might well do it!" he laughed.

After a lengthy discussion with the soldier, the young policeman said, "But I cannot do it. I have written it into the report already."

Looking down at the report, the soldier slowly put the bottle on the metal desk next to the opened report. Then, softly, he said, "Looks like it's only written in pencil, officer."

They stared at one another for a long moment until the young policeman smiled and put the bottle under the desk. "Hm-m, so it is," he said.

Joey, Josef, and the soldier bowed and quickly left the station.

"I wish I had another gift for you," Joey told the soldier.

"You are here, and the Germans are not. What better gift than that?" said Marcel. "I'll see you here at eight?"

Joey gave him the double-cheek kiss he had seen the French do so many times and led Josef back to the jeep for the night. He thought about that bottle of Russian vodka. *I was looking forward to that*, and closed his eyes.

CHAPTER 93

Early the next morning, Joey was awakened by Josef moaning aloud in his sleep and crying out, *"Bitte, er ist gesund. Er kann arbeiten. Er kann arbeiten,"—Please, he is healthy. He can work. He can work.*

Joey shook him awake. "What is it Josef? Who is he?"

It took a few moments for Josef to realize where he was. Looking with tears at Joey he told him about his best friend in Dachau. "He was my friend from kindergarten," he whispered. "We were taken together. But he was a teacher. A gentle, fragile man. They used him for a medical experiment. And the freezing temperatures caused him to lose four toes." He sobbed. "So he couldn't work digging anymore and . . . and they shot him. Standing right next to me. Right next to me. Part of his brains were on my bunk."

Joey took Josef in his arms and rocked him as he would a frightened child. No wonder the Brigaders had formed a revenge unit. He remembered the story Micah had told him about Abba Kovner who tried to mastermind the poisoning of a whole camp of German POWs. They had managed to sneak into a bakery that supplied bread for the German POWs, and by coating bread loaves with arsenic they caused more than two thousand of the German prisoners to be ill. Many were hospitalized. "But no deaths," Micah had said, shaking his head.

They were at the gangplank at eight. A wet gray fog hugged everything, and it was hard to see, so Marcel quickly opened the rope. "Hurry. Before we are noticed. They will take him because I am authorized."

Joey gave the envelope with Josef's JCC papers to the uncertain old man and hugged and kissed him and in German said, "Hurry aboard, Josef. Do not lose these papers. *Verstehst Du?* Write to me when you have arrived."

The tears from both men joined the goodbye. The young soldier added a few of his own as well. Josef took Joey's face in both hands and said in German, "I love, you Joseph. I will never forget what you have done for me . . . and for our brothers." Then, picking up his small suitcase, he climbed as fast as he was able to the deck where a surprised ship's officer greeted him. Josef turned and waved his wrinkled hand slowly, back and forth, and then blew Joey a kiss as the officer ushered him out of sight. For a long moment, Joey stood there staring up transfixed. Then he turned to the young soldier and shook his hand, "*Merci, mon ami. Vive la France,*"—*Thank you my friend. Long live France.*

The boat issued a long mournful whistle while crew members separated the gangplank from the deck. Joey turned and headed to his Jeep, tears once again rolling slowly down his young face. What did Karl call it?

A mitzvah you are doing, Joseph. A blessing . . . getting us into Yisroel.

CHAPTER 94

Palestine, near Kibbutz Givat HaShlosha—

Leah's group of twelve young Palmach fighters were seated around a campfire. As usual after a day of intense training, crawling on their bellies through weed- and thorn-covered terrain and firing at targets planted at various points, they were eating, singing, and telling jokes. A Palmach tradition.

Reading her latest letter from Joey had given a lift to her spirits. He suggested he would see her soon. She frowned as she realized he meant he was planning to make the dangerous trip through Italy and the British blockade. But what if he ended like so many imprisoned in Cyprus? "Horrible," she said aloud.

Dov Hertzog, her assigned unit buddy, was surprised. "What's so horrible? The food? I agree," he laughed. They were given very little to eat on their maneuvers. "Get used to it. You'll be hungry a lot when the battle begins," said the leader.

Already the Arabs were killing Jews in spite of the British orders to stop. And the Jews were killing back. It was like rehearsing for the day when Eretz Israel would become a state by UN decision as the rumors foretold.

Crawling around at night, Dov had asked the leader about rifles. "We are twelve, but we only have eleven rifles. When will we get another?"

"When one of our soldiers is killed, we get another rifle," the leader said. This caused the group to go quiet. The reality of war was not something they thought of often. But it was there, especially when reports came in of Jewish deaths by the Arabs or the British.

One of Dov's cousins was killed recently by an Arab sniper while he was putting up electric poles on his kibbutz's fence. Leah had comforted Dov. He took this in the wrong way one evening, when he shook his head in sorrow, and she put her arm around his shoulders. Looking up at her, he tried to kiss her.

"Dov, no! I have a fiancé." She told him all about Joey and their plans. Dov was embarrassed, "Maybe we should switch to another buddy . . . "

Leah laughed it off. "Don't be silly. We remain friends and unit buddies."

Dov smiled in relief. The Palmach instilled in them the need to trust their fellow soldiers and to learn and understand each mission so that if all the others fell, they could still accomplish the mission. This philosophy would become an important part of Israel's future.

CHAPTER 95

B ack in Fürth, Joey told Karl all about the adventure with Josef.

"Ha!" laughed Karl. "Zat sveet old man wandering off like zat."

"Micah tells me you'll also be wandering off like that soon, so to speak," Joey said. "There's a boat leaving from La Spezia on the Ligurian sea in a few weeks, and he says you will be on it."

Karl beamed. "*Ja*, he told me, *und* zat I must practice not to drink a lot of water *und* not to overeating." The conditions on these ships were notoriously overcrowded, with sparse supplies. Where possible, the refugees were actually training for this, like athletes for an event. These events, however, could be for life or death because of the British blockade and the harsh treatment by their soldiers. Joey had heard too many stories of those who somehow managed to survive the Nazi death camps only to be put in camps on Cyprus by the British, but he took care not to pass that on to Karl.

"The port at La Spezia is called 'The Gate to Zion,'" he said. "It will be 'this year in Jerusalem' for you."

Karl closed his eyes. "*Wenn es Gottes Wille ist*,"—If it is God's will, he said.

Joey shook his head. "God's will? No, it's Micah's will." Again he marveled at how a Jew could believe in God after experiencing the extermination of half of his people.

CHAPTER 96

The next Brigade mission Joey joined was one of secret revenge. It involved going to a hospital for refugees. Because he was a representative of the Jewish Agency, Joey was accepted there as a regular visitor since his job was to help refugees. What amazed him once again was the Brigade's ability to provide fake identities and documents for their members. In this case a multilingual "Doctor Jerrold Fond," who was an "American Army captain," arrived to work with Joey. They spent a week questioning patients to see if they could find someone suspicious that they had been informed was there—a top SS officer disguised as a refugee. At night they would hear horrible dream screams, like the one Joey had heard from Josef, that made him shudder.

One night, night nurse Julie Reston reported to Doctor Fond and Joey that she had seen a patient drop a magazine on the floor from his bed, look around, then reach down very easily with his bandaged arm and shoulder to retrieve it. They looked at each other.

The next day a photographer from the US Army newspaper, *Stars and Stripes*, appeared with a camera and proceeded to photograph the ward for a "story." With a translator, he interviewed a number of patients and nurses and took their pictures. He casually included a photo of the suspected patient. Micah saw Joey and Doctor Fond two days later.

"This is who you have here," said Micah, showing them two photos—one of the patient and another of him as Hans Loritz, a wanted former Nazi concentration camp commandant.

Dr. Fond held the two pictures up and a look of anger crossed his face in a way that made Joey stiffen. "Tonight we will visit the ward, Joseph, and confront him." Joey knew what this meant and stared at Micah, who nodded.

That night, Joey followed along with the doctor and nurse as they gave each patient a brief examination. The nurse had, as requested, first turned up the AFN radio music in the room. "It will help calm them down," the doctor insisted. He pulled the curtains around each bed during this routine. When he got to the patient before the suspect, he sent the nurse off to her desk. "Miss Reston," he said, "you can start your report that all is okay in this ward. I'll check these last ones and come see you."

"I can do that later," she said. "I don't want to leave you." Captain Fond tried to insist it would be okay, but the nurse persisted. He couldn't order her. Joey was sweating when the doctor suddenly dropped a syringe needle.

"Damn it," he said looking at his charts. "Nurse, please get me a clean one. The next patient needs a shot."

"Right away, Doctor," said the nurse and headed off.

"Come. Quickly," Fond whispered to Joey. They approached the suspect's bed. The doctor pulled the curtains around for privacy and went to the side of the bed next to the patient's bandaged arm. Joey went to the other. The doctor carefully pulled a bed strap across the bed and handed it to Joey who gently buckled it around the patient. The German slept with both hands under his head. Fond held a thermometer to the patient's mouth and tapped him. When he opened wide, Fond quickly shoved a wad of cotton in and slapped tape over the German's mouth while Joey simultaneously tightened the strap.

"I wish to examine your shoulder, Herr Loritz," said Fond. The German looked shocked, and struggled as Fond slipped the bandage down a bit and forced his left arm up to reveal the SS tattoo in his armpit. The doctor then held the uniformed picture of Loritz up to the German's frightened face and shined a flashlight on it. "Herr Commandant," whispered Fond, "in the name of the Jewish people, I sentence you to death."

At that point, the German whipped out a Luger with his right hand from behind his pillow and put it to Fond's forehead. With his bandaged left arm he ripped off the tape and spit the cotton out.

"What do you think? I am a fool? I knew who you were immediately," whispered the German. "Unstrap me and move back quietly or I shoot you both before they get me." They obeyed. The German got out of bed. He was fully dressed. He had expected something.

"You vill lead me out of here," he said, "or I will sentence you Jews to death in the name of the Aryan race. Walk slowly." Again they obeyed and led him toward an exit.

Nurse Reston came back to the bed and saw only a syringe. The patient was gone. Puzzled, she picked up the syringe and, looking around, spotted the three heading toward an outside door. Coming up behind them quietly, she realized what was happening and jammed the syringe needle into the back of the Nazi's neck. As he turned in pain, Joey grabbed his arm, yanked the Luger from his hand, and threw him to the ground.

They held him down until suddenly he stopped and died. It was shockingly quick.

The nurse felt for his pulse and said, "Good Lord, he's had a heart attack. There's no pulse," she said.

Fond showed the nurse the SS logo under the German's armpit and said, "Who knew he was an SS officer in hiding? We were so lucky you came along Miss Reston. You saved our lives."

"It was lucky you left your syringe on his bed," she said.

"I've had enough excitement for this trip," said Fond. "I'm due back in Frankfurt tomorrow. Thank you, Nurse Reston, Mr. Goldman. I wonder if you could ask that photographer to send me a copy of the picture he took of us? Come. I'll give you my address."

Once outside, Fond took Joey aside. "This particular injection cannot be noticed, even in an autopsy, so don't worry. They'll stick with the heart attack diagnosis. Thank you for your help." They shook hands and Fond left Joey followed slowly.

Revenge again. Satisfying, maybe, but was it really worth doing? Can it ever compensate for the six million? No. It was revenge for Milton. That's what had made him drop out of college and enlist. He had tried to get into the Air Force, but his eyes let him down—he'd worn glasses since he was eight, so he was either "Four Eyes" or "Shrimpy" growing up on Sans Souci Street. *Sans Souci*, he thought again—"without care." Crazy. He'd had a lot to care about then with his sick father. He turned to look back at the old stone building that was the hospital. All his Charleston cares now seemed so insignificant.

The crystal-clear September days were ending, and the weather was turning cold. Joey got into his Jeep and turned the heater on. As he headed back to Fürth, he remembered what the rabbi had said after the Seder. *He must not focus on revenge, but on getting refugees to Palestine.*

○○○○○○○○○○◖◗○○○○○○○○○

CHAPTER 97

———

W aiting for him were several blue letters. The second one he read twice, in shock:

Joey, darling,

> *I just cannot do what you asked and come with you to live in America. I must stay and fight for this homeland. If you were here you would understand. You would feel the power of feeling that everything is Jewish. At least most of what we experience daily is Jewish. If we can establish a Jewish state then truly we would be living where the butcher, the baker, the candlestick maker are all Jewish, even the police and firemen. There would be no one to look down on you. Well, maybe the ultra-Orthodox, who look down on everyone else. I know how hard it would be for you to be away from your family, but it couldn't possibly be as hard as it would be for me to be without you. I love you so. And I'm so upset to write this to you.*
>
> *Love, Your Leah.*

Again, he read the letter, his heart beating fast. He had thought he would only be staying in Germany as long as possible to help refugees flee. Now he had been given an ultimatum . . . yes, it was an ultimatum to have and to hold or lose forever his Leah.

He barely slept that night.

CHAPTER 98

It was Friday when he returned to the DP camp from a trip with Micah. He had been thinking about Karl's imminent trip to Palestine. *Wait… Maybe he could go, too?* He could protect Karl on what was certain to be a dangerous journey, and then he could be with Leah. *Why not, damn it? But what would Micah say?*

To his complete surprise, Micah thought it was a good idea.

"I've talked about it with Alon and Mordechai, and they think you can accomplish several things," he continued. "We have 650 people ready. Many are youngsters. They have learned Hebrew, weapons, everything to fit in in Eretz Israel. And you can be the shepherd," he added. *"Ivrit shelcha he tova, nachon?"*—Your Hebrew is good?

"Ken, ivrit sheli tova."—My Hebrew is good, yes, Joey answered.

"And you have your British and American officer uniforms. So, you will be able to see that our Red Cross barrels get unloaded safely in Haifa."

"Oh, the weapons barrels?" said Joey. He knew how the Brigade had been smuggling weapons and ammunition for several years by sealing them into Red Cross oak and steel barrels, which the Haganah, disguised as British soldiers, immediately appropriated in Haifa. "I was planning to go as a refugee."

"You *have* to go as a refugee," said Micah. "The Brits would never allow you otherwise. But when you arrive, you have to put on your British uniform quickly."

As October approached, Joey and Karl started to prepare for the journey under Micah's guidance. They were about to review a list of to-dos when the office told him he had a letter. Excited to have something from Leah, Joey rushed downstairs. To his surprise and delight it was a letter from Wilkes-Barre. He rushed back upstairs and sat with Karl to open and read it.

"It's from Josef," Joey said excitedly. "It's written in English from Josef's brother!" Karl closed his eyes to listen.

Dear Joseph,

I am writing this for Josef. He has told us all about your care and concern for which we are eternally grateful. I will write now what Josef tells me to. Thank you forever for what you have done.

Dear Joey and Karl,

I am here safe and sound as you would put it, Joey. The trip was long but uneventful. My dear brother met me on the pier as planned. I was a good boy and didn't lose any of my papers, so it was bureaucratic but successful. You should see me now. They have fattened me up. My brother's scissors were put into action twice! First to cut my hair to make me look almost human again, and then to make me a suit. A suit! I wish you could see me, Karl. You will, because they will take my picture at Rosh Hashanah in my suit and I will send it to you. I wish you would have come with me, Karl, but I know you want to live in Eretz Israel. I have once again started to bake. Just for the family of course but it feels so good.

Joey read on then stopped as he got to the end, which he first read silently, then aloud for Karl.

> *I know you do not pray, Joey, but I do. Every day I pray for you. For God to keep you alive and healthy. I believe he kept me alive because I prayed, so I wish you would think about that.*
>
> *Love to you both. Please write to me. Josef*

They sat in silence. *I don't understand*, Joey thought. *How can he still believe? Maybe there's something I don't know, but I doubt it.*

After a few minutes Joey picked up the list and they began to review it.

Before his discharge, Joey had helped the Brigaders make authentic copies of both Lieutenant Forner's and Colonel Larned's IDs and uniforms, using a photo of Joey on the IDs. The Brigaders also provided him with a British captain's ID: Captain Phillip Jarnmouth. Once again, their ability to create IDs, official orders, uniforms, signatures, you name it, amazed him. His battered suitcase had a secret section in which he could hide these things. He knew all too well that if, or more likely when, the Brits seized their ship, the SS Paducah, they would confiscate all the luggage and herd the refugees into detention areas, then send them in cages like animals on ships to the former POW camps in Cyprus. So, before they docked in Haifa, Joey planned to put his secrets into a small backpack and find a way to don his disguise as soon as he hit land.

CHAPTER 99

The SS Paducah was a former American ship bought by the Aliyah Bet to bring DPs, currently held in Belgium, to Palestine. Although they had been provided with clothing and food for some time now, they were still weary and beaten down by years of incarceration. To their amazement and horror, they were told to don German uniforms, which would allow the lorries carrying them to show official papers and say they were transporting POWs to the southern part of the American Zone.

Then, to get into France, the refugees were to change into civilian clothes and be described in official papers as workers for a particular project in La Spezia. Booze, cigarettes, and chocolates, the currencies of choice throughout Europe, would accompany each negotiation.

Joey took Karl to Brussels to join Micah and the group selected for the journey. In the beginning, quiet reigned as the refugees sat in the abandoned brick barn on the outskirts of Brussels, looking at one another in their German uniforms. You could hear only the nervous breathing of 650 humans who had been terrorized by Nazis wearing these same uniforms. Suddenly, a thin teenager placed his first two fingers under his nose to imitate Hitler and raised his arm, saluting. "Heil Hitler's ass!" he shouted. "It's his only brain!" Laughter burst out.

"Oy! A Jewish parent's worst nightmare," Karl said. "A Jewish Hitler Youth!"

The ice was broken. Laughter and other jokes swirled throughout the huge room. Someone started the *Hatikva*, and the chorus of the hopeful joined to fill the room. Joey and the other Brigaders felt a surge of relief—it was a great start to what they all hoped would be a safe voyage to Jerusalem.

On the way from the British to the American Zone, the convoy stopped at out-of-the-way places that the Brigaders and the Jewish Agency had set up for food and stretching. The difficult part of this trip was keeping the passengers quiet. Their excitement about getting to the Promised Land created occasional bursts of song that Joey and the lorry drivers had to shush. "Sh, sh . . .", Joey said again and again. "A German prisoner would never sing in Yiddish or Hebrew." Needless to say, his words went unheeded. The lorry from which the voices arose would flash its lights to notify the others and put on the brakes to silence the singing—most often choruses of the *Hatikvah*.

When they reached the American Zone, they had to clear both UK and US checkpoints. Joey was doing his best to keep calm. *God knows what will happen to me if we're exposed.* He had always felt confident about the forged documents and permits, but now that it was for his own assignment, he grew nervous.

"Bunch o' Narzi bastards you got there, eh?" the British guard said, chuckling. "Mind if I 'ave a looksee? I'd like to spit on a few of 'em."

Joey laughed along with him. "They're already covered with that," he said, and he reached for his papers from the guard's hands.

Now, moving through the American checkpoint, Joey got out of the truck, his lieutenant's bars, battle ribbons, and Purple Heart in full view of the GI. "Looks like you've been through it, sir," the GI said as he saluted.

"Yeah, well, haven't we all," Joey answered as he returned the salute. "Got a few of them here to deposit in Nuremberg."

"If that's too far, there's a river a couple miles down the road that might do," the GI said, smiling. Joey smiled back, relieved, and got in the truck. Off they went.

Driving all night, they stopped to change their disguises into workers' clothes as they neared the French border. "Speak anything but German or Hebrew when we're in French territory," Joey cautioned each truckload. "You're hired workers for a project in La Spezia. That's all you know."

To the younger refugees this was like playing a spy game. "Do you have some tools for us to carry, sir?" a round-faced thirteen-year-old with red hair asked. It was the first time they had been able to act their age for a long time, and they were really into it.

Joey laughed and put his hands on the boy's shoulders. "No, we don't," he said. "What's your name?"

"Weinstock," said the boy. "Josef Weinstock." Joey showed him his real ID. "I'm Joseph, too," he said and patted the boy's head. "Now let's get moving." He lowered the tarp on the lorry he was in, and the convoy moved out, hoping to reach La Spezia by driving all night.

As the lorries slowly entered the area, the sun was just rising and a pink glow spread over the sea. The red tile roofs on the houses seemed electrified. There were tented centers for the refugees, who could finally speak, sing, or cry, which many of the very young children did. Italian helpers produced food and drink. Weary as they were, the refugees grew more and more excited. They felt as if they were just moments away from the freedom they so longed for. Joey and the others distributed information about the boarding plans and potential problems. The 650 men, women, and children, along with another 300 Romanian refugees, were to crowd into space originally meant for 100 crew members.

At two in the afternoon, the groups took what luggage they owned to the dock where the Paducah was tied up. The ship was one the Aliyah Bet bought for refugees by Jewish Americans as war surplus just after World War II. European shipyard workers had gutted the ship, built enclosed wooden superstructures on the upper decks, and created hundreds of wooden bunks and makeshift latrines.

Prior to arriving at the dock, Joey had changed from his uniform into refugee clothes. He went unnoticed, and took great pains to stay that way, careful not to talk to anyone except the Haganah member, Moka Limon, who would make the journey along with the volunteer American and Canadian crew members. The captain was Rudy Patzert, a non-Jewish ex-Merchant Marine vet.

Joey and Karl went aboard and joined the crowd. The Haganah had reserved two bunks for them. Each passenger had a little less than two horizontal feet of space on the wooden bunks. "Be mindful that these are harsh conditions," said a crewmember. "Your daily rations are minimal." The air below deck was already becoming heavy and acrid with the sweat of so many anxious humans.

"Will we have water, please?" a young mother asked. She had obviously once been very beautiful, but that was prewar. Now her face was hard from terror and grief.

"You will get every day a glass of water, a breakfast of cheese and crackers, some broth and crackers for lunch, and more crackers with sardines for dinner," shouted a Jewish crew member from Chicago. "Be careful, and make it last."

Joey watched as the infants, and women with small children, were quartered on the top deck. A tentlike roof of army blankets gave them some protection from the elements. Down in the hold where he bunked, the air was filled with unimaginable smells. It reminded him of the photos of survivors in their concentration camp bunks that he had seen with Skip. Would they ever be safe in houses again? He marveled that the determination of the refugees helped them suffer the conditions with courage. He made sure Karl was bedded down safely, then went to talk with the captain.

CHAPTER 100

For six days, the Paducah headed for Haifa. It had been shadowed almost immediately by British destroyers, and when it neared Palestinian waters, the order was given to repel British boarders with cans, water hoses, and any sticks or iron bars available. There were five British destroyers. *Destroyers, an apt description for what the Brits were doing to what was left of Europe's Jews.*

They broke formation and an officer started broadcasting. "SS Paducah. You are carrying illegal immigrants. I shall be forced to arrest you. Do not resist me."

Joey knew the Brits had killed and wounded refugees during previous boardings, and decided to fight along with the rest. He made sure Karl did not come up top. *This would be a hell of a place to die.* He found an iron crowbar and joined a line of angry men and women.

Then, at the last minute, orders came from Moka Limon not to resist. "We are so outnumbered we will lose, and I want no more deaths." There were some angry shouts from the crowd to fight on. He continued, "We shall face the hardships of camps in Cyprus, but we shall overcome."

So they put down what weapons they had, but they weren't telling the Limeys. The ships closed in, as they had done so many times to other refugee ships, and sideswiped the Paducah from the port and the starboard side. The old vessel shuddered, creaked loudly, and groaned, just as if it were one of the elderly refugees. The violent shove brought cries of fright from some of the refugees—especially the young mothers with small children.

The crew, meanwhile, was changing into refugee-type clothing so they wouldn't be identified. Crew members were also disabling the engines, so the Brits would have to tow the ship to port. An unsympathetic Royal Marine boarding party leapt aboard and overran the ship after firing tear gas onto the decks. At this, screaming refugees threw cans and bottles at the troops and ran away from the gas. Joey gritted his teeth.

"Goddam Brits," he muttered. "They have always hated us." He was careful not to shout and give away his American identity.

After an hour or so, the occupying force managed to tow the ship into Haifa. It was dusk on October 2, 1947. The pier was set up as if it were being readied for a battle. Lights swept back and forth; armed soldiers were everywhere. Groups of ten refugees at a time, with only what they could carry, were pushed down steep gangplanks. Their luggage, with what little they had managed to keep after leaving the death camps, was flung down onto the docks, often bursting open.

Joey stuffed his two uniforms into his backpack and disembarked with Karl in the middle of a group of elderly persons and mothers with babies. "Stay here if you can," he whispered to Karl. "I'll be back."

Once inside the detention building, he managed to slip into a small hallway, thus escaping the clouds of DDT with which the British were dousing the refugees. He hurriedly began to change into his uniform. Stripping down to his underwear, he stuffed his refugee clothes into his backpack and started to don his British officer's garb when suddenly the door was flung open, and a soldier stuck in his head and his weapon. Joey froze. The soldier, seeing the officer's uniform, was puzzled. "Put your hands up and turn around slowly," he said, pointing the gun at Joey. "Just what's going on?"

"I'm a Canadian with UK Intelligence, Sergeant. I just changed from my dirty underwear," Joey said. "My ID is in my left pocket. May I get it out?"

"I'll do that," the soldier said, and slowly reached in and read the ID. "Turn around slowly, sir, and tell me what's going on 'ere."

Lowering his arms, "I was aboard the Paducah disguised as a refugee to accumulate whatever information I could about what these refugees are up to. I am to report to HQ in Jerusalem with what I have learned."

"Very well, sir," the sergeant said. "But follow me to my officer, please." He picked up Joey's backpack and motioned for him to proceed, still holding his weapon handy. Joey followed. *Oh, God, if this ID isn't good, I'm in deep shit.*

Hoping his American accent would be accepted as Canadian, Joey explained to a bored-looking British captain his secret refugee mission. Fortunately, the officer was more interested in ogling a beautiful, young Jewish refugee being questioned than in listening. "Like to do a strip search there, Captain?" Joey asked smiling.

Startled, the officer looked at Joey and broke into a grin, "Righto, Captain." He reviewed Joey's papers and indicated to the sergeant to give him his backpack. "Sorry, sir. Carry on. One can't be too careful with these Jews, you know." Joey saluted, adjusted his uniform, and ran looking for Karl outside. Alarmed at not finding Karl, he went to the gangplank to get on board.

A sergeant major, standing sentry at the gangplank, stopped him. "Sorry, sir. No one except the crew is allowed back."

"But I have orders to bring this man in," he said, showing him Karl's picture and ID.

"Not without an order from Bureau Four inside, sir," said the sentry.

Joey looked around for the American crew captain, who was in plain civilian clothes now, and saw him coming out from the DDT area. Carefully he slipped him his tattered bag with his American uniform.

"This might come in handy in Cyprus," he whispered to Rudy. "Won't be of use to me anymore. Please look for my friend here." And handing him the copies of Karl's ID, he said, "Tell him I will do my best to get him here."

Then, mastering his anguish, knowing that not only would he never be able to get a permit for Karl, but might jeopardize his own entry into Israel, he strode out of the detention center. For all the world, he appeared a British officer and walked onto a city street next to the Haifa docks. He shook his head and clenched his fists in sorrow and anger that he had failed to protect Karl. As he saw the cages on the ship's decks that would carry Karl and the Paducah's many refugees to Cyprus, he felt despair. They had come so close to the Promised Land, but the Brits were bent on promising the land to the Arabs. They would ship the Jews off to the all-too-familiar barbed-wire camps in the Mediterranean. How could these be the same people who had suffered the Battle of the Blitz in England? Yet here they were, showing what Micah had said were their centuries-old true colors.

CHAPTER 101

Using another set of official-looking papers, Joey entered the cargo area and was approached by a British corporal with a Red Cross armband. He looked at Joey's name badge and saluted. "Captain Jarnmouth? I am Lance Corporal Mayberry." Recognizing the name he had been given by Alon, Joey saluted back and in a low voice said in Hebrew, "*Shalom*. Let's get the barrels quickly."

In the space of a half hour, the work party of disguised Haganah members loaded the many Red Cross barrels onto trucks and high-tailed it out of the area, quickly hiding the load in what they called *sliks*, secret spots hidden from British search parties. "Mayberry," whose real name was Reuvan Smilanski, constantly complained. "The oil-loving bastards confiscate *our* weapons but *supply* them for the Arabs."

The Jews' dislike for the British occupiers had grown with fierce intensity. Small, deadly fights were taking place frequently with the Brits, as well as with marauding Arabs.

It was an eye for an eye, and they were being increasingly poked out.

Joey was taken to a small hotel and told to check in and change into civilian clothes. "Please wait here and do not talk to any strangers," Reuvan commanded.

However, Joey's priority now was to find Leah before he would start any assignment. When Smilanski returned the next morning, Joey convinced him that as an American volunteer with military experience he could and would be a big help, but he first needed to visit Leah. Reuvan agreed to lend him a Jeep and gave directions to Kibbutz Givat HaShlosha. "It is far south of here," said Reuvan. "Near Tel Aviv. It can be a dangerous drive."

"Love drives us to dangerous things, Reuvan," Joey said. "Draw me a map."

"It's very possible you'll be stopped on the way," Reuvan explained as he drew the map. "If it's Haganah, show him this ID." He handed Joey a card. "Don't lose this, *ever.* If it's anybody else, like ETZEL or the Stern Gang, you just speak Hebrew, not English. Tell them your love story and hope for the best."

"I shouldn't show them this card?" Joey said.

"Not if you want your front teeth," said Reuvan. "They're not friendly with the Haganah. You know the expression. Get two Jews in the same room and you'll get three opinions. Haganah is on the mainstream left with the Palmach as their fighters. The Irgun Zvai Leumi is in the center. On the right is the Stern Gang, who shoot first and ask questions later." He sighed. "If we don't all get together, it's going to be difficult when all these Arab countries attack us."

Micah had talked at length with Joey about this, so he understood it was a problem. But it was still foreign to Joey to think that in the face of what was ahead for the Jews there would be such a lack of unity.

"When independence actually comes, we will *have* to pull together," Reuvan said. He gave Joey a pistol, some ammo, and a bear hug goodbye.

○○○○○○○○○◯○○○○○○○○○

CHAPTER 102

———

This was Joey's first look in the daylight at Palestine (*Israel*, he told himself) since he had been transported from the Haifa docks to his room at night. Mount Herman spiraled up majestically, with bright white snow on its peaks. The blue of the sky chorused in harmony with the Mediterranean, which shone with its own deep blue. Blue and white. A Zionist poem from the 1800s said white was a symbol of great faith, and blue the advent of the heavens. They adopted it for Eretz Israel.

The area was lush with greenery. It was nothing like the hot, sandy desert Joey had expected. Reuvan smiled as Joey expressed this. "On your trip south it will live up to those expectations in some places. You'll get some hot, sandy, scrubby land." But he added, "You will also see the beauty of orange groves springing from what was recently sandy earth. If we were only left to ourselves," he added wistfully, "it would soon all be turned from sand to the green of farms and forests, without the red of blood."

His pistol in his waistband, Joey took off in a Jeep along a route that had once been traveled by ancient caravans. It was both physically and emotionally beautiful. Happily, he was not stopped by anyone except an old Arab riding a camel across the road. He held his hand up to stop Joey and glared from atop his centuries-old method of transportation at Joey in his motorized vehicle until he had crossed the road. This was an ancient land, Joey realized with amazement. The Holy Land. Knowing this, he was so entranced with the beauty of the thought that he took his eyes off the road and suddenly came to a stop with his right-side wheels stuck in sand.

Getting out, he cursed his luck and took a shovel from the truck just as a younger Arab came riding by on a mule. Before he knew it the boy had tied a rope from the mule to his front bumper and gestured to Joey to get ready to drive. The mule grunted and moaned but slowly the vehicle pulled out. Joey stood gratefully by the boy and offered him a pack of gum. The boy smiled a wide-toothed grin and they shook hands. *Old Arab, young Arab, just like anybody else,* Joey thought as he drove away.

CHAPTER 103

He was amazed about what he had been told of Netanya. The British were still there. The fights between the Irgun and the Brits were focused in and around Netanya. There had been hangings of Jewish fighters by the Brits, and retaliatory hangings of British soldiers by the Irgun. Reuvan had told him to hurry to the safe house when he arrived. Tensions were high, so Joey left quickly early the next morning. Just as he was about to get onto the newly built road to Tel Aviv, a British patrol car stopped him. Guns drawn and cocked, the soldiers approached his Jeep.

"Get out with your hands in sight," said a lance corporal in Hebrew and English.

"I will, corporal," Joey answered in English, and pointed to his left shirt pocket. "May I reach here with this hand for my ID?" The soldiers looked surprised at hearing English.

"Who the hell are you? I'll reach for your ID," said the corporal, and slowly opened the pocket. It was Joey's British officer's ID. Comparing the photo with Joey's face, the corporal suddenly snapped to attention and saluted. "Sorry, sir. But what's going on?"

"I'm Canadian, with British Intelligence, and am reporting back to my headquarters in Tel Aviv. Been looking for a dangerous chap here."

"Any luck? These bastards are very tricky," said the corporal, handing Joey his ID.

After offering them a smoke and chatting a bit, Joey went on his way, thinking how glad he was he had that ID. His Haganah one would have most likely meant trouble.

He was driving by the amazing Roman viaduct at Caesaria. It was the site of one of the most important cities of the Roman World, the capital of the province of Judaea, founded between 22 and 10 BC by Herod the Great (37-34 BC).

He marveled at its beauty, but decided not to stop anywhere again until he found Leah's kibbutz. He was halfway between Haifa and Tel Aviv when he finally located the kibbutz, and when he inquired about Leah, he was disappointed to find her group had gone on some sort of mission.

"Any idea of when she'll be back?" he asked the young guy who had admitted him into the fortified kibbutz after examining his Haganah ID card. He looked at Joey in disbelief and said, "You think they would give us any information about what they're doing?"

Joey reddened in embarrassment. "Yeah, I, ah, I see what you mean." He took out the photo of himself and Leah in Geneva and showed it to the guard.

"Hey? You were an American soldier and now you're Haganah here to help us?" the guy said admiringly. Joey told him a bit about his ETO experience, and the young man finally said, "Listen, you can sit in her bunk and wait as long as it takes." In the tent, Joey laughed when he saw that same Geneva picture framed and hanging beside her bed.

Later, he was invited to go to the dining room and have some supper. Several of the kibbutzniks asked him questions, including a young doctor from North Carolina who had volunteered to help and had ended up at Givat Hasharon. He was happy to speak with Joey because so far his Hebrew was almost nonexistent, and what he knew was almost impossible to understand when overlaid with his Southern accent. "They just cain't understand me heah."

Joey finally went back to Leah's tent and lay down. His drive had worn him out and he fell asleep without trying. For how long, he didn't know but he was awakened by something moist on his lips. He blinked several times before realizing he was being kissed. Leah had returned in the early morning darkness. She was exhausted and longing to sleep, but finding Joey there was like a miracle and she dropped her belongings and fell on him.

"Is this an angel?" he said. "Am I in heaven?"

"No, it's *me* who is in heaven," she sighed. They had made love before, the last time only with kisses, but now their passion was intense. They slowly undressed each other and felt everywhere, exploring every inch. Leah, eyes bright, breathing heavily, asked, "Do . . . do . . . do you have . . . ?"

Joey, just as excited, reached into his backpack and came up with a condom. "Yes, yes," he exhaled. *Be prepared,* he'd learned as a Boy Scout. They made love until the sun came up, then fell asleep spooning on the small bed.

Joey woke first and looked at the clothes she had removed. They were covered with dirt and sweat. What had she been doing? He wanted to know just how dangerous her role was and after she had awakened and taken him to breakfast, he insisted she tell him.

At first Leah resisted, but finally agreed to speak about it. "We were punishing some Arabs for something they did."

"Punishing? For what?" asked Joey.

"For planting a mine, blowing up one of the trucks, and killing two of our boys," Leah said. "Those Arabs had been warned many times not to take such actions and we would not bother them, but . . . " she stopped.

"But what?" Joey persisted.

"But now we were told to get rid of the village," she said. "We stopped a mile away and got out of our trucks. The moon was very bright so we could see fairly well. Somehow we were not seen or heard. On a whistle, we attacked from three sides and shot a number of fighters. Most of them, as they often did, fled leaving the women and children behind."

"What did you do with them?" Joey asked, fearing the answer.

"We let them get their belongings and go. Then we blew up the buildings and left."

It was hard for him the hear this. Not just because it made him realize she could be in danger, but because it made him understand that this wasn't going to be a simple little skirmish but rather a deadly, hard-fought battle between longstanding enemies, both claiming this as their land.

For the next two days, they spent every minute together. Joey worked beside her picking oranges, washing clothes, watching children, and watching her study medical books. He wished he could stay and protect her, but he could not, nor could Leah miss her Palmach and kibbutz duties. Two days later, in a long, silent goodbye, the two just gazed at each other for several minutes, each breathing in everything about the other to embed their pheromones in their minds, caressing one another's faces.

With a kiss they grasped hands, then Joey turned and walked to his Jeep, turning once to wave. At that same moment, he saw Leah had also turned to wave. A thing that would become a ritual with them.

CHAPTER 104

—————

Arriving back in Haifa, Joey was awakened at sunrise by Reuvan. "Here are your new papers, your new ID," he said. "You are now Menachem Rubin, and here, Menachem, is your introduction to Kibbutz Beit Oren. Be downstairs in ten minutes and a truck will take you there. *Shalom*, and thank you for coming. Take your British uniform. It will be useful."

They shook hands and Reuvan left. Joey stood for a long moment in front of a mirror trying to place himself. He was twenty years old, not yet a legal twenty-one, and looking like a teenager. *Can you believe it? You're standing in Palestine, halfway across the world from home, in love with a Polish refugee. As Menachem Rubin, you who never thought about being Jewish, you're now here about to fight for a homeland for the Jews, and maybe about to die for it.*

He shook his head in disbelief, picked up his gear, and headed downstairs. *How the hell did this all happen?* A dusty two-and-a-half-ton Army truck pulled up in front. *Strange if this were one of those I supplied. It would make a good story.* If this were fiction, it would be, and it would manage to protect me from an Arab ambush.

Louis had always told him he was a good writer. *Jeez, Louis . . . so far away, so far out of touch.* For a moment tears came, but he blinked them away as he handed his ID to the driver, a young, suntanned Sabra.

"R-U-B-I-N?" he said. "Get in quick. You're one of the twelve tribes, eh? *Mazel tov!*" He laughed. "Let's get our ass out of here."

Beit Oren sat atop a hill south of Haifa. It was started by immigrants from Poland and Russia, and was being used by the Haganah and the Palmach as a base of operations. Joey looked up at it as they wound along a narrow dirt road that climbed to the top. As they came to the kibbutz, the guards at the gate asked to see Joey's papers. Only then were they satisfied, even though he was with a member of the kibbutz. The constant sniping from Arabs kept the Jews always on the alert.

Joey was happy to see that. He was beginning to understand that the Jews were already in a war—mostly against Arabs, but also against the British, who generally supported the Arabs.

"Back in 1929," Reuvan had told him, "the Arabs slaughtered Jewish families, even making a savage raid on a rabbi's home. They killed everyone. All the while, they were being watched by the British as Jewish bodies were hideously dismembered. Watched, but not stopped." Joey remembered reading about it in the book he had found at the synagogue in London, but hearing it was still a shock. "They did it again in 1936," Reuvan had said, "including killing many from Beit Oren."

Now, the tit-for-tat fighting was on the increase. Raids by the British were frequent to confiscate arms in Jewish villages and kibbutzim, while at the same time they allowed Jordanian arms to flow into Arab hands. Reuvan likened it to when the American Indian tribes were constantly attacking the first American settlers with arms the French had supplied. This comparison astounded Joey.

"In those days, a wooden wall was good protection," Reuvan said. "But the British are supplying modern arms, ammunition, and vehicles to the Arabs. A wooden wall is obsolete."

CHAPTER 105

The energy of the Palmach group at the kibbutz amazed Joey. They woke early and participated in various jobs from farming to construction for two weeks, then disappeared for eight days of training, and then maybe seven days off. But usually in those seven days, a mission took place. Joey's infantry basic training became a valuable teaching resource for the group. Remembering his platoon sergeant, he made them learn to take apart and reassemble in the dark the recently arrived Czechoslovakian rifles. He even quoted him about diving into some muddy fucking mess in the dark and needing to be able to clean your rifle. Also, he did it in Hebrew, which impressed his Palestinian mates.

They went on rigorous nighttime marches, sometimes creeping into nearby Arab villages and noting every detail for future reference.

On the next to last day of 1947, an ETZEL team sped past a group of Arabs who were standing outside the main gate of the Haifa Oil Refinery hoping to get hired for the day. The team threw a bomb into the midst of the Arabs. Six were killed and more than forty were wounded. It was, ETZEL said in a statement, "retaliation for the many ongoing deadly Arab attacks on Jews." But what it produced was a massacre by the Arab workers of forty of the Jews who worked in the refinery, with forty-nine more wounded. The bomb throwing was denounced as an "act of madness" by the Jewish Agency, but they also authorized the Palmach to retaliate.

The next day, Joey's unit was summoned to join an attack on the Arab village of Balad al-Shaykh near Haifa, where many of the Arab refinery workers lived. The village had been the source of many attacks on Jewish buses for years. Outrage over the massacre at the oil refinery gave many of the young fighters the mental wherewithal to go out and kill for the first time.

Joey led a small squad. They had to devise makeshift methods for carrying the Sten guns on their shoulders. Having no webbing, the boys carried grenades in their pockets and bullets in their socks. As night came, Joey spoke quietly to his squad, giving them encouragement. He was nervous himself. This was his first time in combat as well.

Around 10:30pm, they were given the order and crept single file into the darkness. They usually took to night fighting to take advantage of the smaller size of their army. All told in Palestine, Jews had about fifteen thousand fighters, compared to thirty thousand for the Arabs.

No one spoke, and they walked as quietly as possible. The path led up the Carmel slope. Close on either side of the village were Arab legionnaires and British troop encampments, so a swift, surprise attack was planned. "Kill as many men as possible, destroy furniture, and blow-up houses, but try to avoid harm to women and children," the order said.

It was a misty, moonless night, the village dark and quiet. Dogs barking occasionally made them stop and wait. The units surrounded several sections of the village, and then the attack leader fired a burst from his Sten gun. At that, Joey yelled in Hebrew and English for his squad to charge. Bullets began whizzing. Screams were heard. Joey blasted a window in the first house, then his men threw in grenades.

Rushing in, guns barking, they discovered several dead Arab fighters and a badly wounded woman clutching a small child. Then, firing started from a house across the street. "Mendel's been hit!" yelled one of the squad as he ran to help Mendel get to a medic. Others threw grenades into the window, after which all was silent inside.

The battle raged on for a half hour. Having destroyed most of the houses and killing a number of Arab men, the word spread to leave. Carrying Mendel on a stretcher, Joey's squad hurried away. Another squad in the rear protected the getaway.

Joey was upset by it all. Seeing women and children among the victims, especially the mother with the wounded child in her arms in the first house, was eye-opening. American soldiers were taught to obey the Geneva Convention rules of warfare. *Not that they always did.* War was war, and its object was to kill or be killed. But the next day at breakfast with the others, Joey expressed his concern. "Was it necessary to kill so many instead of just driving them away?" he asked.

Yitzhak Cohen, a burly dentist in peacetime and now a fellow Palmach volunteer, put his spoonful of porridge down and looked at Joey. "My younger brother, Moishe, was bringing us medical supplies from Tel Aviv forty-seven days ago. Forty-seven. Only forty-seven," he said softly. "His route took him near Balad al-Shaykh. They ambushed him. Cut his heart out. Hung him on a tree a kilometer from here so we would be sure to find him, and stuffed his mouth with his genitals." With angry tears he continued, "At his feet, they put his heart, with pictures of his girlfriend, into one of our medical kits. So, as the Bible says, 'an eye for an eye.' Does that answer your question?"

Joey remained silent. What might he do if he saw Louis strung up that way? He just nodded and looked away. It was not going to be a time of law and order. It was a time of survival for what was left of the Jews. The head of the Jewish Agency, David Ben Gurion, himself acknowledged that. "We are conducting a war," he wrote, "and it is impossible to draw individual distinctions in war. That may be unjust to some extent, but we cannot do otherwise."

Cohen growled, "We have to fight for our goddam survival just as we have had to do so many times over the millennia."

Joey dreamed that night about Cohen's brother, hung up like beef in a butcher shop, in the same way the Nazis had used the hooks in the Dachau crematorium.

CHAPTER 106

L eah was now operating full time as a nurse. She wrote:

> *Dearest Joey,*
>
> *The road to Jerusalem has become a constant battleground. Arab forces hold the high ground and are preventing convoys from Tel Aviv getting through without a terrible loss of trucks and soldiers. Jerusalem is under siege and the Jewish inhabitants are in need of food, water, medical supplies, everything. I'm working around the clock caring for young Jewish fighters wounded on the convoys. Too many times they tell me tales of recapturing places and finding their friends not just dead but horribly mutilated. One of the boys died on me this morning. There was nothing we could do for him. I am so worried about you being in such situations. Please be careful. Please, please, please. I so wish this war was not happening.*

The letter reached Joey just after he returned from an exhausting battle at Kfar Etzion, a remote village in Northern Galilee. The battle was led by Moshe Kelman as part of a number of attacks on the Arabs. Thirty-five members of the Haganah had been killed on the way to reach Kfar Etzion, and the feeling was that something had to be done to raise public morale. "We will prove no village is beyond our reach," the orders had read. It said to blow up twenty houses and kill the largest number of fighters possible.

The units under Kelman sneaked into the village at night. Joey headed his squad of seven and had to crawl with them up onto a small hill. When a flashlight blinked, he motioned to his squad to rush down toward the nearest house. Breathing hard as they stumbled over the rocky path, they rounded the corner of a small cottage as shots rang out from a window. Joey threw a grenade into the window. There was an explosion and a hideous scream. After a minute, Joey and two men rushed inside.

"Oh my God," Joey mumbled. Again, a bloodied woman with a child in her arms was lying dead alongside an Arab fighter. The fighters always used the women and children as cover . . . always, and Joey could never get used to it. After a brief exchange of gunfire, the Arab fighters who were not killed fled into the darkness, leaving behind those villagers who survived to follow them unprotected. Only one from the Palmach had been hurt.

Kelman ordered a number of houses blown up to prevent fighters from coming back, and then, since the explosions were sure to bring Arab Liberation Army troops from their nearby base, he ordered the units to head back to the kibbutz. They scrambled over rocks and through thorny sabra patches as quietly as possible, carrying the wounded boy on a makeshift stretcher. When he began to moan, Joey took a wine cork from his jacket and told the boy to bite on it when he felt the pain, so he would stay quiet. It was a trick Micah had told him about. They were, after all, deep in an Arab section, so speed and silence were important. As they crept back toward the armored vehicles, Joey rounded a bend in the gully they were following. Suddenly, there stood a small, frightened Arab girl. Joey silently put his finger to his lips, and motioned to her to leave quickly, which she did just a moment before Yitzhak Cohen came up. Joey held his breath for a moment. *No telling what Cohen might have done.*

When they finally reached the trucks, they quickly boarded to head back to the kibbutz. When Joey had first arrived at the kibbutz and heard about the vehicles, he envisioned them as armored half-tracks like those the Germans used, but they were just ordinary trucks with steel plates around the sides. The steel covered the cabin with only two slits so the driver could see, and several small holes for the boys to fire from.

It provided fair protection from small arms, but that was all. They raced back with the lights out, so the ride was rough, to say the least.

Later, he had to smile reading Leah's plea to be careful. He kissed those words and sat down to write a letter himself . . . to Louis.

> *Dear Louis,*
>
> *I can't tell you where I am but it's in a kibbutz. I am with a Palmach unit and we have been training, fighting, working in the fields . . . and training, fighting, and working in the fields. The Arabs are attacking all over the land. We fight back and are now almost wholly at war. The Brits are terrible to us. They confiscate weapons, and demand curfews but look the other way when Arabs attack. A young doctor here who has been treating our wounded said the British lion has turned into a snake. It's a good description.*
>
> *How this could come to be is depressing as hell. The news is that the UN is going to vote on ending the mandate and partitioning the area into a Jewish State and a Palestinian Arab State. Word is, however, that the Arabs will not accept*

it. Haj Amin al-Husseini, who was the former grand mufti of Jerusalem and a big supporter of Hitler, is lobbying to kill us all. He circulated fake pictures of the Jerusalem Mosque in ruins saying that the Jews had done it. But he doesn't know the fierce, and I mean fierce, determination of the Jews here.

Jerusalem is already under siege. My Leah tells me it's a crisis there so I'm thinking of asking to be sent to help get the convoys through. I understand the Arabs are ambushing them.

Please don't tell Mother and Daddy what I'm doing.

Love, Joey

"Jerusalem is besieged, yes," said Reuvan. "What your girlfriend wrote is true."

"So I would like to go help," Joey insisted.

"Hmm . . . I'm told there's a lot of refugees just off the boat. You could be of help to train them."

"I could do that," Joey said. "But also, I could help chase a few Arab legionnaires away."

Reuvan thought for a few minutes, then left to make a call. When he returned he gave Joey some papers. "Report there to Shlomo Shamir. He will assign you to whatever he thinks is best."

Joey thanked him. "And I will do my best for him . . . and for us."

Packing his materials, he stopped and wrote a brief note to Leah that he would be near her before long. Just how near he did not suspect.

CHAPTER 107

Under the command of Lieutenant Moshe Rashkes, forty trucks rumbled along the Jerusalem Road loaded with sacks of flour, meats, margarine, even a rare treat of oranges. For 100,000 Jerusalemites this would mean not just some desperately needed meals but proof that this road to the sea would continue to be their lifeline. Suddenly, shots rang out and an explosion resounded as a hidden mine went off, throwing the truck carrying the convoy's blockade buster into a ditch. Because the Arabs often pushed boulders across the road, the convoys had to have these bulldozers lead them. Joey was in an armored car at the back of the convoy. "We are surrounded," he heard over the wireless. The commander called for the truck drivers to slow down and not bunch together, but they kept moving until they had to stop, each almost touching the truck in front of it. The way to Jerusalem was blocked, and the Arabs began firing into the sitting ducks, and throwing grenades.

Through the small holes in the trucks and armored cars, the men and boys fired back with Sten guns, but they were trapped in the deadly heat. Several of the trucks tried to turn around but got stuck in the gully. The drivers scrambled out, trying to get into other trucks. Many didn't make it—falling, ripped apart by machine gun fire as they ran. Joey kept calming the terrified youngsters in his car. "Fire back. Fire back," he urged them. "Don't let them get close!"

For several hours the battle raged until, with Joey's urging, the voice on the wireless shouted, "Retreat. Retreat. Back out! Back out! Don't try to turn around!"

Those trucks that could went in reverse, riding on rims whose tires had long ago been shot out. The armored cars covered their retreat as best they could. Nineteen of the forty vehicles were left behind. Sixteen Jews were dead and twenty-one were wounded. Arab soldiers and surrounding villagers pounced on the trucks and, shrieking victory cries, they plundered the food and weapons like ants on sugar, and mutilated the dead and wounded Jews left behind.

When he had led the trucks with the wounded to a field hospital on the outskirts of Tel Aviv, Joey wondered if Leah might be here. He asked the admitting nurse, a stout young woman with a thin scar across her face that reminded him of Mordechai, the Brigade leader back in Germany.

She looked at his battle-stained face and smiled. "Are you the Joey Leah always talks about?"

"Yes. You know Leah?"

"I am Rivka Melsky. Leah is my roommate . . . my tent mate, that is. Come." She grabbed Joey's arm, "I'll take you to her. She was up all night so she may not be awake."

They walked through a room filled with wounded boys. You could see, smell, and hear the pain from all sides. Joey noticed that Rivka had a definite limp. Probably connected to that scar, Joey thought.

Rivka pointed to the camouflaged tent and motioned him to enter, then turned and went back to her post. Joey quietly lifted the flap and saw Leah sound asleep on a cot, fully dressed in a blood-spattered nurse's uniform. He pulled up a folding canvas chair and sat facing her, shivering with the memory of the battle, the heat, the shrieking Arabs, the wounded boys crying from pain and fear, and the mutilated dead left behind. Exhausted, he closed his eyes.

Once again he was awakened when she kissed his lips. He opened his eyes and stared into her blue eyes, threw his arms around her, and kept repeating, "Leah, Leah, Leah." This time she was the one prepared. Rivka discreetly left the tent to them for the night. Joey left just after dawn as Leah went back on duty.

He was consumed with anger now at the Hulda convoy disaster. He wanted to get into a head-to-head battle with the Arabs. When he heard that a young Palmach officer, Yitzhak Rabin, was to head up a mission to raze the villages on both sides of the road to Jerusalem so that convoys could go through without being fired upon, Joey applied for a transfer. It was called Operation Nachshon.

Persistently, he went through level after level until, through Shlomo Shamir, he managed to be assigned to one of the Palmach units. His experience as a trained infantryman who also spoke Hebrew clinched the deal. "We need you, Goldman," Shlomo said. "There are a number of untrained refugees in the force. You have the next five days to give your platoon as much training as possible."

"Five days?" Joey's eyes widened with disbelief.

Shlomo stared back, unblinking. "And you have to conserve ammunition, so you will only be able to let them actually fire their rifles twice."

God knows how they would manage in actual combat.

"Will we be using these . . . these bayonets?" said Roy Weinstein, a young American from Brooklyn who had volunteered over the objections of his family. His face said, "How could I do that?"

"Sure as hell may have to," Joey answered, "so practice it in your mind, like this." He had built a standing figure stuffed with hay like they used in Basic to practice bayonet thrusts. He turned to it and with a loud growl demonstrated a parry and lunge to the wide-eyed boy.

"And you'd be smart to learn some Hebrew quickly," he added. *Jesus, these kids are fresh off the boat with practically no chance to learn how to fight. The goddam Arabs have training and weapons and British officers to lead them.* "It's gonna be awful," he said aloud.

"What?" said Roy.

Joey just shook his head. It's strange how he looked at them as kids when he was only twenty himself. He was so far from the Joey Goldman who went from school into the Army. That Joey was a kid. This one had fought, and killed, and grown up, and, he smiled to himself, fallen in love.

CHAPTER 108

Operation Nachshon was put into operation a week later, in April 1948. Joey asked about it to Uzi Narkiss, who was to lead the first attack, "Nachshon? What does that mean?" he said.

"It's named after Nachshon ben Aminadab," Narkiss said. "He was the first to dive into the Red Sea that Moses parted during the Exodus."

"Why after him?" Joey said.

"Because here there are some firsts, too. This is the Haganah's first attack that uses a brigade-strength unit," Narkiss said somewhat bitterly. He was a short, wiry man with an aggressive manner, often a characteristic of short men. "The Palmach has been urging attacks for a long time, so now finally they listen to us. We will take Kastel."

"What's Kastel?" Joey had become fascinated with military strategy.

"Kastel is an Arab village that sits on top of a big hill outside of Jerusalem," said Narkiss. As he talked, he drew a battle plan in the sand with an olive branch, Joey noticed. *Odd, but it was just a saying.*

"Here is Jerusalem and the road from Tel Aviv. Kastel looks down on and dominates both," he continued. "It has been an important fort since it was built by the Romans. Richard the Lionhearted used it during the Crusades." He spat before he continued, "Many Jews have died around here over the centuries, and many more will die before we're finished. But this time *we* will win."

Joey nodded and swallowed. "Can I go with you?"

Narkiss smiled. "I wish you could, but you're assigned to Yosef Tabenkin. The boys you've been training are his."

Several nights later, Narkiss's unit scrambled up the barren, rocky mountainside and surprised the Arabs who fled after only a brief resistance. Kastel was theirs. Narkiss turned it over to a Haganah unit led by Mordechai Gazit. "Destroy the buildings and dig in. They will counterattack."

And they did, but after four days Kastel was still in Jewish hands. By then, Gazit's force was down to barely seventy, and they were exhausted. But more attacks on the Jews were to come and leading them was Abdul al-Khader al-Husseini himself, a fiery, passionate man who had once led Arabs against the British in 1936. It did not go well for him or for the Jews. Climbing the hill in the fog, with his usual bandoliers across his chest and wearing a red Arab keffiyeh headdress, he was hit by machine gun fire and only discovered the next morning. His followers thought he had been captured, so the word spread that another Arab attack on Kastel would be immediate. Two thousand angry Arabs from Jerusalem and surrounding villages gathered to climb the slopes. They poured heavy fire onto Gazit's weakened band. Finally, Gazit ordered a retreat and fought their way down the hill as the Arabs shrieked victorious cries and raised an Arab flag on the main village house, the mukhtar's home. Kastel was now theirs again.

Suddenly, however, someone stumbled onto the body of al-Khader, and the cries became not those of victory but those of a wake, pain and grief, no longer exhilaration. They carried their dead leader down the mountain shrieking, wailing, and heartbroken. Left behind were only fifty Arab fighters.

Yigael Yadin, outraged at learning that Kastel had been retaken by the Arabs, demanded of Yosef Tabenkin that he immediately take it back. "We need to command the heights for Jerusalem's sake!" he shouted.

A fierce argument ensued. Joey, watching this, couldn't believe the arguing, something he had never seen in the US Army, and probably never would have. The round-faced, beefy Tabenkin stood toe to toe with Yadin. "I only have a platoon of thirty sleep-deprived men who could never win a fight up there in broad daylight." Finally, when calmed by Yadin's assistant, he agreed to attack—but not until that night.

He turned to Joey. "Let's go, boychik. We need some rest and supplies."

Back at their HQ in Kiryat Anavim, Tabenkin downed a cup of vodka in one gulp and told the seemingly lifeless platoon he assembled to rest until sundown.

"I don't expect you to do more than you can," he said, then he smiled at them. "But you always do." They laughed in appreciation and dispersed to find somewhere to lie down for as long as they could.

That night the platoon began climbing the circular, barren-hillside path in several groups. It was difficult to climb, be quiet, and ready for a sniper attack all at once. Joey was in the lead. The bright moonlight gave them little protection, but they didn't know that the fifty fighters who were left after the mass retreat of the Arabs for Abdul al-Husseni's funeral had been told to leave the ancient mountain fortress and were in the process of doing so. With guns and bayonets at the ready, the platoon advanced under the cover of mortar fire. The remaining Arabs, however, began firing as they prepared to abandon the battle-torn village of stone houses.

"Follow me!" Tabenkin yelled. He, David Elazar, and Joey rushed ahead on the rocky path, their guns spitting bullets left and right at the unseen enemy. Joey rounded a battered stone hut and jumped up onto a small terrace wall.

Realizing he needed to reload, he hurriedly grabbed a cartridge clip when from around a wall a young Arab fighter leapt, aiming at Joey. "Hands op!" he yelled in English. "Surendair!"

Surprised, Joey raised his hands, holding his rifle and bayonet like a spear. "Okay! Okay!" he said. Then, calling on his training with Smitty in the Nuremberg stadium, he threw his rifle at the boy, who fired at Joey just as the bayonet plunged into his chest. The bullet tore into Joey's stomach, doubling him over with pain, and he fell over the low wall, landing on his back next to the dying boy.

Whimpering in pain, the boy tearfully cried out, "Mama, Mama!" and turned toward Joey. He stretched out his hand, seeking comfort. Barely able to see or think, Joey reached out and grasped the small bloody hand and closed his eyes.

At the cost of eighteen more Jews, Kastel was once again under Jewish control. The two of them lay there, Arab and Jew hand in hand. Dying in a struggle that had been going on for centuries—a tribal struggle neither of them could accurately define. Now fighting over land that both peoples had sometimes shared peacefully, proving it could be done, until leaders who only wanted their way decided otherwise.

"Louis! Leah!" Joey cried out as his awareness faded into blackness. Little Joey Goldman from the gentle cocoon of Charleston lay now in the Holy Land, on a centuries-old terrace, its stones staining slowly with his blood.

CHAPTER 109

The blackness turned to a soft, bright whiteness. Opening his eyes slowly, Joey saw the face of an angel hovering above him.

"But I never believed in heaven," he whispered, and started to get up.

A jolt of agonizing pain shot through him. He screamed, and the angel gently lowered him back down.

"Easy, Joey. Easy," the angel said.

"You know my name?" Joey whispered.

"Your stomach was in shreds."

He shook his head. What was happening? Where was he? "Where? What?" he stammered.

"You're in the hospital, darling," Leah cried. "You're alive. Alive. They found you just in time."

"My God," he said, his head slowly clearing. "I thought I was in heaven, and you were an angel."

Leah laughed and kissed his forehead. "Well, then, I am your angel," she said with an amused frown. "Or so you've told me several times."

"You are. You are," he said, wincing. "Tell me what's happened."

Leah said they had found him unconscious, holding hands with the Arab boy. "They told me it was such a pitiful, moving scene. Arab and Jew, who used to live together in peace, in that village, now united only in death."

"They can thank the grand mufti of Jerusalem for this," chimed in Rivka, who was standing next to Leah. "The bastard sided with Hitler and now he's siding with the British. He's always hated us"

"The boy is he . . . ?" Joey said.

"Dead?" Leah asked. "No. we were able to keep him alive, but barely."

"Oh, thank God," Joey said. "I didn't want to kill him."

"Why not?" Rivka muttered. "He tried to kill you."

Leah rolled her eyes at Joey, who managed a small smile mixed with a grimace of pain.

Joey passed the next few days in and out of consciousness. Finally, his head cleared and he started worrying about when he would be able to join the battle again, to Leah's strong disapproval. She said the doctors all felt it would be a long time, but Joey had now become just as fierce in his love of this Jewish homeland as those he had met when he first arrived. He was determined to rejoin the Harel Brigade led by Yitzhak Rabin, so he did everything exactly as the doctors advised, and recovered quickly.

When he was able to get out of bed, the first thing he asked Leah was where he could find the Arab boy. "Is he still here?"

"He is," she said.

"I want to see him. Is he doing okay?"

"He's only eleven, so he's gaining strength every day," Leah said softly.

"Eleven? And I bayonetted him. That's so young to be a warrior. It's crazy."

Leah walked him slowly through two long rooms of hospital beds with wounded Israeli soldiers, most of whom were young. *None were as young as eleven, though.*

Crossing into a smaller ward guarded by two Israeli policemen, Joey and Leah walked to the bed where the boy lay. He looked at Joey and his eyes widened and tears began flowing.

"I am sorry. I am sorry," he kept repeating in Arabic, then Hebrew, then English. "I did not want to shoot. Please. Please," he cried. "I was so scared."

Slowly Joey moved to the end of the bed and looked at the information tag. "Adel Bashir? And you speak all those languages?" said Joey. "Don't cry. I am so happy you're alive, Adel."

Adel stopped crying and looked at Joey in wonder. "You are? You are not angry?"

"I am not angry," Joey said, and smiled.

"And I am so happy you're alive, sir, so very happy." The boy tried to sit up and winced in pain.

"Relax," Joey said. "My name is Joey. I will come back to see you soon. *Shalom.*"

"*Shalom,*" whispered the boy.

Walking back to Joey's ward Leah raised his hand and gave it a kiss.

"What?"

"I love who you are," she answered.

CHAPTER 110

———

The State of Israel was declared on May 14, 1948, to huge, joyous celebrations by the Jews, even as the fighting continued.

Five Arab armies attacked in response to the UN's announcement.

The next day, Micah checked in on him. During the months in Germany, and now in Israel, they had become close friends on and off the battlefield. Hearing of Joey's wounding, Micah had come to thank him for all he had done.

"You have taken a . . . a noble journey, Joey," Micah said as he helped Joey walk along the hospital corridor. "But you must take it easy now."

Joey smiled. "Sure, that's me—old take-it-easy Goldman."

But he had to take it easy. His stomach had been badly damaged and required several operations, including removing a chip from his spine caused by the boy's bullet. In the weeks of recovery, Joey and little Adel met for walks and lunches. He found that a bond was forming between them. With Micah's and Leah's help, Joey was given the right to supervise Adel and keep him from being sent to a detention camp.

Now, with Joey's discharge from the hospital, he and Leah returned to the apartment they had taken in Tel Aviv. The insistent Joey also received permission to have young Adel with him. The boy was smart and eager to stay in Israel, as Joey had found out when he questioned him earlier.

"You don't want to return home?" Joey asked. "Why not? Don't you want to be with your family? Your parents must be frantic about what has happened to you."

"My parents are dead," Adel said. "Since I was one."

"What?" Joey said, alarmed. "What happened to them? Who raised you?"

"I was sent to my uncle after they were killed."

"Killed?" Joey asked. "How were they killed?"

"My father was a teacher. He and my mother resisted the bad men led by the grand mufti in 1937. They hanged them both."

"Oh, my God," said Joey. "In the Arab revolt against the British and the Jews?"

"Arabs killing Arabs, too!" Adel spat. "So I was given to my uncle. It was he who forced me to fight," Adel continued. "He has learned nothing from the past. Nothing. I hate him."

"And you think staying in Israel will be a better life?" asked Joey.

"In Israel I think I will not be taught to hate," said Adel tearfully. "Tell me this is true, sir, please."

Joey could not resist. He put his arm around the boy and said, "I believe that is true, Adel. I believe that is true."

CHAPTER 111

A truce was declared in early June 1948 just when Joey wanted to report back to duty. Leah pleaded with him to take more time to be physically ready.

Joey's focus on strenuous exercising each day added to Leah's fear.

"From everything I hear around here, the truce won't last long and I wanna be ready when it's over," Joey said.

Then, on July 8, the Egyptians violated the truce and Joey reported to Yadin's HQ and was accepted for active duty. He fought in battle after battle until a cease-fire and Arab defeat were finally agreed upon in mid-1949 with a working acceptance of Israel. Though this peace was not recognized by the Arab states. In March of that year, the singing of Hatikvah by the Negev brigade soldiers in Eilat, which they had captured, became to many the formal conclusion of the war.

Jerusalem, however, was still in enemy hands. Israel was now a homeland but "Next Year in Jerusalem" was still only a hope. The Jordanians had destroyed all the synagogues. This was now a time for the Jews to clean up and become more than a homeland. Now Israel must become a nation.

Joey and Leah settled in their small flat in Tel Aviv. Joey arranged with Morad Khayri, his Arab teacher friend in Jaffa, to take Adel into his care.

When he heard the news that he would be living with a kind teacher like his parents, Adel burst into tears, ran across the room, leapt into Joey's arms, and hugged both Joey and Leah fiercely.

"He is a good boy, as far as I can tell after this short time," said Morad.

"I am sure he's good, and smart, too," said Joey.

They were having coffee at a small Jaffa place. The city was being repaired after the devastation caused by both local Arabs and British fights with the Irgun just before the war started, and after that from invading Arab armies. Joey had been in Jaffa and helped Morad when the Irgun had tried to loot his home. He had convinced Morad to stay, and not flee.

"Do you know what *adel bashir* means in Arabic?" asked Morad.

"No," said Joey.

"*Adel* means *just,* in the sense of being, how do you say, morally correct? *Bashir* means *the bearer of good news,* said Morad. "His parents were obviously *just* people."

"I hope that's a good omen for him," said Joey. "He told me he wants to be a teacher, like his father."

"I shall do my best to help him in that," said Morad.

CHAPTER 112

———

Leah planned to study to become a doctor and was checking out schools. Joey had no idea what to pursue himself. It could be a career in the Army, which Micah was pressuring him to do, or perhaps another occupation. He was only twenty-one, and there were so many needs in this newborn country.

One morning, they were walking along Dizengoff Street when they passed an Israeli in his car, with his child beside him, arguing with a young English-speaking man sitting in a parking place on his motorbike. He was gesturing badly for the biker to let him have the parking spot. The biker was finishing a coffee and a bun and didn't want to move. The Israeli wasn't nasty but was very frustrated. Joey stepped in and, having heard what the Israeli had asked, said to the man, "Excuse me for butting in, but are you aware of what he is saying?" pointing to the driver.

"I don't know. I don't speak Hebrew," said the man. "All I know is I'm parked here and I'm going to finish my breakfast. Period."

"Well, that's okay, but he has a sick child with him, and the doctor's office is right here. He's asking you to move your bike up on the sidewalk."

The man turned quickly and looked into the car and jumped up. "Sorry. Sorry!" he said. "Sure, I'll move." He stuffed the bun in his mouth, handed Joey his coffee cup, then pushed the bike up onto the sidewalk and smiled at the driver, who smiled back and pulled into the spot. They shook hands with each other and with Joey and thanked him. Leah watched the whole thing, smiling.

"Can I suggest something?" she said as they resumed their walk.

"What?" Joey said, puzzled. "Of course. About what?"

"About what just happened."

"About that argument?" he asked.

"About what you did to solve it," she said. "You knew both languages. How about becoming an English language teacher? They're going to need to know English here for sure."

Joey looked at her for a long moment. "You think so? Really?"

Leah said, "I know so. I looked through the school catalog's courses and I saw a language section."

That night, as they sat on their tiny terrace having a drink, they examined the courses. Joey became enthused about the idea as they talked it through. After sitting in silence for a few moments looking out at the night, Joey smacked his hand down on the table. He got up, squeezed around the table to face Leah. Kneeling awkwardly down on one knee, he grabbed Leah's left hand.

"Leah Chalovitz, you are not only beautiful but very smart and I must, I absolutely must, spend the rest of my life with you."

Leah put her other hand to her mouth, trying to hide a huge smile. "At last . . . you want to marry me?"

"I want to marry you," he said.

She drew him to her, gave him a big kiss, then squealed, "Yes! Yes! Yes!"

They were about to go inside to make love when the doorbell rang.

"Damn it," said Joey. "Let's ignore it."

"We can't," laughed Leah and she opened the door.

"Oh my God," shouted Joey. Karl was standing there, grinning and crying at the same time. Joey knew Karl was coming, having arranged it with the Jewish Agency, but this was a surprise.

"They told me it was next month," Joey said excitedly as he swung Karl around in his arms.

"Your American officer, you remember? He made it happen sooner!" Karl cried out. If lovemaking was forgotten, loving wasn't. They spent the night catching up.

"You are our first wedding present," Leah announced at breakfast.

"Married? You're married?" Karl said, wide-eyed.

"Not yet," Joey explained. "But we will be soon. This is a person I'm lucky to spend my life with." He took both her hands. "That was a wonderful thing you just said to Karl."

Leah blushed and murmured, "Thanks."

"We're going to Charleston to be married," he told Karl.

"Oh, I see. I, ah, I understand, but I wish I could be there," Karl said sadly.

"I wish, too," Joey said, giving Karl another hug. "But you will be here for us when we return."

"You will return? You will live in Israel?" Karl said, now excited.

"We will!" Leah and Joey said in unison.

"A toast, then," Karl said raising his coffee cup. "*L'chaim*. This year in Israel and next year in Jerusalem."

They clinked coffee cups.

CHAPTER 113

—————

Joey brought Leah home to Charleston to meet his family and get married. Being back on Sans Souci Street brought mixed emotions and many memories, both good and bad. He stood on the front porch with Leah and pointed out the Ashley River through the graceful old live oak trees bearded with Spanish moss, and thought of the robin he'd killed with a BB gun. The small dock where he had crabbed with his mother was there, and it reminded him of Micah. And there, too, was the creek where Louis had gone out in his ridiculous homemade boat— Louis, who couldn't swim a stroke but could swim with ease through Tolstoy and Shakespeare. How could he leave all this again?

The family was thrilled. "So, you've finally come to your senses and come home?" his father said. "I'm so happy for you. She'll love it here."

Joey started to say something but held back. *I just can't tell him now that we want to go back to Israel.* Joey's mother couldn't stop hugging both of them. She took Leah to her weekly mah-jongg game, and the ladies "oohed" and "ahed" over the blushing bride-to-be.

"LD," as Joey's mother called his father, was not to be outdone and invited them to come to his Saturday night poker game, held in a special room he had built into the basement, where he proudly introduced them. Leah choked on the smoke from the cigars the players puffed on, so LD turned on a special electric exhaust fan he had built into the only wall that faced the outside. The smoke wafted away immediately. *He hasn't lost his touch.*

Two nights before the wedding, they were having dinner and the phone rang. His father answered it. "It's for you, Joey," he said. "Sounds like some damn German. Who the hell could that be?"

Joey jumped up and went to the phone. "Hello?" he said.

"Hallo to you," Josef said in English. "I vant to say happy vedding!"

Then Josef went back to German and told Joey how he wished he could be there, but that his old beaten-up body told him "don't even think about it." Joey was in tears as he listened, and, switching also to German, said finally, "You will always be with us, Josef. Not to worry, and you know that Karl is waiting for us in Tel Aviv."

"You are going back to Israel?" Josef asked in surprise.

Joey, realizing he hadn't told the family yet, replied in German in a low voice. "Yes, but I haven't told them yet. It will be difficult."

Back in the dining room, Joey told them it was Josef wishing them happiness. His father felt embarrassed and said, "I'm sorry. I didn't realize it was him. I hope you invited him to come to the wedding."

"I did, of course, but he's too fragile to travel much," Joey said. "But at least he wished us *l'chaim*."

His aunt Dodo raised her water glass. "*L'chaim!*" she shouted, and they all joined in. Even his father.

CHAPTER 114

The wedding was held in the Kahal Kadosh Beth Elohim Temple on Hasell Street. When they were there planning the event, Aunt Dodo described it to Leah as if she were a docent: "It was dedicated in early 1841 and is one of the country's finest examples of Greek Revival architecture." Taking Leah by the hand, she showed her a framed letter from President George Washington in 1790, and she read it aloud: "The affectionate expressions of your address again excite my gratitude, and receive my warmest acknowledgment. May the same temporal and eternal blessing which you implore for me, rest upon your Congregation."

Interesting, Joey thought. *Being Jewish in Charleston goes way back. Maybe that's why being Jewish when he was growing up wasn't as up front as it was now?*

Aunt Minnie and Uncle Joe came down from Richmond for the wedding. Joe, who was born and raised in Poland before coming to America, took every opportunity to speak Polish with Leah and learn her history.

"I have not spoken in Polish this much for so long," she confided reluctantly to Joey. "He also asked me three times about the Red Cross visit in Geneva about Milton."

Joey thought he might say to Uncle Joe that, hard as it was to lose your son, it was a lot harder to lose your entire family, as Leah had, but he decided not to. His main concern was how to tell his family after the wedding that the two of them were going back to Israel.

The wedding was classic Reform Jewish, and the celebrations were lively and happy. Milton had been the only family member killed in the war, and now the last soldier was home, safe and sound.

* * *

Two days later, Joey told Louis of their plans. He wasn't surprised, having seen the journey, the change in Joey through their correspondence and now in the flesh.

"I won't try to talk you out of this, Joey," he said. "As long as you've thought it through from all angles."

It was a long passage for the naive young Jewish boy from South Carolina, and he was determined to follow through. "The Arabs are constantly threatening another war, and I couldn't just forget all that we've been through," he told Louis. "I just don't know how to put it to the folks."

After much discussion, Louis suggested an idea: "Everyone's asking what you're gonna do for your honeymoon. So what about saying you're going to Israel where you've both made so many friends? It's gonna hurt them either way, but it'll be a lot easier on you to tell them by mail you've decided to get a degree there and are staying for that."

CHAPTER 115

That's what he did. Gritting his teeth, he watched the now wrinkled faces of his parents, realizing he might never see them again. After many tearful goodbyes to everyone, he and Leah returned to Tel Aviv, where they both started their studies. Joey applied for a teaching position and began a career, just as Leah had suggested. Israel now had to deal with a host of issues: rebuilding towns and cities, accommodating a flood of immigrants—especially Holocaust survivors—and hundreds of thousands of Jews fleeing, mostly with no possessions, from Arab lands because of persecution. Rationing was enforced. There was peace, but none of the Arab nations would sign peace treaties. Only armistice agreements.

Israel and its people applied the same determination for economic growth and self-sufficiency they had applied to win nationhood, but the Palestinian Arabs who fled with the encouragement of the surrounding countries, expecting to win the war and then return, were kept in UN camps and not allowed to prosper and grow. The UN agency, United Nations Relief and Rehabilitation Administration (UNRRA), that had been organized to help Palestinian refugees, was unfortunately staffed mostly by Palestinians who were pressured by the Arab League to resist Israel's offer to build decent housing for their refugees. The result was to keep them in tent cities, with no sanitary facilities like sewers and running water—a decision that was to have deadly consequences later on.

Karl had once again become a history professor, and on a visit to Joey and Leah, he lamented their plight. "These poor people are political pawns. UNRAA won't allow us to do anything for them, not even to build real homes for them. You won't believe the conditions they live in."

"I know," Leah said. "I was there several times with a medical unit from my hospital to help. The sewage smell is everywhere. The unhappiness is, too."

"Micah tells me it's going be serious," Joey said. "They are being taught to hate us. Already there've been some deadly attacks on us."

"Ah, the fedayeen," said Karl. He shook his head. "The news is not always good."

"But my dear Karl," said Joey with a big smile. "There is some good news."

Leah also broke into a big smile, nodded, and put her arm around Joey's neck. Karl looked wondering at them both, then he, too, broke into a big smile and moved to hug them. "Oy!" he shouted. "Am I finally going to be a godfather?"

The three hugged and moved in a dance to celebrate the coming of baby Louis, which reminded Joey of that moment in Fürth so many years ago when he and Josef and Karl had first bonded.

CHAPTER 116

"Tomorrow's assignment is to write about what you plan to do this summer," said Joey. "Assuming, of course, that this is not your year to go into military service."

"Sir!" said a young girl, newly arrived in the class. "All in English?"

Joey and the class laughed, and she flushed but Joey smiled and said gently "In English, yes." Suddenly he stopped and looked at the back of the classroom. Standing quietly there was Micah in a colonel's uniform. *Oh no! In uniform. I know what this means. I'm just getting used to this life.* He nodded hello, and finished the lesson.

Sitting in the school's cafeteria, Micah told Joey about what Israel's intelligence was saying. "They will attack us, Joey," he said. "We need all the strategic help we can get. Your name has come up maybe five times."

Joey rubbed the short beard he had grown over the past few years, and protested, even though he knew his answer. "I have to think of my wife and son, Micah. I can't just drop everything."

"We all have wives and children, Joey," Micah said. "And we need to protect them."

"The bastards won't let us alone," Joey growled. "They don't want peace. They outnumber us in everything: people, land, money, oil, weapons. But that's not enough. They want our land."

"And our blood," Micah added, and paused. "But I want my grandmother to come back to her home in Jerusalem, where she was chased out in 1948."

"Imagine their gains if they'd only made peace," Joey mused bitterly.

"Funny you said that. My friend Schmuel is in finance, and he made a list about just that very thing, but no one has paid attention to it. It is an incredible list of hospitals, schools, housing, parks, airports, libraries they'd have now. It goes on and on."

CHAPTER 117

_____

So it came to pass that Joey put off his studies, his teaching, his quiet family life, and again joined the IDF. It was 1965. He was made a captain based on his prior service and began preparing for what they all knew would be another war. The Syrians were shelling in the Golan. The Egyptians were amassing armies along the borders of Egypt and Jordan, and the Russians were helping both—as well as seeking to prevent any help for Israel from the West.

"We're only nineteen years old, and once again we're threatened with extinction," Joey said after a planning session.

"And we are alone," Micah added bitterly. "Even our so-called friends, the French, have started to suck up to the Arabs. Nasser has closed the straits of Tiran to us and ordered the UN to move out."

Intelligence convinced the government and the military, citing intercepted communications and informants on the ground that an attack was about to begin, and so, just before 8:00am, on Monday, June 5, 1967, the Israeli Air Force began a three-hour preemptive strike that destroyed most of the Egyptian air force. Then, when the Syrian, Jordanian, and Iraqi air forces struck back, the Israelis in turn wiped each of them out, gaining complete superiority in the air.

On June 7, Israeli paratroopers took control of Jerusalem. Entering in force into the Muslim Quarter through St. Stephen's Gate, which the Jews called The Lion's Gate, battle-worn, exhausted crowds of emotional soldiers—many wearing uniforms stained with blood and dust—pushed into a city still dotted with snipers. They took over the Temple Mount and the Western Wall—Judaism's holiest site, where the two temples once stood. They reached the Wall, tears flowing in relief, joy, and the accomplishment of a nineteen-year spiritual goal. No Jew had been allowed there by the Jordanians since 1948.

"*We are on the Temple Mount. The Temple Mount is ours,*" broadcast Mota Gur, the head of the paratroopers. The soldiers leaned against the ancient foundation of the temple and sang, "*Baruch ata Hashem, eloheinu melech haolam, she-hechianu ve-kiemanu vehegianu lazman hazeh.*—Blessed art Thou, Lord God, King of the Universe, who hast sustained us and kept us and hast brought us to this day."

When Joey's unit arrived, he saw Uzi Narkiss, now a general, weeping as he prayed. It had been long, this voyage to the Wall and now, in a lightning-like strike by the Israelis, it was over. Joey stood beneath the huge ancient wall of stones. His journey had been a long and emotional one, but it was not until now that he felt it was complete. This wall was not just a symbol to him of his own voyage, but of the horrendous voyage Jews had taken for thousands of years through wars, captivity, torture, murder, and hatred on a scale unheard of in other religions. He closed his eyes and leaned his head against the stones and breathed in. He knew no prayers to make, nor did he believe in praying, but in his mind he wanted to say something. *I am glad to be a Jew,* he thought. *I am just glad to be a Jew.*

A hand tapped his shoulder. It was Uzi Narkiss. "Goldman!" he shouted. "You're alive. I thought you were dead at Kastel." He gave Joey a huge bear hug. "Our temple was destroyed by the Romans in 70 AD, and the Muslims trashed it as well and built a mosque on top. But goddammit, Jerusalem is ours now, and never again will it not be ours!"

Other soldiers heard this and began yelling, "Never again! Never again!" Joey looked around him and wiped away the tears that were clouding his vision. *I am* proud *to be a Jew,* he thought, looking up at the mighty limestone wall that was once part of the expansion of the Second Jewish Temple begun by Herod the Great.

The celebration went on for hours. The war ended, six days after it began. It became a legend around the world.

"Next year in Jerusalem," Jews had said to each other at Yom Kippur and during Seders over the years. Now next year was *this* year.

○○○○○○○○○○◯◯○○○○○○○○○

EPILOGUE

Joey and Leah lived happily in Tel Aviv although interrupted time after time with several more wars, two intifadas, nine refused peace offers, and 14,000 missile and rocket attacks from Hamas militants in Gaza. They both studied for degrees, and they raised two boys, Louis and Milton.

After finally resigning from the Army, Joey again taught at the Tel Aviv University—now English Literature. Leah became a neurosurgeon at Tel Aviv Medical Center. Once retired and living in Ramat HaSharon, they dwelt in physical comfort but emotional anxiety, with the surrounding Arab countries and the Palestinians still wanting the Jews to disappear, and with global anti-Semitism once again on the rise—especially in Europe. After retiring, Joey volunteered to teach at a small Arab school in Jaffa at the request of Adel, who, true to his desire, had become a teacher there.

It was 2015 and Joey, still active at 88, had just finished a class. As he and Adel were walking up Hatsorfim Street next to the Sha'ar Ra'amses Garden, a young woman in a burqa leapt out of the gardens, knife in hand, and rushed at Joey yelling, *"Allahu akhbar!"*— "God is great!"

Reacting on instinct, Adel turned swiftly and jumped in front of Joey, taking the knife squarely in his chest. Screaming in pain, he fell to the ground, blood welling up around the knife. Several Arabs grabbed the struggling girl as two Israeli soldiers ran up to help. In horror, Joey fell to his knees and cradled Adel in his arms. "Somebody call an ambulance," he shouted. "*Quickly*! Hold on, Adel. Hold on." But he knew it was hopeless.

"*Allahu akhbar*?" choked Adel. "No, no . . . *Allahu mahabbah . . . mahabb*. God is love. God is . . . " His eyes closed and his head fell to the side. A last breath came softly onto Joey's tear-filled cheek. Joey stared at that face he had loved for so many years. Adel appeared to be sleeping but this, thought Joey, was an eternal sleep and his tears fell softly like flower petals onto the dead brow.

At the funeral, Joey talked of Adel's life, and of his parents' deaths by extremists. He stood with the other mourners in an ancient cemetery where both Christians and Muslims were interred. It had been defaced by an extremist Jewish settler group a year earlier.

There along with him stood a large crowd of Arabs, Adel's students, and Jews who were neighbors and fellow teachers of Adel's

"His last words were *Allahu mahabbah*, God is love," said Joey. "It is time for us, all of us, to seek peace and end hate. Adel told me only last week that if all the blood that has flowed had been water, then the red sands would have turned green." He blinked back tears. "Are we so ignorant that we can't stop continuing this hatred? It is not too late. It is never too late." After a long pause he said, "Goodbye, Adel. I love you."

Morad stood up next. "I love you too, Adel," he said. He paused and wiped his eyes before he could continue speaking. "Adel grew up under my care. Jewish extremists killed Rabin, a Jewish man seeking peace. Now here an Arab extremist kills an Arab, also a man of peace. The powers that be of both sides—*both sides*—must stop preaching hatred and killing and make it happen. Yes, Allah is *mahabb*, love. But peace, or *al-salaam* as we say, is also one of the names for God. God is peace."

Adel's young class was there. The students ended the ceremony with a song, "I Dream of Peace," which Adel had taught them. Tears of sadness, frustration, and uncertainty washed all the faces there that day.

A month later, on a particularly beautiful spring morning, Joey and Leah were on their small balcony at the sounding of an air raid siren commemorating Yom HaShoah, Holocaust Remembrance Day. Slowly they rose. During this day with an 11 a.m. siren blast, for two minutes, all activity—including traffic on the streets and highways—ceases suddenly. People stand in silent devotion in memory of the millions of Jews murdered in Europe before and during World War II.

Holding hands now wrinkled and spotted with age, but still firm with love, they listened as the radio played the Hatikvah, Israel's national anthem. With tears, Joey once again remembered the Seder in Wiesbaden so many years ago, when the boy who survived the Holocaust sang the lyrics in English for him.

> *As long as the Jewish spirit is yearning*
> *Deep in the heart, with eyes turned*
> *Toward the East, looking toward Zion,*
> *Then our hope will not be lost,*
> *The hope of two thousand years*
> *To be a free nation in our land,*
> *The land of Zion and Jerusalem.*

After it ended, and life renewed below, Joey thought of Adel and the children singing another song. He drew Leah's hand to his lips, nodded his head, and thought *I Dream of Peace*. He said softly, "I've learned it is hard to be a Jew."

She sighed, "My grandmother would say that in Yiddish: '*Schwer zu sein ein yid*.'"

Joey nodded slowly. "It always has been," he said.

Acknowledgements

To Josh Weil in whose writing class I did this as a short story and he encouraged me to make it into a novel and then edited much of the beginning drafts, and taught me a lot.

And Robert Rubin who initially advised me about creating scenes and ultimately edited the finished manuscript. He's so like his father, my late brother Louis whom I miss daily.

And Frank Nicolo who encouraged me and helped with insights and comments along the way and designed a great cover. And Hal Friedman who also encouraged and helped me often with comment. And for my interview in Israel arranged by Judy Goldman, my wonderful sister-in-law, with Professor Mordechai Gichon, who was the intelligence officer for the Brigade and afterwards an important Intelligence officer for many Israeli military organizations.

And thanks to my beloved wife Jane who so often commented helpfully as I was into it for these past 10 years. And to Ken Jacobson of the ADL (Anti-Defamation League) for his meaningful preface.

And to all the important folks who so generously wrote wonderful things after reading my manuscript. Their comments are on the covers and in full in the end of the book.

And Jessica Bushore who shepherded me through the production by Gatekeeper Press with so many copy edits and suggestions.

And, of course, my buddies in the 318th Ordnance Battalion and their high jinks and support they gave me. And my HQ CO, Lieutenant Colonel Royce P. Larned and our Adjutant, Lieutenant Hershel Forner for the support they gave me. I would also like to remember my dear, departed friends- Al Markim (born Al Moskowitz) who led me to helping the two Dachau survivors and the Wiesenbad Seder, and Skip Say who took me to the Trials.

And to my little dachshund, Schatzie, who always seem to know how to make me feel better when I felt down or anxious in those WWII days.

And finally to my late close friend of eighty years, Joseph Bruce Goldman, whose name, Joey Goldman, I gave to my protagonist. At least he got to read the manuscript before he passed away last year.

And to these important leaders who were kind enough to read my manuscript and offer these insights:

Abraham Foxman, *Director of the ADL, 1987-2015*

Manning Rubin's partially autobiographic novel, *Voyage to the Wall*, is a great read and an important story.

It recounts the transformation of a highly assimilated Jew from the south and how the revelation to him of details of the Holocaust brought him to a new understanding of his place in the world and in the Jewish community.

At a time when Holocaust denial and Holocaust ignorance are rampant, Rubin's telling this highly personal story of exposure to the Nuremberg trials, Dachau, and other Nazi-related experiences is timely and relevant.

At a time when delegitimization of Israel is afoot, Rubin's saga connecting Jews to the Holy Land and the Jewish struggle for independence is persuasive and moving.

And today when the American Jewish community is facing weakened identity among many of its constituents, this evolutionary tale of heightened Jewish motivation emerging from indifference is instructive and hopeful.

A good read and a source of inspiration, not a bad combination.

Mark B Sisisky, *President, Joint Distribution Committee—JDC.org*

Voyage to the Wall brings to life, in a uniquely sensitive way, the dark years of post WW2 and what is left of Europe's Jews to find their way to a homeland. The horrors of the Holocaust, the War Crimes Trials, Dachau, the struggle for Israel are, for the first time, connected in an intensely human way through the eyes of a naive young Southern Jewish boy.

Joey Goldman enlists in the war, is stationed in Nuremberg, Germany after VE Day, meets Micah of the Underground Jewish Brigade risking his life by helping assassinate top Nazis in hiding and getting refugees to safety in Palestine, despite the harsh British embargo and Arab attacks.

Joey falls in love with Leah, a young Polish survivor, and follows her to Palestine, where he joins the desperate struggle to re-establish a homeland for what he now realizes is his people. *Voyage to the Wall* articulates in deeply personal terms a moving story of how the war changed the life of an innocent young American soldier and reminds us of the horrors of the Holocaust.

Shoshana Bryen, *Senior Director, Jewish Policy Center*

In the 21st century, it has become frighteningly possible to believe that the Holocaust is just another bit of history and "Holocaust" is just another word. "Holocaust literature" has become so pervasive that it is hard to open another cover. But the Holocaust is not comprehensible to those of us who weren't there—and that's now about 99% of us - and more books about the destruction of European Jewry don't generally help.

But I did read *Voyage to the Wall* by Manning Rubin, and you absolutely should as well. Rubin takes a different path. Semi-autobiographical (he calls himself Joey Goldman), this is a single-eye view of someone who believes he is unaffected and how he becomes aware that he is affected. He doesn't ask you to experience what you cannot. He doesn't ask you to put yourself in the shoes of someone you can never be and never want to be and hope your children won't be. You are an initially disinterested observer as Joey was—and, as observers often are, you are drawn into the object of your study. But outside, where you belong. Until you aren't.

You feel the impact of his learning and the attachment of one man to all of Jewish history—the worst parts and the best.

This is not "Holocaust literature," it is modern Jewish literature and a great read.

Rabbi Abraham Cooper, *Simon Weisenthal Center*

It was both humbling and inspiring. I hope it will be read by many people, young and old, Jew and gentile. Your narrative is the narrative of the Jewish people spanning a hundred years. From Shoah to a flourishing State of Israel.

James Patterson, *World's Best-Selling Author*

Voyage to the Wall should be read by anyone interested in the Jewish experience—especially non-Jews. It is incredibly readable, intelligent, and highly emotional. Manning Rubin is ninety-five years old, but he writes, and thinks, like a young lion.

Author Manning Rubin.

About the Author:

Manning Rubin's debut novel is based in part on his experiences as a naïve, young Jewish soldier in Germany in WWII who discovers the Holocaust and the death camps. In his debut novel he uses his Army position after the war to help the Underground Jewish Brigade collect military supplies for Palestine and to help desperate Jewish refugees reach there, the only place that wanted them. He falls in love with a Jewish survivor from Poland and follows her to Palestine to fight in all the wars to establish Israel as a Jewish homeland.

Rubin previously published KEEP YOUR BRAIN ALIVE (Workman) and 60 WAYS TO RELIEVE STRESS IN 60 SECONDS (Workman and Manning Rubin Publishing). Manning was an award-winning creative executive for major New York Advertising firms. His clients have included a Who's Who of major corporations.

He holds an MA in Writing, Speech, and Drama (Johns Hopkins); a BA in History and English (University of Richmond, Virginia); and is a member of Phi Beta Kappa.

As volunteer Creative Director for The Anti-Defamation League, he created and consulted on scores of public service ads for over 30 years to fight prejudice and to support Israel. He has lectured extensively on Neurobics, the new science of brain exercise, which he helped develop with the late Dr. Lawrence Katz. He is a member of the American Society for Neuroscience and The Cognitive Neuroscience Society.

References:

The Center for Jewish History (New York, New York) who helped me in selecting all sorts of information from articles, letters of fighters before and during the various wars, books, recordings . . . just an amazing wealth of Jewish history.

The Beit Hagdudim Museum of the Brigade near Netanya (Israel) where I saw actual pictures of what I wrote about and learned even more.

Plus books from which I wove actual situations and events into my novel:

The War Against the Jews, by Lucy Davidowitz, *The Brigade,* by Howard Blum

The Revolt, by Menachem Begin

A History of the Jews, by Paul Johnson

Israel, The Forgotten Ally, by Pierre Van Passen

The Palestinian Covenant and Its Meaning, by Yehoshafat Harkabi

Jerusalem: One City, Three Faiths, by Karen Armstrong

The Oslo Syndrome, by Kenneth Levin

The Genius of Judaism, by Bernard Henri Levy

Concerning the Jews, by Mark Twain

The Plot, by Will Eisner

A Convenient Hatred: The History of Anti-Semitism, by Phyllis Goldstein

Stealth Jihad, by Robert Spencer

Genesis 1948: The First Arab-Israeli War, by Dan Kurzman

1948, by Benny Morris

O Jerusalem!, by Larry Collins and Dominique LaPierre

Of Guns, Revenge, and Hope, by David-Lawrence Young

History of Israel's War of Independence, Volume II, by Uri Milstein

Rebirth and Destiny of Israel, by David Ben Gurion

Dual Allegiance, by Ben Dunkelman

The Complete Idiot's Guide to Middle East Conflict, Mitchell G. Bard

The Holocaust: Victims Accuse, by Reb Moshe Shonfeld

Torn Country, by Lynn Reid Banks

Exodus, by Leon Uris

Exodus 1947: The Ship That Launched a Nation, by Ruth Gruber

The Brigade, by Hanoch Bartovvise

The Jewish Contribution to Civilization, by Cecil Roth

Days of Pain and Sorrow, by Leonard Baker

The Chosen Few, by Maristella Botticini and Zvi Eckstein

The Case for Israel, by Alan Dershowitz

The Trial and Death of Jesus, by Haim Cohn

Constantine's Sword: The Church and the Jews, by James Caroll

Between Arab and Jew, by Yosef Olmert

Disraeli: The Jew, by Benjamin Cardozo and Emma Lazarus

Myths and Facts, by Mitchell G. Bard

The United States and the Middle East, by Philip L. Grosisser

The Story of Israel, by Meyer Levin

Chuck Olin's films: "Is Jerusalem Burning" and "In Our Own Hands"

Lightning Source UK Ltd.
Milton Keynes UK
UKHW020648310722
406617UK00005B/450